PRISONER OF PASSION

"Damn you, Rance Taggert, I don't want to be your woman," April cried. "You've caused enough trouble in my life. I should've let my father kill you when he had the chance—"

He silenced her with a kiss that tasted of warm, sweet wine. Startled, she did not move, and he released her quickly and got to his feet, jerking her along with him.

Suddenly his face became a thundercloud of fury. "Now *you* listen to me," he ordered. "You belong to me now, just as if you'd been a horse wagered on a race. And you're going to obey my every command. Disobey, and you'll be punished."

Terror coursed through April's veins as her mind conjured images of what life would be like if she did not escape. . . . For this time, there would be no one to save her from a man's lust and passion.

PASSION'S FURY

PATRICIA HAGAN

AVON
PUBLISHERS OF BARD, CAMELOT AND DISCUS BOOKS

PASSION'S FURY is an original publication of Avon Books. This work has never before appeared in book form.

AVON BOOKS
A division of
The Hearst Corporation
959 Eighth Avenue
New York, New York 10019

Copyright © 1981 by PHH, Incorporated
Published by arrangement with PHH, Incorporated
Library of Congress Catalog Card Number: 80-69910
ISBN: 0-380-77727-4

First Avon Printing, July, 1981

AVON TRADEMARK REG. U.S. PAT. OFF. AND IN OTHER COUNTRIES, MARCA REGISTRADA, HECHO EN U.S.A.

Printed in the U.S.A.

10 9 8 7 6 5 4 3 2 1

For my brother, Dr. Garrett Hagan, Jr., who loaned me his courage, borrowed my patience, shared my joys and sorrows, and gave me the loyalty and guidance only a big brother can bestow upon a little sister.

PASSION'S FURY

❧ Chapter One ❧

APRIL stood at the top of the long curving mahogany stairway and shook her head in wonder at the activity below. Her father had proclaimed that tonight's ball would be an event no one in Alabama would soon forget, and the Pinehurst Plantation servants were scurrying about, busily trying to make his words come true.

She watched Buford, her father's valet, and Posie, the housekeeper, argue about the holly draped over the stair railing. "Pink bows just don't look right," Buford snorted.

"What do you know?" Posie countered. "It ain't Christmas, you old fool. Red wouldn't look right. If it was spring, we could use dogwood. And look there! You got so much of that stuff draped around nobody can see that pretty wood I worked so hard to polish this mornin'."

"This ain't my job, nohow. Why don't you just do it like you want to. I got other things I can be doin'."

He turned to leave, but Posie cried, "You just get right back here, Buford. Somebody's gotta wrap ribbon around that chandelier—" She looked up to the crystal piece hanging from the ceiling and then saw April. Her hand flew to her mouth. "I'm sorry, Miss April. I didn't see you standin' up there."

"Don't mind me," April laughed, lifting her skirts to hurry down the stairs. "There's so much going on around here. I can see why anyone would be irritable. You're doing a lovely job. Everything looks wonderful."

1

Buford had turned back, contrite that his mistress had heard him complaining. April waved him away with a smile. "You do whatever it is you need to be doing. I'll help Posie with the garlands."

"You ain't supposed to be helping," she protested. "You're supposed to be getting dressed. It ain't long till folks start arrivin'."

"There's plenty of time for that." She picked up a holly branch and looked at it skeptically, wondering if the stairway wouldn't be pretty with just ribbons wrapped around the banisters. "Besides," she continued, "I'm enjoying all the excitement. A girl doesn't have a presentation ball every day. Where's Vanessa? She might want to help, too." She trailed off at the look on Posie's face.

"I ain't seen her since early this mornin' when she flounced out of here to go ridin'." Posie bent down to begin tying pink bows among the green foliage. "Ain't seen her since and don't care if I don't, the hateful way she was actin'. She don't care nothin' about this party, nohow."

"Of course she does. You know Vanessa's moods. It probably has nothing to do with the party."

Posie shook her head. "Believe me, missy, she don't care nothin' about it. It's a shame, too, especially after you had that big fuss with your poppa, 'bout lettin' the party be for her, too. That girl just don't appreciate nothin' nobody does for her. I tol' her she didn't have no business out ridin' when there was so much to be done, and she told me to shut my mouth."

April frowned worriedly. "Posie, Vanessa doesn't know that Poppa didn't want to include her in the ball. I don't want her to find out that I had to talk him into it. She would be so hurt."

Posie snorted. "I don't see how you *was* able to get him to. He and that girl been fightin' since the night she was born."

April began taking off the holly garlands, deciding the ribbons and bows were decoration enough. "We had quite an argument," she admitted. "Poppa said he didn't want her included because he considers her so unladylike. He doesn't want her around his friends. But that's all his own fault. He's the one who has always allowed her to run wild, never requiring her to study or learn ladylike graces."

"She didn't want to," Posie pointed out. "She wanted to do just what she did do, what she's doin' now—as she pleases."

"I didn't want to learn either," April said in defense of her twin. "At least not as rigidly as Poppa required. Goodness, Posie, there are other things in life besides music and reading poetry and learning to make idle chitchat over tea."

Posie straightened to point a shaking finger at April. "You hear me good. I'm sayin' that girl will do somethin' to embarrass your daddy before this night is over."

"Oh, I don't think so. Besides, I told Poppa that if he didn't include Vanessa, then I would lock myself in my room and not come downstairs. I can't stand the way he treats her, Posie."

Posie shook her head. "No matter how mean that girl is to you, you always take up for her. I knows I ought to keep my mouth shut, but I can see how come your poppa didn't want her at the party. Just wait and see. You gonna be sorry you talked him into lettin' her come."

April started to speak but Posie rushed on. "I ain't sayin' it's right the way he's treated her all these years. Heaven knows, your momma would turn over in her grave if she could've seen it. But what's done is done. Miss Vanessa is like she is and ain't nothin' gonna change it. She hates you and she hates yo' daddy, and she hates ever'body in the whole world."

"Perhaps with good reason," April murmured sadly. She threw the ribbons aside and sat down on the bottom step, not caring if her skirts were crushed. Folding her hands beneath her chin, she stared wistfully through the diamond-shaped glass on the side of the double oak front doors. Beyond her was a winter world, ice-sheathed trees creaking like great crystal hands reaching toward the gray February sky. She whispered, "If it'd been me instead of Vanessa, I probably would've grown up feeling bitter, too."

Posie sat down beside her and placed a plump brown arm around her shoulders. "I was there the night you was born, honey. You knows that. And I been with you most ever'day since. I knows what happened that night, and I knows how your poppa has acted ever since."

April had always known the story of her birth. There were times when she felt sure it was etched in pain across her heart. Her mother had endured agony. April had been the firstborn, delivered by her father because neither midwife nor doctor had arrived. She had almost died. Her father had breathed life into her tiny body and then, jubilant, named her April Lorena for her mother, Lorena April, whom he adored with an almost insane devotion. Even in her weakened condition, her mother had protested such favoritism.

Time dragged on. A midwife arrived and, after realizing what a struggle Lorena April Jennings was having, told Carter Jennings that unless he could locate the doctor, his wife was going to die before giving birth to the second baby. Carter galloped into town in the middle of the night, found the doctor drinking and gambling in a saloon, and threatened to shoot him if he did not come to Pinehurst and save his wife.

Vanessa finally was born, but not before everyone was sure that Lorena April would die very soon.

"Mastah Carter, he say he wished the baby would die," Posie had confided to her. "He blamed that child for Miz Lorena's sufferin', and he blamed her fo' Miz Lorena never bein' right after that night. And the day she died, when you young'uns was only three years old, he blamed Miss Vanessa all over again."

Posie clucked sympathetically. "It won't Miz Vanessa's fault. No, it sho' won't. It was just the Lord's will. And it won't her fault that yo' momma was poorly from that night on and finally died. That was the Lord's will, too. But yo' poppa, he ain't never gonna see it that way, and nobody can tell him different. Goodness knows, folks tried. Finally, they just gave up. Yo' daddy ain't the kind of man you can tell somethin' to when he's got his mind set."

To make matters worse, April reflected painfully, he had lavished all his love on *her*, neglecting Vanessa, almost pretending she did not exist at all. April had tried to make it up to her. Each time her father showered her with gifts, she shared them with Vanessa. She lost count of the number of toys and dolls her sister had maliciously destroyed.

Posie had said many times that it was beyond her why April did not hate Vanessa, for Vanessa seemed to go out of her way to be cruel. April had tried to make Posie understand. "She behaves as she does because she doesn't feel that anyone loves her. I do love her. And I'll never stop trying to make her believe that.".

Posie and April looked up as they heard the sound of footsteps clicking along the polished hallway leading toward the entrance foyer. Carter Jennings stepped into view, a wide grin on his face. He was a powerfully built man, tall, with an authoritative air about him. He was successful and wanted the whole world to know it. Some thought Carter Jennings arrogant, but all were awed by his immense wealth and political influence.

"My darling." He walked over quickly to kiss April's upturned cheek as she stood to greet him. He clasped her hands and smiled with fatherly pride. "Tonight is your night. All of Alabama will know how proud I am to present you to society."

April returned his smile, but tightly. "Posie and I were just discussing our party, Poppa . . . mine and Vanessa's," she added with emphasis.

Posie glanced up to see Carter Jennings's frown.

He rushed on. "It's going to be quite an affair. I've checked everything, and I find nothing out of order. The pigs are roasting, and the smells coming from the kitchen make my mouth water."

He put his arm about her and gave her a quick hug. "Some of the most important people in the South will be here tonight to see my little girl presented."

"Not just to see me,". she corrected him gently. "And I happen to know that you planned this party for tonight because President Davis is being inaugurated on Monday. You knew that important people would be in Montgomery this weekend."

He winked. "Perhaps. There are many parties being held in Montgomery tonight, but you will see which one they all attend. I wouldn't be surprised if President Davis himself made an appearance."

"Speaking of surprises," he added mysteriously, "I have one for you."

"What kind of surprise?" April asked.

He snapped his fingers at Posie. "Get a wrap for April. It's quite chilly out, and we're going to take a little walk."

Posie scurried to obey, while April attempted to pry the secret from her father. But he laughed mysteriously and refused to say more.

Posie returned with a long green velvet cape, which Carter draped about April's shoulders. Pulling the hood up to cover her long golden hair, he whispered, "Beautiful. Just like your precious mother. An angel come down to earth."

April always felt uncomfortable when he looked at her so adoringly. It made her feel eerie, somehow. A strange look would come into his eyes, and she shivered to think that, for one fleeting moment, he was not really seeing *her*, but her long dead mother.

"Poppa, let's go wherever it is you want to go." She stepped out of his embrace and moved toward the door. "It will soon be time for me to begin dressing."

He made a grand bow, then winked mysteriously once more before opening one of the doors. "All right, my beautiful daughter. Let's be on our way."

April stepped onto the wide marble porch that ran the length of the great house. She took her father's arm, and they descended the long steps between the tall white columns. A blast of cold wind pushed back her hood, sending her hair flying about her face.

"Poppa, you've given me so much already," she protested once more as he led her across the lawn. "There is no need for whatever it is you're about to do."

"Nonsense." His arm went about her as he tried to shield her from the icy wind. "A father certainly wants to give his daughter a gift on the day she is presented to society. But this isn't to be your only gift, by any means. I have something to give you later that is very precious . . . something that belonged to your dear mother."

April realized it was useless to argue. She just hoped he would also have a gift for Vanessa.

They passed beneath an archway of bare crepe myrtle trees. In the spring, when the pink and purple blossoms burst forth, it would be a myriad of beauty. Now the passage only reminded her of the ugly gloom of winter.

The stables loomed ahead, two large buildings which housed all the fine horses that Carter took such pride in. Many of his horses had been brought over from England.

Besides showing his stock in the ring from time to time, he also entered many of his horses in match and heat races.

"Virginia calls itself the horse capital," April had often heard him scoff. "I defy anyone to show me horses from the state of Virginia any finer than mine. One day I will make Alabama the horse capital of the whole damned world!"

April had attended a heat race one Sunday in Montgomery and had been completely enthralled. Four-year-old horses competed the full distance of four miles, and that day, her father's entries had won.

She always had loved to ride, but, due to her father's insistence that she spend most of her time in pursuit of genteel interests such as books and music, there had not been much time for riding. Vanessa, on the other hand, went riding as often as she pleased. April had often watched in wistful envy from the windows of the great house as her twin romped across the lush green lawns of Pinehurst.

They neared the stables, and April could not stand the suspense any longer. "Poppa, would you please tell me what all this is about?" she begged, shivering in the cold despite her cape and his arm about her.

He stopped just outside the door leading to the smaller of the buildings. "Do you remember my prize Darley Arabian?" he asked proudly.

"Yes, of course. He's a magnificent creature. People come from all over just to see him."

"Do you remember all I told you about him?"

She nodded. "He has a pedigree, is full-blooded, and is a descendant of a famous horse named *Eclipse*, bred by the Duke of Cumberland."

"And I had him brought over here from England at great expense," he added with a wry smile. "Well, I've a wonderful surprise for you, and it's been quite difficult keeping it a secret. I've had to keep you away from the stables and leave strict orders to the groomsmen that your surprise be kept out of sight."

"Poppa, whatever are you talking about?"

Bewildered, she watched as he reached to open the stable door. The glow of a lantern spilled out into the gathering twilight. He looked inside, nodded to someone, then turned to her and said in a voice trembling with pride, "I have hidden Virtus's colt from you, April, because he is my gift to you on this day."

He laughed at her stunned expression and reached to pull her inside the stable. She gasped, catching sight of a shiny black colt prancing in the center of the room. His coat shone like satin, and his eyes sparkled with gold and red fires. He was the most magnificently beautiful horse she had ever seen, even among her father's thoroughbreds.

"You . . . you mean he's *mine?*" April looked from the black colt to her father in disbelief. "You are giving the son of Virtus to me?"

"He's all yours." He was beaming with pride. "Now he hasn't been broken yet, and I certainly don't want you riding him until he is. Like his father, he's high-spirited. But you should be able to handle him after he's trained."

"She'll never be able to handle this horse."

For the first time, April noticed a man standing in the shadows outside the ring of light, holding the colt's reins. He stepped forward, and she dimly recognized Rance Taggart, who had arrived at Pinehurst when his father became ill. Frank Taggart had been in charge of the stables for as long as she could remember, and his son Rance had often been at Pinehurst.

Vaguely, she recalled her father saying something about Mr. Taggart's son arriving a month or so previously, but since she had not been in the stables of late, she had not noticed him.

Now, she felt her father stiffen with indignation. He was not accustomed to being challenged.

"What do you mean by that, Taggart?" Carter Jennings growled.

Rance's eyes flicked over April briefly, then met the challenge of Carter's glare. April noted that he was a full head taller than her father, with wide shoulders. Beneath his open suede shirt, she could see a heavily furred chest tapering down to a flat belly and narrow hips. He was well-proportioned, lean, yet muscular.

Her gaze moved to his face. His hair was ebony, and his eyes, a smoldering chestnut brown, were intense, probing in their alertness. He was quite handsome. Something about him was disturbing . . . something she did not understand just yet. Something dangerous? She was not quite sure, but the man possessed a quality that caused her to tremble at his nearness.

Rance spoke to Carter Jennings in a firm confident tone. "This colt is very high-spirited, and even after he's broken, it will take an experienced rider to handle him. April isn't that experienced. If you want to give her a horse, there are some gentle mares—"

"You forget your place, Taggart!"

Rance Taggart did not wither before her father's angry, booming voice as other men did. He stood straight, erect, eyes unwavering. He had no intention of apologizing.

"I own this colt, just as I own everything else at Pinehurst, and if you think I will tolerate your telling me what I may or may not give my daughter—"

Rance's smile was arrogant as he tilted his head to one side. "Mr. Jennings, I don't give a damn if you give your daughter every horse you own. Along with every cow and mule. I'm just telling you what I know. This colt is too dangerous for her to ride. She could get her neck broken."

As if to emphasize the statement, the colt suddenly reared up on his hind legs, forelegs thrashing wildly in the air above. Startled, April stepped back. She would have fallen, but Rance's free hand shot out to steady her. He gave the reins a yank with his other hand, bringing the colt down on all fours once again. "See what I mean, Mr. Jennings?" he drawled.

Carter Jennings's hands were clenching and unclenching at his sides. "You made him do that. I find you insolent, Taggart. Tell me, just how is your father? I'd like to know how much longer Pinehurst will be subjected to your presence."

Rance was unswayed. "My father is still in bed, Mr. Jennings, flat on his back. But if you would like me to leave before he's able to take over the stables again, I can oblige you."

Despite his anger, Carter knew that it would not do to turn the care of the expensive stock over to the Negroes. Until Frank Taggart was able to resume his duties, his son would have to be tolerated.

"You may stay," he said tightly, "but remember your place. I won't tolerate insolence from you or anyone else in my employ."

He turned to April, forcing a smile. "Well, what do you think, darling? He's a beauty, isn't he? And, I might add, worth a fortune."

Her first reaction had been to protest the extravagant gift, but suddenly she found herself resenting the arrogance of the man who stood there smirking, insisting that she was inexperienced. A quiver of rebellion sparking from deep within, she stepped forward and touched her fingertips to the colt's velvet nose. "I think he's wonderful, and I love him already. I can't wait to ride him."

She turned to look at Rance, expecting to see—what? Anger? Alarm? Instead, she saw that his mildly mocking expression had not changed. His mouth twisted to one side in a knowing grin, as though he *knew* she was actually frightened and realized he was right—she wouldn't be able to handle this horse.

April and Rance locked eyes, each silently challenging the other.

Suddenly the stable doors creaked open. Turning quickly they saw one of the servants scrambling to get out of the way of a thundering horse. Vanessa was riding him. She reined her lathered mount to a stop only a few feet from where they were standing.

Carter began swiping with annoyance at the dust settling on his coat. "Vanessa, in the name of heaven, do you have to charge in here like that? You could injure someone. And that is no way to stop a horse. You have the manners and the grace of a nigra field hand!"

Vanessa threw her right leg up and over the horse's neck and dropped to the ground with a thud of booted feet. She was wearing worn, dirty breeches, and her golden hair was tossed wildly about her wind-flushed face. She tossed the reins to the stable hand, who led the animal away to walk him down.

Her blue eyes swept over the three of them curiously. She ignored her father's admonishment. Then her gaze narrowed suspiciously on the colt. She addressed herself to Rance. "Why is the colt here?"

"Your father just made a present of him to April."

"Oh, he did, did he?" She placed her gloved hands on her hips and turned to April, lips curled back in a snarl. "Well, you did it again, didn't you? You begged and wheedled Poppa into giving you something just because you knew I wanted it."

"Oh, Vanessa, no!" April gasped, shaking her head quickly from side to side. "I knew nothing about this."

"What do you mean, something *you* wanted?" Carter snapped. "I would never give you something as valuable as this colt. I know how you handle the horses. You haven't got sense enough to appreciate something of value."

Vanessa gave her hair a toss and turned her sneering grin on him. "Really, Poppa? Well, tell me. When have I ever been given anything of value? I've never had anything except April's leftovers!"

"This is neither the time nor the place," he sputtered, face coloring. "Get out of here at once."

"Oh, I'll go"—she took a step backward—"but I won't forget this. You win again, sister dear!" She gave April a snapping salute before turning on her heel and walking toward the door.

"Vanessa, listen to me, please." April started to follow, but her father caught her arm and held her back. "It isn't what you're thinking," she called to her twin. "You must believe me. I had no idea—"

"Don't argue with her." Carter gave her a gentle shake. "She's just trying to make trouble as she always has."

Vanessa paused at the door to look over her shoulder at Rance and cry, "Maybe you can see now that I was telling you the truth about my life, the way I've been treated!" With a sob, half anger, half anguish, she rushed into the night.

Carter turned to Rance and told him to put the colt away. "And see to it that Vanessa never rides him."

"Whatever you say, Mr. Jennings." Rance began walking toward the stall, pulling the colt along. But he cast one final look at April. Was it contempt? Anger? She did not know and she admonished herself for caring. She had not seen Rance Taggart in years. But, strangely, she felt touched by him now.

Her father took her arm and led her from the stable. "This is a special night. Your night," he murmured quietly as they walked toward the house. "We won't let Vanessa ruin it for either of us."

She did not speak. There was too much turmoil inside her. Oh, why couldn't Vanessa see that she loved her and despised the way their father treated her?

Suddenly, April felt an impulse to turn and look back. Rance Taggart was leaning against the stable door, tall in the moonlight, arms folded across his chest. He was not smiling. He was staring boldly at her.

Once more, she felt a strange trembling from deep within.

❧ Chapter Two ☙

THE great plantation of Pinehurst had come to full life. The tall, regal Lombardy poplars lining the long, curving drive swayed in apparent anticipation of the evening ahead. The white, columnar, two-story mansion glowed and glittered, as though bragging to every tree, rock, and blade of glass, that *it* was host to this magnificent affair.

April stood in her room before the oval, gilt-edged mirror above the dressing table. Surveying her hair critically, she decided that Cora had done a good job. A great roll swept from behind each ear and down below her neck, creating a silken, glistening hoop of golden tresses. The hair was carefully parted above her smooth forehead.

She turned her head this way and that in the lantern's glow, satisfied with the way the tiny diamond teardrops sparkled in her hair.

Cora stepped forward with an enormous powder puff, which April took and began dusting her chest. She loved the fragrant smell and, feeling just a bit wicked, allowed a bit of rice powder to settle into the ravine of her cleavage.

"You sho' got nice bosoms," Cora said admiringly. "If I hadn't nursed nine young'uns, maybe mine wouldn't hang to my belly. 'Course I ain't never had a fine body like you got, Miss April."

April felt her cheeks grow warm. Such talk embarrassed her, and she always hated dressing in front of her maids.

13

She much preferred to stand behind the brocade screen in privacy, but tonight she was in a hurry and had no time for modesty. The visit to the stables had delayed her, and the guests were already arriving. The musicians were beginning to tune their instruments. She wanted to make a grand entrance with Vanessa, but, as angry as Vanessa had been, she might just go on down alone if April weren't ready when she was.

"The hoop, Cora," she said quickly. "I must hurry."

"I'll have to get Lucy to help," Cora said as she rushed from the room.

"While you're doing that, have someone check and see how long before Vanessa will be ready."

Oh, why did Poppa have to be the way he was? He seemed to be getting worse, too. He just wasn't himself at all lately. It was the war, she told herself. He was worried. South Carolina had seceded from the Union in December. Mississippi and Florida followed in January, and her own state, Alabama, seceded one day after Florida's decision. Then Georgia and Louisiana announced their severance, and Texas was close on their heels.

War was imminent, and although her father tried to shield her, she knew enough to be afraid.

The door opened with a bang and Cora and Lucy hurried in, each carrying a tall stool. Cora brought the big iron cage hoop from where it stood in the corner and fastened it about April's tiny waist. Then the two Negro women climbed up on the stools. They each took a long pole and lifted the first of three horsehair crinolines.

April raised her slender arms, and they lowered the first crinoline over her head by the poles, careful not to muss her hair as they dropped it over the iron cage. As they reached to maneuver the second, April asked about Vanessa.

"She's in there with Mandy, dressin'," Cora told her. "She say she ain't goin' downstairs with you nohow, and you is to just go on alone. She sounded mad, so I wouldn't waste my time arguin' with her if'n I was you. You know how ornery that girl can be. Don't do no good to try to talk to her when she's in one of her hateful moods."

"Well, I'll try to reason with her when I've finished

dressing. This is one night she should be happy. Let's hurry now, please."

When the three crinolines were in place, Lucy brought the velvet ballgown that had arrived from Paris only a few weeks before. The sleeves were short, puffed, draping to leave her shoulders bare and her bosom provocatively displayed. The skirt, nearly six feet in diameter, hung in deep swags, each caught with a tiny gold lace rosette. Cora buttoned the bodice in the back and stood back to gasp her approval. "Lawdy, you is a lovely thing, Miss April. That green just sets off yo' hair, and those little gold things on the skirt makes it all look so pretty."

"Those are rosettes," April said quietly, then smiled at her reflection in the mirror. "Thank you, Cora. I don't want to sound conceited, but I don't think I've ever *felt* prettier, whether I look that way or not."

She had not heard the soft knock on the door. Her father's voice, filled with pride, startled her. "You aren't pretty, my darling. You are absolutely magnificent! Never have I seen a more beautiful woman." He walked over and kissed her cheek lightly.

"You look magnificent yourself," she said affectionately as her gaze took in his fawn-colored trousers and brown velvet waistcoat.

He went on as though she had not spoken, placing his hands on her bare shoulders. His eyes seemed to burn into hers as he murmured, "You look like your dear mother. In the name of God, it's as though I am seeing Lorena April again after all these years. The eyes, the hair, even the sweet, delicate smile, the touch of your skin . . ."

April stepped back, suddenly frightened. She could see the curious glances Cora and Lucy were exchanging. Her father turned suddenly and snapped his fingers at them. "Leave us now."

They scurried from the room, and April turned to follow. "I suppose it's time to make our entrance. I'll just go and tell Vanessa."

"No!" he said sharply. She paused, turning slowly, and saw that his eyes were almost glassy. "I have something for you . . . something I have waited till this night to present to you. I know your mother would have wanted it this way."

She felt a flicker of relief, and she realized that she was constantly afraid he would think she *was* her mother. But that was silly. She chided herself for thinking such a thing. He was merely a man who had loved his wife deeply. And because she resembled her mother, she triggered memories which made him behave strangely at times.

He was holding out his hand to her. "This belonged to your mother. I gave it to her on our wedding day. It has been in the family for generations, always being given to the oldest son to present to his bride. Since I have no sons, I want you to have it, April darling, to carry on the tradition of the Jennings family."

Curious, she moved closer, then covered her lips with both hands in a gasp of astonishment. He held out a ring— a ring more beautiful than any she had ever seen. There was a large diamond, surrounded by fire-red rubies and glistening green emeralds covering the band. When she could find her voice, she whispered, "I . . . I've never seen anything like it, Poppa."

"I don't suppose you have," he grinned. "As legend goes, my great-great-grandfather had it made for his bride. The stones are pure, and the ring was fashioned in France by a famous jeweler who designed for the royal family. It's priceless, of course, but its worth is not only in money." He paused significantly. "The possessor of this ring has undisputed claim to Pinehurst.

"Of course, it was worn by the mistress of the house," he went on, "but it was designated that the bestower was the rightful, legal heir. This is my gift to you this day, April. I bestow on you not only this valuable family heirloom but also undisputed title to this plantation."

She was speechless. With a trembling hand, she took the ring from him, astonished at its beauty. Then, suddenly, she thrust it toward him and said in a rush, "I can't take it, Poppa. It isn't right. *You* are the owner of Pinehurst. And besides, there is Vanessa to consider."

His eyes narrowed. With quick, jerky movements, he grabbed her right hand and twisted the ring into position on her third finger. It fit perfectly. "It's yours, and there will be no arguing. Of course, I am the owner of Pinehurst as long as I live, but everyone will know now that you are my heir. We won't speak of Vanessa. You were the first-born. Pinehurst is rightfully yours, even if she were deserving, which she most assuredly isn't."

He placed her hand in the crook of his arm. "Now we will make *your* grand entrance."

Stunned, April could only allow him to lead her out of the room, down the thickly carpeted hallway. When they passed the closed door to Vanessa's room, her heart constricted painfully. How much more grief would the girl have to bear, she wondered, feeling guilty over her own blessings.

They reached the top of the stairway. The guests were mingling below the huge crystal gas chandeliers, sipping champagne and talking above the music of the string orchestra playing in one corner of the large foyer. One of the musicians was watching for Carter Jennings's signal. When it came, he motioned to the orchestra for silence. The guests, sensing what was about to happen, began gathering in the foyer, looking upward toward the top of the stairs. The music began once more, and they smiled up in approval as April made her entrance on her father's arm.

Everyone clustered about as April and her father reached the bottom step. April shook hands, received kisses, hugs, and exchanged pleasantries till she felt weak from it all. Someone handed her a crystal glass filled with champagne, and she turned to smile gratefully. But her smile quickly faded as she looked up into the lascivious gaze of Graham Fletcher.

He took her hand and began to lead her away from the crowd, whispering when she held back, "Come along now. You don't want to make a scene now, do you?"

When they were away from the others, she snapped, "I didn't know my father had invited you, Graham. I certainly didn't ask him to."

"Now is that any way for you to behave when I have just rescued you from all those vultures?" He made a disapproving sound as he shook his head, but then his eye caught the ring her father had just given her. "Well, I see Carter Jennings has decided to let everyone know officially who is going to inherit Pinehurst. But there was never any doubt in *your* mind, was there, my love?" His grin was mocking.

He had clasped her hand, but she snatched it away and hissed, "I don't care for your impertinence, Graham, and I will thank you to go away and leave me alone. It was not my intention for you to be here, so please be a gentleman for once and respect my wishes. Stay away from me while you are here!"

She started to move away, but he caught her arm. "Now that is not being neighborly, April, and I hardly think your father would approve. You know he's always tried to maintain good relations between Pinehurst and Fletcher Manor. After all, where would Pinehurst be if it weren't for my family? Must I remind you that the underground stream that supplies water for your father's land originates on my family's property?"

"And he has paid you well for those water rights." April was struggling to keep her voice down. If there was one human being in the world whom she could not stand it was Graham. It was not that he was unattractive. Far from it. All the young ladies swooned over his good looks. But he was disgusting. Twice she had slapped his face for pinching her breasts, and he had boldly asked her to meet him in the barn some evening for her "pleasuring."

Graham continued to smile down at her. "That is a fetching dress, April. My, how I would love to see the bodice dropped just a wee bit lower. I've seen some fine breasts in my time, but I envision yours as the most luscious a man could ever ask for."

April clasped her fingers tightly around the glass stem. "Graham, if you persist in your filthy insults, I am going to tell my father, and he will give you the sound thrashing you deserve!"

"You're merely reacting indignantly because society demands it of a lady. One of these nights, you'll stop your little charade and be the passionate, wanton vixen I know you want to be."

His hand still clasped her arm. She picked it off carefully as though it were a loathsome bug. "Say just one more word to me, Graham, and I will throw this champagne in your face. I don't care how big a scene I make."

He struggled to keep smiling though anger was washing through him. "I could have that wild sister of yours any time I want, you know." He straightened his cravat with trembling hands. "But who wants her when she's probably frolicked with all your nigra field hands? You're the one I want, April. And you, I shall have."

She lifted her hand quickly, ready to splash the champagne in his face as she had promised, but he fastened tight fingers over her wrists. "Don't do it," he hissed ominously.

Their eyes locked in a gaze of fury, each challenging the other. "I'd rather be dead than lie with you, Graham," April whispered.

He released his grip, stepping back. "I think you'll change your attitude when the day comes for me to inherit Fletcher Manor. When your wells run dry, and your horses and cows die from lack of water—*my* water. . . ."

"I pray a Yankee shoots you dead, Graham," she said quietly. "I pray you are the first Confederate soldier killed in the war."

His face reddened. April did not wait for his retort, but moved away quickly. He had asked her father's permission to court her, but when April expressed disfavor, permission was refused. But Graham was not one to give up. Once rejected, he had resorted to vulgarity whenever he had the opportunity to torment her without being overheard.

She walked into the mammoth ballroom, taking a fresh glass of champagne from a passing footman and giving him her empty glass. The buffet was laden with giant silver platters of fruit, glazed ham, turkey, iced caviar, and a variety of lavishly decorated cakes and cookies. She nodded her approval to Posie, who stood by in a simple gray dress accented by a large white collar, a big white apron covering her large stomach.

"Have you seen Vanessa?" she asked.

Posie shook her head. "I just asked Lucy, and she ain't seen her, either. Ain't seen Mandy, though, so I reckon she's up there helpin' her get dressed. But I wouldn't be at all surprised if Miss Vanessa didn't even come down. Lucy says Mandy told her that Miss Vanessa knowed all along you had a fuss with yo' poppa over her bein' included in the party. She heard you two when you was arguin'. Maybe she just decided she didn't want to come where she wasn't wanted."

April's eyes widened in stunned surprise. "You mean Vanessa overheard my conversation with Poppa? Oh, no! I'll go talk to her, make her see—"

"There you are, my darling."

She looked around to see her father approaching with a distinguished-looking man.

"April, I want you to meet Lester Warrick. He is an aide to President Davis."

She held out her hand, and the man bent to kiss her fingertips. "Miss Jennings, this is such a pleasure. I have heard what a beautiful woman you are, and now I see for myself that all I've heard is true."

"You're too kind," she said, forcing herself to sound demure. She was anxious to go to Vanessa. "I know you must find your work with President Davis fascinating."

"Oh, quite. He's a remarkable man. Do you know him?"

"April hasn't met him," her father interjected. "We had hoped he would be able to attend tonight."

Lester Warrick looked contrite. "I'm sorry, sir, but the President was invited to so many social functions this weekend that he just decided to stay at home and work on his inauguration address rather than choose which invitations to accept."

"I understand. I'm sure April will meet him later. Now if you two will excuse me, I see someone I haven't spoken with yet."

He walked away, leaving April with Mr. Warrick, who began to expound on why Jefferson Davis was an excellent choice for President of the Confederacy. "He was a respected member of the cotton aristocracy, and is renowned not only as a soldier but as a statesman as well. He graduated from West Point, then served seven years at various frontier posts before quitting the army. Then, in 1845, he was elected to Congress but resigned a year later to command a regiment in the Mexican War. He came home a wounded hero and was sent to the United States Senate by appointment."

Warrick paused to take a fresh glass of champagne from the buffet. Behind his back, April looked at Posie and rolled her eyes.

"Where was I?" He smiled. "Oh, I remember. The South is indeed fortunate to have a leader like Jefferson Davis in this time of crisis."

April could not contain her sigh of relief when her father returned. "Well, are you two getting along well?" he greeted them.

"Mr. Warrick is quite interesting," April replied, "but if you will excuse me, I would like to go upstairs and see what is keeping Vanessa."

"Of course, of course." Lester Warrick gave a slight bow, then cried, "Oh, there's Franklin Overby. Excuse me." And he hurried away.

Her father leaned over to whisper, "What's this about Vanessa? She hasn't come downstairs yet?"

"No, and I think I should go talk with her."

"She's pouting about this afternoon." Her father was irritated. "Just leave her alone. If she wants to sulk in her room, she won't be missed. It's *you* everyone wants to see, and we both know I'm having this party just for you, anyway."

"Oh, that's just it, Poppa." As always, April felt totally frustrated trying to make him understand. "I just found out that Vanessa overheard our arguing over her being included in the party. She's terribly hurt. She's been hiding that hurt all these weeks. She doesn't feel you want her here. And it's not true that everyone wants to see just me. They want to include Vanessa, and it *is* her party, too. Now I'm going upstairs and try to reason with her."

He sighed, then said, "All right. I will go with you. If she's sulking, I'll tell her that if she doesn't come downstairs to make you happy, I'll drag her down."

"No! I'd rather go alone. You'll only make things worse, Poppa. You and Vanessa just bring out the worst in each other."

She started making her way across the ballroom, but he was right behind her. "I'm not going to put up with her selfish, ugly behavior tonight of all nights," he said quietly. "If necessary, I'll tell her she misunderstood, and I do want her at the party."

Gratitude washed over April. "Poppa, it would be so wonderful of you to tell her that."

He scowled. "I'd only do it for your sake, April, to make you happy. I certainly don't want her here. Mark my words, she will do something to bring disgrace on this family. The girl is uncontrollable."

"She is not. She just feels that no one loves her. I've told you before how unfairly you treat her, Poppa. She's as much a part of you as I am—"

"Oh, there's the lovely belle of the ball!"

April stopped short at the bottom of the stairs as Graham's mother moved in front of her.

"I've been wanting to speak to you, dear. This is such a lovely party. Your father should be very proud of himself. You are such a beautiful girl, and now that you are being formally presented to society, I'm going to have a difficult time with Graham. He's going to be so upset when all the eligible young men start hovering around you."

April had never cared for Mrs. Fletcher. She was such a gusher, forever going on and on about something. She looked to her father for help, but he was kissing Mrs. Fletcher's hand, being gracious, as always.

"Will you excuse us, Mrs. Fletcher?" April turned sideways to slide around her, inching her way toward the stairs. "We're going upstairs to see what's keeping the *other* belle of the ball, my sister, Vanessa."

Mrs. Fletcher's nose wrinkled in distaste. "Oh, I see." Her voice was stiff. "Graham didn't tell me the party was for her, too."

"Well, why wouldn't it be?" April snapped. "She is my twin, and the invitations plainly stated the party is for the debut of April *and* Vanessa Jennings, and—"

"Uh, April, it's all right." Her father touched her shoulder, nodding apologetically to Mrs. Fletcher. "You must excuse us. April is worried that her sister might be ill since she has not come downstairs yet. Enjoy yourself, please."

"I was going upstairs myself." She tilted her head upward. "I would like to freshen up." With an icy glare in April's direction, she lifted her skirts and began to make her ascent.

April gritted her teeth and followed. She lagged behind her father so he would have to be the one to make idle chitchat with Isabelle Fletcher.

"I'm so worried about Graham," Mrs. Fletcher sighed. "He's so anxious to march off to war. He thinks it's so grand and glorious. Bless his courageous heart, he just doesn't realize he could get killed. It's frightful, all this dreadful war talk. Graham is my only son and the love of my life. I declare, if anything happened to him, I just couldn't stand it."

If he doesn't leave me alone, April thought with gritted teeth, *he'll be safer going to war.*

"I'm sure the war will end quickly," her father said, trying, April knew, to be polite. He didn't really care for the talkative woman any more than she did. "I hear all the young men are afraid it will be over before they have a chance to shoot any Yankees."

Isabelle Fletcher made a clucking sound. "To think our young men actually want to shoot someone. It's just terrible! If the Yankees would only mind their own business."

April started to comment that if everyone would mind their own business, life would be wonderful, but she couldn't be rude. After all, Mrs. Fletcher was a guest in her home, and she wasn't being any more annoying than usual.

They reached the second floor. "I will see you and your sister downstairs, April," Mrs. Fletcher said, smiling.

April nodded and hurried in the opposite direction, wishing her father were not following. She would stand a better chance of reasoning with Vanessa if he weren't present.

She paused outside Vanessa's door, took a deep breath, then lifted her fist to knock.

Her hand froze in midair. There was laughter, and not just a woman's laughter. She was sure she heard the deep, throaty chuckle of a man!

Her father joined her, looking impatient. "Well, what is it? Won't she answer the door? We haven't got all night."

Before April could stop him, he reached around to grab the knob. The door swung open.

Vanessa was lying across her bed, her mussed ballgown twisted about her. Her bodice had been pulled down, completely exposing her breasts.

The man on top of her jumped up, and April gasped as she recognized Rance Taggart. His shirt was unbuttoned to the waist. She had seen his hand slide quickly away from Vanessa's breasts.

Vanessa's eyes glittered maliciously. Her long hair whipped about her face as she said, "Don't tell me I was missed at your party, sister, dear. Since I wasn't wanted, I decided to have one of my own and neither of you were invited."

Rance struggled to his feet, stuffing his shirttail into his trousers. Vanessa continued to lie there languidly, exposed, challenging anyone to admonish her.

Carter Jennings stood rigid with shock, his bulging eyes taking in the scene. Then, suddenly, he came alive, lunging forward, arms outstretched, hands reaching for Rance Taggart's throat.

Behind her, April heard a scream and was vaguely aware that Isabelle Fletcher was in the hallway, watching.

"I'll kill you for this!" The force of Carter's lunge at Rance took both of them to the floor. Rance was trying to get the older man away from him without hurting him, while struggling to breathe through Carter's grip on his throat.

Vanessa continued to lie there and watch, expressionless, making no move to cover her nakedness.

Sobbing, April hurried to pull her father away from Rance. She tripped and went sprawling to the floor. "Poppa, no!" she screamed, trying to get back on her feet, impaired by the giant hoop beneath her heavy skirt. "Poppa, you'll kill him!"

Mrs. Fletcher's screams had brought others to the upstairs hallway, and several crowded into the room to pull Carter away from Rance. It was difficult. In his wrath, the older man had a viselike hold on Rance's neck.

When they were finally able to get him to his feet, they led Carter out of the room and into the hall. He was still struggling fiercely, cursing and swearing, demanding that they release him at once.

Rance staggered to his feet, rubbing his bruised throat. He saw April struggling to stand, and he reached down and jerked her to her feet.

"If you stupid women wouldn't wear those silly iron bird cages, you could get up when you fall down," he commented.

"How dare you?" April's hand cracked across his face. "How dare you stand there and look so smug when you tried to rape my sister?"

His eyes widened as he looked from her to Vanessa, who started giggling. "You . . . you think I tried to rape her?" he asked incredulously.

"Oh, I wouldn't take anything for this," Vanessa laughed shrilly. "Poppa didn't want me at your party, and I had one of my own, and now everyone is upset. This is just marvelous!"

She saw Isabelle Fletcher watching in horror from the open doorway. "Well, what are you looking at?" Vanessa yelled. "If you'd open a few doors around your house, you'd find your son doing the same thing with your servant girls!"

With a gasp of outrage, Mrs. Fletcher backed out of the room and out of sight. Vanessa slowly tucked her breasts back into the bodice of her dress, then looked at Rance and said, "I think you'd better go now."

"Yeah," he said quietly, calmly, his eyes burning strangely into April's. "I suppose your party is over now."

"I think you should leave the way you came." Vanessa pointed toward the door leading to the veranda. "If Poppa sees you again, he'll kill you."

With a crooked smile, he looked at April and rubbed the red imprint of her hand upon his cheek with the back of his hand. "Don't ever do that again, blue eyes. I don't allow a woman to make more than one mistake."

April was speechless, staring as he walked out the door and disappeared into the night.

"He *is* a handsome devil, isn't he?" Vanessa got up and stood before her mirror. She picked up a brush and began stroking it through her wildly tangled hair.

April fought to speak. "How . . . how can you stand there so calmly after . . . after what you just did?"

Vanessa laughed shrilly. "We did not *do* anything, sister dear. We were merely, shall I say, enjoying ourselves? Rance would make a wonderful lover, though. He's so powerful, so strong! Couldn't you and Poppa have waited a few moments longer? Then you might have walked in on something quite fascinating."

"Vanessa, just shut up!" April stumbled toward the

veranda door, peering miserably out at the carriages now hurrying down the curving drive. The guests were leaving. The ball was over. "You ruined it all," she murmured. "I hope you're satisfied."

The sound of the hair brush slamming on the dresser made April turn quickly, startled. "Yes, I am quite satisfied." Vanessa's nostrils flared. Her face was starting to redden. Her whole body shook with her wrath. "You think I don't know what goes on around here? I heard Poppa say he did not want me at the party. And I heard you tell him what gossip it would provoke if I weren't there. The two of you—talking about me as though I were the family disgrace, some kind of poor, demented soul to be locked away where no one can see me! I won't stand for it, April. Not now or ever!"

As she moved forward, April shrank back, thinking Vanessa was about to strike her. But Vanessa grasped her hand and held it up, displaying the huge ring. "I see Poppa bestowed the precious ring upon you. That *is* the official family ring, isn't it?"

April nodded, numb. How could she explain to her sister that it was all right, she intended to share everything with her? In her present mood, Vanessa wouldn't listen.

"So! Pinehurst will be all yours, one day," Vanessa said. She slung April's hand away, her breath coming in gasps as she continued her furious explosion. "You go on and enjoy yourself for now, my father's precious darling. But one day *my* day will come, and then you will pay for all you have ever done to hurt me."

"I never tried to hurt you. I love you, Vanessa. I hate the way Poppa has treated you all these years. It wasn't fair for him to blame you for Mother dying, and I've told him that over and over. You can ask Posie. She's heard me argue with him and defend you."

"Lies! All lies!" Vanessa whirled away, starting to pace up and down the room, wringing her hands as tears streamed down her face. "Get out of here. I don't want to listen to you anymore."

"I must make you understand," April begged. "You arranged all this tonight so you would be discovered. You wanted to embarrass Poppa. But don't you see? You've only embarrassed yourself. You ruined the party, if that was your intent, but I don't care about that. I care about you and what you've done to yourself. I'd rather you tell me that Rance forced his way in here and tried to rape you than—"

"Perhaps that might have been true, once." Vanessa stopped pacing to smile at her. "But Rance does not have to rape his women. All he has to do is kiss them and touch them in a special way, and they beg to be taken, as I did."

"He's been around animals so long he's become one himself."

"But a wonderful animal," Vanessa gloated. "The kind a woman is born to please."

"I won't listen to any more of this. Tomorrow, when we've all calmed down, we'll talk. Good night, Vanessa." April hurried from the room, grateful to see that the hallway was empty.

She walked to the stairway and looked down at the empty house. Posie was just closing the front door. "Is that the last of our guests?" she called down softly.

Posie looked up at her, tears streaming down her dark cheeks. "Yes'm. It didn't take 'em long to clear out. Missus Fletcher, she invited ever'body over to her house. I think most of 'em went. Prob'ly just to gossip. It's a shame. A terrible, terrible shame." She shook her head from side to side.

"Where is Poppa?"

"Buford took him some whiskey and said he was gonna sit with him till he got hold of hisself. He wanted to get a gun and kill that Taggart boy. He's mad at Miss Vanessa, too. She's sho' gonna hear about this fo' a long, long time."

"I don't think any of us will ever forget it, Posie," April sighed. "I'm going to bed now, though I doubt I'll sleep."

"Want me to bring you up somethin' to eat? We got plenty of food left. Won't hardly none of it touched."

"I can't eat. Thank you." She went to her room and started to pull the bell cord for Lucy, but decided she would rather be alone. She struggled out of the crinolines and hoops by herself. She put out the lantern, crawled under the satin coverlet and stared into the darkness.

Sleep would not come. It was a nightmare. She knew she would never forget the sight of Vanessa lying there, her breasts exposed, being fondled by Rance Taggart.

Rance Taggart. She could feel only hatred for him. Cold, consuming hatred. She trembled with it.

It was difficult now to recall the cobwebs of childhood memories when they had played together. The times had been rare, for as soon as her father discovered she was with the son of a hired hand, he had reprimanded her. But there had been some warm summer afternoons splashing in a secret pond, and hours spent whispering in the shadows of the stable as he confided his love of horses, and dreams of growing up to conquer the West.

Then he had gone away, she could not remember exactly when. The years passed, and when he returned, he was a man. A very handsome man. One day, while strolling through the woods and savoring the sweet smell of spring's arrival, she overheard two Negro stableboys talking nearby. Hearing Rance's name, she paused and listened. Perhaps it was the pity in their voices that caught her interest. The gossip was that Rance Taggart had returned to Pinehurst after his wandering years to escape some anguish over a young Mexican girl. She had wondered about that for some time.

Now her thoughts wandered back to the way Rance had looked, there on the bed with her sister. A warm flush crept through her body, making her feel ashamed. He was a fiercely desirable man.

He had not looked the least bit frightened when he and Vanessa were discovered. There had been the play of an arrogant smile on his full, sensuous lips. It was difficult to imagine *any* woman being capable of breaking *his* heart. Had the Mexican girl done so?

But after tonight, she found him unbearable. Her father had been good to Rance, paying him well and giving him a comfortable place to live. Nothing justified his being a party to Vanessa's vicious scheme.

Slowly, the great hand of sleep waved over her weary body. There would be ample time tomorrow to remember the agony of the evening. She would talk to Vanessa again, and to Poppa, and maybe she could make peace between them.

April's eyes flashed open. She stared into the darkness, struggling to bring herself to full awareness. What was that strange noise?

She heard it again—the rhythmic sound of dull thuds. Throwing back the covers, she sat up, her feet touching the cold floor. There was another sound—as though someone were grunting and someone else was struggling to breathe. It was coming from across the hall. Vanessa's room!

She groped for her robe, jerked it about her shoulders, then padded quickly across the floor to fumble for the door-knob. She stepped into the hall. The sound was louder, and now she was sure she heard muffled cries.

She did not pause to knock at Vanessa's door but opened it and rushed in. She screamed.

Vanessa lay across the bed on her stomach, completely naked. Her back was crisscrossed with bleeding welts. Their father towered above her, methodically wielding a leather strap. Vanessa was writhing in pain beneath the onslaught, her fists bloodied as she bit down on them to stifle her screams.

"Poppa, no!" April lunged forward, flinging her own body across Vanessa's, catching the next blow herself and crying out with pain.

"April, get out of here!" Carter Jennings cried, reaching down to jerk her from the bed. "Go back to your room. This is none of your business."

April twisted away from him, once more shielding Vanessa with her own body. "I won't leave, and don't you dare strike her again. You're beating her to death."

"I don't care! The she-devil deserves to die. Now get out of the way. She's needed this for a long time. I'll beat the demons out of her."

He reeked of whiskey, and was struggling to stay on his feet. She began to scream as loudly as she could, until he begged her to stop.

Footsteps thundered down the hall, and April was grateful to see Buford standing in the doorway. "Do something," she cried out to him. "He's killing Vanessa. He's drunk, and he doesn't know what he's doing."

Buford came forward reluctantly and put his arm around his master's waist. "This ain't the answer, Massa," he said in a trembling voice. "You had too much to drink, and tomorrow, you gonna feel bad about all this. Now let's go on back to yo' room, and I'll help you into bed."

"No!" Carter lurched away, giving him a shove that sent the old Negro staggering backward. "Get Mandy in here. Tell her to put some clothes on this trollop. Then I want you to drag her out the front door. She's no longer my daughter."

"I never was your daughter," Vanessa rasped feebly. "You've always hated me, and for something I couldn't help! I'll leave this house, gladly. I don't want to spend another night under your roof."

Carter stood swaying, eyes opening and closing slowly as he watched her crawl from the bed, blood trickling from her back. April tried to help her, but Vanessa used what little strength she had to fend her sister off. "Leave me alone. I don't want you to touch me," she cried. "I don't want any of you hyprocrites to touch me. I just want to get out of here."

"Vanessa, you can't leave. Where would you go? Please, listen. We'll talk all of this out tomorrow. I'll send for Reverend Filmore. He'll help us. I know he will. You just can't go, Vanessa. Please listen to me!" April began to cry.

". . . wasn't my fault my mother died," Vanessa panted as she struggled into a dress she had yanked from her wardrobe. "Only a crazy person would blame me for that." She cast hate-filled eyes at her father.

Carter raised the strap ominously and yelled, "You watch your tongue, or I'll finish beating every scrap of skin from your worthless hide."

"You won't!" April turned on him. "You touch her again, and I'll leave, too, Poppa. Now stop it! You're drunk!"

"He's crazy as a loon!" Vanessa jerked a shawl from a drawer, wincing as it touched her back. Blood was already seeping through her dress. Suddenly she whirled on April.

"And you're crazy, too, if you think I'll let you just take over and have everything! You won't get Pinehurst, April. I have a heritage, too!"

"I never said you didn't, Vanessa. I will always share with you, you know that!"

Carter started around the bed, but Buford blocked him. "You won't get a goddamn thing I own, you little bitch!" he screamed, waving the strap as Buford struggled to hold him back. Vanessa inched her way to the door. "I'll see to it that your name is never mentioned in this house or on my property again. If I ever see your face, I'll kill you— just as you killed your mother!"

He sagged against Buford, knees buckling, and the old Negro lowered him quickly to the bed. "I think he's havin' some kind of attack, Miss April," he cried in fright. "You better get somebody to fetch the doctor quick."

"I hope he dies!" Vanessa paused at the door to scream. "I hope all of you die!"

"Vanessa, wait!" April wanted to go after her, but she knew that her father really was stricken. Vanessa would not go far, and help had to be summoned for her father. She told Buford to open his shirt, try to help him breathe.

She ran into her own room and yanked the bell cord, then decided that Posie might be so sound asleep she would not hear it. Returning to the hall, she saw Mandy standing beside Vanessa at the top of the stairs, holding a candle. "Don't let her leave," she called out to the black girl as she made her way to the first floor. "I'll be back in a few minutes. Get her into bed. I'll want the doctor to check her after he sees to Poppa."

She found a lantern, lit it, then went to the rear of the house to awaken Posie and send her up to help Buford. Then she made her way through the chilling night to the servants' quarters, ordering one of the men to fetch the doctor at once.

By the time she returned to the house, Vanessa was gone, and Mandy was sitting on the bottom step crying brokenly. "She wouldn't listen to me. She say she'd rather die than stay here another night. She just walked out the door. Wasn't nothin' I could do to stop her, and I tried, Miz April, I swear to the Lord, I tried."

April gave her a quick pat on the shoulder as she moved by. "She won't get far, Mandy. It's cold out there, and she's hurt. Let me see to Poppa, and then we'll find her and bring her back. I know you did all you could."

She ran up the steps, her heart racing. Though she was indoors, the night wind still surrounded her, wrapping icy fingers around her.

Somehow, April Jennings knew that this night marked the beginning of an agony such as none of them had ever known.

❧ Chapter Three ❧

THE women were gathered in front of the fireplace in the Pinehurst parlor. The fire had begun to die down, and Buford entered to place fresh logs in the grate. The first chill of autumn was in the air, and a cold north wind blew, rattling the windows. Posie kept the teapots filled and promised that a lunch of chicken and drap dumplings would soon be ready. Even in a region where drap dumplings appeared regularly on everyone's table, Posie was famous for hers. A creation of flour and water, they were dropped into hot fat and cooked quickly.

The women were working deftly on a quilt which was mounted on a stretching rack. Katherine Downing complained, "It takes so long to make these. We could put our time to better use if we went to Mary Dobbins's house, where the ladies are making bandages."

Isabelle Fletcher made a face as she pushed a threaded needle in and out of the material. "It's depressing to make bandages and lint, Katherine. I'd rather think my efforts were being used to keep a poor, freezing soldier warm than to sop up blood."

Katherine stiffened, lips pursing tightly. "But bandages could save a life and keep a soldier from bleeding to death. I think tomorrow I'll just go over to Mary's and work there."

"You won't hear all the latest gossip," laughed Thalia Morrow, a plump woman with apple-red cheeks. She had

33

always disliked Isabelle Fletcher. "Mary frowns on gossip. But it's doted on around here, it seems."

"I do not gossip," Isabelle retorted, "and I get so tired of your sniping, Thalia. The only reason you come here is to try and start a quarrel."

Thalia stopped stitching to glare across the blanket at Isabelle. "That's not true. I come because it's closer to my home. And I love April Jennings and feel she needs company, with her father so sickly—"

"Sickly. Hmph! The word is crazy. Everyone says so. Ever since that night he caught that trollop daughter of his naked in her own bed with that stableboy, he's been tetched in the head. Everybody says so."

"He had a stroke," Katherine interjected. "The doctor said he just got so angry that something happened inside. I say it's his spirit that's broken. That was a terrible thing. After all, it was the most lavish ball in all of Montgomery. People passed up invitations to several others to be here. To have Vanessa do what she did . . ." She shook her head in pity. "It was awful. I'm surprised the poor man didn't just drop dead."

Isabelle sniffed. "Stroke, my eye. The man went crazy, that's all. Where do you think April is this minute? Upstairs coddling him, trying to get him to eat. One of their servants told one of my servants that all he does is sit and stare out the window. He never says a word unless it's to call out to his dead wife."

She glanced about to make sure none of the servants was hovering about, then spoke so softly that the rest of the ladies had to strain to hear. "The servant also said that she heard him talk to April like he thinks *she* is his dead wife. If you ask me, that's proof that he's tetched."

"I don't know." Katherine sighed. "I grieve so for April. She's had so much on her shoulders these past months. She's tried to run things, but it's just too much for her. I hear the Pinehurst cotton crop was so poor that they didn't make a thing from it this year. You can tell things are getting run down."

Isabelle commented, "It's a shame. But in one way, it's what Carter Jennings deserved. He always was pompous. Now he's getting his comeuppance."

Thalia laughed. "Carter was a powerful man and you know it, Isabelle. Heaven knows, that son of yours tried his best to court April. He wanted to marry into the family and get some of that wealth and power. But April wouldn't have him."

"That's not true! *She* chased *him*! I was the one who put a stop to that romance. I didn't want my son marrying into trash, and that's all you can call it. *I* was there that night, remember? I saw Vanessa Jennings lying naked in the arms of that stableboy, and I *knew* what they were doing."

"I should hope you would," Katherine giggled. "Or did you find Graham under a collard plant?"

"Go on. Laugh. How would you two have felt if your son had been smitten by one of those girls?"

Katherine quickly said, "Well, I would have no qualms whatsoever if my Thaddeus married April Jennings. She's a sweet and beautiful girl. I'd be proud to have her for a daughter-in-law."

"Not I!" Isabelle shook her head firmly. "I'd disinherit Graham, and his father and I both told him so. Thank heavens he's put that woman out of his mind. He's so involved with the war. He's Company Captain now, you know. He was at Wilson's Creek in August. He came out without a scratch."

"Maybe he wasn't really *in* the battle," Thalia pointed out slyly. "Maybe he was behind the lines in a tent, mapping strategy. I've heard that's what the officers do. They seldom get into the fighting."

Isabelle's cheeks reddened. "That's not so. I will have you to know that the Union commander, General Lyon, was killed in that battle. Officers are always being killed or wounded. Graham just happens to be a good soldier and a good officer, and he's careful. His father and I are quite proud of him.

"Besides," she continued, her fingers working fast and furiously, whipping the needle in and out of the quilt. "According to all reports, the war won't last much longer. The South has won most of the battles so far."

"Only because both sides are just unruly mobs," Thalia snapped. "My brother, Monroe, is up in Richmond, and he wrote his wife that we haven't begun to see the bloodshed."

Katherine sighed, "Well, I'm just thankful they decided to move the capital out of Montgomery up to Richmond. That makes Virginia the major battleground and Richmond the primary Union target. It keeps the war out of Alabama, which suits me just fine."

"You're forgetting Selma," Thalia was quick to point out. "They're making powder there, and once they finish building that big arsenal, they're going to start making cannons. You can be sure the Yankees will want to do something about Selma, and that's not too far from here, ladies."

"Oh, hogwash and turkey feathers!" Isabelle laughed. "The Yankees will never, ever, get this far. My Graham promised it."

April entered the room, and they all fell silent for a moment, taking in her haggard appearance. Katherine was the first to speak. "Dear, I hope you don't mind that we came on in and got started. You look as though you don't feel well. If you would like to go upstairs and lie down, we can work without you. I think we'll even finish this quilt today and be able to start another."

"Yes, you do that," Thalia spoke up, voice filled with concern. "Posie said she'll be bringing in lunch soon. Chicken and dumplings. You could eat a bite and then go lie down."

"No. I'd like to work for a while. I like to keep busy." She sat down next to Isabelle only because it was the last place left from which to work on the quilt. After that horrible night so many months ago, when the woman had witnessed the awful scene, April had not wanted to be around Isabelle Fletcher. She knew Isabelle was responsible for a lot of the gossip about her family.

"Is your father not feeling well today?" Isabelle asked in a too-sweet voice.

"He had a bad night," she answered quietly. "He hardly slept at all."

Isabelle turned to stare directly into April's face. "Seems to me he gets worse all the time. Tell me, is it true that he has spells when he thinks you are your mother? That must be dreadful for you, dear."

"No, that isn't so. I don't know how you could have heard such a thing." April kept her head down, working her needle in and out, afraid that the lie would show on her face. Which one of the servants had been gossiping again? she wondered furiously. "Actually, Poppa is better. He just feels bad once in a while and needs to rest. There's no need for concern."

Isabelle glanced around the parlor significantly as she said, "Goodness, April dear, you can tell he's allowing the place to become run down. The crops weren't good this year, and I hear he's lost all interest in those expensive horses of his. It's such a pity that despicable Rance Taggart stole your father's prize colt when he ran away that night."

April held her temper with great effort. She was aware that Thalia Morrow and Katherine Downing were waiting to see what she would do. This confrontation with Isabelle had been coming for some time. In the weeks they had all been gathering to make quilts, Isabelle had been goading her methodically.

Isabelle Fletcher was watching, too. She enjoyed seeing April squirm. It compensated a little for the callous way April had rebuked Graham's request to court her. "Do you ever hear from Vanessa? I don't see how she could have survived on her own. I understand she left with only the clothes on her back. How many months has it been now? This is October, and that ugly thing happened in February, just before President Davis was inaugurated. So, let me see . . . that would make it about eight months. And what if she were *pregnant* when she ran away?"

April stood so quickly that the quilting frame tilted and fell to the floor. She pointed a trembling finger. "Mrs. Fletcher, I will thank you to leave this house at once. I've tolerated your nosy questions and cruel remarks as long as I can. You only come over here to see what you can find out so you can gossip about my family."

"Well, of all the nerve—" Isabelle stood, stunned.

"Yes, I would say you do have a lot of nerve, Mrs. Fletcher. What I would like to know is why? Did that spoiled, lecherous son of yours tell you I refused to allow him to court me? I would rather die an old maid than marry that revolting despicable cad. When I think of all the times he practically attacked me, I wish I'd had my father give him the thrashing he deserved."

"How dare you talk about my son that way? How dare

you? I would never have him court you, you little trollop. Why, you're no better than your sister. I saw her naked in the arms of that stableboy."

"You saw them kissing and caressing and no more. My sister's breasts were exposed but the rest of her clothes were intact. Mr. Taggart was fully clothed. But you had to make the story worse than it was! Why? What possible pleasure could you derive from doing such a thing, Mrs. Fletcher? I think you have a warped mind, and as angry as you make me, I still pity you. But I also want you to leave my house and never come back. You are no longer welcome."

"Oh, I'll leave, all right." Isabelle Fletcher grabbed her shawl from the back of her chair. Her chin jutted upward. Her eyes were narrow slits of malice. "And I promise you one thing, you little snit. Pinehurst has not seen the problems it is going to encounter. When I tell my husband about this, you may be sure your water rights will be curtailed."

The others gasped, but April said coolly, "I have carefully studied all my father's business papers, and I know that there is a legal binding agreement concerning the water rights. Before you make threats, I suggest you know what you are talking about. If you attempt to break the agreement, you may rest assured the matter will be dealt with in court."

Buford had heard the loud voices and appeared then, standing apprehensively in the doorway. April saw him and spoke in a cool, controlled tone. "Show Mrs. Fletcher to the door, please, and advise the other servants that she is not to be admitted to Pinehurst again unless I inform them otherwise."

Isabelle's eyes flashed fire. "You will pay for this, April Jennings. Just wait and see! Who do you think you are?" She whirled toward the door, then stopped to look back at Thalia and Katherine. "Why are you sitting there? Aren't you leaving with me? Certainly you don't want to be in the company of such a rude woman!"

"No, we certainly don't," Thalia said quietly as she picked up her needle and began stitching once more. "That's why we aren't leaving with you, Isabelle."

With a final cry of indignation, Isabelle stormed out the door.

April sat down again, suddenly very tired. "I apologize to you ladies. I'm sorry you had to witness that."

Thalia gave her hand a comforting pat as Katherine clucked approval. "Dear, we understand. We're glad you stood up to her. She's had it coming for a long time.

April bent her head over the quilt and began to stitch. She hoped they would not notice the tears that filled her eyes. Lately, she felt as though she spent most of her time around others fighting to hold back, not give way to the turmoil inside. Only when she was alone, could she succumb. Dear God, how much longer would this go on?

There had been no word from Vanessa. The colt had disappeared when she did. Perhaps Rance Taggart stole the animal, and he and Vanessa had left together. What was worse, her father was crumbling before her eyes. Since that night, he seemed to be only a shadow of himself, and she often wondered whether it had been caused by his stroke or by the humiliation Vanessa had caused him.

The doctor had said there was no medical reason to explain her father's condition. Carter Jennings spent almost all his waking hours sitting in a chair, staring out his bedroom window, the expression on his face suggesting that he was somewhere far, far away, in a world of his own.

What frightened her most, and what she could not tell anyone, was the way he often looked at her, smiling as he whispered: "Lorena, my beloved. You've come back to me."

She had tried to reason. "No, Poppa. It's me, April. Not Momma. Momma died a long, long time ago."

The first few times it had happened, a sad awareness had washed over him, and he'd blinked several times and murmured in a sad voice, "Oh. It's you, April."

Then one day the awareness did not come. He had laughed, "Don't tease me, darling. I know it's you. Could I ever forget your beautiful face?" And April had run from the room to weep.

Perhaps she would not have lost all patience with Isabelle had it not been for a scene that morning. Once again,

he had seen her as her mother, but before she could turn
and hurry from the room, he had reached out for her with
a strength she did not realize he still possessed. She cried
out, startled, as he pulled her into his lap, his arms about
her, lips seeking hers, and whispered huskily, "My darling,
how I've wanted you. I could never find the passion with
another woman to match what I knew in your arms."

"No!" April screamed in horror, struggling to release
herself. "No, Poppa, stop! It's me! Not Momma. Momma's
dead!"

"Let me hold you." He slipped a hand upward to caress
her breast. "I want to hear you moan with pleasure."

With a lunge that caught him off balance, April managed to spring to her feet. He was right behind her, catching her skirt as she rushed through the door. The fabric
tore, and he stood there clutching it in his hand, staring
after her with a lost, pained look. "I don't understand,
Lorena," he called after her. "You never refused me before. You always wanted me to make love to you. . . ."

April locked her door and stood there gasping as a great
chill spread through her. Dry sobs racked from her throat,
and then her stomach pitched and rolled, and she staggered
quickly to the chamber pot barely in time to lose her
breakfast. She sagged onto the bed, shuddering in horror.
If she had not escaped him, he would have taken her. Dear
Lord, her own father!

He was losing his mind. She was sure of it. Perhaps the
death of her mother had been the start of it all, and ever
since, insanity had been digging into his brain. That might
explain his rejection of Vanessa over the years, the feeling
that had eventually turned to hatred.

Lost in thought, she did not hear Thalia tell her that
Posie had announced lunch. A firm hand was clamped on
her shoulder, shaking her, and she glanced up. "My dear,
you are in a stupor." Thalia was looking at her with great
concern. "Perhaps when Dr. Grainger visits your father
next, he should have a look at you."

"I agree," Katherine chimed in. "With your father ill,
you're probably doing too much. After we eat lunch, you
just go lie down. We'll finish up this quilt."

"Yes, you need the rest," Thalia agreed, and then the
two women took up positions on either side of April, as

though afraid she would not be able to make it to the dining room unescorted.

April forced herself to eat, though the food was tasteless to her. When Mandy appeared in the doorway and beckoned to her, she excused herself gratefully and followed her into the back hallway.

"It's Mastah Moseley." Mandy grinned secretively, holding on to her full skirt with her fingertips and swaying from side to side. "I reckon he's come to court again, 'cause he's hidin' down in the stable and told one of the hands to send word to you he was there."

April bit her lower lip thoughtfully, then asked, "Have you said anything about this to anyone, Mandy?"

The Negro girl's eyes grew wide, and she shook her head. "No'm. I ain't said nothin', just like you tol' me not to. I come right heah to tell you, just like the other times. I ain't even said nothin' to Posie."

"I can trust Posie. I just don't want you talking to all the servants. Someone here has been gossiping to the servants at Mrs. Fletcher's, and I don't know who it is, so I'm not taking any chances. Now you go to the stable yourself and tell Master Moseley that I will be there shortly."

Mandy started to turn away, but paused, looking thoughtful. Her eyes danced mischievously. "Seems funny fo' me to be callin' Mastah Moseley, Mastah, when he's 'bout as poor as I is."

April stiffened, felt her cheeks coloring. Mandy scooted down the hall, lifting her skirts as she skipped along.

April knew that the girl had been quite fond of Vanessa. Mandy was about the only human being Vanessa had ever been even slightly tolerant of. Several times Vanessa had even given her old gowns to the girl. As a result, Mandy defended her mistress when the other servants criticized her.

After Vanessa left, Mandy had cried for days. But then almost overnight, she seemed to be her old self again. She hovered around April, as though replacing her devotion to Vanessa with devotion to her. April accepted this graciously, wanting to ease her loss. Gradually, Mandy became her personal maid. Everything had worked out satisfactorily, except for those distressing times when Mandy became uppity, even sassy.

Mandy did not like Alton Moseley. April was aware of that. Mandy had belligerently hinted that he had no right to be calling. April reminded her angrily that she was out of place. There had been an apology, but the slips still came.

True, Alton was poor. April had seen the two-room shack that was home for Alton and his parents and the seven other Moseley children. But wealth made no difference. He had been a friend to her when she needed one most. And now that Frank Taggart and his wife were gone, as well as Rance, it was Alton who had charge of the stables.

April began to spend a lot of time at the stables. At first she meant only to get away from her father. But then she and Alton became friends. She found herself confiding in him, telling him of her miseries, except for her father's thinking that she was her mother. She could not make herself divulge that to anyone, not yet.

She thought of him only as a friend, but had lately realized that he had more in mind than friendship. It disturbed her, but what could she do?

Now April went to her room and changed to something warmer. Even as far south as Alabama, the October afternoons could be quite chilly. With a shawl wrapped about her shoulders, she walked quietly down the back stairway, careful not to be seen; then slipped out the rear door and hurried toward the stables.

The crepe myrtles had bloomed all summer. Now the leaves were patches of gold and brown against the cloudy sky. A few already skittered and danced their way to the ground. In the field to her left, the parched, gnarled cotton plants were already dead. On her right, she could see the Negro slaves—or *servants* as she preferred to call them, or field hands, anything but *slaves*—moving through the cornfields, gathering the last of the crop. She hoped the corn would bring a lot of money. Goodness knows, they needed money.

When she reached the stables, she entered the larger building. Alton had improvised sleeping quarters in the back room there, so he would not have to return to his home every night. April suspected he liked the extra room, even if it was in a stable.

The warm smell of manure mingled with the faint odor of polished leather. April loved the stables and the horses. She felt peaceful here. Back in the huge house, she felt as though she were suffocating.

Alton stepped out of a nearby stall, a bucket of feed in his hand. "Hello," he greeted her, a bit uneasily, she thought. "I see you got my message. I never know if Mandy will deliver it. She's a funny one."

"She . . . she teased me. Said you were coming to court me." April tried to sound light, humorous, but her brows were already knitting together.

They made the usual small talk, discussing the horses as she followed him from stall to stall to fill the feed bins. She sensed that there was something wrong and soon she asked bluntly, "What's wrong, Alton? You're behaving quite strangely."

He set the bucket down at his feet, then reached to brush a golden tendril back from her forehead. She waited, sensing that he was gathering courage. He took a deep breath, let it out slowly, then said, "I've got to go to war, honey. There's just no getting around it any longer. I've hung back, because of you, wanting to be around to look out for you. Now things seem to be getting ready to bust loose. I've got to go fight for the South. I feel I must. Can you understand that?"

She felt as though the air were being sucked from her lungs. Alton leaving? His friendship was all that kept her going. To lose him was more than she could bear.

Suddenly, she was washed with shame. Her thoughts had been only of herself, not of the dangers he would face in war. And he was right. All the able-bodied men were marching off to defend their homeland.

She wiped at her tears with the back of her hand and whispered, "I'll pray for your safe return, Alton, and I shall miss you deeply."

"I knew you'd be this way," he cried suddenly, joyfully. He placed his hands on her shoulders and gathered her close, his lips touching hers. Strangely, she felt herself responding, but even then she knew her reaction had nothing to do with love. She did not love Alton. He was shelter from the storm.

He stepped back to give her a lopsided grin, his hair tumbling down over his forehead. "I knew you'd be upset when I told you, April. You do care for me! Maybe not a whole lot, but you feel something. And I want you to marry me. I want you to be my wife."

He was speaking rapidly, as though he knew if he hesitated, for even a second, she would begin reciting reasons for refusing. "You don't have to go live with my folks, though you could if things got real bad here. Shucks, they might not have a big house, but they all got big hearts, and they'd take you in and see you didn't go hungry. Maybe you think I'm a fool to ask you to marry me, when I'm poor as a church mouse, but when you love somebody like I love you, you act like a fool, I reckon.

"I mean," he rushed on, brushing away the tears that were slowly moving down her smooth cheeks, "I see that big mansion you live in, your fine clothes and all, and I know I can't ever give you those things. But God knows, I love you with every beat of my heart, April, and I'd never do anything to hurt you, I swear to you."

It had all happened so quickly, like the flash of lightning in a summer storm. Her brain was spinning. Her lips moved but she made no sound.

"I'm going to speak to your daddy," Alton said firmly as he folded her in his arms and held her tightly against him. "I'm going to go to him and respectfully ask for your hand in marriage."

Once more, April was ashamed, for her mind was now telling her that this was the way out of her misery. This was the chance to get away from her father and his increasing insanity. As wrong as it might be to marry a man she did not love, there seemed to be no other answer.

He cupped her chin, lifting her face for his kiss. "I'll make you happy, April," he smiled. She saw the glimmer of unshed tears and knew he was ecstatic.

She responded to his kiss and, as he held her, she prayed silently that God would understand and forgive her.

🍂 Chapter Four 🍂

NOON shadows danced along the ceiling. April knew she should get out of bed, but she did not move. She was weary from crying since early dawn. More than that, she was frustrated from the constant struggle to hide her tears. Most of all, she hated herself for not being able to do anything about the miserable existence her life had become.

Coward. She winced as she scalded herself with the word. That's what she was. A coward for finding only one road left open—escape. Marriage to Alton would be an escape. But even if she remained at home, there was nothing she could do for her father.

True, there were times when he seemed his old self, but these occasions were becoming rare. The servants were gossiping openly now, and only faithful old Posie and Buford would even go near him. The others whispered fearfully that their master was mad . . . and dangerous.

Dangerous. The word danced about in her mind, stabbing painfully. He did not mean to harm her. But only that morning, in the early hours, he had come to her door and, finding it locked, rapped softly and called out, "Lorena. Why are you locking me out? I want you, darling, and you know how good it will be."

She had covered her face with her pillows, trying to shut out his voice. When she did not answer, he began to pound on the door with his fists. She had huddled beneath the

45

covers, sobbing in terror, frightened that he would break down the door.

Finally he petulantly called, "This isn't like you, Lorena. You've never refused me before. I'm quite angry with you. I'm your husband, and I have my rights."

After what seemed forever, he gave up, and she heard the sound of his shuffling footsteps as he returned to his own room.

Dear God, how much more could she take? How much longer could she fend him off?

Someone knocked on her door, and she cringed. She would not answer. Let him think she had gone out for the day.

"Miss April, is you sick?"

Posie! She leaped from the bed, almost tripping in her haste to unlock the door.

"How come you ain't been downstairs?" Posie looked at her suspiciously as she entered the room. "Mandy said she knocked early this mornin', and you didn't answer. What's wrong child? You look might poorsome."

April turned away, not wanting Posie to see her red-rimmed eyes. "I'm fine. I must've been asleep when Mandy knocked. I guess I'm just being lazy."

"Well, I come up to tell you this is one of yo' daddy's good days. He's up and dressed and been downstairs in his study workin'. He tol' me to come up here and see if you is comin' down for lunch. I got collards and fatback and some sweet tater puddin'."

April sighed with relief. If her father was having a good day, then he would behave normally, and there was no need to be afraid.

Then, with a wave of joy, she thought of Alton. It would not do for him to speak to her father when he was in one of his dazes. She would send for Alton today.

There was no other way. She could only pray to God that Alton would never know she did not truly love him, and she vowed silently to do everything in her power to make him happy.

She took a deep breath, gathering her wits about her as she turned to face Posie. "I want you to send Mandy to the stables to find Alton," she said. "I want her to invite him here for lunch today."

"Mastah Alton Moseley?" Posie's eyes bugged. "You ain't serious, is you, chile? You know how yo' poppa is, and he ain't gonna want no po' white trash eatin' at his table."

"Alton is not white trash!" April flared.

Posie was instantly contrite. "I'm sorry. I know he's a fine young man, but he is po', and yo' poppa ain't gonna want him eatin' here. You mark my words. Yo' poppa gonna be mad. All Mastah Moseley is around here is a stable hand, and yo' poppa ain't never had none o' them at his table. Not even the Taggarts, when they was here."

She paused, then glared at her. "Now I done tol' you he's havin' a good day. How come you wants to go and ruin it?"

April would not back down. How could she? "Do as I say, Posie. I don't have to explain myself to you." She hated speaking so sharply, but she was too desperate to argue. "You see that Mandy invites Alton here for lunch today."

Posie murmured "Yes'm" and bustled from the room, mumbling to herself.

April splashed cool water on her face from the porcelain bowl on her dresser, then began to brush her long golden hair. She chose a light green wool dress with a high, lace-edged collar and long, fitted sleeves. Finding a matching ribbon of green velvet, she tied her hair back so that the natural curls fell about her shoulders. Dabbing a touch of cologne about her ears, she looked in the mirror and decided that she looked as mature as she should look for the occasion.

On her way downstairs, she met Mandy coming up. Her face was bright with excitement, and she spoke breathlessly. "I did what you asked, Miss April. Mastah Alton, he say to give him time to clean up a bit, and he'd be here. He was cleanin' out stalls, and you know what he smells like!" She held her nose and giggled.

"Don't say anything to anyone, Mandy," April warned. "I want to be the one to tell my father we have a guest."

She started on down the stairs, but Mandy made her pause. "He ain't gonna like it. Not one bit. He's gonna have a pure fit. Ain't no stableboy ever set his boots under his table before."

She paused to giggle and cover her mouth with her hands before rushing on. "How come you's sweet on Mastah Alton, Miss April? You could have yo' pick o' rich boys. How come you likes him? If you could've smelled him a lil' while ago, you'd know why I think it's so funny, you likin' a man what smells like—"

"Mandy!" April stared at her incredulously. "I don't care what you think. I'll thank you to keep your thoughts to yourself. I happen to be quite fond of Mr. Mosely, and there is nothing wrong with his being a stable hand. It's honest work. And speaking of work, isn't there some *you* could be doing, instead of tending to my business?"

Mandy's eyes dropped. "Yes'm," she murmured.

"Besides," April added, "would you rather I were interested in Graham Fletcher?"

"Oh, no ma'm!" Mandy's eyes grew large as she shook her kinky head from side to side. "No, ma'm! I's scared of that man. I hears things about him. I hears he goes down to the slave shacks at their place and rapes the young girls any time he wants to. They say one was just ten years old. They say she's gonna have a baby, and—"

"Mandy, please don't gossip." April was losing her patience. The girl was young, perhaps only fourteen or fifteen years old, and while she was fond of her and found her youthful innocence amusing at times, there were other occasions when she was annoying.

She gave her an affectionate pat on her shoulder and told her to run along. "And I want you to watch that tongue of yours. I don't like the servants gossiping."

April moved on down the stairs and turned to go to the rear of the house and speak with Posie. But his voice boomed out, "April? Is that you? Come in here, please."

April stiffened, then walked to the door. She saw him sitting behind his huge oak desk, which was covered with ledgers and papers. He wore a white ruffled shirt, open at the throat. With the intent, concentrated expression on his handsome mature face, it was ludicrous to think him insane. He looked so calm . . . in complete control.

He looked up. "April darling, you look beautiful," he smiled, pushing a ledger aside. "Where have you been all morning? I missed you at breakfast. I'd hoped we could go riding."

"I'm glad you're feeling better." She stepped inside but did not take the seat he gestured to. "There's so much work to be done around here, Poppa, and you might get stronger if you tried to do a little each day when you're feeling like it. I've been worried about how run down things are getting—"

"I know, I know," he said airily, waving his hand as though to dismiss the subject. "But with the war it's hard to concentrate on everyday things. If I were younger, I'd be out fighting the goddamn yankees myself. Sometimes I think I should join up, anyway. There are plenty of good men my age in battle."

"After your stroke, your doctor would never agree to your going off to war," she said quickly.

A frown touched his forehead, and his eyes shadowed briefly. "I was upset, April. I became physically ill, and what man wouldn't? But I've told you, I don't want to discuss it. It didn't happen."

"It *did* happen, and you aren't well, Poppa, and you know it. This is one of your good days, and I'm glad, but you have to acknowledge the fact that you aren't completely well."

"I'm fine." He rose from his chair and walked around to stand before her. "That was a long time ago, and life must go on. I'm going to get things in shape around here. You'll see."

"Poppa," she pressed on hesitantly. "On your . . . your *bad* days, do you remember anything? I mean, I find you sitting in your room, staring out the window like you're not really here. I speak to you, but you don't answer me. Do you remember those days? What happens when you seem to be in a fog?"

"What is this?" he demanded. "You think you're my doctor, April? What does it matter what I'm thinking then? I told you. Sometimes I don't feel well. I don't feel like talking to anyone."

"But do you remember anything, Poppa?" she repeated. "Anything at all about . . . what you do?"

He turned away. "It doesn't matter. Why are you needling me? Have I done anything to offend you?"

"You think I am my mother."

For a moment, he stood frozen. Then he turned slowly,

a bewildered look in his eyes. "Are you trying to tell me that I speak to you as though you are your mother? That's insane, April. You look like her, true. You're as beautiful as she was, but—"

"I didn't mean to bring this up." April squeezed her hands together to stop their trembling. "I didn't want to mention it, but it worries me. You aren't yourself on those days, and you think I'm my mother, and—"

"This is nonsense." He turned abruptly and walked briskly to his desk once more and began to shuffle his papers around. "I tell you, I'm fine. I suffered a great shock, but I've chosen to forget it. Now let's have lunch. Later, we can go for a ride. And there will be no more of this kind of talk."

The sound of the heavy brass knocker banging on the front door surprised both of them. "I wonder who could be calling at this hour," Carter murmured. "I'm not expecting anyone."

April took a deep breath. In the anxious moments while Buford answered the door, she looked at her father through a mist of emotions. She loved him. She respected him. Despite the way he had treated Vanessa, she still loved him. Of late, as he drifted in and out of his stupors, she had come to fear him, even to loathe him. But even so, she knew she did love him deeply, and she grieved over the anguish of their lives.

Buford appeared in the doorway, looking bewildered and, April thought, also frightened. "It's Mastah Alton Moseley at the door, suh," he said with a bob of his cotton white hair. "He say he come for lunch, that Miz April invited him."

Before Carter could ask any questions, she told Buford to bring Alton in, then said briskly, "Poppa, I invited him here. He wants to talk to you."

"Talk to me? About what? I have nothing to discuss with my groomsman. If I do, I'll go to the stables. Since when do my servants come as luncheon guests to discuss business?"

April was relieved when Alton stepped into the room. Better to get this over with quickly, she thought frantically, before her father really had time to become angry. "Shall

we go into lunch now?" she said before Alton could even
step forward to shake the older man's hand.

"No, we will not go into lunch now." Carter sat down
behind his desk. Looking directly at Alton, who stood with
his straw hat in his hands, twisting it around and around
nervously, he snapped, "What's the meaning of this,
Moseley? My daughter doesn't entertain hired help, and
neither do I."

Alton looked beseechingly at April, silently asking what
he was supposed to do next. "Go on," she whispered. "Do
it now."

"Do what now?" Carter stood, hands clenching the edge
of his desk. "I think someone had better tell me what this
is all about. My lunch is getting cold while I stand here in
front of a dawdling stableboy."

"Poppa, will you just listen to what he has to say?" April
cried, near tears. "Please?"

"I'm waiting. And so is my lunch." To Alton, he said,
"If you're wanting more money, boy, this is a stupid way
to go about asking for it. And you aren't worth it. You'll
never be the groomsman the Taggarts were."

"It isn't money. I'm joining the Confederate Army. I'll
be going off to fight the Yankees soon." His adam's apple
bobbed up and down as he glanced at April in misery.

"Well, that's commendable. I'll have to find someone to
replace you, but that shouldn't be hard. Now we'll just talk
about this later. April and I were planning on going for a
ride after lunch. We'll talk later." He held out his arm to
April. "Now it's time for us to eat. If you will excuse
us—"

"I want to marry your daughter, sir."

Carter whipped his head about to stare at him, then
shook himself slightly as he whispered, "I don't believe I
heard you correctly, boy."

"Don't call me 'boy'!" Alton's cheeks flushed. "I'm no
boy. I'm a man, going off to fight for the South. I love your
daughter, and I want her to be my wife. I want to marry
her before I go off to war. She can live with my folks,
and—"

Alton was speaking in a rush, as though he would lose
his nerve if he didn't get the words out rapidly. April was

watching, trancelike, praying he would say it all in the right way. Neither of them had been concentrating on Carter. The veins in his neck began to throb. His fists opened and closed convulsively. And suddenly the explosion came. He leaped for Alton, knocking him to the floor, his fingers squeezed tightly about his throat.

"I'll kill you, you no-good white trash," he screamed. "No one is ever going to take her away from me, do you hear? And I'll kill anyone who tries."

April screamed as she watched her father choking Alton, pounding his head against the floor. When she was able to will her wooden legs to move, she entwined her fingers in her father's hair, trying to get him off Alton.

Buford and another servant ran into the room. "Stop him," April screamed as she was knocked to the floor. "Stop him before he kills Alton."

The two Negroes grabbed Carter by his shoulders and pulled with all their strength, but his grip on Alton's throat was a death-lock. April could see Alton's eyes bulging, his face turning color as he struggled to breathe . . . turning to red . . . to white . . . to a sickly blue-gray. And all the while the men were pulling at Carter, begging him to let go, telling him he was killing the boy.

April, hysterical, glanced around and saw the heavy ledger book at the edge of the desk. Struggling to her feet, she grabbed it, stumbled forward, and began to beat her father over the head again and again, all the while screaming for him to stop. The force was stunning enough that he jerked backward and loosened his hold. The two Negroes yanked their master away, though it took all their strength to restrain him as he struggled with them.

April scrambled to kneel beside Alton, who lay choking, coughing, clutching his throat. She watched as the color began to return to his face, the deep welts and bruises in his neck turning vivid red. "Alton, Alton, I'm sorry," she sobbed. "Dear God, I didn't know he'd react this way—"

"I'll kill you," her father was still yelling as his servants dragged him from the room. "No man is good enough for my daughter, and I'll kill anyone who tries to take her from me. Do you hear me, you bastard? I'll kill you."

"Buford, have someone ride out and find the doctor," April called, helping Alton up to a sitting position.

"Yes'm, I'll do that," he yelled, "but you better get Mastah Alton outta here, 'cause I don't know how long we gonna be able to hold yo' daddy down."

It was true. Alton had to leave at once. Not only the house but the area as well. Posie appeared, wide-eyed with fright, and April motioned to her. "Help me get him out of here. Now."

"You're going with me." Alton's arms went about her as soon as he got to his feet. "I can't leave you here with that madman, darling. Come with me."

Pain constricted her heart, as April watched her father being dragged up the stairs like a tantrum-stricken child. "I can't leave him," she whispered in anguish. "Not now. Not when he needs me."

Alton grabbed her arms, squeezing painfully as he held her so close she could feel the wild beating of his heart. "I love you, April. And I want you out of all this. Everybody's talking about how your daddy's turned into a lunatic. Now I've seen for myself, and I'm afraid for you."

She could not tell him that she shared his fears. At that moment, she was thinking only of how much she loved her father. He had always treated her with love and kindness. He was sick. Could she ever forgive herself for walking out on him? Who would care for him? Buford and Posie and the others would probably run away. They would never remain to care for a man who scared them witless. "Alton, listen to me, please—" she begged, blinking back tears. "I'll send word to you to meet me somewhere when it's safe. We'll talk then. For now, just go. Please, just go!"

He looked at her searchingly, then nodded solemnly. "All right. For now, I'll leave. But I'll be back. And I'll drag you away from here if I have to. I'm not going off to war and leave you with that crazy man. I know you love him. He's your father, but damn it, April, you've got to think of yourself."

His lips came down on hers in a bruising kiss. With hands pressed against his shoulders, she gave one mighty thrust and pushed him back. "Alton, please go! Leave here now, before something terrible happens."

She stared at the vivid purple bruises rising on his throat. He whispered raggedly, "All right. But you'll come to me, April. Promise me you'll come."

"Yes, yes. Anything, Alton. Just go . . . now!"

Then they heard it, and they followed Posie's terrified eyes past the doorway and the stairs leading up. The sound thundered through the great house, echoing, reverberating with fury. "Lorena!" The scream exploded. "Lorena, I'll kill you if you leave me. I swear to God, I'll kill you!"

"Oh, Lordy, Lordy!" Posie covered her face with her apron. "That man done lost his mind. That man crazy fo' sho'." She scurried from the room sobbing.

April faced Alton as he gripped her arms once more. "He's mad. And you aren't safe here."

"He's sick. I told you, Alton, he's sick. Now leave. As long as he knows you're here, it's only going to make matters worse."

"I'm afraid for you. I can't walk out of here not knowing what that lunatic is going to do. Go get your things, and we'll leave now."

"I can't leave him the way he is!" she cried, gesturing wildly. "Can't you see that? I—can't—leave—him!" she cried hysterically.

He stepped back, shook his head, and sighed. "All right. I can't force you. I leave in a week. There's time for us to get married and get you out of here. After I'm gone, I won't be able to help you, April."

"I know," she said quietly. "I need time to think. Poppa needs a doctor. I must hear what he says. I promise I'll send word to you, Alton. Just give me time."

He kissed her forehead, then turned and walked out, but she did not miss the flash of anger in his eyes.

The sound still echoed all around them. April ran her fingers up and down her arms, the flesh crawling.

"Lorena, for God's sake don't leave me. I love you, but I'll kill you if you try to leave me."

Yes, April told herself in silent anguish, Poppa was truly insane.

❧ Chapter Five ❧

APRIL looked up from her father's desk as Posie entered the room, obviously upset. "What is it?" she asked tonelessly.

"You know what it is, missy. It's yo' daddy. He's just sittin' up there snifflin' and a'cryin' like he's been doin' since that fancy doctor from Birmin'ham come down here. Snifflin' and a'cryin' and a'talkin' to yo' momma." Posie shook her head from side to side and took a deep breath. "I can't get nobody else to go in there 'cept Buford. Everybody's scairt to death o' him."

"He has not been violent for three days now," April pointed out. "He's a pitifully sick man. Why should anyone be frightened of him when all he does is sit and cry?"

"You heard what that fancy doctor said, that he's real sick, and you ought to send him to that hospital fo' crazy people in Tuscaloosa." Posie glared at her accusingly.

"Dr. Wermer is one of the best doctors in all the state, Posie. It's true he suggested that I have him committed, but he also said that this might be temporary, because of what happened with Vanessa. I think all he needs is time. I can't send him off to a place for crazy people when he's just plain heartsick."

Posie snorted. "Then you ain't scairt o' him, like the rest of us? You ain't scairt he'll hurt you? I reckon it just don't bother you none a'tall that he don't even know you no mo', that he thinks you is yo' dead momma?"

55

"Yes, it bothers me. More than you can know, Posie," she said wearily. "But perhaps, with time, he'll come out of it. Right now, I'm bone-tired and I'm going to bed. Would you ask Buford to see that my father is put to bed? We'll call in all the household servants and talk about it in the morning. That's all I know to do. Now good night." And, with a swish of her skirts, she brushed by Posie and made her way out of the room and up the stairs.

Once inside her room, she flung herself across the bed, wanting to cry. But no tears would come. Too many had already been shed, and perhaps she had none left. So much had happened, and she did not know what to do. Alton kept sending messages, begging her to come to him, reminding her that time was short. She wanted to escape the misery but could not will herself to leave her father.

The room grew dark, as silent as the rest of the house. She rolled over on her back to stare up into emptiness for a moment, then got up to grope about for her gown. The night was chilly, but rather than ring for Buford to make a fire, she decided to just snuggle beneath the covers.

Memories of the past settled upon her like a giant spider's web. There had been happy times, despite her father's dominant, iron will. But through it all, there had been his ever-present pain over the loss of her mother . . . his resentment of Vanessa . . . Vanessa's hatred for her . . . so much pain. Escape would be paradise. But she owed her father her devotion.

Slowly, sleep took over and she felt herself slipping gratefully away. Tomorrow she would plan the journey to Birmingham. She would talk at length with Dr. Wermer. And she would meet with Alton, ask for his patience. She would do all that tomorrow.

She felt hot, moist lips on her face. She stirred, moaned, struggled to awaken. Groping hands sought and found her breasts, squeezing possessively.

"Lorena, my beloved."

April awoke, the scream of terror locked in her throat. She struggled to breathe beneath the bulk of the figure pressing down on her. His mouth covered hers. Seeking, probing fingers were everywhere at once, ripping the sheer gown.

With great effort, she was able to twist her face to one side, away from his hungry mouth, and the scream fought its way past her constricting throat. "Poppa, no . . . no . . . it's me, April! You don't know what you're doing. Please, no. . . ."

"I'm going to love you." He threw one leg over her, pulling himself up so that he straddled her struggling body. With one hand, he jerked her arms upward, pinning them above her head so that she was powerless beneath him. Twisting and writhing, she begged him to come to his senses.

"My wife," he grunted. "My wife, my love, mine. . . ."

He held her tightly, and for one fragile moment, she felt that she was lost. There was nothing she could do. But this could not happen. She would not let it happen. In that one fleeting moment he loosened his hold on her wrists just long enough for her to bring her hands, wrapped together in a giant fist, slamming downward across the bridge of his nose. With a cry of pain he grabbed his nose, his head jerking backward. Her knees came up into his crotch and he rolled to one side.

She scrambled from the bed, found the door, and reached up with trembling fingers to grasp the knob. Then the door was opening, and she plunged into the hall and ran as hard as her trembling legs would carry her. Posie would not have heard her screams. Posie slept in the servants' quarters, away from the great house. She would hear nothing. Oh, God, why hadn't she begged her to sleep inside?

Stumbling along, she found the hallway leading to the kitchen. Forgetting her nakedness, she opened the back door and was about to leap into the night when a frightened voice called out behind her, making her scream in surprise.

"Miss April? Lordy, what's goin' on?"

April pressed her back against the door, struggling to breathe. A match was struck, a lantern lit, and she saw Mandy staring at her, mouth gaping. "Why, Miss April, somethin' terrible's happened. I knows it." She was moving toward her, holding the lantern above her hand. "I's glad Posie said I had to sleep in the pantry tonight. She was afraid somethin' would happen. Oh, Lordy, Miss April, you want me to have somebody fetch a doctor? Did yo' daddy *rape* you?"

April shook her head slowly from side to side. She hated, even in her shocked state, to have anyone know what had almost happened.

"Mandy, you listen to me," she said when she could find her voice. "You are not to say anything about this to anyone. My father did not rape me. He isn't himself. He . . . he's sick."

"Lord, I knows he's sick," she cried, bobbing her head up and down. "So does ever'body else. That's how come nobody wants to go near him. Lord, look what that man done to you."

"He did not *do* anything!" April realized she was screaming and checked herself. In a low whisper, she attempted to explain. "I told you, Mandy. He's a sick man. He did not *do* what he tried to do. I doubt he even knows he tried. But I don't want you to repeat this to a soul, do you understand me?"

Mandy's feeble, hesitant "Yes'm" was barely audible as April made her way to a chair beside the long wooden kitchen table and sat down. She gratefully accepted the blanket the young girl draped over her shoulders.

"What you gonna do now, Miss April?" Mandy asked once she had sat down opposite her and placed the lantern on the table between them. "What you gonna do about yo' daddy now?"

April sucked in her breath, held it, then let it out in one long rush as her body trembled convulsively. "I don't know. Oh, God, Mandy, I just don't know."

Several moments passed in which neither spoke, then Mandy said, "You just sit right here, and I'll fetch Buford to see to the mastah. He's gonna have to know somethin's goin' on, 'cause we can't just not do nothin'." April nodded in reluctant agreement, and Mandy hurried out of the house.

Buford was silent as he returned a short while later, merely glancing sympathetically in April's direction. Mandy sat down again opposite her. "You want me to get you some clothes?" she asked gently.

"Let Buford get my father back to his own room first," she said quietly. Then, slowly, she lifted her gaze for the first time to stare at the young Negro girl. "I want you to get a message to Alton for me, Mandy. At break of day."

"Oh, Lordy, Miss April, you ain't gonna tell Mastah Moseley about this, is you? He gonna kill yo' daddy, even if he is plumb loco."

"No, I'm not going to tell Alton, and neither are you." April was surprised at her sudden calm, her sudden decision. It was as though the sun had come out after a storm. "I want you to tell him I will meet him. At midnight tomorrow."

"At the stables?" Mandy's eyes were shining. "You gonna meet him at the stable and run off with him and marry him, ain't you? That's what you wants me to tell him?"

"Tell him only that I will meet him. But not at the stable. That's too close to the house. Do you know the boat landing? Down by the river?"

Mandy nodded, shaking with excitement over being included in such important, secret plans.

"I will meet him there."

"You goin' to run off with him?"

April reached across the table and touched the girl's hand. "I must be able to trust you, Mandy. You must give me your word that I can trust you." Her eyes were pleading, searching for the truth she wished to see in the girl's face.

"Yes'm. Oh, Lordy, yes'm. You can trust me."

"All right. Yes, I am going to go away with Alton, and I'm going to marry him. It's the only way. I can't stay here now. Poppa would destroy himself if he ever knew what he's been doing. Plans must be made, and they must be made quickly."

"You want me to go to Mastah Moseley. Is there anything else?"

"You can help me pack what few things I intend to take with me. Then, after I'm gone, I want you to send word to Poppa's brother in Mississippi—James Jennings—and ask him to come here and look after things. He will be able to keep Poppa from losing Pinehurst. I'll also leave it up to my Uncle James to decide whether or not Poppa should be sent to that hospital. But for now, I just have to get away, or I'm going to lose *my* mind."

She laid her head down on the table, willing the tears to come. She could think of only one thing to do—escape. She hated giving Mandy so much responsibility, but she was afraid to trust Posie. Posie, she knew, was ready to run away herself. Mandy was young enough to be enthralled by all the excitement. Posie was older, and not so resilient.

"James Jennings," she reminded her. "I'll write everything down. He may not even come. I don't know. They were never close. I only remember seeing him once, and that's when my grandmother died, when Vanessa and I were ten years old. He came to the funeral. I haven't seen him before or since.

"Something happened between him and Poppa, something I never knew about. I think it had to do with Poppa being heir to Pinehurst. I once heard that Uncle James was disinherited by my grandfather for marrying a girl who was not pure white. I don't know. I don't even know why I'm telling you all this, Mandy, except that there's no one else." She shook her head from side to side, shoulders slumped in defeat.

"I'll take care o' things. Don't fret."

Buford stepped into the doorway, looking shaken. "I got him back to his room," he said in a sad little voice. "He didn't even know where he was, missy. He looked like a dead man walkin' around, just shufflin' along and mumbling to hisself, wonderin' how come Miss Lorena wouldn't let him . . ." His voice trailed off and he looked away, embarrassed.

"I know," April whispered, squeezing her hands together as she held the blanket tightly about her. Hesitantly, she asked, "Do you think he needs to be restrained?"

"I can lock the door to his room from the outside, but you knows yo' daddy, honey, and if'n he takes a notion to come outta there, ain't no lock gonna hold him."

She nodded. "Will you just stand by today? In the hall? You will have to pick someone you trust to be on guard tonight."

"Yes'm." She had to strain to hear him. He was deeply upset over his master's condition. She told him to return to the room for the rest of the night, and he left.

"Are you afraid to ride to Master Moseley's, Mandy?" She turned to the girl. "At first light of day?"

"Oh, no'm." Mandy was almost smiling in her enjoyment of all the excitement. "I'll be all set and ready to go. Then I'll come back here and help you pack. You wants me to stay in yo' room the rest of the night?"

"No, I'll be all right. Buford will be with Poppa. I want you to go on back to bed now. That's what I'm going to do."

Once in her room, she stood for a long, long time staring out the window that overlooked the rolling lawns of Pinehurst. Would she ever see her home again? She did not know. Perhaps one day her father would be well. But that might not happen, and she had to face the fact that she might never be coming home again.

Suddenly, her hand felt heavy. She glanced down to see the diamond and ruby and emerald Pinehurst ring her father had so proudly given her months ago. She could not take it with her, not when, by running away, she was denying her heritage.

The eastern sky was streaked with gold and pink rivers as the sun struggled to rise. Somewhere a bird sang his song of joy. A rooster crowed. It was a new day, a new beginning . . . and, she realized painfully, an ending as well.

The ring must be hidden before she did anything else. But not in the house. What if the Yankees did make their way South and into Montgomery? She could not take a chance. It would have to be hidden outside the mansion, in case of looting.

April hurried to dress in the early morning chill, selecting a warm blue muslin and a thick cape. Then she quietly tiptoed out of her room and into the darkened hall.

She jumped, startled, as Buford stepped out of the shadows. "Oh, dear God, you scared me," she cried, hands clutching her throat.

"I'm sorry, missy," he said quickly, careful to keep his voice low. "I just been standin' out here, listenin' out fo' yo' poppa. He's sleepin' good now, and I don't want nothin' to wake him up."

April tensed. "Buford, what do you think happened?" She had hoped the servants would not speculate but knew that was impossible.

Buford glanced away uncomfortably. "Well, it don't take

much figurin', missy. It ain't none o' my business, and I ain't gonna say nothin' if'n you don't want me to."

"Of course I don't want you to say anything." She spoke more sharply than she had intended. "Poppa is sick. I don't want anyone gossiping or blaming him for things he cannot help. You just stay here in case he needs you. Right now, there's something I must do."

Suspicion shadowed his chocolate eyes. "Where you goin' this time o' the mornin'? It ain't hardly light out yet."

"I won't be gone long. Just do as I say, Buford, please." Turning away, she made her way on down the stairs, through the back hallway, and into the crisp morning air.

Where could she hide the ring? She looked toward the stables. The Yankees might burn those. True, the enemy would probably be defeated soon, and she might be worrying for no reason, but she couldn't take foolish chances with the inheritance ring.

She looked down at the red Alabama clay. She did not dare dig a hole, for if the terrain were changed in battle, the burial place might not be found again.

Burial! That was it. Even if the Yankees did come, they would not desecrate the burial places of the dead, would they? Even Yankees would not be so barbaric.

She walked briskly to the stables, then cut around them to follow the path that led down to a peaceful, sloping hill overlooking the creek that ran from the Fletcher land. In the spring, dogwood trees dotted the lush green woods with dollops of white blossoms, and pink and red azaleas abounded, nature's magnificence standing guard over the Jennings family burial ground.

The graves toward the front of the cemetery were raked of leaves and dead limbs, as the field workers knew it was a standing order from Carter Jennings that they be kept cleaned. Long ago, her father had identified all the graves for her, and April knew where each of her great-great-grandmothers and grandfathers and aunts and uncles was buried. As she moved farther along, there were hand-carved stone monuments.

In the most picturesque spot in the cemetery, stood a small, square, red brick building, the family mausoleum.

As a child, April had refused to play around the cemetery at all, particularly the red brick building with its double iron gates across the doorway. The ornate gates were adorned with a flowery scrawled "J."

Poppa had forced her to come here on special occasions, such as her birthday, or her mother's, or Easter. He would bring flowers, and he would unlock the iron doors and go inside and make her go with him. Then he would lay the flowers on top of the brick box and get down on his knees and pray for a long, long time. April would be obediently and respectfully quiet, but she hated those times. She did not mind listening to his tales of how wonderful her mother had been, how much she had loved her, but she wished he would talk of these things in another place . . . anywhere but inside the damp building with its spider webs and unseen creatures scurrying about in the shadows.

"I could not put your mother in the ground," Poppa had told her each time they visited. "She was a special, rare beauty, and I wish I could have preserved her for all time. To lay someone like your mother in the ground would have been a sacrilege."

Once, April had said, "Posie told me that the Bible says that it's supposed to be 'ashes to ashes and dust to dust' when somebody dies, and it's not right not to bury someone in the ground so they can turn into ashes."

"Posie can't read," he had retorted angrily. "What does she know?"

"She says a preacher said that once at a funeral she went to."

"I'll beat her hide off her back if she ever speaks of such a thing again." He had ground out the words so vehemently that April vowed never to repeat anything else Posie told her.

Then one day, when she was perhaps eleven or twelve, her father had taken her to the cemetery on an ordinary day, a day of no special occasion. He had held her hand as they walked. When she asked him fearfully why he wanted to take her there, he murmured quietly, "You'll see, child. You'll see."

They stood before the closed iron gates, and in the faint sunshine that filtered through the thick magnolia trees above, he pointed out two new brick boxes. "For you and me, April darling. We'll rest with your mother here, not in the ground."

She had shivered to think she was staring at the place where her dead body would one day be placed. Her father had hugged her tightly against him and told her not to be afraid. "I think I will welcome death," he said in a trembling voice. "Then I can be with your mother for all eternity. For now, I find peace only in being with you, child, for you are the living proof of the love your mother and I shared."

April stood before the gates now and stared inside. It was as though time never touched this place. Nothing had changed. It was still a room filled with gray light and cold breezes. The sound of unseen creatures still reached her ears as they scurried along the hard clay floor. Like a giant gray hand, a spider web was wrapped around the brick tombs.

On each side of the gate, there were little niches built into the brick. The niches held tiny marble statues imported from Italy. Her eyes went to the left, to the statue of the kneeling angel. With trembling fingers, she reached beyond, found the tiny, chipped brick that slid outward to reveal a small hole. Groping with her fingertips, she found the key she was looking for.

April took a deep breath, commanded her throbbing, pounding heart to slow down. And with icy fingers, she fitted the key into the lock, and swung open the creeking gates. The doors to the mausoleum swung open with a creak.

🐚 Chapter Six 🐚

A HALF hour before midnight, April crept from the dark, silent house. There was neither time nor reason for tears, she told herself as she hurried through the purple night toward the stable. After all, her leaving now did not mean good-bye forever. Mandy would see that word was sent to Uncle James, and he would come to Pinehurst. Then, after she and Alton were married, she would return. With Uncle James's aid, she would be able to help her father and keep Pinehurst from disaster.

There was no moon, and she had to follow the path from memory. The stable loomed ahead, a hulking shadow. Any other time she might have been frightened, but there was no time now to be afraid. Alton would be waiting by the river, and they would leave together, probably going to his family's home. By sundown tomorrow they would be married.

Married! She trembled at the thought. To lie in a man's arms, to be possessed—the idea of doing so with a man she did not love made her feel ill, sick at heart. Yet, she might learn to love him in time, and just *wanting* to love was important, wasn't it? Yes, she told herself as she hurried along. She *wanted* to love Alton, wanted to make him happy, to be a good wife to him. And there was a war going on. Many people were getting married even though they were not starry-eyed in love. War made people desperate.

She reached the stable and set her tapestry bags down while she wrestled with the heavy doors. With a loud creak, they opened. The smell of hay and manure reached her at the same time she heard the horse whinny. Just before dark, she had hitched one of the mares to a wagon. The stable hands had left for the day, and she was careful that no one would notice.

She moved toward the horse, wrapped her fingers around her harness and led her from the barn. When her bags were in the rear of the wagon, she lifted her thick skirts and hoisted herself up onto the rough wooden bench.

The mare moved forward, and soon they were out from beneath the wall of crepe myrtles. She breathed a sigh of relief. Her eyes were adjusted to the darkness, and with care, she would be able to see her way.

The horse moved slowly, but April did not dare urge her on lest she lose the sight and feel of the road. Finally, the sound of gurgling water reached her ears. She could make out the black ribbon of the twisting river and the boat landing just ahead. She gave the reins a jerk, and the mare snapped to a quick halt. April scrambled from the wagon to the ground so quickly that she almost fell.

"Alton . . ." Her voice was a whisper, lost in the wind. She admonished herself for being afraid to call loudly, and then called out, "Alton? Are you here?"

There was no answer. She could hear only the night wind dancing through the cottonwoods and cypress trees lining the riverbank. She trembled involuntarily and pulled her cape tightly about her shoulders, moving closer to the mare as though the horse could protect her from the darkness.

It was ridiculous to be frightened. He might have been detained. There was nothing to do but wait, and there was no need to be nervous.

Suddenly, leaves crackled. April whirled about and looked toward the dark river, the thick underbrush and trees. "Alton, is that you?" She called out, her voice a shaky whisper.

The crackling sound was louder. Then there was another. Someone was walking toward her. "Alton, for God's sake, will you answer me?" She laughed, a high-pitched, tinny sound that belied her growing fright. "This is no time to tease me."

The sound was closer . . . a few feet away. April pressed back against the mare, feeling her warmth.

"Alton, answer me, please. . . ." She could not keep the tears from stinging her eyes. Her fingers laced around the leather harness, squeezing. Alton would not frighten her this way, no, not Alton.

She wondered frantically if there were time to climb up into the wagon, to ride away. She had to get away—now! Her mind was spinning and her body began to shake, as though in the throes of a deep chill. She gave her frozen body the silent command to move . . . now!

"Hello, April."

She spun completely around, searching for a face to go with the voice. Was it fear playing tricks on her?

"Can't you even speak to your own twin sister?"

"Vanessa?" April gasped, finding the direction from which the voice came. She could make out only a figure in the shadows. "Vanessa? Is . . . is it really you?"

"Yes, it's really me." The voice was mocking, with the hint of an angry snarl. "Did you really think you could get rid of me forever, dear sister?"

"*Rid* of you?" April echoed, stunned.

"Yes, like you planned. Like you always planned. You wanted me out of the way so you could have Poppa and Pinehurst all to yourself."

"Oh, Vanessa, that's not true." She took a step toward her, but something felt, rather than seen, made her stop. She swallowed hard. "I've worried about you so much, prayed you were all right—"

"You can stop your lying, April. I had eighteen years to learn how cunning and convincing you can be."

"I'm not lying," she cried in exasperation. "What's wrong with you, Vanessa? *I* had nothing to do with what happened the night of our party. But let's not argue about that. Why didn't you come to the house to see me? And how did you know I'd be here tonight?"

Vanessa's laugh was taunting. "Come to the house? Are you serious, dear sister? You made sure that could never happen. Poppa would've had me beaten or killed me himself. Who can say what a crazy man might do?"

"Crazy man? Who told you that? He's sick, but—"

"Sick!" She spat out the word. "I suppose you blame his trying to rape you this morning on the influenza? He *did* try to rape you, didn't he? He's had spells these past months. He thinks you are our mother, doesn't he?"

April was furious. "Who told you all this? And I asked you how you knew I'd be here! Suppose you tell me what's going on, Vanessa."

Vanessa moved closer. April could see her face now, but she felt the hatred even before she saw her sister. "I'm here because Mandy told me you would be here, just as she's told me everything that's gone on since I was kicked out of my own home. She's very loyal to me. I know all about your plans to marry Alton despite Poppa's objections—"

"If you wanted to talk to me," April interrupted sharply, "why didn't you just have Mandy bring me a message to meet you somewhere? I would've come to you. You've no reason to hate me. I've always loved you, and—"

She reeled as a hand whipped out of the darkness to slap her cheek. "Shut up, damn you!" Vanessa screamed shrilly. "Just shut your lying mouth! You've plotted and schemed against me all your life, because you wanted Poppa to disown me and disinherit me. You wanted Pinehurst for yourself. And I know how it's falling to ruins because Poppa's too crazy to keep it going. And *you* aren't smart enough to take over. But *I* am. Poppa can't stop me now, and neither can you."

April faced her with fury blazing through her. "How dare you strike me? And you've no right to accuse me of all these things. You're the one who's behaving like someone insane. When Alton gets here—"

Again the shrill laughter pierced the air. Vanessa gave her long hair an insolent toss as she taunted, "Do you really think Mandy gave him your message to meet you here, you little fool? She told Alton what *I* told her to tell him—which was that you don't ever want to see him again, because you would never go against your dear father's wishes."

She rushed on and April stared in horror. "She also told him that you don't love him and wouldn't marry him anyway, and that you want him to leave you alone. I'll wager

Alton's so angry with you that he wouldn't come now if you begged him."

"He'll listen to me. I'll tell him what you did, and he'll understand. He'll help me keep you from hurting Poppa."

"You won't be around to help Poppa, dear sister."

Before April understood the threat, a torch appeared and she whipped her head about to see two men approaching, ominously smiling in the orange glow.

"I don't believe you've met these gentlemen," Vanessa mocked. "I'd like to present Zeke Hartley and Whit Brandon. They're going to be looking after you for a while, so it would be a good idea to make friends with them."

The man called Zeke grinned at April, displaying yellowed teeth. He was short and stocky and wore heavily soiled clothes. His face was craggy and lined, and April winced at the sight of a zigzagged scar that ran all the way from his left temple to the corner of his mouth.

Whit Brandon looked much older, and while he appeared as scruffy as his companion, there was something less ominous about him. Perhaps it was the flicker of sympathy that she saw briefly in his eyes. She turned back to Vanessa and cried, "Just what are you planning to do? You're my sister, but so help me, Vanessa, I'll not tolerate—"

"You'll shut your mouth or I'll have the boys gag you!" Vanessa growled as she gestured to the two men. They came closer. "You're going away with them. They're going to take you to a convent up in the mountains near the Georgia border."

"A convent? Please, Vanessa—" She was fighting to hold back tears, and she did not want to beg. "You won't get away with this. Now let's talk. You can go home with me, and we'll try to talk to Poppa. I've sent for Uncle James, and when he arrives, he can help us—"

"Uncle James won't get your message. Mandy showed me the letter you wrote him, and I burned it."

April shook her head. "But why? Why are you doing all this? And to think that all this time I've trusted Mandy."

"Mandy's loyalty is to me. I've already told you that I am not going to let you cheat me out of what's mine. You're going to a convent, and my men will tell the monks there that you're incorrigible. Your family can do nothing with you. You can't leave men alone, and you're a disgrace. They'll take you in and keep you there to protect you from your sinful ways. You will be well cared for, but you won't ever be permitted to leave unless someone comes for you. And I assure you, no one ever will."

"Vanessa, don't—"

"Silence her!"

April struggled as Zeke grabbed her arms and twisted them behind her back. Whit jerked the scarf from about his neck and stuffed it into her screaming mouth. Then she was lifted and thrown over Whit's back. Vanessa yelled, "Take the wagon, like we planned. Get as far away from here by daylight as you can."

"We know what to do," Whit replied gruffly. "We'll get back as quickly as we can."

"Yes, I want you to hurry back to me." Vanessa was now leading a horse from the bushes where it had been hidden earlier. "I know I'm going to need help, but I can manage on my own for a while. My father is in no condition to argue with me, and I can handle the servants."

April was carried to the wagon and dumped roughly into the back. She lay there staring up into the cloak of night, frantically twisting her hands about inside the rope that bound them. She saw Vanessa peering down at her from on top of her horse. "I'll tell everyone that you ran away because you were ashamed of what happened this morning. I'll say that Poppa raped you, that he is insane and won't remember whether he really raped you or not."

April strained wildly against the gag, and Vanessa laughed.

It would kill her father, April knew, to be told he had raped her. He could not face thinking that he had done something so loathsome. *For the love of God, Vanessa, don't do this evil thing*, she screamed silently. She heard the sound of Vanessa's laughter once again, rising above the clip-clopping trot of her horse. Then the wagon moved and Vanessa disappeared into the night.

The wagon moved slowly. Zeke's horse, Satan, was tied behind it, and the beast snorted with impatience. After a while, Zeke began complaining about the pace, and Whit murmured, "This is a rough road. I can hear that girl rolling and bumping around back there now. If I go any faster, she'll be bruised from head to toe."

"So who cares? I don't want to risk—"

"You ain't risking nothing. Nobody's gonna look for her, 'cause ain't nobody gonna doubt Vanessa's story. If you don't like us goin' so slow, you get on that fancy horse of yours and ride just as fast as you want to."

Zeke snickered. "It really tears you up, don't it? Knowing I got such a damn good horse. Can't nobody beat him."

"That don't bother me. What makes me sick is the way you're so almighty cocky about it. Always bragging and running that mouth of yours. Someday somebody's gonna beat you and then you'll shut up."

"Well, when that day comes, you crow about it, you hear? Till then, you just remember I own the fastest horse in the state of Alabama, and if it hadn't of been for what I won this past year racing that horse, we wouldn't have had the money to keep you in that rotgut popskull you love so good."

Whit did not reply, and after another snicker, Zeke fell silent. April stared up into the black sky once more.

She suddenly found herself hating the sheltered life she had led. She had always envied Vanessa her freedom, but until now, she had not fully realized just how much she resented the useless life she had been forced to lead. Had she been allowed more independence, perhaps she would be better equipped to cope with this horrifying situation. Survive, she ordered herself. Survive and fight back. She would fight. Then she would deal with Vanessa.

Her eyes closed, opened, then closed once more as sleep mercifully took her. After what seemed only moments, the wagon lurched to a stop and the sun was shining on her face. Raising her head, she looked about to see that they were stopping beside a dilapidated old barn. She could hear the two men discussing spending the day inside.

"We can pull the wagon right inside," Zeke was saying. "Ain't nobody around. Nobody'll see us. We can get some sleep and start out again once it's good and dark."

"Suits me. I'm about to fall asleep in my tracks."

"You want me to take that outta your mouth?" Whit asked her. "I will if you promise to be quiet so's I can get some sleep. I reckon you're hungry, too." He reached down and jerked the scarf away. As she gasped for the sweet air, he warned, "Now don't you give us no trouble, girl. I'm just doin' a job. I don't want to see no harm come to you. Now how about some corn dodgers? That's all I got to offer you. There ain't nothin' to drink 'cept whiskey, and I got a feelin' you ain't a drinkin' woman."

Zeke appeared at Whit's side and looked down at her, grinning with yellowed teeth. "Naw, she ain't no drinkin' woman. She's all lace and velvet and fluffy stuff. I'll bet she sips her tea from a china cup." He threw back his head and laughed. "Bet you'd never see *her* match drink for drink with a man like her sister can!"

"Leave her alone." Whit walked to the back of the wagon. "I guess we better take her for a walk so's she can tend to her, uh—personal needs."

Zeke spoke up quickly. "You go on and take the wagon inside. I'll take her to the woods."

Whit ignored him. He reached into his pocket and brought out a knife and, with one quick movement, slashed through the ropes around her wrists. She rubbed her hands together and stared down at the bruised flesh. He said, "You been strugglin' against them ropes, girl, and that's how come you got rope burns. You best just settle on down. You ain't doin' nothing but hurtin' yourself."

He reached in and clamped strong hands around her waist to lift her up and out of the wagon. Her legs felt weak as her feet touched the red clay ground, and she sagged against him briefly but quickly regained her balance and stepped back. She did not want help of any kind from either of these men.

"Come along." Whit started toward thick underbrush at the edge of the road.

She held back. Zeke laughed, and Whit shot him a furious look. "Might as well come on, girl," he snapped. "Or else I'll tie you up and you can wet yourself. Now come along. I ain't gonna look."

With flaming cheeks, April stumbled along behind him. When they were out of Zeke's sight, Whit said, "Okay, you get behind that tree over yonder, and I'll wait right here. Don't get no ideas about runnin' off, 'cause these woods is full o' bobcats and wild hogs, and I'll just let them tear you to pieces if you try anything."

For the first time, April spoke. "Mr. Brandon, if I do try anything, you may rest assured it won't be just an attempt. I'll succeed."

"Well, I'll be doggoned." He slapped his knee. "The little filly's got some spunk after all. Glad to hear that, little lady. I figured we had us a real milksop."

With a swish of her skirts, April moved behind the tree, tended to her needs, then returned to follow him to the barn. Zeke had already moved the wagon inside and out of sight. Three blankets were spread side by side in a corner. She snapped, "I've no intention of lying down beside you two."

"I don't see where you've got any choice." Whit sounded annoyed for the first time. "Now stick out them wrists, 'cause I'm going to tie you up good."

"Let her have her way." Zeke strode over and snatched up one of the blankets, then walked to the other side of the barn and threw it down in the shadows. "Let her lay over here with the spiders and horse dung if she's too good to bed down with us. And once you get her hands tied, tie up her legs, too, so she won't be up wandering around."

Whit nodded. When he'd finished binding her, he lifted her as unceremoniously as a bag of flour, flinging her easily over his big shoulder to carry her across the straw-littered floor. But when he laid her down on the blanket, he did it gently. Despite his gruffness and hard drinking, something told her she had nothing to fear from this man.

Once the big doors were closed, there was little light inside the barn. She tried to sleep but soon gave up and let herself become lost in worry.

She heard movement before she saw the hulking shadow moving stealthily around the wagon. Footsteps, soft, muted, sneaking. Her skin prickled as she saw Zeke creeping toward her, eyes gleaming as brightly as a cat's in the dark.

Sticken by terror, she waited too late to scream. He was upon her, covering her mouth with his hand as he fell on top of her, straddling her body. She bit down on one finger, but before she could make a sound, he had gripped her throat so tightly she could not even breathe.

"Now, you just be still, or I'll have to hurt you." He leaned close and she could smell the sweet-sour odor of whiskey. "It won't bother me none to slit your throat. I'll just tell your sister you tried to get away and you drowned or something. She'd probably be relieved to know you was out of the way for good. So you just relax, and ol' Zeke'll show you a real good time."

He pulled a sweat-stained handkerchief from his pocket and stuffed it quickly and tightly into her mouth. "You'll choke on that if you struggle much," he said matter-of-factly. His laugh was nasty, taunting, as he held her by the neck with one hand and used the other to hold her down. "Me and you gonna have ourselves a time. You better get your fill while you can, 'cause them monks ain't gonna give you no lovin'. You can bet on that. Now, I gotta untie your feet."

April began to struggle once more as soon as the rope was removed from her ankles. Zeke rasped, "Better be still now, or I'll kill you."

"What in the hell is all that racket about?"

Whit's anxious, angry voice caused Zeke to freeze. April knew he was scared of the bigger man, older man. She continued to twist beneath him, even though he wrapped his fingers tightly about her throat once more and hissed, "Shut up, damn you. Don't you make a sound."

"Zeke, what are you doing?"

Whit Brandon got up and moved quickly across the barn.

Whit came around the wagon, stopped short, then moved quickly to grab Zeke by his shoulder and sling him to one side. "You sorry bastard, I ought to kill you dead right here and now! I told you you won't gonna lay a hand on this girl, and I meant it."

He reached down and yanked the gag from April's mouth. She began coughing and gasping and crying all at once. "How bad you hurt, girl?" Whit demanded, roughly pulling her up to her feet. "What did he do to you?"

April could only shake her head as she pulled her tattered clothing about her.

"I didn't do nothing," Zeke whined, cautiously moving back, out of range of Whit's fists. "I was just foolin' around. Didn't see no harm in that. I wasn't gonna really do nothin'. You can see she's got her clothes on."

"You lying sonofabitch! You think I don't know what you would'a done if I hadn't heard and woke up? Now you get the hell out of here before I give you a beatin' you won't forget."

Zeke stiffened, and his eyes narrowed. "You ain't got no right to talk to me like that. You ain't my boss. You can stop threatenin' me, 'cause I ain't scared of you."

Whit whirled around, fists doubled menacingly. Zeke took a few shuffling steps backward before turning to run the rest of the way out of the barn.

"You all right, girl?" His eyes were filled with concern as he faced April once again. "You sure he didn't hurt you?"

"He didn't succeed, thanks to you," she whispered, rubbing her throat.

"I should've kept a closer watch on him. Zeke can be a mean one when he wants to."

The words came rushing out. "Why don't you just let me go, Mr. Brandon? You seem like a nice man. Not at all like Zeke. Have mercy on me, please." Her wrists were still bound, but she reached out to clutch the front of his shirt. Anguish was mirrored in her eyes.

"Now, I can't do that, girl," he said gruffly, gently pulling her hands away. "I got a job to do. That sister of yours has promised to pay me well, and what with the war and all, I've got to find some way to make a living without folks noticing, or else they'll wonder why I ain't off fightin' in the war. So you're just wastin' your breath."

Her pleas turned to anger. "Then why did you bother to help me just now? Just what kind of man are you? You don't want me raped, yet you'll kidnap me, while my sister torments my father. You're scum, Whit Brandon! Scum!"

"Well now," he said after a long pause. "I reckon I am at that. But I figure you ain't no angel, not after you got your own sister kicked out of her own home. So don't you go preachin' to me."

"Lies! I never did any such thing," she screamed. "Can't you listen to my side of the story?"

"No." He turned and walked toward the door. "I'm going

out to the wagon and bring your bags in so's you can get a decent dress on. That one's kinda torn. Then I'm gonna bed you down close to me so's I can keep an eye on you. Zeke might try something again."

He paused before leaving the barn and gave her a long, searching look. "I ain't asking you to understand me, girl, 'cause once we reach that convent, I'll just forget I ever knew you. But you should know one thing about me. I've done a lot of bad things in my life, but I ain't never raped a woman, and I'll kill a stranger to keep him from raping a woman I ain't never even met. That's just how strong I feel about it."

"How noble!" April snapped. "I'd be interested to know why such a filthy rogue would have even that scrap of virtue about him."

He stared at her, trying to decide whether he should answer. When he finally spoke, his words were choked, as though he were fighting tears. "My mother was raped. Raped to death. I found her body. I was only eight years old. If that gives me the scrap o' virtue you're talkin' about, then maybe she didn't die in vain."

He lurched from the barn, and April stared silently after him.

❧ Chapter Seven ❧

THEY set out on their journey once more at sundown. Zeke grumbled about having to travel at night, and Whit assured him that by morning they would be far enough from Montgomery and Pinehurst that they could relax and move when they felt like it.

April did not feel well, and as the night moved on, she felt even worse. Once they stopped to boil coffee and eat corn dodgers. She was not hungry but forced herself to put some food in her stomach. Almost as soon as she swallowed, she vomited.

"Oh, hell, she's sick!" Zeke cursed, watching her as she doubled over, clutching her stomach. "That's just what we need."

Whit walked over and put a gentle hand on her shoulder. "Girl, what's the matter? You ain't gettin' sick on us, are you?"

Her knees buckled, and he quickly grabbed her around her waist and helped her to the wagon so she could sit down. "I don't know what's wrong. I feel dizzy, and I think I have a fever."

He placed his hand on her cheek and nodded. "Yep, you sure do. We're gonna have to get you to a doctor. We ain't far from Sylacauga. It ain't much of a town, but they ought to have somebody around who knows a little medicine."

77

"Sylacauga?" Zeke cried. "Are you serious? We got to keep on ridin'. I want to get on up in them mountains and get rid of her."

"Well, we can't have her get sick and maybe die on us," Whit snapped, giving him an angry look.

Zeke threw up his hands. "So what if she does die? It won't be our fault. And if she does, we can just bury her and turn around and head back."

"You just want to get back before some other man gets sweet on Vanessa."

"And you just want to stop in Sylacauga 'cause you know there's a saloon there where you can get drunk."

April struggled to speak over the whirling heat that was making her so dizzy. "Please. Don't fight over me. Just let me go . . . just let me go and be on your way."

Whit reached in to tuck a blanket around her. "Don't you fret, girl. I'm gonna look after you, and I ain't gonna let you die. Maybe it won't be so bad livin' with them monks. I hear they live a real peaceful life. You might like it."

He finished covering her, then turned and walked straight to Zeke and poked an angry finger in his stomach. "Now you listen to me, boy. You hush up that kind of talk around that girl. Ain't no cause to mistreat her. I ain't gonna let her die, you hear?"

"Oh, hell, Whit! It don't matter to me what happens to her." He stepped back. "What's gotten into you, anyway? How come you're so worried about her? Maybe you're wantin' her for yourself."

Whit went around the wagon and crawled up on the bench. Taking the reins in his burly hands, he said, "I had a daughter once. She died. That girl back there reminds me of her. The way she might've looked if she'd lived to grow up. Nice and pretty and sweet."

Zeke sighed and got up on the bench beside him. "I don't mean to rile you none, but I'd like to know something."

Whit gave him a warning glare.

"You don't believe in rapin' a woman 'cause your momma was raped. Now you don't want to see that girl hurt because she reminds you of your daughter. Every time something comes up you don't like, you've got a reason for why you don't like it."

The angry look faded and Whit began to look amused. "Maybe that's true, boy. You know why I don't like life?"

Zeke snapped, "Naw, I don't, but I'll bet you got a reason for that, too!"

"Yep. It's on account of havin' to live around bastards like you, boy." He chuckled as he popped the reins over the mare's back.

The wagon began to lumber forward, and Zeke slumped into an icy silence as Whit continued to snicker over having bested him.

The moon hung low in the sky as they moved into the sleepy little town of Sylacauga, Alabama. April was only dimly aware that they had arrived. She did not know much about the town, only that the name "Sylacauga" was an Indian word, meaning "buzzard's roost."

Whit pulled to a stop in front of the only hotel, and after ordering Zeke to fetch a doctor as quickly as possible, he lifted April in his arms and walked through the swinging doors. The sleepy-eyed clerk behind the desk eyed him suspiciously, but Whit gave him no time to ask questions. "This girl's sick," he bellowed. "I want to get her to bed right away. I've sent for a doctor."

The clerk was tripping over his own feet as he grabbed a key from one of the slotted holes on the wall behind him and rushed around the counter. "This way, sir. Right up these steps. We'll take care of registering you later."

Whit followed him, and once inside the room, hurried to place April's limp body on the bed. "Get me lots of blankets," he ordered, and the clerk rushed to obey.

He pulled up a chair, sat down, and leaned over to clutch her small hand. "Girl, can you hear me?" he whispered. April's eyelids fluttered as she feebly nodded her head. He moved closer. "Listen to me now. I'm gonna take care of you. I ain't gonna let nothin' happen to you. You just trust ol' Whit, okay?"

She tried to smile, but she felt herself fading away again.

She focused her eyes on him, but he was drifting away into a gray cloud . . . farther . . . farther . . . and then she was floating higher. It was so pleasant to just let her body float away . . . away from the sickness . . . the misery . . . the agony her life had become.

People came and went, murmuring softly. It was dark, then light. She could not keep up with the passing of time or what the people were saying. Finally came the deep sense of peace that was so wonderful that she wanted to remain there forever.

Annoyance washed over her as she heard someone call her name. What did they want? Why wouldn't they leave her in peace?

"How do you feel, my dear?"

The man standing to the right of her bed was tall, stoop-shouldered, and had a large beaked nose.

"You gave me quite a time," he said, when she continued to stare at him. "I'm Dr. Benedict, and I've been caring for you for the past five days. You had a nasty bout with the fever, but you're recovering nicely."

He wasn't one of them, her heart sang joyfully. With great effort, she pulled her weak body up to a sitting position so she could see him better. "You've got to help me," she croaked. "I've been kidnapped. I've got to get back to Montgomery . . . to my family."

He stepped away from the bed and said, "You need rest. Now I'm going to have some collard soup sent up to you, and I want you to eat all of it."

"I don't care about that!" she cried desperately. "Doctor, you've got to help me! Go to the sheriff and tell him to come up here at once. I've been kidnapped!"

She watched in disbelief as the doctor shook his head sadly from side to side. "It's a pity when a young girl goes astray. I've a daughter about your age. It would break my heart to have to put her somewhere to protect her from her own moral decay, but I *would* do it. It's for the best, my dear. Someday you will realize that."

He opened the door and called out, "She's awake. She's doing what you said she'd do."

In an instant, Zeke was inside the room, grinning his yellow-toothed smile. "Well, well, the princess awakes. That's fine and dandy. Now we can be on our way without too much more delay." He turned to the doctor. "How long before we can move outta here? I want to get rid of her as quick as I can. She's too much responsibility."

"I can imagine she would be." The doctor stared at her thoughtfully. "Such a beautiful thing. A pity she has such a hunger for men."

"What has this bastard told you?" April struggled out of bed, ignoring the weakness that made her legs tremble. "I demand to see the law. He's lying! You must believe me—"

"April, get back in that bed." Zeke strode over and gave her a shove. She lost her balance and would have fallen, but he quickly lifted her and dropped her roughly on the sagging mattress.

"I wouldn't be rough with her," the doctor spoke hesitantly, as though wondering if he should interfere. "She is still weak, and—"

"I don't need you anymore, doc," Zeke snarled, whipping about to face him, "except to tell me how soon we can be on our way. You see what I've got to put up with. I want to get her tucked away safely with those monks in the mountains just as quick as I can. Hell, she's all the time pawing *me*, and I promised her pappy I wouldn't breed her."

Dr. Benedict glanced at April and then looked away as his cheeks flamed. "I understand. Let her rest today, and then be on your way tomorrow. If she gets tired, then stop along the way."

"We've only got about two more days travel. She can stand that." He walked to the door and waited for the doctor to gather his things and put them into his worn leather bag.

"Bundle up good, doc. It's plenty chilly out."

"Yes, it is," the doctor agreed, wrapping a woolen scarf about his neck. "I pray we don't have a bad winter, for the sake of our brave soldiers out in the fields."

Zeke snorted and waved his hand. "Don't worry about them. That war will be over any day. You'll see."

"I do hope you're right." He stepped into the hall. "If you should need me—"

"She's going to be fine, doc, just fine. Thanks for everything. See Whit downstairs at the bar, and he'll pay you up."

He closed the door, then waited till the sound of the doctor's footsteps disappeared. All the while his eyes were blazing at April. When he was sure the doctor had gone, he crossed the room and shook his fist over her.

"You try that again around anybody else, girl, and I'll beat the hell out of you, you understand me? I'd already told that doctor you'd tell him a bunch of lies, so he didn't believe you. Somebody else might, and it might just get 'em killed if they do, 'cause I ain't gonna let nothin' stop me from gettin' you out of Vanessa's hair. So you best wise up if you want to keep that pretty face of yours. You understand me?"

April stared at him icily and refused to answer.

Infuriated, he sat down quickly on the bed and reached out toward her breasts. "You know what I oughtta do, you little spitfire?" he spoke in a husky voice. "I oughtta go ahead and breed you right here and now. That'd tame you down."

"Get away from me," she cried, twisting her arm upward, bringing her hand down to rake a nail across his eye. With a yelp of pain, he leaped to his feet and stumbled away, cursing.

"You blinded me!" he roared, staggering over to the cracked mirror. "You put my eye out, you bitch!"

April jerked the covers up around her chin and cowered against the head of the bed, eyes darting wildly about for a weapon. The sound of the door opening filled her with grateful relief.

Whit came in, took one look at her, then saw Zeke staring at his bloodied eye in the mirror. "Well, what in thunderation is going on in here?" he yelled.

"The bitch blinded me!" Zeke yelped.

"Hell, she should've. I can just imagine what you were up to." He walked over to Zeke and knocked his hand out of the way so he could examine the eye. Then he laughed. "She just caught the edge with a fingernail. It's torn and bleedin', but you ain't blind. Serves you right for tryin' somethin', boy. I told you to leave her alone."

He turned to study April. "You must be feelin' right smart if you put up a fight like that, little lady. That's good. You had me worried for a time. Thought maybe you weren't gonna make it."

"I am going to welcome being with the monks," she said evenly. "At least I won't have to worry about them attacking me. Can we leave right away?"

"In the mornin'. The doc says you need that much time to rest."

"Come on, Zeke." He motioned to his partner. "I want you to leave her alone. Doc said he's sendin' some collard soup up. She can eat that and take a nap."

Zeke was still covering his eye with his hand, and on his way out, he paused and whispered fiercely, "I'm gonna get you for this. You just wait. You won't get away with this."

"You touch me again," April lashed out, "and so help me, I'll claw both your eyes out!"

He started toward her, but Whit slammed a beefy paw on his shoulder and shoved him toward the door. "Get the hell out of here, boy, and leave her alone. I'll be so goldarned glad to get you away from that filly. I've never seen you with such a hankerin'."

The door closed behind them, and April sighed with relief. Exhausted from the encounter, she fell asleep.

The sound of voices out in the hall woke her. The room was dark. Night had fallen. Instantly, she was alert, and she slipped out of bed and tiptoed quietly across the cold, rough floor to eavesdrop by the door.

Whit and Zeke were drunk, and their voices slurred as they argued. Zeke was more belligerent than Whit. "I tell you, we're gonna do it. I ain't passin' up a chance like this, no matter what you say."

"You're crazy!" Whit was struggling to keep his voice down. "Vanessa told us to get her sister up to that monastery and high-tail it home, and we shoulda been up there and back by now."

"This ain't gonna take long. How long do you think a horse race takes, you old fool? All we gotta do is be at Cheaha Mountain by mornin'. It'll all be over soon and we can be on our way. That sonofabitch downstairs says this man's got a horse that can beat my Satan, and you and me both know that ain't so."

"Yeah," Whit countered. "And he also says this man up at Cheaha has got the fastest horse in three states. You just might get beat this time. What you got to bet, anyhow?"

"I tell you, I ain't gonna lose." They argued awhile and then April heard Whit sigh in defeat. "All right, all right. We'll go have your dadblamed horse race, but if'n you get beat, don't say I didn't warn you. And I 'magine since we ain't got no money, you're gonna have to put Satan up against his horse. You just might lose him, boy."

Zeke laughed. "I ain't never lost a race yet, and I ain't gonna lose this one. Now I'm goin' downstairs and send word that at daylight, we're havin' ourselves a horse race at Cheaha mountain. I'm gonna watch the bettin' start."

She stumbled wearily back to bed and fell asleep again. Soon, Zeke was shaking her roughly. "Wake up and get dressed. I'm racin' my horse this mornin', at first light. If I ain't there on time, folks will think I forfeited. We gotta move. Now get dressed—fast."

She dressed hurriedly, while he waited outside. Then she left the room and, as she started through the door, he reached out to dig his fingers into her arm. "Remember," he warned. "You kick up a fuss, and you'll be sorry. I don't want to break that pretty neck o' yours, but I will if I have to."

They stepped out into the hall, and from the glow of Zeke's lantern she saw that Whit was passed out cold, dead to the world. He lay on the floor, stretched out and snoring. Zeke snickered and steered her by. "The old goat never could hold his liquor," he murmured.

Outside, the wagon was waiting, the mare hitched up. Behind, Zeke's proud black stallion pawed and stamped his feet in anticipation of the race, as though he fully understood what was going to happen. Zeke checked to make sure he was tied to the rear of the wagon, where he had been tied since they'd kidnapped April. Then he helped April up onto the bench before climbing up to take the reins.

April was frightened to be alone with him. Oh, why had Whit drunk so much?

The wagon lumbered along. Zeke didn't speak. Deep inside, April felt an ominous chill. Something about this was not quite right. Would Whit catch up with them? She was sure of only one thing. Before the day ended, she had to escape Zeke Hartley, even at the risk of her life.

❦ Chapter Eight ❧

ZEKE knew exactly where he was going. They left the main road leading to Talladega and headed eastward over a rough trail. Ahead, she could see the big mountain known as "Cheaha," dense with tall green pines.

The gray light of dawn melded into a blue brilliance, but even the sun's glow could not ward off the damp chill in the air. The peak of the mountain was invisible, hidden by a giant gray hand of fog.

She knew Zeke would be racing in a dash race, when horses and riders are pitted against each other for a particular distance. With a backward glance at Satan, she decided he would probably be capable of running two, even three miles at a stretch. He was a strong, powerfully built horse, obviously of good stock, and would probably win the race.

If he lost, what would Zeke pay his debt with? Had Vanessa given him any money yet? Surely not. Vanessa didn't have any money. Had Zeke perhaps wagered his horse?

They rounded a banked curve, and Zeke gave the reins a quick jerk bringing the wagon to an instant halt. There was a man standing in the middle of the road with a rifle pointed straight at them. "That's about as far as you're going, mister," the gunman's voice boomed.

April looked at the stranger with interest. While he seemed dangerous, she decided he was a cut above Zeke's caliber. He had a nice face, stern, but not sneering. He was tall, well-built, and wore clean clothes.

She watched as Zeke forced a smile to his lips. "My name's Hartley. I come to race, and—"

"Yeah, we heard you were coming." The gunman moved closer, his eyes flicking over April. With a polite nod in her direction, he turned his attention back to Zeke. "This is as far as the wagon goes. The woman stays with us."

"Us?" April blinked. She only saw one man.

He swung the barrel of his rifle upward to the bank and she saw another man perched up there, also holding a gun.

"I'd rather keep her with me," Zeke laughed nervously. "See, she's a bit crazy in the head. Keeps tryin' to run away. Her family asked me to take her to the monastery up in the mountains so the monks can keep her from runnin' wild. I'd feel better if—"

"The boss don't care how you feel, mister," the gunman snapped. "We got this place well posted, and we're a bit particular about who comes around. We been watching you ever since you left the Talladega road. Now if you want to race the boss, you just untie your horse and go with Tom up there. The lady stays with me.

"Otherwise"—his hands gripped the rifle tighter—"I suggest you turn around and head out of here pronto."

Zeke held up his right hand and said, "All right. We'll do it your way. It won't take long nohow."

April saw the gunman smile. His eyes met hers, and he said quietly, "My name's Edward Clark, ma'am. You don't have no call to be scared of me. The boss just don't want no women around when he's racing."

She returned his smile. She liked this blond young man with the dark eyes and neatly trimmed blond beard. "I won't be any trouble," she said demurely, wondering how soon she could slip into the woods and escape.

Zeke untied his horse and then snapped, "Look, I'm holdin' you responsible for this girl. If she gets away, so help me, I'll have your hide. Now the best thing to do is let me just tie her to that tree over there."

"She won't get away, Hartley." Edward returned the challenging glare. "I've got strict orders from the boss not to let that happen. He also said she's not to be mistreated, and I think that includes not tying her up. So you best just be on your way, before he changes his mind about this whole thing."

April was listening to the exchange of words, and suddenly she blurted out, "How did your boss know I was even along? Does he know about me? That I was taken from my home against my will?"

Strange looks passed between the two men. They remained silent, and she cried, "Well, answer me, Mr. Clark. Does he know I'm being held against my will?"

"Yes'm, he was told you'd say that," he answered quietly, reaching to grip her arm tightly with a leather-gloved hand. "You just come on with me. There's a shack close by, and I've got some hot coffee. I expect you could use some."

To Zeke he said, "Tom's waiting around that other bank. He'll take you to the boss. It's about another mile on up that road."

April allowed him to lead her through brambles and beyond thick scrub underbrush. In the summer, when there was new foliage, the way would probably not be passable.

As the shack loomed ahead, she gave him a quick smile and said, "Thank you for not letting him tie me up."

"I just take orders like the other men around here," he replied gruffly. "And I sure hope you don't give me no trouble, miss. I'd hate to get rough with you."

It was not, she realized, going to be as easy to escape as she had thought. It would be best to pretend defeat and catch him off guard. "I won't give you any trouble, Mr. Clark," she whispered, putting a whimper into her voice.

He grinned. "That's good. I find you awful pretty, miss, and I wouldn't want to hurt you. The boss wouldn't like it, either, but he'd kill me if anything happened to you."

Nodding, she started walking once again, but this time she took sneaking glances around her. The woods were quite thick, but if she kept her bearings and used the mountain as her point north, she could move southwest and eventually find the Selma railroad. There was also the Coosa River and the possibility of a flatboat heading down to Montgomery. All she had to do was get away and stay out of sight. Freedom was at hand! Her heart was beating with excitement, and she hoped Edward Clark did not notice.

He opened the door of the shack, and she stepped inside to the shadowed light. There were two bunks, neatly made up with sheets, blankets, and pillows. The floor was swept. There was a small fireplace with a coffeepot hanging over the smoldering logs. A crude table and two rickety-looking chairs were the only other furnishings.

"Why is the shack hidden so deeply in the woods?" she asked innocently as Edward took a tin mug from the mantle and reached for the coffeepot. "It must be hard to get to."

"We keep watch," he said simply. "There are always two men. One on post. The other staying in here most of the time. It's closer than the main house, and when strangers come up, we don't like them to know they're being watched till we know what they're doing and who they are."

"Makes sense." Her voice was casual and she gave him an appreciative smile as he handed her the steaming mug of coffee. "Thank you. I haven't had anything to eat or drink since yesterday."

"I thought you looked a little pale and cow-eyed."

She told him she was recovering from a fever, and he nodded and suggested she sit down.

"What kind of race is it to be? A dash race? How long will it be? Two miles? Three?"

He laughed and sat down opposite her, propping his booted feet up on the table. "My, you got a lot of questions. And how come you're so interested in horse racing?"

She explained that her father had raised some of the finest horses in the South, and she was puzzled to see a furrow of suspicion appear upon his forehead. "What's wrong?" she asked suddenly. "Did I say something I shouldn't have?"

"No," he snapped, then added quickly, "They'll be racing two miles. There's a course marked off. We have a lot of dash races around here. Especially on the weekends. The boss likes to try out his horses. He breeds and raises horses. We've got some mighty expensive stock around here."

"Which explains the heavy guard," she offered, but he just looked at her closely and made no comment.

Perhaps a half hour had passed since they had left Zeke, on his way to race his horse. In an equal amount of time, he could return. Hoping she did not sound as nervous as she felt, she took a deep breath and said, "I would like to go outside."

Edward had been staring into the fire, and he glanced up sharply. "Huh? What did you say?"

She glanced away, trying to look embarrassed. "Sir, there are things a lady must do, and—"

"Oh, sure, sure." His feet hit the floor with a thud and he stood up. "We'll go outside. I didn't think—"

"You aren't going with me?" she asked incredulously, widening her eyes.

Now his cheeks flushed. "Well, ma'am, I can't let you just up and go outside. I was told to keep an eye on you, and—"

She got to her feet and pretended indignant anger. "Sir, there are some things a lady does that a gentleman does not 'keep an eye on.' Surely you can grant me five minutes of privacy."

He ran his fingers through his beard, his eyes boring into hers. "All right," he said finally. "But I'll walk outside with you and stand in front of the shack. You step around back, and I'll give you just five minutes. Now don't you try to run off, because you'll just get lost in these woods, and—"

She cut him off by snapping, "I have no intention of wandering out there among the snakes." She walked by him, swishing her skirt as she passed.

Once outside, she walked quickly around the corner of the shack, down the side, and to the rear, out of Edward's vision. She kept right on going, moving as fast as she dared but careful not to step on a twig that might snap and signal that she was moving beyond the rear of the shack. Neither did she want to stumble and go toppling headlong among the weeds and rocks. It was important to make as much distance as possible in only five minutes, but she could not take any chances.

She lifted her skirts as she stepped along, feeling her pantalets rip and tear as she scraped bushes along the way. Her heart leaped with joy when she saw the washed-out ravine just head. Free of debris, it was like a clearly cut path leading downward, and once she stepped into it, she broke into a run.

The ravine cut sharply to the right, but she feared Edward would see her footprints imbedded in the soft red clay. A little distance was now between them, so she leaped from the gulley and plunged once again into the thick brush, winding westward. Ahead, there was a wall of tall pines clumped close together. They would give cover while she caught her breath.

"Hey, girl, where are you?"

His angry shout caught on the wind, floating to her in the distance.

"You better come back here! You're gonna get lost. There's bobcats in these woods!"

She pressed herself tightly back against the trunk of a tree, feeling the ragged bark cutting into her back. Gathering her skirts up tightly, she tucked them between her knees and clamped her legs together so the light fabric would not make her visible.

There were crashing sounds. "Girl, you better come back here!" he yelled, furious, his voice echoing through the still forest.

It seemed forever before she could tell that he had moved on in the opposite direction. His movements could no longer be heard. Carefully, stealthily, she began to pick her way along, taking only a few steps at a time, moving between the pines to hide until she was sure no one was around. Then she would make a dash forward to yet another pine. She kept this up for hours.

The day wore on. Still weak from her illness, April was tired and cold, hungry and thirsty. She had no idea how far she was from the ranch, and each time she looked up, Cheaha mountain appeared to be the same size, taunting her efforts.

She stopped awhile to gasp for breath. It was too much. She was weaker than she thought. It would be so easy to give way to the weariness . . . to just slide down into the fragrant pine needles below and let sleep come. Perhaps she would sleep for a little while. She was so weary, and she had run for hours. They would not find her now.

Her eyes opened reluctantly, then blinked rapidly as she

struggled to awaken. How long had she slept? Judging from the sinking sun, it was quite late. Total darkness was only a few hours away. She could not remain where she was. What if there were wild animals? A tremble went through her as she forced herself to stand. Shelter had to be found, but where?

She stood up and stretched to try and get the stiffness from her body after being in such a cramped position for so long. Despite her peril, it felt good to just lift her arms to the sky and gulp in sweet, fresh air.

And then she saw him.

Slowly, she brought her arms down from over her head to wrap them about her shoulders. She stepped backward in retreat. He made no move toward her, just continued to stare from beneath the rim of his hat. He was leaning against a tree, arms folded across his leather-vested chest. Beneath the neatly trimmed mustache, there was an amused smile on his lips.

"Hello, April."

She glanced about wildly, trying to decide which way to run. Could she escape the towering stranger who seemed to be enjoying her plight?

"Don't you remember me? You had such a low opinion of me once, I figured you'd never forget me."

Panic took over, and she turned and began to run back across the clearing. Behind her, she heard the sound of a long, low whistle, but there was not time to wonder about that, for on top of the sound came another . . . thundering hooves pounding through the forest right behind her. Someone on a horse. He was going to run her down. She would be killed. She opened her mouth to scream in terror but no sound came out. Instinct told her to keep running . . . to try and make it to the safety of the trees where a horse could not move so fast. If she was going to die, then by God, she was going to give them a fight first.

The horse was upon her. In a split second, he charged past her, cutting back to block her path. In that moment, she realized that there was no rider. She stopped so quickly that she lost her balance and tumbled to the ground. The horse also stopped, then snorted and trotted over to stand beside her, giving warning that she should stay right there.

"Good boy." The man came up behind her. Strong arms reached down to scoop her roughly to her feet. "Now then," the man said gruffly. "Suppose you realize that you aren't going anywhere, April, and let's stop all this nonsense. I'm hungry, and the cook's got our supper waiting."

She looked up and gasped as recognition flashed. "My God!" she whispered. "Rance Taggart! My Lord, it is you!"

His eyes flicked over her, and seeing blood on her arm, he examined the wound quickly and said, "That could be nasty. We'd better get you back to the house and wash it out. Come along."

"I'm not going anywhere with you." She felt herself coming together once more. "I don't know how you came to be here, but if you want to help me, then see to it that I get home. I'll pay you well when we get there, and—"

"April, you aren't going anywhere except with me." He sounded quietly amused.

"No, I don't understand." She was getting angry. "And I really don't have time to stand here and listen. There are men back there looking for me, and I can't let them find me."

"They aren't looking for you anymore."

"They aren't?" She looked at him hopefully. "How can you be sure?"

"Because I found you." He seemed to think it was all quite simple. "Come along now. It's going to be dark soon. Virtus will take us back."

"Virtus!" She stared at the horse.

"It's Virtus's colt, April. Don't you remember? Your father gave him to you. When Vanessa left, she took him with her. Some months ago, she got word to me that she was interested in selling him because she needed money. So I bought him. His name is Virtus, like his sire's."

"I . . . I don't understand any of this. How did you come to be here, and why did those men stop searching for me? Did Vanessa have a change of heart and send you to bring me home?"

He mounted the horse, then reached down easily to bring her up behind him. Reluctantly, she wound her arms around his narrow waist.

They began to move toward the mountain in the gathering dusk. They had not gone far when April cried out in exasperation, "Why won't you answer my questions? I can't believe Zeke Hartley isn't out there looking for me."

"Zeke won't be after you. I imagine he's gone back to Sylacauga to pick up his partner and head back to Vanessa." He laughed to himself and murmured, "I just wonder what kind of lie he's going to tell her about all this."

She tensed. "Why do you know all this? And why were *you* in the woods looking for me if Vanessa didn't send you?"

He was silent for a few moments, then said, "April, *I* was the one riding against Zeke in the dash race. I was riding Virtus. I won. Zeke lost. It's that simple."

"So? You won!" she cried, flinging her arms out, then quickly grabbing him as she felt herself sliding from the horse's rump. "What difference does that make?"

"In the race I won you."

"You *what?*"

He laughed. "Zeke wasn't about to bet that horse of his that he takes so much pride in. He made a deal—if he lost, I'd win you. And I did."

She began to beat on his back with her fists, screaming in protest. This time, she did slip from the horse, falling to the ground, but the soft pine needles cushioned her fall. Rance dropped from the horse and fell to his knees beside her, chuckling in amusement.

His face only inches away, she could feel his warm breath as he whispered, "April, you're going to enjoy being with me. Believe me, you'll have more fun as my woman than you ever would stashed away in the monastery they were taking you to."

"Damn you, Rance Taggart, I don't want to be your woman," she cried. "You've caused enough trouble in my life. I should've let my father kill you when he had the chance."

He silenced her with a kiss. She was shocked to find that it tasted of warm, sweet wine. He released her quickly and got to his feet, jerking her along with him.

"Will you listen to me?" she pleaded, struggling. "My father is very sick. Vanessa is going to take advantage of that. That's why she wanted me out of the way."

Suddenly his face became a thundercloud of fury, and he reached out and shook her.

"Now *you* listen to me," he ordered. "I can see why Vanessa would want you out of the way, to give her a chance to make peace with your father. You've always been the apple of his eye. Let Vanessa have him to herself now.

"You belong to me, and you're going to obey my every command, just like a well-trained animal. Disobey, and you'll be punished. It's up to you, sweet."

He lifted her and placed her in the saddle, then began walking through the woods, leading Virtus. April wrapped her trembling hands around the saddle horn, staring at Rance's broad back, too stunned to speak.

❧ Chapter Nine ❧

THE house was nestled at the base of the mountain. It was neatly constructed of logs and provided a homey setting in the rugged terrain. Beyond, there were stables and corrals, where horses pawed and stamped the ground. Rance Taggart had good stock and plenty of it.

Edward Clark bounded out the front door to greet his boss. "How'd you find her? I gave up. Figured she'd fallen in the river or something."

Rance swung down from the horse's back, then set April on her feet before replying. "I know every inch of these woods, Clark. I also know how to track. Learned it from the Indians."

Edward shrugged and said, "Well, I guess all that makes a difference."

Rance withered him with a look. "I also don't give up, Clark. *That's* what makes the difference."

Edward nodded. He started for the bunkhouse, calling over his shoulder. "Cook brought your supper up a while ago. Smells like chicken and drap dumplings. See you for breakfast."

April shivered as his eyes flicked over her knowingly. She was now his boss's woman—or so he and his boss thought.

Rance clamped a possessive hand on her shoulder and steered her toward the front door. He called to Edward to see that Virtus was rubbed down and put in his stall. They stepped up onto the porch, and April froze.

"I told you not to give me any trouble, sweet," he said. "I own you now. Maybe you'd rather sleep in the barn like a horse. I'm offering you a nice hot meal and a warm bed."

"A bed with *you* in it, I imagine," she snapped. "No thanks, Rance. You'll have to kill me. I'm going home!"

He picked her up easily and kicked the door open with his booted foot. The room was large, with a fireplace, sofa, and chairs. In one corner was a desk littered with papers. He walked across the floor and kicked another door open. This one led to a bedroom, and he dropped her roughly on the bed covered with a bright patchwork quilt.

"Hell, yes, I'm in the bed, too," he cried, jerking off his vest and ripping off his shirt. "So let's just go ahead and find out who's boss around here, April. Your daddy pampered you all your life, and you think everybody is going to scrape and bow to you. You've got a jolt coming."

"Don't you touch me!" She scrambled to the far side of the bed, huddling against the wall. Tears sprang to her eyes. "Rance, please. I don't know what lies Vanessa told you, but you've got to believe me. She's going to hurt Poppa."

She was talking quickly. "I hated the way Poppa treated Vanessa, but now he's so sick—"

Rance sighed. "Whatever is wrong with your father, I'm sure Vanessa can get him a doctor as well as you can. And it's important that they have some time alone together, to work things out, without you being there. You always did stand between your father and Vanessa."

When she began to protest, he said evenly, "You're going to love being with me, April. We'll talk about your home another time. Right now, *this* is your home—for as long as I want you. You're mine, and you're going to be happy being mine."

He sat on the bed and drew her into his arms. His lips were only inches away as she stared up at him. "You want me, and you know you do. You just think you should pretend you don't. But I'm going to make it so goddamned good you'll forget all about pretending. I'm going to make you beg me. You'll be glad I won that race."

His lips closed on hers, his tongue moving inside her mouth as she struggled in vain. His hand moved from her breasts to her stomach, a teasing demon. Moving to one side, he slid his knee between her thighs to force them apart. Skillfully, he removed her clothes, one piece at a time. His fingers touched where no man had ever touched before. April could not control the spasms of pleasure that shot through her body, making her arch her back beneath his caress.

Never had she wanted a man to possess her, never had she felt this way. What was happening to her?

He raised his lips, and she looked into his taunting eyes. "Tell me you want me," he commanded.

"Yes," she whispered, hating herself. She wanted him. Dear God, she wanted him. She had never dreamed of such desire. "Yes, yes, Rance. I want you."

She gasped as she felt his finger slip inside her, moving to tantalize. She clutched at his smooth, hard back, feeling her nails digging into him as she fought to pull him even closer to her. But he held back, staring down at her so arrogantly. "Beg for it," he commanded.

Fury mingled with her desire. He was trying to humiliate her, and she could not let him do that. "No, damn you," she hissed, her body on fire. "I want you, but I won't beg."

He shifted his body so that he was on top of her, and suddenly there was a new sensation. Something hot and hard and pulsating was touching her, about to enter. She waited, but he moved no farther. She whispered hoarsely, "Damn you, please! Please take me!"

He chuckled and bent to kiss her, slowly and lingeringly. Then, grasping her hips firmly, he moved back and then forward. She felt a sudden pain, but it was far overshadowed by the ecstasy that followed.

He held her tightly against him but did not move again. Her eyes flashed open and she saw that he was staring down at her once more, and this time all the arrogance was gone. His gaze was puzzled, probing.

"Rance?" she asked.

"You were a virgin."

He said it almost accusingly, and she continued to cling to him, trembling with desire. "Did you think I wasn't?"

He began to move, as though he could no longer hold back. Faster and faster he plunged in and out of her, and she felt the explosion coming from deep within. She wrapped her legs around his back to hold him tight and bit her lip to hold back a scream, but it pierced the stillness of the night all the same.

With one final thrust that threatened to impale her to the bed, Rance took his release. He held her for a moment, then rolled to the side and onto his back, to stare silently up at the ceiling.

April was in tears. She was shaken by the wonder of it all. But suddenly she could stand the silence no longer. "Well, have you nothing to say? Now that you've got what you wanted from me, am I free to go?"

"You aren't going anywhere, April."

"But what do you want from me?" She exploded into tears of rage. "Why do you want to hurt me?"

"I didn't want to hurt you."

"Then why are you doing this?"

"Why didn't you tell me you were a virgin?"

"What makes you think I would be otherwise? Did you think because you made love to my sister that both of us were easily seduced?" She started to get up, but his hand snaked out to hold her down.

"I never made love to your sister. And certainly not the way we just did. I was merely kissing her, touching her."

"The two of you set it up to hurt my father and humiliate me and ruin the party. You can admit it now, Rance. It's all over. There's no need to lie."

"That's why I'm not lying. I didn't know Vanessa set the whole thing up. She asked me to her room and said it was important. I knew she was upset about your father giving the colt to you. I felt sorry for her."

"Is that why you were in bed with my sister? Because you felt sorry for her?" April lashed out, glaring at him.

He shrugged. "Once I got there, she let me know she was willing. I've never turned a beautiful woman down. But you and your father arrived before we had time to do anything."

April chewed her lower lip nervously. "It doesn't matter. I just want to go home."

"You aren't going anywhere, April. You belong to me

now. I wish I'd known you were a virgin. I never would've had you as the wager on a race. But it's too late now. You enjoyed making love, and I suppose someone had to be the first."

"You bastard!" She raised her hand to slap him, but he caught her wrist and flung her back on the bed.

"I told you once, blue eyes, never to do that again. I don't allow a woman to make but one mistake." His brown eyes smoldered. "I think it's time you learned your place around here."

He ignored her screams and thrashing arms and legs as he jerked her roughly over his knees. She screamed even louder as his broad hand began to smack soundly across her bare buttocks.

"I'll kill you, Rance Taggart," she shrieked. "So help me, I'll find a way to kill you!" She twisted and rolled from side to side, but she could not escape the hard, stinging blows.

Abruptly, he stopped. "Have you had enough?" he asked gruffly. "I'll beat you black and blue if I have to, April—"

"Yes, yes, stop!" she pleaded, slumping across his lap in defeat. "Just let me go, please," and she dissolved into tears once again.

"I'm getting a little tired of that bawling, too," he snapped, rolling her over on her back and cradling her in his arms. "You're a fine-looking woman, April Jennings, and it makes me mad to see you whimpering like a spoiled brat. I'd rather see you whimper with desire."

His hand shot between her legs once again, and he lowered his lips to her breast and began to suck gently. At first, she remained rigid, determined that this time he would not arouse her, but, as before, she was betrayed by her own body. Soon, she was wrapping her arms about his neck, pulling him closer, and her legs were spreading beneath him to offer herself wholly and completely.

He was gentle this time, knowing her bottom smarted. But the lovemaking was good and warm, and April felt a deep sense of contentment as she allowed herself to be carried away once again on the sweeping, raging tide of fulfillment.

She felt him reach his pleasure and was surprised that he continued to move within her until she had touched that

peak of ecstasy herself. Then he held her for a long time
without speaking. She found this surprising but said nothing.

"All right," he said finally, moving from the bed and
jerking on his trousers. "I think it's time we ate. That stew
is going to be cold, and I imagine you're starving."

He slipped on his shirt, buttoning it quickly as he stared
down at her. "Your bags are in the corner. There's water
for bathing in the pitcher on the dresser. When you get
dressed, come on out in front of the fire and warm yourself."

She called to him as he walked from the room, but he
did not answer. He closed the door soundly behind him.

Surely, she reasoned as she hurried to bathe and dress in
the cold room, he did not intend to keep her imprisoned.
He only wanted her for his pleasure and would let her go
when he'd had enough. The thought made her feel some-
what better.

She chose a high-necked dress of blue wool, then found
her silver brush and began to smooth her long, golden hair.
It was difficult, for there were brambles and leaves and
pine needles from her journey through the woods. Finally,
her tresses hung smoothly about her face, and though she
was tired, she felt more confident because she was clean
and fresh.

She opened the door and stepped into the big room.
Rance stood before the fireplace, ladling stew from the
big black pot over the flames into bowls. He glanced up
and saw her, then gestured to the round wooden table. "I
had to heat it up, but the delay was worth it," he smiled.

Suddenly, she felt terribly embarrassed. Moments before, he had ravished her, making her scream. Now he
stood there calmly serving her supper.

"Well, let's eat." He gave her a lopsided grin and sat
down at the table.

He was, she admitted reluctantly, quite attractive. His
face was strong and handsome, his black hair full and as
dark as Virtus's. And his brown eyes held a depth she
had not noticed until today.

She sat down across from him and began to spoon the
thick golden broth into her mouth, delighting in the taste.
The chicken was plentiful, the dumplings crisp on the out-

side and soft and juicy inside. There were also generous portions of hot spoon bread, and delicious coffee.

They ate in silence, and then Rance got up and walked over to the mantle where he got a long cheroot from a wooden box and lit it with a straw ignited in the fireplace. He turned to stare at her thoughtfully. She decided to let him carry the conversation. So far, every attempt she had made to talk with him had turned out disastrously. She moved to the sofa and waited for him to speak.

"You're awfully quiet," he said finally. "Still pouting over the thrashing you so richly deserved?"

She bristled but was determined not to let him rile her. "How long have you been living here?" she asked quietly, hoping to change the subject.

"Since shortly after your father ran me off," he answered, smiling. "I wanted a place to raise horses, and this was a likely spot. I rounded up some good men, men I could depend on, and we built this place. I suppose you could say your father did me a favor. I'm doing quite well. We're breeding the best horses in the state right here."

"Why aren't you in the Confederate Army fighting Yankees?" she asked suddenly. "After all, the *good, brave* men of the South are volunteering."

"Oh, I wouldn't say that," he challenged. "The war is probably not going to last all that long. If it does, I will be performing a much better service to the Southland right here, rather than marhing off gloriously to catch a Yankee ball in my heart."

"I don't understand."

"Cavalry horses, sweet. We're raising horses for the Confederate Cavalry. Someone has to do it."

Suddenly April was tired of skirting the issue. Quite abruptly, she leaned forward, extending her hands in pleading gesture. "Rance, I must leave. I have to return to Montgomery."

The pleasant atmosphere disappeared. An angry furrow appeared between his eyes and he gazed at her grimly while drawing on his cheroot. "You'd better remember that you belong to me now."

She leaped to her feet, waving her arms wildly. Was there no reaching this man? "I am not an animal, Rance.

I cannot be bought and sold like a horse. I cannot be won and lost like a horse. You have to let me go!"

His laughter infuriated her almost as much as his taunting words. "Now wouldn't your father be happy to hear that little speech, April? What about all those slaves he owns? Do you suppose they just might feel as you do about being bought and sold like animals?"

"You are a traitor to the South, sir!" she retorted hotly. "Why don't you go fight for the Yankees?"

"And you're just a stupid female who doesn't know beans about the war and why it's being fought, or you'd know the war isn't all a matter of slavery." He held his cheroot between his teeth, talking around it as he leaned over and began pulling off his boots.

"You'll like it here, April, once you calm down and accept things the way they are. Cheaha Mountain is the closest thing there is to heaven. There's peace here. You'll be happy if you let yourself. I'll even let you ride Virtus. After all, I guess by rights he's yours. I knew Vanessa had stolen him when I bought him. But he's such a prize, I won't do the noble thing and give him to you."

"I don't imagine you've ever done a noble deed in your entire life, Rance Taggart."

He chose to let the tart remark pass and continued, "It does get lonesome around here at times. I let the boys bring some women in from town once in a while when they get randy. As for myself, I like to have one around when *I* want her. I don't want to be bothered with having to go out and find one. That's why I was willing to take you on the wager today."

"And, of course, knowing it was me and wanting revenge on my father had nothing to do with it," she snapped. "Well, my father won't know, Rance. You won't get satisfaction from that. I'm afraid he's too ill, and—"

"I didn't know the woman was you."

"You didn't?" She blinked, surprised that she felt a wave of disappointment. "Then how could you be sure you would like your prize?" she goaded him. "Or do you get so *randy* that you're willing to take *any* woman?"

He grinned insolently. "I had you checked out, sweet. I was told you were quite lovely. When I found out it *was* you, that made it all so much better. I only regret that you were a virgin. I don't like to take virginity."

"I'm surprised you have any scruples at all, however shallow they might be." She shook her head from side to side. "Rance, it will not work out. You cannot keep me here."

"I am keeping you here, blue eyes, and it's been a long day. I suggest we get to bed. The day begins early around here, even before the sun wakes up." He began banking the fire. "You will be expected to help the cook, and there are plenty of other chores to be done. Washing. Cleaning. In the spring, we plant a garden."

"I won't be here in the spring!" She clenched her fists, her body rigid with fury. "I won't be here tomorrow if I can help it. I'd rather challenge the bobcats than spend a night under your roof."

He silenced her with a kiss and held her against him for a moment before stepping back to smile down at her. "You aren't going anywhere, April. I have guards posted all night, every night. You wouldn't make it to the woods before you were spotted. Now don't make me tie you to your bed to keep from giving everyone a rough night. Why can't you admit you're defeated?"

She did not trust herself to speak, for she was afraid that if she became any angrier than she already was, she would lose control and slap him again, and there was no doubt where that would lead.

He led her to the bedroom, then brushed her cheek with his lips and said, "I'll be right next door if you need me, but there's nothing to be afraid of. I'll see you in the morning."

He turned and walked away, leaving her staring after him in wonder. He was leaving her to go to his own bed, alone. While she was relieved not to have to sleep with him, she was still surprised.

As though reading her thoughts, Rance turned at his bedroom door and said, "Come to me when you feel the need, April. In some ways, you are still very much a virgin."

Exasperated, she cried, "Well, what is that supposed to mean?"

His arrogant smile infuriated her. What was worse was the way her body flushed when he looked at her as he was doing then. "I don't like to take virginity, April. I let women make the overtures till they become truly experienced."

"Well, you'll freeze in hell before I make an overture," she yelped, but he closed his door on her .

The man is insane, she thought furiously as she changed from her dress to a sleeping gown. He didn't believe in raping women, did he? Well damn him, if he ever took her again, it would have to be rape!

She crawled beneath the quilts, trembling with cold. Memories of what had taken place in that bed only a few hours earlier made her body feel even colder.

He was on the other side of the wall. All she had to do was call to him and he would come, to hold her and kiss her and lead her to heights of joy.

She would not call. No! There were more important things to think about. How soon could she escape and return to Pinehurst?

Rance Taggart meant nothing to her. He was an animal, regarding a woman as a stud does a mare—something to couple with and then forget. And though she did not truly love Alton, she knew that he would have been different. He was the man for her. Not Rance Taggart.

She rolled on her side, beating the pillow down with her fist. She would dream of Alton, and of how it would be when they were married, making love, warm, secure, decent, respectable love.

But in her dreams, the face of the man who held her was not Alton's. She saw raven hair, smoldering brown eyes, and an arrogant smile that annoyed and excited her, all at once. His kisses tasted of warm, sweet wine.

On the other side of the wall, Rance Taggart lay in his own bed, arms folded behind his head. Damn! he cursed himself silently. Of all the women in the world, why did he have to win April Jennings in a race?

He had no time to get involved with a woman. There was a war. He had to train his horses for the Confederacy. She could only mean trouble. The thing to do was let her go. Let her get the hell out of his life.

Limpid blue eyes framed by lashes that seemed to have been dusted with silver and gold floated before him. He felt soft golden hair entwine about his fingers. Her beautiful body was alive in his embrace.

Savage desire burned Rance, there in the darkness.

No, he had no intention of letting her go.

🐾 Chapter Ten 🐾

RANCE Taggart was stripped to the waist. The March winds were chilly, but the sun beat down upon his back, so he did not feel any cold. He had also worked up quite a sweat with the horse he was breaking.

He rubbed the gelding's back, smiling with satisfaction. Captain James Randolph had asked for the best possible cavalry horse, and Rance was going to give it to him. He was going to show the Confederate army he could produce the very best mounts.

Already people were saying that the Confederate cavalry was far superior to the Yankees'. He wanted to keep it that way. The South, for the present, was aided by its own background and tradition. Reb recruits came from rural areas and were used to horses. Many Yankee recruits could barely sit a horse. The North just wasn't horseback country. And legends of chivalry made it so much more gallant to go off to war on horseback instead of on foot.

But there was a problem to come, and Rance figured he saw it quicker than the government did. The Southern soldier was riding off to war on his own horse. But after several battles, when his horse had died, he had to get another one himself. Sometimes he could get a furlough and go home for another, and sometimes he had to do without.

That's where Rance was going to come in. He already had 300 horses ready to take to Dalton, Georgia. Captain

James Randolph had agreed to buy the whole lot even if he had to pay for them out of his own pocket. Surely there would be other officers just like Randolph who would need horses.

Rance's one big problem was going to be finding the animals, because he couldn't raise them that quickly.

Everyone was saying that Jeb Stuart's Reb troops could teach tricks to circus riders. Tales of Stuart and his men were already widespread, and Rance also had a lot of respect for what he had heard of Joe Wheeler and Nathan Bedford Forrest. Forrest was called an untaught genius. He had no military training and not a shred of social status, but he was probably going to be the best cavalry charger in the whole damned war.

"Git thar fust with the most men," said Forrest. Rance, too, believed in the speed and prowess of mounted soldiers, and by God, he was going to see that the Confederacy had the best horses.

A movement caught his eye, and he turned to see April walking toward the cabin, carrying two chickens with freshly wrung necks. He was not close enough to see, but he knew her tiny nose would be wrinkled in disgust. In the two months she had been with him, the cook had taught her the cooking chores at the main house, but he knew she would still be repelled by having to clean chickens.

Before going inside, she stopped to gaze at him across the expanse of cleared land. She did not smile, merely looked at him for long, silent moments, then disappeared inside.

He turned his attention back to the horse. She probably hated him. If he could have seen her eyes, the hatred would have been glittering in their sapphire depths. He knew the look. He saw it every time they sat down to one of their silent meals together. Sometimes she glared at him and other times she just looked at him like she was hurt. Plenty hurt. Maybe she had a right to be. Hell, it wasn't her fault that he had won her in a damn race. And it wasn't her fault she had been raised as she had.

He still regretted the remark he had made to her when she accused him of treating her like property, when he'd thrown her daddy's slaves up to her. He knew full well that April Jennings did not hold with slavery. He could remember her sitting and reading to the Negroes, because they were not allowed to learn how themselves. He had even suspected that, when nobody was around, she was *teaching* them.

Sure, she was spoiled. No way to avoid that, the way her daddy doted on her, giving her anything she wanted. The only time she had not gotten her way was when she tried to make him stop treating Vanessa badly. But nobody could have changed Carter Jennings's mind about his other daughter.

Rance figured that the man had coming whatever he got. And knowing Vanessa, he imagined she was giving the old man a pretty rough time.

Damn it all, he was doing April a favor to keep her here, he thought defensively. She wasn't up at the monastery in the mountains living with monks, and she wasn't back at Pinehurst fighting with Vanessa. She was living here, and living good, as a matter of fact. Nobody bothered her. Especially him. He was not going to force himself on any woman. The only reason he had made her want him that first night was because he figured she expected it. And he never would have thought a woman who looked that sexy could possibly be a virgin. Still, he was sorry about that night. Kind of.

Rance Taggart had had many women, but he had never loved any of them. He made love to them, and in a strange sort of way, he figured he needed them, but he was rough and selfish with them. One pretty woman was like another. He had sense enough to know that some of the women in his past had only pretended to be aroused. The whores in Birmingham and Montgomery and others along the way were only performing. They could not possibly have been as eager as they pretended to be. That hadn't bothered him. It just made it that much better when he found one who didn't pretend.

Like April.

She had wanted him. Oh, hell, yes, she had wanted everything he had to give her. When she got her pleasuring, it was no act. The realization made him want her something fierce.

"You're gonna brush the hide right off that horse."

He whipped around quickly at the same time his right

hand moved, lightning fast, to the gun in his holster. By the time he recognized Edward Clark, he had his gun pointed straight at him.

"Hey, watch it!" Clark's face paled.

"I don't like anybody sneaking up on me," Rance snarled, putting his gun back in the holster. "Why aren't you watching April like you're supposed to be?"

"She's not going anywhere. I can see the house from here, anyway. How come you're brushing that horse so hard? You got something eating on you?"

"If I have," Rance replied, giving the gelding one last swipe, "it's my business. What's she been doing today?"

"Watching the cook kill chickens, or at least trying to watch," he added with a laugh. "She covered her face when he started wringing necks. She's no farm girl, that's for sure."

Rance led the horse from the stable, Edward right on his heels.

"There's something I've been wanting to ask you, Rance," he spoke hesitantly. "Some of the boys were talking, and we're wondering just how long you plan to keep her here."

Rance flashed him an annoyed glance. "That's also my business. She's not giving you a hard time, asking you to let her go, is she?"

"No. That's kinda sad, too. Like her spirit's broke, like she just don't care for nothing, no more. She just does what she's told and never says a word."

When Rance made no comment Edward rushed on boldly. "You know, she's a fine-looking woman. About the finest-looking woman I ever saw. Hair the color of sunrise, eyes that make you want to just crawl in 'em. Lord! Anyone can see she's got a body that would drive a man wild, and the boys don't blame you for keeping her around, but they still don't like it. I mean, a woman out here—"

"That's enough!" Rance whirled around, a muscle twitching in his cheek. His eyes flashed ominously. "You and the others would be wise to keep your mouths shut."

"Hey, don't get mad." Edward threw out his arms in a pleading gesture. "We just wonder how long this is going to go on."

Rance took a deep breath, trying to get his temper under control. Clark had seen him lose it. He had also seen, lying on the floor beaten to a pulp, the man who had *made* him lose it. He knew he was treading on dangerous territory. "You're my best hand, Clark," he said quietly, evenly. "That's why I trust you to look after her. But stay out of my personal life, or we're going to have problems."

Edward glanced away nervously, uncomfortable in his boss's angry, challenging glare. "Okay, okay. I'm sorry. I just thought I'd let you know the boys don't like it."

Rance began to trot the horse around in the circle while he held on to the end of a rope fastened to his harness. "He's a fine one, isn't he?" he asked, dismissing the tension. "I broke him for that cavalry captain who's buying three hundred horses for his company."

"Yeah, next to Virtus, I'd say he's about the finest piece of horseflesh on the whole ranch," Clark nodded. "When do we take them horses to Georgia?"

"Tomorrow. I told the boys to round them up today and be ready to leave at dawn. You're going with us."

"Who's going to watch April?"

"She won't give anybody any trouble. She won't even go near the woods now that we're having warm weather and seeing a few snakes around. I'll leave Hinton and Mulhern. Hinton's still limping on that ankle he busted, and Mulhern's got a bad foot from that horse stepping on him. They can keep an eye on things."

"It's fine with me. We shouldn't be gone over a week, anyway."

"Well, me and you aren't coming back right away. Selling off three hundred horses is going to cut into our stock. We've got to do some scouting around. The war is going to pick up this spring, for sure, and we've got to have horses. The Rebs are going to realize before long that they've got to buy their own, and when they do, I want to be ready to supply them."

Edward Clark whistled and shook his head. "Boy, that's going to take some scouting. Don't you imagine the Yankees have got the same idea?"

Rance grinned. "I sure hope they do. I plan to steal the horses from them."

Before Clark could react, they looked up at the sound of a door closing and saw April on the front porch. She did not look at them, but sat down on the steps to stretch her arms toward the azure sky and the warm sun.

Rance touched the tip of his mustache and stared at her for several seconds, then said, "Go tell her to come over here."

Edward was surprised. Rance usually ignored the girl and she ignored him. He figured the only contact they ever had was in bed, after dark. Nobody ever saw them talking, and even though Rance would kill him if he knew it, Joe Townes had peeked in the window once and watched the two eating supper. He said neither of them spoke a word all through the meal.

Having riled his boss enough for one day, he made no comment, but approached April. "Boss wants to see you," he said tonelessly.

For a moment, she continued to sit, staring straight ahead. Finally she got to her feet, smoothed the skirt of her bright gingham dress, and started toward Rance.

Edward shook his head and moved off toward the bunkhouse. He would never be able to figure out the situation. Knowing Rance's temper, maybe it was best not to try.

April said nothing when she reached Rance, just waited for him to speak. She kept her head down, staring at the ground.

"You never did learn to ride a horse well, April," he said pleasantly.

She looked up at him, and he saw just a spark of defiance in the sapphire eyes. "I know how to ride a horse!"

She sounded defensive, almost angry, and he was glad. Maybe she still had some spunk, after all. "But you aren't good at it," he said gently. "Would you like to learn?"

"Why?" she asked suspiciously.

He shrugged. "I guess I'm tired of seeing you stuck in the cabin all day cooking and cleaning. Soon it will be spring, and I'l like to see you outside more. So, would you like to learn to ride?"

She chewed her lower lip thoughtfully, then murmured, "I suppose there's no harm."

"Wait here, and I'll go get a side saddle."

He started toward the stable and tack room, but she said, "I don't want to ride on a side saddle. I want to either use a stock or learn to ride bareback."

"Well, you aren't riding bareback," he laughed, "and if you're going to ride in dresses, you can use a side saddle like a lady."

"Vanessa used a stock."

"Vanessa is no lady."

The two challenged each other with their eyes, then April placed her hands on her hips and said, "All right, we can just forget the whole thing."

He disappeared inside the stable and returned with a stock saddle. April carefully hid her smile of triumph as he placed it on the horse's back.

"The stirrups are going to have to be pulled up, and you aren't going to like the high pommel horn," he said as he fastened the saddle in place.

She smiled demurely. "I might need it to tie my lariat. Who knows? One day I might just start roping calves, since it appears I'm going to live the rest of my life on a ranch."

He ignored her tartness and helped her mount. "Now listen carefully." He handed her the reins. "There are four natural gaits—the walk, the trot, the canter, and the gallop. I've broke this horse to all four."

He stepped back. "A walk is a slow, four-beat pace, and the trot is two beats, light and balanced. You can either sit there and bump your butt or you can rise to the movement of the horse's gait. That's called posting. Rise up out of the saddle slightly and let more of your weight fall on the stirrups.

"Okay." He motioned her forward. "Walk him around in a circle and see if you can get him into a trot."

April dug her heels in slightly, and the animal began to move. She had no problem nudging him into a trot.

"Rein him in," Rance called.

She paid no heed, wanting to show him that she *could* ride. She kicked the horse's flanks. Suddenly he reared up on his hind legs, and Rance cursed, yelling at her to hold him tight. Instead, she kicked him again, thinking he was only confused. "Whoa, boy," she called to him over the panic that began roaring in her ears. "Down, boy, down!"

He stopped thrashing the air with his forelegs and brought them crashing down to earth. When he hit the ground with a thud, she almost lost her hold.

"April, hang on, I'm coming!" she heard Rance screaming behind her as the horse streaked across the field and headed for the woods. She could only pray that he would slow when they reached the congestion of trees, but then they were upon them, and the horse maneuvered his way about, darting here and there. He seemed to move even faster.

She did not dare loosen her hold. To fall now would mean she could land on a jagged stump or break her neck against a tree trunk. There was nothing to do but hold tightly. She realized she was too frightened to even scream.

A clearing loomed ahead. Did she dare let go and take her chances falling on the ground? Dear God, what should she do?

From behind, there came the sound of thundering hooves, faster than the ones below her. She did not even have time to turn her head before she felt the strong, powerful arm wrapping around her waist to lift her easily up and out of the saddle. She clung to Rance as he rode Virtus like the wind.

He slowed, stopped, then lowered her to the ground and leaped quickly down behind her. He gave Virtus a hard slap on his rump and hollered "Go get him, boy!" Virtus took off at a hard gallop.

Rance's concerned face loomed above her. Looking her over from head to toe, he gripped her shoulders and asked, "Are you all right?" When he saw that she was, he scolded, "You had to show off, didn't you? I should've known better than to let you on that horse. I thought I had him broke, but I guess he was just waiting for some nitwit like you to come along so he could prove his spirit's not as broke as he had me believing."

"I'm sorry," she mumbled, dizzy and sore from the rough ride. "I guess I was trying to show off. Don't blame the horse."

"You're going to be pretty sore tomorrow," he told her, glancing up and smiling as Virtus trotted up, the run-away horse following docilely behind.

He mounted the large black steed and pulled April up behind him, knowing without asking that she did not want to get back up on the other horse again. "I've got a gentle mare you can ride," he told her as they headed back toward the ranch. "Though I don't imagine you're going to want to ride again any time soon."

"Oh, I'd like to go out tomorrow," she said quickly, then realized that a ripple of pleasure was moving through her as she sat close behind him. Why does he have to affect me this way? She cursed herself silently. The man is a savage.

"I'll leave word you can go out for an hour or so every day, as long as you don't give anybody any trouble."

"Leave word? Are you going somewhere?"

"Me and the boys are taking some horses over to Georgia. I'm leaving Hinton and Mulhern to look after things. Don't give them any trouble. And I don't want you riding alone."

"I don't want to go out alone with the snakes moving around." She made herself shudder so that he would feel it. "When we were out at the chicken pen this morning, I saw one. The cook said it was just a chicken snake and harmless. But I'm scared to death of them. I don't want to go near those woods."

"Good. I won't worry about you." He was silent for a moment, then teased, "Are you going to miss me?"

It took every bit of self-control not to give him a sarcastic reply. Now was not the time, she reminded herself. For two months, one week, and three days, she had kept her temper in check. Through the silent meals, the glances he gave her, she had managed to keep silent. Everyone thought she had resigned herself to imprisonment here. That was what she wanted them all to think, and she was not about to be goaded into exposing her true feelings.

"You didn't answer me, April."

"I'd rather not discuss it. We were getting along well. I see no reason to argue."

"All I asked was if you'll miss me."

She sighed, kept her voice even. "Not really. Do you think prisoners miss their jailers?"

"I suppose not," he said, after a pause. "But tell me something else. Don't you ever get lonely? Seems to me I hear you tossing and turning in that big bed of yours at night."

"No," she could not help snapping at him. "I do not get lonely."

He reached to tug playfully at a strand of her long hair. She moved back quickly as he murmured, "I think you're lying. I think you do get lonely, and that you'd like to come to my bed. You can't help remembering that it was good for us once."

"Once was enough." She removed her arms from about his waist and maneuvered so that her hands were twisted behind her to grip the back of the saddle. If she fell off, so be it. She was not going to sit there hugging him.

He murmured, "Once is never enough, sweet. You'll realize that sooner or later."

They rode the rest of the way in silence, and he let her off in front of the cabin. She hurried inside.

Later, plucking the chickens in back of the cabin, she saw Rance working around the stable, and her gaze kept moving back to him. His back glistened in the sun, muscles rippling. He had a strong, powerful body, and his thighs strained against the tight britches.

Once he turned to face her, and she looked away quickly lest he see her watching him . . . but not before she caught a glimpse of that massive chest. A flush went through her. She had seen the dark curling hairs that tapered downward, and she trembled to remember that other time, when she had seen him naked . . . seen the way those thick hairs curled below to his manhood.

He was rugged. He was rough. He was unlike any man she had ever known. And how, she wondered angrily, had he known that she did, indeed, toss and turn in her bed at night?

It was thinking of her escape that made her toss and turn at night, she told herself furiously as she stole another glance in Rance's direction. Certainly she had not been longing for him!

Slowly, the idea took hold. The more she thought about it, the better it seemed. Rance would be even less suspicious of her if she could bring herself to do it. He would think she was mad about him, and would never leave him.

Why, it was even better than pretending to be afraid of snakes in the woods.

She hurried to finish making dinner, and then went into her room to bathe and change. She chose a green velvet gown that she had not worn since leaving home. The bodice dipped down to expose the pink ridges of her nipples. She took a deep breath to shove her breasts even higher, before struggling with the fastenings.

She stood before the mirror and brushed her hair up into a sweeping coiffure, leaving little ringlets to curl saucily about her face and ears. She had only a tiny bottle of perfume, which she had packed into her bags that long-ago night. Dabbing the fragrance behind her ears and between her abundantly exposed breasts, she decided she looked lovelier than she had since arriving at the ranch.

It was almost dark when he came in, the masculine smell of leather clinging to him. April was sitting before the fire, waiting, and he raised an eyebrow as his surprised gaze swept over her.

"Are you ready to eat now?" she asked softly.

He nodded, a strange expression on his face. "I'll go wash up," he mumbled.

When he returned, he was wearing clean clothes and smelled faintly of lilac water. His black hair was damp and smoothed back, but tendrils clung to his neck and about his ears.

He sat down opposite April, and they ate in silence. She hoped her nervousness did not show, and she had to force every bite past her lips.

When he had finished, he got to his feet and said pleasantly, "You're getting to be a good cook, April. Now if you'll excuse me, I've got to be up before dawn, and I'm tired. I think I'll call it a day."

The word rang out before she realized it. "Wait!"

He stared at her expectantly. When she said nothing more, he cocked his head to one side and asked, "Well, what is it, April?"

There was no light in the room except from the fire, bathing them in a golden hue.

"You didn't say anything . . ." she began hesitantly, shyly. Taking a deep breath, she rushed to finish, ". . . about my dress."

"You look lovely." He continued to stare at her, puzzled. "But you always look lovely, April, no matter what you are wearing."

When she did not speak again, he nodded and said, "I will try not to wake you when I leave. Good night."

She stared after him as he disappeared into his room and closed the door quietly behind him. Damn it, she thought, furiously twisting her skirt in her trembling hands, I *have* to do it.

With trembling legs, she stood and began to unfasten her dress, letting it fall to the floor at her feet. Stepping out of the garment, she removed her chemise and pantalets. Her body shone gold and bronze in the glow of the fire. She reached to remove the pins from her hair, letting it fall softly around her face and shoulders.

Quickly, before she could lose her nerve, she walked to his door. She did not knock. She turned the knob and let the door swing open. He sat up in bed, and she saw the stunned expression fade to one of pleasure and desire.

"My God!" he whispered hoarsely.

She moved slowly to the side of the bed. "You were right, Rance," she spoke tremulously.

"About what, April?"

"Once was not enough."

With a groan, he flung the covers from him with one hand, exposing his naked body, bathed golden from the fire's glow behind them. With almost savage strength, he reached out to pull her roughly down beside him. Her soft breasts squeezed against his chest, and his hands moved to cup her buttocks and pull her tighter still. She could feel his immediate hardness between her thighs as she lifted her face for his kiss.

His mouth was warm, hungry, fierce with passion. His tongue touched hers possessively, then he moved to devour her face, her neck, then swiftly lick upon her thrusting, heaving breasts.

April closed her eyes. Sweet delight seemed to consume her entire body. She opened her thighs to receive his probing hand, gasping out loud as the hot needles of pleasure soared through her loins. "Take me, Rance," she whispered raggedly, shamelessly.

"Oh, no, my lovely." His lips were moving downward. "Tonight you're going to become my woman for all time. I'm going to show you what it means to be a real woman in a man's arms."

She screamed out loud as she felt his probing tongue, there in that secret place. Her body jerked and writhed in spasms as he held her firmly, not letting her struggle away, paying no attention to her protests. She felt as though she were on fire. A great roaring began in her ears and then she was being swept higher, higher. Molten waves of pleasure flooded over her body, consuming her. Just as she felt she would surely die, he moved to thrust himself inside her. The explosion charged through her loins and up into her belly to move onward, upward, to the depths of her soul. Her nails dug mercilessly into the rock-hard flesh of his back as she fought to bring him closer, closer.

She could feel his hot, harsh breathing in her ear, the pounding of his wildly beating heart against her breasts. He moved furiously, hammering into her body relentlessly as she opened her legs wider to receive as much of him as possible. With a strangled cry, he gave one mighty push and released his passion inside her.

They clung together, naked flesh wet with the perspiration of their almost savage consummation.

He rolled away to lie on his back, pulling her close against him so that her head lay against his shoulder. Nuzzling her soft damp hair with his chin, he whispered teasingly, "After that, my sweet, even twice won't be enough."

She did not speak. A terrible sadness was wrenching her because she knew that twice would have to be enough. After this night, they would never again be together.

And she cursed herself for the silent tears that flowed down her cheeks as he lay sleeping beside her through the long, long night.

✿ Chapter Eleven ✿

SOMEWHERE in the woods an unknown animal screamed mournfully. April ran her fingertips up and down her arms as she sat in her bed, felt the goosebumps upon her flesh. She would not let herself be frightened, she told herself. There was nothing to be afraid of. After all, when she left the ranch, there would be only an hour or so of darkness. She knew the road, had made sure that Mulhern or Hinton took her in that direction during her daily rides. She felt she knew every curve and bend in that road, and she figured it was only a distance of about three miles to the main road that would take her south, into Sylacauga. From there, when it was daylight, she would be able to cut through the woods, out of sight.

She knew that one of the two men would be outside sleeping on the porch, following Rance's orders. She also knew that whichever one was on post, he would be sleeping soundly, probably snoring. With their boss away, they drank as much as they pleased. They usually fell into a drunken slumber and would not awaken till the morning sun hit them full in the face.

A week. It had been a week since Rance and his men left for Georgia with the herd of horses. How she had ached to leave during that week! But she had made herself wait in order to learn the route she would be taking in darkness.

The animal screamed again. A bobcat. There were plenty of them around, she had been told. She really had no reason to fear them, except at night. They were, Edward had explained, nocturnal animals, preying on small animals, chickens, and the like. But get one mad, he had warned her, or cornered, and the cat could be quite dangerous.

That last night with Rance still made her tremble and she knew she would always remember it. If he were another kind of man, and they had met under different circumstances, perhaps they might have shared a real love. But all they had was lust, plain and simple, and she would have to forget she had ever known Rance Taggart.

Her eyes grew heavy from want of sleep, but she did not dare give way to slumber. Moving slowly from the bed, she padded over to the window that opened onto the front porch. She pushed the curtain aside slightly. A quarter moon gave enough light that she could see a man's sleeping form on the porch floor. He turned his face just a bit. It was Mulhern. Good. He drank more than Hinton. He would be dead to the world.

How much longer till day? She dared to strike a match and allowed the flame to burn just long enough to see the clock on the wall. Five o'clock. Another half hour, and she would leave.

She returned to the bed and sat down, drawing her knees up beneath her chin. Rance was going to be livid when he returned to find her gone. But there would be nothing he could do about it.

Restless, she paced the room. Finally, she decided she could wait no longer. As long as she remained in that room, she was going to work herself into a nervous frenzy.

She knelt beside the bed, felt beneath for the bundle of clothing she had taken earlier from Rance's room. There was a pair of trousers—much too big, but perhaps there would be a rope in the stable for tying the waist. There was also a thick woolen shirt and an old coat. When she had dressed in Rance's clothes, she pushed her long mane of hair up into an old straw hat she had found in the barn and hidden away. She hoped she looked like a man. She stared down at her high-top pointed shoes. They would be awkward for riding. But there were no boots to be had.

Her own clothes would all have to be left behind, for it would be an unnecessary nuisance to try and lug her bags along.

It was time to leave. Slowly, ever so slowly, she turned the doorknob, holding her breath and praying there would be no sound. There was not. Gingerly, she steppped into the big room, then moved slowly, stealthily to the door that led out behind the house. Once outside, the moonlight filtered down through the pines, guiding her toward the stable. Halfway across the clearing, she turned and could barely make out the sleeping form of Mulhern. Good. He had not awakened. Hinton would be in the bunkhouse, and that was farther away still, not even in sight. There was slim chance that he would hear her.

She went to the rear of the stable, carefully opening the wide doors. Earlier, she had rubbed lard into the hinges. Inside, the smell of manure, hay, and animal sweat made her nose wrinkle. It was deathly dark, and she moved from memory. The mare was in the third stall on the left. The saddle was slung over the railing on the right, the harness right beside it. For an instant, she panicked as one of the horses whinnied, pawing the ground, and she whispered to it soothingly. They were used to her. Good. The hours she had spent here memorizing every part of the building had paid off. The horses were not frightened of her.

She reached the mare's stall, opened the gate, and slipped inside. Running her hand down her neck, she whispered to let the horse know who she was. Then she began to move faster. The saddle was heavy, awkward. She prayed she had the cinches adjusted right or she would spill to the ground when she tried to ride. The mare did not want to take the bit, and there was momentary struggling until it was in place.

She led the mare from the stable to the woods. Twigs snapped beneath the horse's heavy feet, and April stopped to stare through the night toward the house, silhouetted vaguely in the shadows. If Mulhern did awaken, perhaps he would think there was only a possum or racoon out here.

She moved deeper into the woods. The trees were thick and darkness was absolute. A panicky chill danced up and down her spine as she realized she was taking a chance on getting lost. No, she thought fiercely. She knew this path. She had to keep going and make that road. Thorns ripped at her trousers, but she jerked ahead. Nothing could stop her, nothing. She had been away from home too long. She had to go back—had to.

It has to be here somewhere, her mind churned anxiously. The rocky, red clay road, just below the bend and out of sight of the house—that was where she would leave the woods. Behind her, the mare snorted, and she jumped, startled, stood still for a moment before moving on.

A soft cry of joy escaped her lips as the moon pointed the way to the road ahead. She quickly mounted the mare, urging her forward, still keeping her to a walking gait.

Was she far enough away? Dear Lord, she prayed so. Nudging the mare with her heels, she took her into a trot. The clip-clopping sound was not too loud, she decided. It was all she could do to restrain herself, for she wanted to move, get as far away from this place as possible. Be calm, she told herself, be calm.

The scream erupted everywhere at once. She was caught in the middle of it, as though sucked into a maelstrom of sound. The horse reared up on her hind legs, front legs flailing the air. Something snapped beneath her—a cinch that had not been properly tightened. She dropped the reins and clutched the horse's mane, knotting her fingers in the silky hair as she fought to hang on, to keep from falling to the ground beneath those wildly thrashing hooves. Her grip began to slip as the mare twisted, heaved, side-dancing in frenzy. April's fingers were slipping, and then suddenly there was nothing to hold onto anymore, and she was falling to the ground. Instinct commanded her to roll quickly away from those deadly thrashing hooves. Rocks cut through her clothing, into her flesh, scraped the soft skin of her face. Scrubby undergrowth halted her spiraling movement. A moment later, she realized that the horse had turned and was running in panic back to the ranch.

She lay there struggling to breath against the churning choking pain that squeezed her chest. Her gaze turned upward, toward the shadowed trees above, and a silent scream parted her lips. Above, staring down at her like the eyes of satan, were the eyes of a bobcat.

The bobcat's scream ripped through the night once again.

It was as though an unseen hand had suddenly, silently, drawn back the great curtain of night. A pale grayish pink mist swept across the sky. April could see the snarling yellow-gold cat as he perched upon the limb perhaps only ten feet above where she lay. Every instinct told her to run, but something held her still. She dared not breathe. Slowly, she allowed her constricting lungs to drink of the sweet air.

The cat's mouth opened once more, displaying shining, ominous teeth. A thin rope of saliva connected pointed fangs. The growling from his throat was deep, gnarling. She watched in horror as he sprang easily, silently, to a limb even lower and closer. With small, stalking steps, his padded paws, claws protruding, moved along the limb until he reached a position directly above her face.

Was her life to end so abruptly and horribly? Was there to be no chance to return home to save her father? Was she to die here, like a wounded bird, as that vicious beast tore open her throat? She was helpless. One leap, and he would be on her. Silent prayers formed in her tortured brain, but she was unable to put words together.

She watched in astonishment as the lithe cat lowered himself to lie down on the branch. His eyes shone with hatred, and he licked his lips, as though enjoying her torment. She was his, and he could take her any time he pleased.

Moments passed. The cat continued to lick his face, but all the while he stared down at her with those glittering yellow teeth. The sky lightened. Now she could see every hair on his body.

Suddenly, in the distance behind her, the sound of thundering hooves filled the air. The cat heard it too and raised up once again, arching his back and howling another heart-stopping screech. He was poised, ready to leap, ears up and alert, his eyes steadily on his prey. Noise meant an intruder. Would it take away his treasure?

He sprang. April screamed at the same moment she rolled to her stomach and covered her head with her arms. Let it come quickly, she prayed.

And then the shot rang out.

The cat hit the ground just beside her with a dull, heavy thud. She raised her head. Those eyes were still on her, but they were no longer menacing. A clear glaze clouded them, and blood spurted from the opened mouth, staining the sharp fangs. With one great spasm, the cat lay dead.

"April, what in tarnation are you doin' out here?" She turned her head, her neck painful from lying so long in fear. Mulhern was coming toward her, a smoking rifle in his grasp. "Are you all right?"

He knelt down and helped her sit up. "That mare woke me up when she came running through the yard, and it's a damn good thing she did," he said anxiously, his eyes scanning her for some sign of injury. "I saw the harness, saw the saddle draggin', and I knowed somethin' was wrong. I grabbed my gun, and when I heard that cat screamin', I could tell from the sound he had somethin' trapped."

He stared at her reproachfully. "You was runnin' away, weren't you, April? You had it all planned! Look at you! You 'bout near got yourself killed. Well, I'll tell you one thing. I'm gonna do just what the boss said to do if you did try somethin' foolish. I'm gonna lock you in that house, and you ain't comin' out again till he gets back."

He turned to look at the dead cat. "Now that's a nice one," he said proudly. "Good shot, too. I ain't never got one from that far off. On horseback, too. The boss will be plenty proud of me when he hears about this."

He had turned his back on her. She had to act at once or lose her chance. Springing to her feet, she grabbed his rifle and brought the stock crashing down across his head. With an agonized grunt, he toppled forward onto the clay and lay motionless.

She did not wait to see if she had killed him. She could not allow it to matter. If Hinton had heard the shot, he would be right behind. She grabbed the mare's reins and swung herself up onto the smooth bare back. Evidently Mulhern had untied the remaining saddle cinch. No matter. She had never ridden bareback before, but by God, there was no time like the present to learn.

Kicking the horse's flanks hard, digging in her heels, she gripped the reins tightly. Leaning forward, pressing her body down for balance, she rode hard and fast. The sky was light. She could see everything clearly. Now it was all up to her.

When she reached the main road, some twenty minutes later, she immediately crossed over into the dense forest beyond and allowed the horse time to rest. By then she had decided that Hinton was not following. If Mulhern was alive, then Hinton would have to care for him.

April urged the mare back onto the road toward Sylacauga. She could be there easily by midmorning and, with luck, be halfway to Montgomery by late afternoon. A night's sleep somewhere, and she would be fresh tomorrow morning and ready to give Vanessa the surprise of her life.

Her stomach rumbled with hunger. She had no money with which to buy food. After all her careful planning, she cursed her stupidity for not thinking to bring along something to eat. Thoughts of the corn pones she had fried for herself and the men the night before made her feel even worse. There had been a whole basketful sitting on the table when she left. Even one would quell some of the twinges she was feeling.

Then it dawned on her that, if she had no money, she couldn't telegraph Uncle James. I'll find a way, she told herself.

The balding, potbellied man stared at April over the narrow wooden counter. "You gotta be kidding," he said around a mouthful of tobacco. "What you think I got going here? You think I give credit?"

April looked down at the floor, hot with embarrassment. "I'm sorry." She lifted her eyes to meet his once again. "But I must send a message, and I just don't have any money with me."

He shifted his wad of tobacco to the other side of his mouth, cocked his head to one side, and grinned. "Lady, I feel sorry for you, but I don't own this place. I just work here, and if I don't have the money to turn in for what telegraphs is sent, then I got to come up with it out of my own pocket. And I can't afford that."

If she could not get word to Uncle James, then she would have to deal with Vanessa and Zeke and Whit on

her own. Of course, she could go to the sheriff and tell him
her story. But what if the sheriff refused to get involved?
"After all," he might say, "Vanessa is your father's daughter and entitled to live in that house, too. I can't just throw
her out." Then he would brush her aside.

Her hands felt cold and clammy. She moved them to her
throat, slowly, and touched the tiny gold locket she had
worn for years and treasured so dearly because it had
belonged to her mother. Her father had told her it was
pure gold and quite valuable. But she had never thought of
the monetary value . . . until now. Quickly she unfastened
it and thrust it at the man. "Can you take this as a gesture
of faith in my promise to pay you? I *will* get the money to
you, but you can hold this until I do."

He extended a fleshy hand, and she laid the locket in his
open palm. As he turned it over, scrutinizing it carefully,
she rushed on, "It was my mother's. It means more to me
than I can say. Surely you can see that I would never give
it up for good. All I ask is a few days—a week at the
most."

"Oh, all right," he said in a bored voice as he stuffed the
locket in the pocket of his stained silken vest. He picked up
a piece of paper and a pen. "Give me the message and tell
me where you want it sent."

"James Jennings, Hattiesburg, Mississippi," she told
him, gripping the edge of the counter and leaning over to
watch him scrawl her words. "Just say, 'Please come at
once. Poppa sick. Many problems. I need you desperately.
Love, April.'"

Her voice broke slightly at the last, but the man looked
at her with the same bored expression, unmoved. "Is that
it?" She nodded. "Okay. I'll give you a week to get back
here with the money, or the locket is mine. Understand?"

"Yes, of course. You don't have to worry. I'll be back.
You can count on that."

The sinister chuckle stopped her as she hurried toward
the door. "I'll be worrying that you *do* show up, lady. This
locket is worth somethin'. I wouldn't mind keeping it."

"I'll be back," she said firmly.

Outside in the dusty street, April felt sick with hunger,
but since there was no means of buying food, she decided

she would be better off to hurry on her way. There were smells of bacon frying from a restaurant next door to the telegraph office, and the odor made her dizzy.

The mare had drunk her fill from the wooden trough, so she mounted and headed out of town. From time to time, she looked over her shoulder, still worried that she would see Hinton and Mulhern charging toward her. Each time she saw only an empty road behind, a wave of relief washed over her.

It was becoming apparent that she had miscalculated the time it would take to reach Montgomery. She had to allow the mare to walk leisurely because she did not know enough about horses to know how much exertion they could stand—particularly this chunky little mare. The mare was also going to need some hay or corn or something, she thought anxiously. And she herself must eat soon.

Rounding a curve, she saw what lay to the right and reined the mare in so sharply that she reared up. The sight had taken April by surprise—a church, people milling about, the smell of pigs roasting over open pits, frying chicken. It was a picnic, and the smells were too much to bear. She jerked the reins to the right and rode onto the church grounds. A few people glanced up at her curiously as she got off the horse and tied her to a tree.

She dusted off her trousers and stood there awkwardly, not knowing what to do next. She knew she looked a sight, and oh lord, she hated to beg. A kind-faced man came walking toward her. The preacher, she thought nervously.

"Bless you, brother, and welcome to Shady Grove Baptist church—" His voice trailed off and his eyes widened as she removed her hat. Her hair tumbled down about her face and shoulders. He smiled quickly. "Excuse me, sister."

"It's all right." She licked her lips nervously and began to twist her hat in her hands. "Look, parson, I've never begged before in my life, but I'm on my way home, and I haven't eaten since yesterday. I smelled your food—"

"Of course." His smile quickened to a broad grin. He offered his arm and she took it as graciously as though she were making a grand entrance. "You just come with me. The lambs in my flock are always ready to open their

hearts—and their picnic baskets—to a child of the Lord.
Just come with me."

The others were as friendly as their preacher, and while
she received a few curious stares, no one asked any questions. She was given a generous portion of roast pig, along
with baked sweet potatoes, corn on the cob, green peas,
and hot biscuits dripping with butter. While the crispy,
bubbly dish of apple pie was tempting, April declined.

"Then you'll take a basket with you," a woman smiled
kindly. "You might get hungry again before you reach
your destination."

Though she protested, the good people of Shady Grove
Baptist Church would not take no for an answer. They
even showed her a grazing place for her mare. She left
them carrying a bag of food that would see her through the
rest of her journey. "I don't know how to thank you all,"
she murmured, tears in her eyes.

"Just help another stranger along the way," the preacher
smiled and waved. "Pass along the good work of the Lord."

"And pray for our soldiers," the woman who had packed
the basket called to her. "Pray they defeat the Yankees and
save our homeland."

April promised she would and moved the mare on down
the road, feeling a gratitude she had never felt before.

At dusk, she found a deserted barn set back from the
road and shrouded with thick vines and weeds. The door
hung from rotted hinges, leaving the opening a black and
yawning mouth for the green monster that framed it.
Poking her head inside, she leaped back, startled at the
sound of something unseen scurrying in the dark. All of a
sudden the hard ground below her feet seemed a more
welcome bed than that black pit.

After a restless night, she continued on her way. She had
never been so tired. Every muscle ached from the long
hours of riding.

By midafternoon, familiar sights told her she was close
to home. She began to pace the weary horse slower, not
wanting to get too close to Pinehurst before dark.

At dusk, she reached the stream that ran through the
woods far behind her home. After unsaddling the horse
and making sure she was secured out of sight, April

crouched behind a tree to watch for signs of movement near the plantation.

The field hands had already finished the day's plowing. Wisps of smoke rose above the trees surrounding the slave cottages, telling her that the workers were inside, preparing their evening meal.

She waited until total darkness covered the land, then made her way slowly toward the house. It was her plan to find out as much as possible, then find a place to hide out until Uncle James arrived. Perhaps she could go to Alton's family. When they heard her story, they would take her in. She really ought to have gone there first, but curiosity about Pinehurst was eating away at her.

She came to the very edge of the woods. Nothing lay between her and the front of the house except the rolling green lawn. The house looked quiet. Deathly quiet. There was a light in her father's room, and in the study. The rest of the mansion was dark.

Taking a deep breath, she ran across the lawn, moving as fast as she could. When she reached the side of the house, she crouched down once more and waited. There were no sounds. One quick look, she promised herself, one quick look to make sure Poppa was all right, and she would leave and hurry to the Moseleys' farm. But she *had* to know about Poppa.

Slowly, stealthily, she made her way up the wide marble steps to the sweeping porch. Pressing her back against the white wood side, she inched along till she reached the parlor window. Slowly she turned to peer through the glass and felt an ominous chill when she saw Vanessa sitting behind their father's oak desk, looking at the papers spread before her.

Vanessa looked quite at home, and April was briefly surprised to see that she wore a rather formal gown of pale mauve, the sleeves and collar edged in delicate lace. Vanessa had never cared for ruffles and frills, preferring plain dresses if she were forced to wear dresses, but being happiest in breeches and shirts.

A bitter flash moved through April as she caught sight of Zeke Hartley sitting opposite her sister. His booted feet were propped on the edge of the desk, and he held a long cheroot between his teeth. His fingers tapped on the sides of a brandy glass. He, too, looked quite at home, she thought angrily.

Their conversation could not be heard, and April decided she had seen enough. What she wanted desperately to know now was how her father was. She turned and left the porch, slipping around to the rear door, praying all the while that she would not run into anyone. All she wanted was a quick peek in her father's room and then she would be on her way to the Moseleys.

She tiptoed up the dark back stairs, making her way from memory. She reached the second floor and wrinkled her nose at the musty odor. How many of the servants had run away? Probably many, for Vanessa was often cruel to the Negroes.

A thin shaft of light shone through the crack between her father's door and the floor. She placed her trembling hand on the knob and turned it ever so slowly. Then she opened the door just far enough to see inside. Her father lay in his bed, eyes closed. She watched the rise and fall of his chest. He appeared to be all right.

Then she scanned his face. Even in sleep, much misery and heartache were etched there. She blinked back the furious tears.

She realized she was gripping the glass knob so hard that her fingers were hurting, and she relaxed her hold. She had to have help. *Had* to. That shadow of a man lying before her did not deserve his treatment, no matter what his sins.

"Hello, April."

Her spine stiffened. Very slowly, she turned around. A lantern was suddenly lit, flooding the hall with a sickly yellow light.

Vanessa was smiling evilly, blue eyes glittering in the glow of the lantern Zeke Hartley was holding. He was not smiling.

"Welcome home, sister dear," Vanessa said softly.

April looked about wildly. Was there a chance to run? Any chance at all? She would not give in without a fight.

Zeke handed the lantern to Vanessa and took a step forward as he whispered between clenched teeth, "We've got some things to talk about, girl."

In that moment, April realized that she had never awakened from the nightmare her life had become.

❦ Chapter Twelve ❧

APRIL was furious. Zeke had twisted her arm painfully behind her back, squeezing hard and lifting
her up till she was forced to walk along on her tiptoes,
down the stairs and into the study. Vanessa leaned against
their father's desk to watch while Zeke shoved April into a
chair, then handed her a glass of brandy. It was taking
every ounce of self-control to keep from throwing it at
Vanessa's smugly smiling face.

"Well, this is quite a surprise." Vanessa folded her arms
across her bosom. "When Whit told us he had spotted you
prowling about, I decided to just sit back and wait and see
what you were up to." She cast an accusing glare in Zeke's
direction. "I think someone is going to have some explaining to do about how you came to be here. I never thought
you would be able to escape the monastery."

April explained in a furious, staccato voice. "Didn't
Zeke tell you that, instead of taking me to the monastery,
he used me as the wager on a horse race with Rance
Taggart and then lost? I've been at Cheaha mountain,
Vanessa, held prisoner by that savage, Rance."

Vanessa raised an eyebrow. "Oh, really? Well, then, I'm
sure you can't be *too* disappointed that you never got to
the monks. Knowing Rance—and I do—I'll bet you found
him much more entertaining. Much more, shall we say,
gratifying?"

"I don't want to talk about it." April started to get up

but Zeke roughly pushed her back down. "Don't you touch me, you bastard," she hissed through clenched teeth.

Vanessa moved to sit behind the desk. "Now, now, let's not get emotional, April. As you can see, I'm quite in charge here, and I'm not about to have you around to mess up things."

"I'm not leaving."

Vanessa and Zeke exchanged looks and simultaneously broke into hearty laughter while April watched in seething silence. "You have no choice," Vanessa told her when she had stopped laughing, adding, "You didn't see Poppa awake. Too bad. You would have seen how completely docile and helpless he is. He never gets out of bed these days unless Buford picks him up and sits him in a chair. He even has to be spoon fed."

"Did he have another stroke?" April leaned forward anxiously, gripping the arms of the chair as Zeke kept a watchful eye. "What have you done to him, Vanessa?"

She shrugged. "Naturally he demanded to know what *I* was doing back here, so I told him how he'd raped you and you'd run away, filled with hatred and shame. He started screaming and yelling and then fainted. He's been like he is now ever since. Yes, I guess you could say he had another stroke or whatever."

"You heartless bitch!" April moved so quickly to sling the brandy that Zeke was unable to stop her. Vanessa shrieked as the liquid hit her full in the face at the same time Zeke backhanded April and sent her reeling to the floor. He reached down to grab her and yank her back up into the chair. April cried, "You're going to pay for this. Both of you. How could you do it?"

"Shut up!" Vanessa's eyes glittered as she clenched the edge of the desk with quickly whitening fingertips. "Pinehurst is mine now. The war may hold things up a bit, but it's going to be the finest plantation again one day. Until then, I'm holding onto it."

"Look around you, Vanessa. It's falling down. How can you keep it from falling to ruins? Why don't you just get out and let me care for Poppa? He can't live much longer in his condition. Why do you want to keep twisting the knife and torturing him?"

"He didn't mind torturing me all those years he blamed

me for Mother's death. The old fool!" She spat the words. "Do you honestly think I don't want revenge on the both of you? I have it now, dear sister, and no one questions me. When the good neighbors heard what Poppa did to you, they praised me for returning to care for him—him being completely insane, of course. They think I'm marvelous to be so forgiving after the way he drove me away.

"And we're not completely in ruins," she continued excitedly, confidently. "The hands are making the fields ready for spring planting. There will be a good crop of cotton this year, and even if there isn't, there's money to tide us over, because I sold those valuable horses of Poppa's for top prices."

She leaned forward to stare right into her face. "So don't get your hopes up, dear sister. I'm going to survive. The sooner Poppa dies, the better. He's only in the way . . . like you. But I'm going to take care of *you* quickly enough."

April knew that her only hope was Uncle James, but it would be several days before he arrived. "When do you plan to have me sent to the monastery?" she asked quietly, trying not to sound as desperate as she felt. Time was her only weapon. "I'm very tired. I'd like to rest."

Vanessa nodded, then took a few steps to the long braided bellcord which hung by the door and gave it a quick yank. "I'm not totally heartless, April. I'll see that you're fed before you're taken away, and—"

Posie appeared in the doorway. When she saw April, her eyes widened and she screamed and ran for her with outstretched arms. Zeke was quick to step between them and stop the embrace, and his elbow caught the old Negro painfully in her bosom. She staggered backward, clutching herself and moaning as April threw herself at Zeke, clawing, scratching, screaming her rage.

"I've had about enough of you," he muttered, slapping her once, twice, then doubling up his fist and drawing back his arm just as Vanessa told him to stop. "Leave her be, Zeke. I'm getting a bit tired of all this drama." To Posie she said, "Get hold of yourself. This isn't a family reunion. Get out to the kitchen and get April something to eat. And be quick about it."

With a muffled sob, Posie ran from the room.

April covered her stinging face with her hands, glaring

at the two of them. "You're both going to pay for this. Somehow, someday, I'm going to get you both—"

Again they shared laughter.

"Let me break her," Zeke snickered. "Just give her to me for the night. I guarantee that by tomorrow morning she'll be cowering as a whipped dog—"

"Aren't you forgetting something, Zeke?" Vanessa whipped her head about to stare at him with rising fury. "You sleep with *me*. Not my sister. You lay one hand on her *that way*, and I'll cut your throat."

Zeke's face paled. He fully believed her. "Baby, I meant I'd beat the hell out of her. You know I didn't mean nothing else." He laughed nervously. "Hell, I sure ain't never looked at another woman as long as we been a-doin' it."

April looked away in disgust. To think Vanessa could actually sleep with that filthy creature—it made her sick to her stomach. Vanessa sensed what she was feeling. "Don't you go acting high and mighty and sitting in judgment of me. If Rance Taggart won you in a horse race, and considered you his property, then you haven't come home a virgin after all this time . . . if you even were one before you left." She looked to Zeke, who obligingly joined her in a snicker.

Time. April kept reminding herself that she had to stall for time until Uncle James arrived. "Will you allow me to rest for a few days? I don't feel well. It was a terrible journey." She pressed her fingertips to her forehead, feigning sickness.

"I want you out of here as soon as possible, before anyone sees you. Zeke, take her upstairs and lock her in her room. I want you to stand guard outside all night, and I want Whit to post himself below should she get any ideas about climbing from her portico."

Zeke advanced toward her, but April threw up her hands to fend him off. "You can't send me off with this . . . this monster again. Do you know he tried to rape me before? Whit stopped him. . . ."

"Aw, she's lyin'," Zeke whined, looking to Vanessa for understanding. "She knows you an' me are romancin', and she wants to make trouble. Don't believe her. She's too prissy. Who'd want a cold fish like her, anyhow?"

"You would," Vanessa said coolly. "You'd hop on any woman, Zeke, and you and I both know that."

She looked at April once again. "I'll decide what's to be done with you by tomorrow morning, but you can rest assured that this time you *won't* be coming back. Get her out of here, Zeke."

April struggled in vain as he once more twisted her arm up behind her back. He pushed her along up the stairs, and when they were halfway up, Vanessa called out softly, "Don't get any notions about making noises to wake Poppa, April. He can't help you, and you'd only upset him."

Once inside April's room, Zeke slung her across the bed. "I'm gonna tell you somethin', bitch!" he whispered raggedly, pointing an unwavering finger as he towered above her. "I'm gonna have some of you, and this time ain't nobody gonna be around to stop me. I'm gonna have you till I get my fill, and you're gonna pay for acting like you was too good for me."

"You filthy bastard!" April gave her long hair an insolent toss. "If my sister finds you desirable, then she has a taste for horse manure."

His face contorted with fury and he raised his arm to strike her. She shrank away, but then he lowered his hand, smiling with the satisfaction of a man with the upper hand. "Naw, I ain't gonna bruise you. Might make your sister mad. There'll be time for taming you later, you little spitfire. That's one bet I *will* win."

He turned, then paused at the door. "Remember. I'll be right outside all night long. Don't get no ideas."

April let her breath out, relieved that he was gone. With the door closed, the room was plunged into darkness. She fumbled about on the bedside table till she found the sulfur matches, then struck one to light the oil lamp. Glancing about in the mellow glow, she saw that not much had been changed about her room. The perfume bottles were absent from the dresser, but she was not surprised. Vanessa had always resented Poppa importing expensive French perfume for her. She had tried to share, but Vanessa would smash the bottles, so she had finally given up.

She got up and walked over to the chiffonier and opened the drawers. Some of her nicest nightgowns were missing, along with delicate lace chemises. An inspection of her wardrobe closet disclosed that several expensive gowns had also been removed. She didn't bother to look in her jewelry chest, for Vanessa would surely have taken any valuable pieces. This brought to mind the treasured locket left with the cipher clerk in Sylacauga. Now it was his, she thought sadly.

A key clicked in the lock, and she looked up, expecting to see Zeke. Instead, a quick flash of anger made her stiffen as Mandy walked in, head bowed, a tray clattering in her trembling hands. "What are *you* doing here?" she snapped bitterly. "You're about the last person I want to see."

"Yes'm," Mandy murmured, setting the tray down on the bed. "I reckon you hates me, and I reckon I don't blames you. I didn't want to come up here, but Miz Vanessa, she sent fo' Posie."

"Well, just get out!" April struggled to keep her voice down, for she wanted to scream at the little black girl. "I don't want to see your face ever again."

"Yes'm. I'm sorry." Mandy turned and shuffled toward the door, shoulders stooped. "I'm real sorry, Miz April. Don't blame you fo' hatin' me one bit. Not one bit a'tall."

"Wait," April called. "Don't go. Come over here."

She sat down on the bed and removed the linen cloth from the tray, looking hungrily at the plate of cold fried chicken and sweet potatoes. Posie had also sent a cup of steaming herb tea and a dish of fig cobbler. She nibbled on a piece of chicken, keeping her eyes on Mandy, who stood before her fidgeting and twisting her white apron in nervous hands.

"I didn't know," the girl whispered miserably, tears trickling from her eyes. "I just didn't know. Miz Vanessa, she made me think she only wanted to help yo' daddy, and she made me feel sorry fo' her, gettin' beat and run off like she did. But it just didn't work out like she said it would."

"What has it been like, Mandy?"

She hiccupped, then said, "She's mean to ever'body. You remember Lolly? She beat her so bad she lost her baby, and then she run away and drowned in the river. Some o' my people say she kilt herself."

Mandy covered her face with her hands and began to

sob loudly. April quickly told her to quiet down or Zeke would make her leave. "I's so sorry. . . ." she hiccupped over and over. "Oh, if only I could undo what I did—"

April felt a flash of hope. "Would you help me escape?" The aspiration left her as quickly as it had come when she saw Mandy's reaction upon her face.

She shook her head. "They watchin' you close. If I was to try and help you, they'd kill me. Anything but that, Miz April. Please don't ask that o' me."

"Well, then," she sighed, "could you at least tell me how Alton reacted to the message he thought came from me?"

Mandy stared at her feet. "I couldn't read it, Miz April. I gave it to him and left. Ain't heard nothing, either. Miz Vanessa don't allow none o' us to leave the plantation, and she don't let us talk to nobody what comes here. Not that anybody evah comes. We just does our work and tries to stay out of her way." She made a clucking sound and murmured, "She one mean woman, she is."

April pressed her weary brain. She dared not confide in Mandy that she was expecting Uncle James.

"Mandy, I don't hold any hope of escaping this time," she finally said, "but if anyone *ever does* come looking for me, anyone at all, would you at least try to find out where I am and tell them? Could you try to do just that much for me?"

"Yes'm, I'd try." Her curly head bobbed up and down. "I sho' would find a way to do that. I promise."

April continued to eat while Mandy spoke in whispers, telling her what little she knew. Then the door opened suddenly and Zeke stepped into the room to snap, "Okay, get that tray and get out of here, nigger. You ain't supposed to be in here gossipin'."

Mandy looked terrified. "Yassuh, yassuh," she said quickly, looking at April's tray in hopes she had finished. April handed it to her, and she turned to scurry out, not looking at Zeke.

When they were alone, Zeke stared at her with hooded eyes, as though he could see her naked beneath her dress. She faced him arrogantly, silently. Finally, he twisted his lips in a smirking grin and whispered, "How did you get away from Taggart? I'd really like to know."

She did not reply.

He took a step closer. "Tell me. Was he any good? I mean, did he make it good for you? Did you bounce all over the bed and cry and carry on 'cause it felt so damn good? Or did he just jump on top of you and grunt off his pleasure and not give a shit if you was pleasured."

"You are disgusting!" She spat the words.

"He couldn't have found you too good," he sneered. "Or he never would've let you get away. I imagine it'd take a lot of fuckin' to teach you how to really please a man. Maybe Taggart didn't know how. Maybe he knows how to ride a horse but don't know a damn thing about ridin' a woman. Maybe—"

She interrupted to cry, "Maybe you just have a filthy mind and a mouth to go with it. Maybe if I scream loud enough Vanessa will come in here and shut you up! I doubt that she wants her lover talking this way to her sister—"

"Shut up!" he snarled, lowering his voice and looking over his shoulder nervously as though he expected Vanessa to be standing in the doorway. Then he turned to stare down at April once more, lips curled back in an angry grimace. "I just wish I'd taken the time to lay you proper before I turned you over to Taggart. But I'll have my turn. You wait and see!"

He left her, and she felt only relief when the door closed, and she heard the sound of a key in the lock. She found one of her own gowns and changed, then extinguished the lantern and crawled beneath the down comforter.

Without Uncle James, without someone to help, she was useless to her father. So far she had only succeeded in getting herself into trouble.

Perhaps, she thought sleepily, she would have been better off staying with one whose kisses tasted of warm, sweet wine. . . .

❧ Chapter Thirteen ❧

THE bright sunlight struck her face abruptly. April sat up quickly, struggling to awaken, and saw Vanessa standing near open drapes, a gloating smile on her face.

"My goodness, sister dear," Vanessa said. "You can't sleep all day. There is much to be done. But tell me, did you rest well?"

"I wish you would just stop playing with me, Vanessa," April swung her legs around to the side of the bed, her feet touching the soft India rug. She reached for the robe she had left on the chair. "Tell me what you plan to do with me, and be done with it."

Vanessa looked at her through squinted lids. "*You* do not tell *me* what to do, April. The days of your being queen of this household are gone forever. I am in control. Remember that."

April saw that Vanessa was dressed quite elegantly in a powder blue dress of spun taffeta. The bodice was edged in lace, and the skirt was covered in tiny white velvet bows. Her hair was twisted back in braids that wound upward to form a twisting crown. Vanessa smiled. "Don't you think I look nice? I really hate these ruffles and frills, you know, but the mistress of Pinehurst must look the part. Now then. Suppose you get yourself bathed and dressed. Mandy is going to fix you a nice, hot tub. Then I want you to pack all your belongings, what I've left you, that is," she added, smirking.

"Posie is preparing some nice gruel and sausages for you," she continued. "Once you have packed and eaten, you will be on your way."

"I don't feel well," April said quickly, panicking. She couldn't leave yet. Not today. Not for several days. She had to be there when Uncle James arrived. She rushed on to explain that the trip, the hardships she had endured even before leaving the ranch, had all combined to make her ill. "Surely, it isn't imperative that I leave right away, today—" she said pleadingly.

"I don't want anyone to know you are here. So far, you haven't been seen. The servants know better than to gossip, but I want to get you out of here as quickly as possible, and this time, Zeke won't fail me. He has learned"—she smiled as though thinking of some wicked secret—"that it does not pay to go against me. I expressed my disappointment earlier this morning."

Miserably, she faced Vanessa and whispered brokenly, "My God, why do you hate me so? I've told you over and over how I pleaded with Poppa not to mistreat you. Why do you want to hurt me?"

"I just want you out of the way. You've been a thorn in my side all my life." She laughed softly. "Funny, isn't it? I mean, when you think about it, it could have been the other way around. Suppose *I* had been the one to leave Mother's womb first? *You* would have been the one Poppa blamed for her death, and I would have been his darling – princess."

April shook her head in defeat. "At least tell me what is to become of me. I have the right to know that much."

"You have *no* rights, but I will satisfy your curiosity by telling you that you are going to be taken somewhere far away. All the way to New Orleans."

"New Orleans?" She was bewildered.

"Zeke knows of a madam there who runs a house of pleasure with such iron control that there will be absolutely no chance of your escaping. Should you even try, she will have you taken to the Bayou, tied to a tree, and left for alligator bait," she continued with glittering eyes. "She makes every one of her girls witness what happens to anyone who tries to leave without her permission. If you behave yourself, you should get along nicely. It will be up to you, dear sister."

Sheer terror rippled up and down April's spine as she cried, "Send me to the monastery. Don't do this to me, Vanessa."

"I must. You see, I thought you were such a spineless ninny that you didn't have it in you to escape. But Zeke tells me that if you escaped Rance Taggart, then you must be quite cunning. I agree. I cannot afford to risk having you come back. I'm fortunate no one saw you, so there won't be any questions. Everyone thinks you ran away, shamed and brokenhearted because your own father raped you. That's the way I want it.

"Now get up and get dressed," she snapped, weary of the conversation. "I want you out of here as soon as possible. And let me warn you against putting up a fuss. Either you do as I say, or I'll send Zeke in here to dress you. He would enjoy that, but I don't think you would."

She was almost through the door when April asked, "Is Whit Brandon going to take me to New Orleans?"

Vanessa shook her head. "No. Whit may be a good hand in some ways, but he has some traits I find annoying. He doesn't mind killing or stealing, but he refuses to mistreat women. When he heard about Zeke wagering you in that stupid horse race, he was almost as angry as I was. He would never take you to a whorehouse."

"But what about Zeke?" April asked desperately. "He threatened me last night. He wants me. Do you honestly think he will take me all the way to New Orleans without having me? Does he mean so little to you that you would share him with me?"

Vanessa's face contorted with rage. "Zeke learned this morning what happens when he displeases me. I've already told you that. You have nothing to fear from him now."

April stood, eyes imploring wildly. "He isn't afraid of you, Vanessa. He never was and he never will be. The man is a savage!"

"Get dressed!" she screamed, taking a menacing step forward. "You have five minutes, and then I'm sending in Zeke. Don't push your luck with me, April."

She walked out and slammed the door. The key clicked once more.

With shaking hands, April began gathering the few clothes left to her, but when Mandy came in with the hot water, she all but threw herself at her. "You've got to help me. You're my only hope."

She told her of Vanessa's plans, and with each word, Mandy looked even more frightened. Her body began to shake, and the water she carried sloshed against the pail. "All I'm asking of you," April rushed on, "is that you tell anyone who comes looking for me where I have gone. Can you do that much?"

"I . . . I don't know, Miz April." Mandy would not meet her gaze, and she twisted from her grasp and set the pail on the floor. She tried to turn away, but April grabbed her once again.

"Mandy, you can do it. You can whisper through a door if you have to, not let anyone know it's you doing the talking. Just tell them I've been taken to a whorehouse in New Orleans. Dear God, girl, you've caused me enough hell. Can't you do something to cleanse your soul?"

"It ain't . . ."—Mandy swallowed hard and rubbed at her large, flat nose with the back of her hand—". . . like you thinks. I can't say no mo', Miz April. I heard somethin', and I . . . I just can't say no mo'. Now I's gettin' outta here, 'cause you gonna get me killed."

She ran from the room before April could make a move to stop her, and she had no sooner disappeared from sight when Zeke walked in. April gasped at the sight of the crude, blood-soaked bandage covering one side of his face.

"This is your sister's idea of teaching me a lesson," he said in a voice so ominous that her heart wrenched. "The bitch cut me with a knife. She says if I lay one hand on you, she'll cut off my cock."

April was too shocked to speak and continued to stare in horror at the bloody bandage. To think her own sister had cut the man! She shook herself, for a loud ringing had begun in her ears. Was Vanessa insane?

Zeke's effort to grin threateningly became a grimace of pain as he jerked a thumb toward his wounded face and said, "The only thing this means is that your sister don't find out nothing from now on. Now you hurry up and get ready, 'cause me and you is goin' on a little trip."

After Zeke stalked from the room, she dressed and

searched for some answer, but she couldn't think of anything. Finally, she went to the door and called to Zeke,
knowing he would be right outside. He bulled his way in,
shoving her aside roughly as he maneuvered her tapestry
bags through the door.

April saw a chance to speak to her father as she realized
that Zeke had his hands full. She turned and ran down the
hall, with him yelling and cursing after her. She heard him
drop the bags to come after her, but by then she had
reached the door to her father's room. She flung the door
open, bosom heaving with the tension that was winding
through her.

"Poppa! Poppa!" she screamed hysterically as she felt
Zeke's arms wrapping about her. She struggled against
him, fleetingly remembering his wound and moving to
strike her fist to his face. With a cry of pain, he released
her. She rushed to the bedside, clutching her father.

"Poppa, it's me, April. Don't you know me? Oh,
Poppa—" Dry sobs escaped her throat as she shook him.

Slowly he turned confused eyes on her. She looked into
their depths, saw the silent, inward struggle to return to the
living. He was emaciated. His face was gray and skeletal,
the flesh clinging to the bones. There were black hollows
beneath his eyes, and his too-long hair was dirty and greasy
as it fanned out on the pillow.

"Poppa, please listen to me—" she begged.

"You little fool!" Vanessa's irate voice sliced across the
room. "Zeke, get her out of here."

"Hell, she hit me in the face. It's bleedin' again," he
whined. "You shouldn't have cut me, Vanessa—"

"I'll do worse than that if you don't get her out of here.
You can hear her screaming all over the house. Do something, damn you!"

April was still clutching her father, shaking him, as Zeke
grabbed her and dragged her away. Suddenly she realized
that her father's lips were moving. He was trying to speak
her name. She knew he was. And if Zeke had not been
yelling she knew she would have heard him. He knew her!
He wasn't completely lost! He just needed help.

Zeke threw her over his shoulder and started out of the
room. April beat his back with her fists and her legs kicked

wildly. "Vanessa, he knows me!" she cried. "He does. He *isn't* hopeless. He needs help!"

As Zeke carried her down the hall toward the stairway, she could see Vanessa standing in the doorway of her father's room, gloating. Had it been dark, April knew those evil, glittering eyes would have shone through the blackness. Dear Lord in heaven, she was powerless to do anything to save her poor father from that she-devil. She had known her sister was bitter, but was she actually insane? She had asked herself this question twice in the last hour.

"I ain't carrying you outta here screamin' like a banshee," Zeke yelled. He took her back to her room and threw her on her bed, then began ripping a sheet apart. Her struggles were in vain as he bound her wrists and ankles, then stifled her cries with a gag. Yanking the coverlet from the bed, he wrapped her in it, then hoisted her over his shoulder once more. She heard him talking to Vanessa as he walked with her. Vanessa snapped icily, "You get back here as quick as you can, Zeke. There's work to be done. And you see that she gets to New Orleans. I don't ever want to see her face back here again."

"What if she runs away?" he growled.

"You got a gun, haven't you? I'd rather see her dead than back here, Zeke. Don't you forget it."

April felt herself being placed in the back of a wagon. She knew Posie and Mandy were watching, because she heard Vanessa yelling at them. "And send Buford up to the old man," she ordered. "He's crying and carrying on, and I want him calmed down."

Oh, Poppa, April thought. *What will happen to you? If only I could help.*

It seemed hours before the wagon finally lumbered to a stop. She heard footsteps coming toward her, and then the coverlet was yanked away. She blinked her eyes at the sudden brightness of day and looked into the ugly face of Zeke Hartley.

"Welcome home, April," he displayed his yellow, chipped teeth in a menacing grin.

She looked around. The terrain was familiar. Then, slowly, it came to her. They were perhaps five miles from the house, at the farthest southern point of Jennings property. It was low here, and marshy, and had never been cultivated for crops. This was actually a small valley, shielded by high hills.

Zeke was not going to bother with taking her to New Orleans. He was going to kill her and leave her body for the buzzards to pick.

He climbed up in the wagon beside her and began to jerk the strips of torn sheeting from her feet and ankles, then removed her gag. He motioned for her to get out of the wagon. Stiff, sore, paralyzed with fear, she could only look at him in silence.

"Come on, April. Don't make me get rough. I want to show you your new home." He got out of the wagon and stood waiting.

She made herself move. If I must die, she thought with a sudden calm, then I won't beg this bastard for mercy. I will face death and pray that my father soon faces his so he, too, will be out of his misery.

Zeke wrapped a beefy hand about her arm and started walking. He led her toward a crude shack that looked as though it had either been hastily put together or had stood so long it was falling apart. Nestled among trees, it was hidden from view by a large red clay hill. There were no windows. The shack was about twelve feet square.

"I built this," Zeke said proudly, kicking the door open. Sunlight spilled through to show the only furnishings, a crudely constructed bed with sagging mattress, a table, and two chairs. "It's where I come when I want to get away from that bitch sister of yours. I can bring my women friends from town here, too. She don't know it exists. I ain't even told Whit."

He gave her a rough shove. "Now get in there. This is your new home."

April looked around, then back at Zeke's grinning face. "I'm going to bring your things in from the wagon, and then I gotta go into town and get some supplies. You'll be needin' food every once in a while, I guess."

He laughed with real pleasure as she stared at him with increasing understanding. *Here? She was to stay here?*

"But . . . what about New Orleans?" she cried, her voice trembling.

"Vanessa'll never know the difference. She'll think you're there. But I'll have you where I can get you. This is where you'll be stayin'," he chortled, gleeful over his newfound prize and his own cleverness.

Without another word, he reached under the bed and came up with a six-foot length of chain. She turned to run, but he caught her at the door and held her tightly, wrapping one end of the chain around her ankle and fastening it with a steel clip. The other end was double-bolted to the wall. He walked from the shack and quickly returned with her bags. Giving her chain a significant tug, he winked hideously at her and said, "I'll be back in a few hours, and then me and you will start gettin' along real cozy-like."

After he was gone, she stood staring out the door, not moving and barely breathing.

❧ Chapter Fourteen ❧

WITH each plodding beat of Virtus's hooves, Rance felt a synchronizing pain stabbing through his temples. They should have started back the day before, as planned, instead of sitting around drinking with Stuart's men, but one thing had led to another, and while he did not often get drunk, he had really tied one on this time. Now he was paying for it.

Several yards behind, Edward Clark was slumped in the saddle, chin drooping to his chest. He had given his horse the reins as he dozed.

Rance had not intended to go all the way up to Franklin, Tennessee. But when General J. E. B. "Jeb" Stuart, himself, had sent for him, he had wasted no time getting there. Rance had a hell of a lot of respect for Stuart, the best horseman in the Confederate cavalry, some said, and already a legend. He was busting proud that Stuart had heard of his horses. He had sat opposite Stuart before a roaring campfire up on that big mountain in Franklin and reveled in the knowledge that the general shared his ideas about the importance of horses to the Confederacy.

Rance intended to supply them, even if he had to steal from the Yankees. General Stuart had slapped his knee and laughed and said if Rance ever got tired of horse trading, he would be proud, by God, to have a man with his grit ride with him.

Rance smiled. He liked the man.

Stuart and his men were headed for Virginia now, and Rance had promised to round up horses and try to keep a good supply available. He had discussed with Edward a plan to send out scouts regularly to locate horses for either buying or stealing.

Now, Rance had a need to get back home. He hadn't meant to be gone so long. He had done a lot of thinking about that last night with April, wondering why she had suddenly warmed to him.

He did not consider himself arrogant to suppose that she would eventually come around. It had been good between them, so why should she remain aloof?

Thoughts of April brought back memories of another woman, the gentle, doe-eyed, dark-haired Juanita, and Rance tried to shield himself from those memories, which were both tender and raw. Juanita. Good Lord, had it really been three years?

He had never been able to truthfully admit that he loved the beautiful Mexican girl, but who could say that he had not? He only knew that now she was gone from him forever, and he would never know what might have been.

They met when he went to Mexico to buy horses for a man he had been working for in Kentucky. They had shared hot, sweet passion unlike any he had ever known. When it was time for him to leave, she had begged him to take her along. He refused, preferring his freedom, while promising to return to her one day.

But that day did not come until a year later, and when he did return to the squalid little village on the border, Juanita's mother had tearfully told him that her daughter had died in childbirth. Was it his child? Who could say? The baby, a boy, had also died.

He swam in Tequila for a month, finally fighting his way back from hell by telling himself that fate was responsible. Fate, not him. And he sure as hell couldn't spend the rest of his life hating himself for something he could not help now.

But on a lonely night, with the wind in the pines and the sound of a bobcat calling lustily to his mate, he thought of those doe eyes and knew that he had loved her in his way. And if he had not left her, she might still be alive. He lived with that, every day.

Rance shook his head to clear it. The past was just that—past. No need to torture himself. Juanita was dead. His son, if it was his son, was also dead. There had been women before and after. And now, there was April.

April Jennings was a beautiful woman. Long, silky hair the color of gold. Eyes as blue as the sky beyond a rainbow. Her body was sculptured to perfection—large, firm breasts like honeydew melons with nipples as succulent and sweet as wild mountain berries.

He reflected, briefly, on her twin. Damn, but Vanessa was a cunning bitch. He had sent a scout to check out April's story. It was all true. Vanessa was running things, and the old man was said to be tetched. The fool he had beat in the horse race was still around, along with his partner, another low-life.

Rance figured he was doing April a favor by keeping her. She was better off away from Pinehurst. There was no telling what a she-devil like Vanessa might do if April got in her way.

And he planned to make April like staying with him. It was going to be good for both of them. He had been sure of it since their last night together.

He looked about him at the rolling hills. Along the road, beside the thick growth of firs, he could see honeysuckle blooming, and plums and blackberries. Beyond, in the distance, balsam forests trailed upward to mountains that tried to kiss the sky. He loved the Alabama land. He once heard an old man say that the state was so pretty God must have spent a few extra hours on creation day to make Alabama extra beautiful.

Rounding a bend, they crossed a rickety plank bridge built over a rolling, silver stream. They were in a valley, and Rance drank in the sweetness of the cool air here. Tranquil. Peaceful. It was hard to imagine a war near here.

Suddenly, he sat upright in the saddle. Something was wrong. Virtus also noticed, his ears twitching slightly as he lifted his nose to the wind.

He spoke Edward's name, and the man behind him was instantly alert. The two had not traveled the wilderness without learning to sense danger.

Edward knew better than to make a sound. His hand, like Rance's, moved slowly to his sidearm.

Their eyes darted from right to left and above to the low-hanging branches. Rance saw it before Edward did—the flash of sun against metal. With a movement so quick it was invisible, he drew his gun and fired, and not a second too soon: The shot fired by the man waiting in ambush went wild . . . the shot meant for Rance.

The man pitched forward, head slamming into the dirt as blood gushed from the hole in his neck. Rance and Edward slipped quickly from their horses, diving for cover.

"What in hell is going on?" Edward whispered as they crouched together in the bushes, tensely waiting. "We aren't in Yankee territory, for God's sake. This is Alabama. We're almost home."

Rance signaled for him to be quiet. He had heard a faint sound, like someone crying. He called out, "Throw down your guns and come out with your hands up, or we're going to start shooting."

"No, don't shoot!" the female voice screamed in terror. "I don't have a gun. Please, don't kill me."

Rance and Edward watched as a woman stepped out into the road, holding her trembling arms above her head. She was young, slender, and underneath the mud and grime that streaked her face, she was quite lovely. Her hair was the color of coal, and even from where they crouched they could see smoldering brown eyes, now wide with fright.

"There's no one else here," she called. "I promise. You must believe me."

Rance straightened, fingers still tight on the gun. He whispered to Edward to stay down and cover him until he could be sure the girl was telling the truth. Then he stepped out into the road, slowly, his gun drawn but not aimed. The woman dared to hope he wouldn't shoot.

"Start talking," Rance said quietly.

She took a gasping breath and pointed to the dead man. "He made me come with him. I didn't want to. My daddy said he was a traitor and ought to be killed."

"Who is he?"

"Leroy. Leroy Pearson. We're from Selma. He wanted

your horses." She lifted the skirt of her tattered yellow
dress and showed him her bare, bloody feet. "We've been
walking. Leroy made sure we stayed in the bushes, off the
roads. He was afraid my daddy would come after us, but I
told him Daddy would never want to see my face again.
He would call me a disgrace to the family."

Rance waved a hand for silence. "Who are you?"

"My name is Trella . . . Trella Haynes."

"Miss Haynes," he nodded. "Spare me details that don't
concern me. That man would have killed me and my partner. You were with him. That makes me suspicious of you.
But since I don't go around killing women, suppose you
just get on out of here now."

Her hands flew to her throat as she cried, "No! You
can't send me back into those woods. I showed you my
feet. I haven't eaten in two days, and, oh—what kind of
man are you?"

She crumpled to the ground. Rance watched, expressionless. One thing about women, he thought grimly, they can
always faint at the most convenient times. A man can't just
close his eyes and fall down. He's expected to stay awake
and face things.

Edward scrambled from the bushes and knelt down beside the woman. Lifting her head, he looked up at Rance
with concern. "We can't just go off and leave her. She's
telling the truth. . . ."

"How do you know?" Rance snapped, "There's something about this I don't like. Someone else will come along
to help her out. We've got to get home."

Edward smoothed her long black hair away from her
face. "I'm not leaving her," he said gruffly.

Rance stiffened angrily. He was not used to his men
arguing with him. "I said," he repeated firmly, "that we're
leaving her. Now let's go."

The girl moaned, moving her head slowly from side to
side. Another thing about women, Rance thought wryly, is
that they can also wake up from a faint any time they
choose. Like now . . . with Edward staring down at her
solicitously. She opened those warm brown eyes and
looked up at him with all the heart-shattering appeal of a
wounded doe.

He waited silently while Edward moved quickly to his horse for his water canteen, then bent beside her to give her a drink. Rance listened without speaking as the girl told Edward that Leroy Pearson had courted her until she learned his views about the war, that he refused to fight with the South, and then she agreed with her father that he was not the man for her. But Leroy was crazy, she said. He had kidnapped her. And look what he had done to her, she was sobbing against Edward's shoulder now. Her father would never let her come home. She did not want to return, anyway. He was a hopeless drunkard who beat her whenever he took the notion. She had no place to go.

She kept darting anxious glances at Rance, beseeching him to believe her. He looked away, gritting his teeth. The girl was a liar. He had been around enough women in his life to know there was just no truth to the story. It was the sneaky, suspicious look in her eyes and her whining tone that told him. Hell, Edward was so damn dumb.

Too disgusted to listen any longer, Rance turned and walked over to the dead man. He ought to just fire Edward on the spot, he thought. Fire him and get back to the ranch. But he knew he couldn't do it. The man was his friend, his closest friend. And if he was letting that little vixen get to him, then he was going to need someone who understood her kind to stand by him.

The very dead Leroy Pearson was lying on his stomach, eyes staring sightlessly, ants already beginning to scramble about the thickening blood that covered his face and neck. A puddle had formed on the ground, mingling with the red clay. With his toe, Rance turned the dead man over on his back. He searched him absently, knowing he would find nothing important. He took the gun and stuffed it into his coat pocket. Then he clasped his hands about the man's heels and dragged him from the road into the thick bushes alongside. There was no need to report the incident to the sheriff. Nor was there time. The death of a would-be murderer and horse-thief was of no consequence. The only ones who cared were the buzzards hovering overhead in eager anticipation. Let them have him.

Rance brushed his hands on his trouser legs, straightened his hat, and turned to face Edward once more.

"I'm taking her with me," his friend said with an expression that pleaded for understanding. "She hasn't got anybody, Rance. She won't be no trouble. We can use her around the ranch, and she'll be company for April."

"I don't want her around April!" Rance spoke louder than he meant to, and he did not miss the girl's reaction. Her chin jutted up just a bit in defiance.

"Hell, just keep her out of my way," he said finally, walking quickly to where Virtus waited. Mounting, he gave the two a final glare. "Do what you want. You know the way home. I've going on."

"I'll be along," Edward called to him, relief in his voice, "I'm going to give Trella some food. She's hungry—"

Rance kicked Virtus, moving him to a faster gait. He wanted the hooves to strike the ground hard and loud so he would not have to listen to Edward. Hell, you don't go around picking up women and taking them home with you like stray animals, he thought furiously. Especially one whose man friend tried to kill you and steal your horse.

He sighed. He knew he had a problem on his hands. Even dirty and tattered, Trella Haynes was lovely. Cleaned up, she was going to be beautiful. Edward was not very experienced with women, and she would be able to handle him like a well-broke colt. He shook his head. The girl was going to be a problem.

They caught up with Rance several minutes later. She was sitting behind Edward, her arms wrapped around his chest. Every so often Edward would laugh softly. The two were becoming close, fast. Damn you, Clark, he cursed silently, we don't need this on top of everything else.

They did not slow the horses until the ranch was in sight. Once again, Rance had a strange feeling. Something was not as it should be. No one was around.

The hands would be out with the horses, but even the house appeared empty. Where was April? He had figured she would come outside when she heard a horse approaching. He reined to a stop and dismounted. In quick strides, he was across the porch and flinging the door open to call her name—once, twice, three times. Cold apprehension growing, he looked in her room, then his.

He stepped back onto the porch, chest heaving with rapidly growing fury, just as Tom Stilley came riding up from the trail where he had been on watch. He scanned the man's face, quickly saw the frightened look. He demanded, "Where the hell is April?"

"Boss, listen—" Tom leaped from his horse but kept his distance. "When we got back, only Mulhern was still here."

Rance waited, teeth and fists clenching. If his suspicions were correct, Hinton was a dead man.

"Mulhern left, too," Tom Stilley rushed on. "He got scared of what you'd do when you got back and found out—"

Rance forced the words from a throat constricting with rage. "Where did Hinton take her?"

"That's just it," he said quickly. "Hinton didn't take her. She ran away. Mulhern said she left in the middle of the night. They tried to catch her, but couldn't, and Hinton took off and told Mulhern there won't no way he was gonna hang around for you to blame him. Mulhern was gonna stay, but when the boys started talkin' about how mad you was gonna be, he got scared and took off, too."

Rance whirled around to smash his fist into a post. Tom Stilley backed away, holding his hands up as he stammered, "Look, boss . . . I didn't have nothin' to do with it. I'm just tellin' you what was told to me."

"When did she run away?"

"I don't know. Mulhern said it wasn't too long after you left. She took that mare she'd been ridin'. They don't know where she went. Mulhern said they woulda gone after her, but she whopped him over the head and dang near killed him. He was out cold till the next mornin', and Hinton hung around to see if he was gonna die before he took off after her. By then, it was too late to track her."

Just then Edward Clark rode in, Trella still clinging to him, her face flushed with excitement. Edward took one look at Rance and knew not to ask any questions. He looked to Tom, who spread his hands in a helpless gesture and murmured, "She's gone."

Grimly, Rance walked over to Virtus, mounted, and reined him about. He headed back toward the road.

"Where you goin'?" Tom Stilley yelled after him. "You ain't gonna find her now. And Mulhern and Hinton are long gone. Won't do no good to raise hell with them."

"Well, where in tarnation does he think he's goin'?" Tom

asked Edward incredulously. "He don't know where Hinton and Mulhern went, and it ain't gonna do no good to beat them up."

Edward quietly replied, "He isn't going after them. He's going after her."

Tom's eyes bugged out. "Well, what in hell for? She's just another filly, and he damn sure ain't never lacked for them." He seemed to notice Trella for the first time and stared at her curiously. "And who might you be?" he demanded.

Edward answered for her. "This is Trella, and she's with me. I'm looking after her."

Tom looked her up and down and smiled. Then he turned his gaze back toward the rapidly disappearing horse and rider. "What in hell is he goin' after her for?" he repeated in wonder.

Edward took Trella's hand and began to lead her up the porch steps. "Well, Tom," he began wearily, the play of a smile on his lips, "It's like this. Right now, Rance just figures he's going after something that belongs to him. But the truth, and he don't even know this himself, is he loves the girl."

"Rance Taggart?" Tom hooted, stamping his feet in the dust as he danced a little jig of delight. "Rance Taggart in love? Boy, you're crazy. He ain't never loved nothin' but a horse."

Edward paused on the porch to stare after his friend. He could be wrong. Rance Taggart had confided once when he'd had too much to drink that he had only fancied himself in love with one woman—a little Mexican girl—and Edward had suspected something tragic had happened there. The look in Rance's eyes had been startling. Edward had never seen him look that way before. Something strange was going on inside his friend.

"Well, when's he coming back?" Tom Stilley demanded.

Edward looked at him and grinned as though it were all quite simple. "When he finds April, Tom. That's when he'll be back."

❦ Chapter Fifteen ❧

APRIL had lost track of time. Zeke brought her scraps of food from the house, and she wondered if Posie would notice and suspect what was happening. Zeke had tormented her one evening when he had laughingly told of her Uncle James arriving in response to her telegram. Vanessa had handled the situation by explaining how grieved she and everyone else was over April's disappearance. April had turned into a trollop, finally running away.

Zeke grinned smugly as he described the scene. "That Vanessa is some woman. She stood right there with tears in her eyes and told him how you probably was wanting him to come so you could get some money out of him, 'cause your old pappy quit doling it out to you once he saw your wicked ways. Your stupid uncle believed every word. Just stood there shaking his head with disgust. Ate a big dinner that night and then went on his way home the next morning."

So now there was no more hope that Uncle James would help. One day blended into the next as her life shrank to the size of the shack.

At first, Zeke had come nightly to torment her with descriptions of what he planned to do with her. He hadn't carried out any of his threats, however, merely making her cringe with fear as he towered over her, ranting. Why hadn't he touched her? She guessed it was his fear of Vanessa that stopped him, for his hand moved unconsciously to his face every now and then, fingering the raw scar. And she dreaded his coming. Some night, he really might rape her.

One twilight evening, she dragged herself out of the hovel as far as the chain would let her go. Zeke wouldn't be back until later. She wanted to sit in the sun, wanted just to be out of that horrible shack.

She wondered, as she did so often, about her father. Was he still alive? And, if so, what kind of torment was Vanessa inflicting upon him?

She hung her head wearily. She had accomplished nothing in escaping Rance. Nothing.

A twig snapped. April stiffened and began to rock back and forth in dread anticipation. He was coming. It had been two nights, and even though she had long ago eaten the jerky and corn dodgers he had left behind, and her stomach cramped with hunger, she would rather have endured starvation than his insane rantings.

With a shudder, she rose and backed toward the cabin door.

She closed the door and crept through the black cabin to kneel in a corner and wait. But when several moments passed, she dared hope that he wasn't really coming.

Then, slowly, the door squeaked open. April burrowed her head in her hands. She knew Zeke was inside, but he had made no move toward her. Was this a new game? She strained to see in the blackness. Suddenly, she could stand the tension no longer and screamed, "Damn you, why are you torturing me this way?"

"April, shut up!" The voice cracked like a whip.

She could not believe it. No. It was not possible.

"Get over here. Hurry up. We may not have much time." He spoke in a harsh whisper, and when she did not move he said, "Damnit, April, move!"

He stepped back to open the door, and twilight rushed in to give some light. He saw her and crossed over to jerk her to her feet. "We don't have much time. I don't want any trouble."

And then his eyes raked over her, and he gasped, then cried. "April! What's happened? And what is this?" He held up the length of chain, the rattling sound ominous in the stillness.

He shook the chain angrily, trailing his hand down to the cuff about her ankle. "What have they done to you? What's this connected to? I'll have to try to break it."

Impatiently, he gripped her shoulders to shake her roughly. "April, you must come out of it. I've got to get you out of here. Now what's this chain connected to?"

"The . . . bed," she croaked. "Over there."

He released her and walked to the bed, found where the link was connected and began to jerk with all his strength. "I can't break it," he said finally. "I'm going to have to shoot it. Stand back." She obeyed, and he drew his pistol, pointed, and fired. The explosion shook the thin plank walls, but the chain broke open.

"We'll have to worry about that ankle cuff and the chain dragging later. Let's go." He lifted her in his arms effortlessly, then paused to glance about. "I don't suppose you've got anything here you need to take along. It looks like you weren't left with much."

"How did you find me?" She struggled to get the words out.

"I hid out in the woods around the house for a couple of days, watching. When I didn't see you, I finally cornered that little Negro girl, Mandy. I scared the hell out of her, and she told me where she thought you might be."

He maneuvered her through the door as he said in a gruff tone, "We'll talk later, April."

He froze. His eyes narrowed and she turned her gaze and gasped at the sight of Zeke standing a few yards away. His lips were twisted in a sneer that was both mocking and angry.

And he held a gun pointed straight at them.

With a whispered oath, Rance quickly set April on her feet and pushed her behind him protectively.

"Don't go for it!" Zeke snapped, nodding toward the gun in Rance's holster. "Don't make a move till I tell you, and then move real slow. I want you to reach down and unbuckle that belt and let it fall to the ground. Then I want you to kick it over here to me."

Rance made no move, holding his arms out slightly from his sides, right hand inches from his gun. His feet were spread apart, body rigid.

"I told you to unbuckle that belt," Zeke's voice was

louder, betraying his own tension. "I ain't gonna tell you
again, you sonofabitch. I'm just gonna start shootin'."

Slowly, Rance's hands moved toward the buckle of his
gunbelt. Unfastening, he let it drop to the ground, where it
hit with a dull thud.

"Now kick it over here," Zeke ordered.

April suddenly felt herself being shoved roughly to the
side, her knees raking the dirt. Rance had hooked his toe in
the belt and kicked it upward, sending it into Zeke's face
and taking him by surprise. Rance sprang for him, hurling
his body against Zeke's knees and knocking him backward, just as the gun went off. She heard the whine, the
crashing impact of splintering wood as the bullet hit the
cabin wall inches from her head.

Zeke and Rance rolled in the dirt, pummeling each
other, their guttural shouts and oaths breaking the stillness
of the evening.

April came out of her trance. Scrambling for the gun
Zeke had dropped, she grabbed it with ice cold fingers.
Where were their horses? Now was the time to escape from
both of them! She knew these woods. She could find a
place to hide during the night, and get help in the morning.

Her eyes darted about desperately, looking for the
horses. Behind her she could hear the sound of flesh hitting
flesh, the grunts and curses of the desperately fighting men.
Then there was a cracking sound, an agonized cry, and she
started to spring forward for the cover of the bushes,
knowing, somehow, that the fight was over. She had to flee
at once. The victor would claim her, and by God, she was
not going to belong to any man!

"Hold it, April!"

Rance's voice. He had won the fight. She turned slowly,
hating the tremor of joy that moved through her. Not joy,
she admonished herself, it was only relief. Yes, that was
it.

"Virtus is tied over there." He pointed to a thicket. "Go
get me a rope, and don't try anything funny, April. You
try to get on Virtus and ride out of here, and all I've got to
do is whistle. He'll throw you to the ground. Now move."

April forced herself to obey his command, knowing that,
for now, there would be no escape. Wading through the

shrubs, she found Virtus, took the rope from his saddle with quick, jerking movements, then carried it to Rance.

He took it from her in silence. Bending down, he looped one end around Zeke's left ankle, then dragged him, screaming, across the ground roughly to where two trees stood about four feet apart. He twisted the rope around the trunks, connecting the other end to Zeke's right ankle, tugging until he was spread-eagled in the dirt.

Rance mounted the waiting horse, then lifted April to perch behind him.

"Rance Taggart, I don't want to be with you," she said firmly.

"Leave me here," she challenged. "I want to go home."

"And tangle with that wildcat sister of yours and wind up dead?" He shook his head from side to side. "Your father is probably being cared for just as well in his house as he would be in a hospital. Didn't you tell me he's got his old Negro with him? If you go back there, you'll only get yourself into terrible trouble. And you can't do anything for your father. You're coming with me, April, and that's how it is."

He urged Virtus into a faster gait as they reached the road. April sat quietly behind him, taking in what he had said. The terrible thing was that he was probably right. What could she do for Poppa now, with a war raging and the hospitals probably filled with soldiers anyhow?

They paused briefly while Rance took food from his saddlebag and gave it to her, silently cursing Zeke for half-starving his prisoner. He began to regret leaving Zeke alive, but it was too late to change that.

A little later, April looked warily skyward at the sound of heavy, rolling thunder. Lightning pierced the sky, splitting the blue-black heavens as the wind picked up to send leaves and small branches swirling down.

"This is dangerous," she screamed above the howling wind, holding tighter. "We can't keep riding in this."

He did not answer but continued to urge Virtus onward. The rains began to fall, slashing down on them. A bolt of lightning struck not too far to the left. A distant tree erupted in yellow-red flames, smoke soaring skyward.

"We have to stop!" she cried, terrified. "For God's sake,

Rance. You're going to get us killed." Already the rains had soaked her to the skin.

He slowed the horse as he shouted above the storm. "I remember an old barn around here somewhere. We're on Fletcher land. I don't think we have to worry about Zeke slipping up on us in this storm. And as soon as it breaks, we'll move on."

"There!" he yelled as a white streak punctured the darkness. He headed straight for the barn and, within moments, he was dismounting, yanking her down beside him and leading her and Virtus inside.

The sweet smell of hay touched her nostrils along with the odor of decay. Then she became aware of him standing just behind her, and she heard him say, "Take your clothes off."

"I will not!" She whirled about, trying to see his face in the darkness. "I'll never give in to you again, Rance Taggart."

"Oh, hell, April, I'm tired of arguing with you."

He spoke with maddening calm. "There's a pile of hay. You can burrow down in it to get dry and warm. I don't want you getting sick on me."

He pushed her toward the prickling hay. "I'm going to do the same thing. I'm soaked to the bone."

"You stay away from me," she warned, quickly removing her ragged dress and burrowing into the hay.

She lay there tense, waiting for him to make some move toward her. He, too, had burrowed down in the sweet-smelling hay, after removing his own clothing.

Did she dare venture out in the crashing storm? She could not return to Pinehurst. She would have to seek refuge with the Fletchers.

Slowly, she raised up to her knees. Pausing to listen for Rance's even breathing, she began to crawl along, pausing every few seconds to make sure he was still asleep.

She was almost out of the hay, about to stand, when she felt a sharp crack across her buttocks. She pitched forward. Rance's amused voice echoed mockingly all through the old barn. "How can I sleep with you wiggling around, April? Get back up here."

Enraged, buttocks still stinging, she turned around and threw herself down beside him. "Only God knows how much I hate you, Rance Taggart," she hissed. "I'll find a way to get away from you. I swear it!"

He murmured, "Calm down, blue eyes. If you're real sweet, I'll make it so good that I couldn't drive you away from me."

Oaths bubbled in her throat, but she forced herself to remain silent. She lay perfectly still, her back toward him, not touching. Despite the fury within, matching the storm's, she finally slept.

❧ Chapter Sixteen ❧

SUNLIGHT streamed down through a slit in the rotting roof. April opened her eyes to stare upward at the azure sky. The storm was over. Glancing about, she gasped at the sight of Rance, lying inches away, brown eyes staring at her intently, the play of a smile on his lips. He was no longer covered by the hay, and his naked body was entirely displayed.

"Good morning, blue eyes," he whispered. He was so ruggedly handsome, and he seemed to exude a special kind of strength. Under different conditions, she might have been vulnerable to his charms. But not now—not when she had come to resent him so fiercely.

She told herself that the desire swimming through her was only a normal reaction to such a magnificent display of manhood. It certainly did not mean that she cared. She would never lose control of herself where Rance Taggart was concerned. Never.

"Go ahead and take me!" she challenged suddenly. "It's why you insist on keeping me with you when you know how I loathe you. Go on and take what you want from me. Satisfy yourself and be done with me." Her voice cracked, and she turned her face away.

"What makes you think *you* could satisfy me?" he asked mockingly, and she turned to see the twinkling in his eyes. "What makes you think you're so special that I would go to any trouble to keep you with me?"

She shook her head, bewildered. "What other reason could there be? When you returned to your ranch and found me gone, then why didn't you just forget about me? Why did you come after me?"

"Would you have preferred to be left in the hands of Zeke Hartley?"

"No. I don't want to be in the clutches of *any* man!" She sat up, too incensed to care that she was naked. "Why is it all men seem to think a woman's sole purpose is to be mated? Did you ever stop to think that maybe we can live without you? That maybe there are those among us who would prefer to be alone than to have some man pawing at us night and day? Sweating and grunting like a boar hog?"

His eyes darkened and she knew she had finally broken through that cool facade. He reached out to cup her chin in one large hand, squeezing firmly. "Listen to me, damn you. You can lie to yourself all you want, but you can't say you were pretending either of those times we made love. That was no act. You wanted me. You enjoyed it. And you're a goddamned liar if you say you didn't."

He rolled over, pinning her beneath him, holding her wrists tightly at the sides of her head. She could feel his warm breath on her face, and there was no escaping the blazing fury of his eyes. "You wanted me then, and you want me now. You challenge me to rape you, but I've never had to rape any woman, you conceited little fool. I've never had to. Heed me well, April. You're nothing but a spoiled brat, and you think I'm just panting now from wanting you, but I'll never take you again until you beg me."

"That will never happen," she cried. "I'll never want you, you smug bastard, and I'll die before I let myself."

Abruptly, he silenced her with a smoldering kiss that left her gasping for breath when at last he raised his lips. She trembled, hoping it was anger and not desire that made her do so.

He looked straight into her fiery eyes and murmured, "You liked that, didn't you? You won't admit it to me, but you can't hide the truth from yourself."

His lips mashed down once again, and she tried to struggle, twisting her head from side to side, but she was powerless. She was fighting a battle within herself as she commanded her body to freeze. I won't let him, she cried silently. I won't let him do this to me . . . dear God, not again.

"You were made for this." He dipped his head to fasten hot, seeking lips around one nipple and suckle. "God never made fruit so sweet." He began to flick his tongue across each nipple in turn, pausing every so often to draw them into his mouth hungrily. "Say you want me, April. Say you want me, and I'll take you all the way."

"Damn you, never!"

She was hanging from the precipice by her fingertips. Never had she known such a driving, gnawing hunger. Pain began to swoop down into her belly. But she would not give in.

She struggled up to a sitting position. "With every breath I draw, Rance Taggart," she whispered raggedly, "I will hate you more than the last breath I drew."

"Strong words, young lady." He gave her a lopsided smile.

For an instant, she thought of slapping his smugly smiling face but she remembered what had happened the last time. It was not worth the trouble. There were other ways of taking revenge, and she vowed to find them.

She got to her feet and walked away, fists clenched at her sides. "I've got an extra shirt in my saddlebag, and a pair of trousers," he called. "Put them on. They'll do till we get back to the ranch. Can't have you riding around naked and exciting all the farmers."

He watched as she walked to the saddlebags and took out the clothing, then disappeared outside.

He shook his head in wonder. Why hadn't he taken her? Because he wouldn't do so unless she wanted him, wanted him and said so. There was no other way.

He finished dressing and walked outside. She heard him approach but did not acknowledge his presence. He touched her shoulder, felt her stiffen. "April, I've got something to say to you."

"Say it."

"I need your help. That's why I'm going to keep you with me. When I'm done with you, you can be on your way."

"And just how long do you think you will be needing my services?" she asked bitterly, still not turning to face him. "I do have business of my own to tend to."

"I can't say. Maybe for as long as the war lasts."

She whirled around, eyes wide. "You can't do that! Rance, I *must* get home. You don't know—"

"Yes, I do know," he snapped. "And I know you can't do a damn thing about it, so I don't want to hear about it anymore. Now I'll be good to you if you'll let me. But I want it understood here and now that I'm not putting up with any of your foolishness. You do as you're told, and we'll get along."

She blinked back furious tears. "I suppose that includes repeating that sordid little scene back there."

"No, April. I proved to you that I don't have to have you. I won't touch you again unless you ask. Now let's go. I'm anxious to get back."

Edward Clark was waiting when they arrived at the ranch. The guard at the main road had signaled ahead. Edward stood in the clearing in front of the house, and Trella was standing quietly beside him.

April was startled to see the strange girl, and her curiosity was further aroused when she realized she was wearing one of her dresses.

"I see you got her," Edward drawled. "Have any trouble?"

"Not really," Rance replied casually, swinging down from the horse. He turned to fasten his hands about April's waist and lift her down. She stepped away from his touch immediately, and he gave her a knowing smile before turning back to Edward. "What's been going on? Any news of the war?"

"Yeah, and it's all bad." His face took on a grim look. "All hell's busted loose, Rance. We got word that the biggest battle yet was up in Shiloh, Tennessee. Some say we lost ten thousand men."

"Oh, my God." Rance looked about in misery, then fastened his gaze once more on Edward. "We can't stand a loss like that."

Edward shrugged. "It could have been even worse. Grant and another Yankee general by the name of Foote got delayed. That gave Johnston and Beauregard just enough time to get their forces together at Corinth, Mississippi."

He knelt and picked up a small stick and began to draw a diagram in the dirt to illustrate how the battle took place. Rance bent to a squatting position to observe. With a sweeping glance at the strange girl, who continued to stare so rudely, April looked downward, anxious to hear the story.

Edward pointed with the stick. "Grant had put his army on the western bank of the Tennessee, here, at Pittsburg Landing. Most of his men were in camp near a little meeting house called Shiloh Church, here, which was just about twenty miles from Corinth." He gestured once more with the stick before continuing. "We hear Johnston figured to strike Grant before that Yankee Buell and his troops could get there to help. So he marched up from Corinth and took Grant on. He caught him off guard and, the first day, he almost pushed his army into the Tennessee River."

He paused, a wave of sadness making his voice crack slightly. "The damn Yankees rallied, and Johnston got killed. By dark, Buell's troops were arriving, along with one of Grant's divisions that had been delayed. The next day, the Yankees hit with everything they had. Ten thousand men. It don't look good, Rance. Not at all. Now our Confederate Congress has voted that all men between eighteen and thirty-five gotta go fight."

"Conscription," Rance mused thoughtfully. "I'm not surprised. When the war started, Confederate soldiers were enlisted for just a year, and that year is up. I imagine the glory has dissolved. Our army could be in danger. I'm glad to hear Congress has passed a conscription act."

April could contain herself no longer. "Why would you be glad?" she asked scathingly. "Now you can't be a coward any longer. You'll be forced to join the army."

Without looking at her, Rance murmured, "You don't know what you're talking about, April." To Edward he said, "What is the reaction of the men?"

"They're willing to stick it out with you. They figure the way you got it planned, we aren't gonna be seen around too much, anyway. Most of our work is going to be done at night. This conscription thing is going to mean trouble, though. There's an exemption that says the owner or over-seer of at least 20 slaves can't be called to serve. They also say that, for $500, you can hire somebody to take your place."

Rance shook his head. "We can't be worried about that. We've got plans to make." Remembering April, he ges-tured for her to move to the house. "We've got things to talk about that you don't need to hear. Should you get captured, you won't have anything to tell the enemy."

"Captured?" she echoed, suddenly frightened. "Why should I be captured? There are no Yankees around here."

With a silent look of understanding between him and Edward, Rance murmured, "There will be where we're going. Now get along."

She turned toward the house, anxious to fetch water from the creek and heat it for her first real bath in a long time. She went to the room that had been hers and began to see whether the rest of her belongings were intact.

"I only took two dresses."

She whirled about to see the girl standing in the door-way, an apprehensive smile on her lips.

"I'm really sorry," she said as though she meant it. "I only came here with the clothes on my back. I had to have something to wear. Edward said it would be all right if I borrowed something of yours. Of course, I had to let the seams out. You're such a tiny thing."

"It's all right," April replied, more sharply than she intended. "If those two mean to make a women's prison out of this ranch then they should stock clothes of all sizes to accommodate everyone."

"Hey, you sound bitter."

"Why shouldn't I be?" April crossed over to sit on the bed and began to rub at her sore, swollen feet. "Why do you think I ran away? I'll run away again, too, the first chance I get."

"Yeah, that's what Edward said. He said if Rance found you, he'd have to keep a good watch or you'd do it again. As for me, you couldn't run me off."

April raised an eyebrow. "You mean you're here of your own free will?"

She laughed. "In a roundabout way." She recounted her story as April listened, astonished, then added, "I really like Edward. Maybe I even love him. He makes me happy, and I know I make him happy. I never had it this good at home. I hope I can stay here forever."

"Well, that's your business," April sighed and got up to walk toward the kitchen. "I have a home that I'm very anxious to get back to. The last thing I want to do is be around Rance Taggart, anyway."

"I just can't believe you said that."

April cocked her head to one side. "And why not?"

She smiled, slowly, almost insidiously. "As much as I like Edward, I'd give anything to be Rance Taggart's woman, if only for one night. He's so handsome . . . so dashing." She wrapped her arms about herself and began to swirl around the room, a dreamy look upon her face. She stopped abruptly, eyes shining, and cried, "Tell me. What is it like with him?"

April backed away from her. "I'll tell you nothing. I won't discuss something so sordid."

"Sordid?" Trella echoed with a whooping laugh. Placing her hands on her hips, she twisted from side to side mockingly. "Well, listen to little miss goody-goody. You must be one of those sick women I've heard about who don't have a need for a man. So what does a magnificent specimen like him see in you?"

April shrugged. "Ask him, if it means so much to you." She picked up the water pails and breezed by her toward the rear door.

❦ Chapter Seventeen ❧

APRIL hated being in Washington. It seemed an effrontery to the Southland just to be here, in this Yankee capital city.

She could find no fault with the hotel Rance had chosen. Oh, no, he had made sure that they were all afforded the most elegant accommodations to be had. He and Edward had separate rooms, opposite the one she shared with Trella. And while Trella made almost nightly visits to Edward's bed, she always returned promptly to take up her station as April's bodyguard.

April had accused Rance of having Trella spy on her, and he had not denied it. "Of course, sweetheart," he had laughed. "You don't think I'm going to give you another chance to escape, do you? Especially now, when I need you."

Need, indeed, she thought furiously, pacing across the room to pull back the lace curtains and stare down at the bustling street below. Forced to pose as his wife for all the ridiculous social functions he insisted they attend. That was his need. He had not been to her bed or insisted she come to his. Well, for that much, she was thankful.

Trella liked to goad her about that, too. She would quite brazenly talk of her bedtime activities with Edward, then demurely hint that perhaps the reason Rance did not come to her was that he had other women.

"You think I care?" April stared incredulously. "I hope

to God that man never touches me again. He's evil and vile and—"

"And good-looking, and I'll bet he's hell in bed," Trella interrupted flatly. "What I wouldn't give for a tumble with him, but I wouldn't want to risk losing Edward. *He* talks about getting married, something that would never enter Rance Taggart's mind."

"There are other things in life besides getting married," April pointed out.

It was Trella's turn to be shocked. "I'd like to know what! Maybe you was raised all fancy and rich, but I know what it's like to crawl through a cotton field on your hands and knees dragging a sack behind you in the dirt, with the sun boiling down on your back and blistering through the rags you call a dress, 'cause you ain't got no better. If I was to marry a fine man like Edward Clark, I'd never be on my knees in red Alabama clay again. No sir! You see the way he dresses me now, don't you? Well, this is the way I'm gonna live from now on. Elegant and fancy. You think you can do better, you go ahead. You just don't know when you're well off."

April sighed, recalling the conversation. She left her post at the window and stood before the ornate oval mirror that hung on the wall over the ruffled dressing table. Yes, Trella probably was wearing the nicest clothes she had ever had. But it was not Edward supplying them. Rance picked out everything she and Trella wore, and while she would never tell him so, he did have excellent taste. The gown she was wearing for tonight's party was of pale blue watered silk, yards and yards of it, the skirt supported by a large metal hoop and five crinolines. The front of the skirt was embroidered in white rose-shaped patterns, sheltering a bouquet of daisies in the center. Each flower shimmered, catching the light as she turned. The same white embroidery adorned the daring bodice, enhancing her ample bosom.

The door opened, and she saw Rance enter. She did not turn around. He never knocked, she thought furiously. She had to make sure that she never moved from behind the tapestry dressing screen unless fully dressed.

As she watched him stride across the scarlet and gold rug, she could not help wondering once again why he

chose not to take his pleasure with her. Each time their
eyes met, he sent her a secret challenge. He was sure she
wanted him, and was merely teasing her, making her wonder when the magic time would come.

Magic, indeed, she sniffed with disdain. She did not want
him or any man. And he was a fool if he thought she had
enjoyed those moments of passion. Her body had betrayed
her then. It was her body, not *her* that he had ravished.

She felt the light pressure of his fingertips on her bare
shoulders and looked up, hating to admit that he did look
quite handsome in his dark blue waistcoat and white satin
cravat. His dark hair curled ever so slightly about his face,
and his mustache was neatly trimmed above the ever-smil-
ing arrogant lips.

"When I see you this way," he murmured, lips so close
to her ear she could feel his warm breath, "it's as though a
magician and a designer put their heads together to create
a masterpiece. Your hair, exotically golden, framing that
beautiful face, your eyes glowing as the blue silk of your
dress. No earthly creature could be so lovely. You must be
bewitched. Merlin himself created you."

She returned his smug smile, eyes meeting his with cool
defiance as she said, "It's a pity I am *not* bewitched, or I
might be swayed by your poetic words. But I know you for
the rogue you are, and you would do well to remember
that. Nothing you can say will make me despise you any
less."

"Ahh, April, why must you always be so unpleasant?
Why can't we at least be friends?"

He looked her over again and said softly, "You are a
rare and treasured beauty, and I am proud to introduce
you as my wife."

"But I am not your wife, and I would rather be dead
than make your lies a truth. Why do you persist in this
game? What difference does it make whether these people
accept you or not? You're supposed to be fighting for the
South, not sipping brandy with the enemy, you coward."

He flinched, ever so slightly. It was enough. She knew
she had hurt him.

"I wish you wouldn't talk that way, April. Someone
might hear. I've told you—for all intents and purposes, we
are happy to be here. We sympathize with the Union

cause. I am a horse trader, and my sole purpose is to supply the federal army with the best stock available. You are my loving, dutiful wife. Edward is my partner, and his wife is your dearest friend."

"None of it makes any sense to me. We've been here so long. What is it now? September? How much longer must we stay here?" She shook her head. "I'm sick of the parties, the charades, and one of these nights I'm going to scream to high heaven that you're a spy, and I'm not your wife, and—"

His hand moved quickly to her throat, squeezing her to silence. Terror made her eyes widen. Why did he react so violently? "I don't want to hear any more of that kind of talk, April. I don't want to hurt you, but damn it, you aren't going to mess things up."

His brown eyes smoldered with bright crimson fires as he stared down her. "If you ever expose me, I swear you will live to regret it.

"When I have finished with you, then you can go home and do battle with that she-devil twin of yours. But until that time comes, you are not going to give me any trouble. For the last time, do you understand me?"

She was frightened of him and agreed quickly.

"I will play your game . . . for now."

"That's all I ask." He took a breath, straightened his coat and bowed slightly. "Now then, shall we join Edward and Trella downstairs?"

She swished by him, and moved down the hall quickly.

Below, she could see guests arriving to mingle in the lobby before moving to the spacious, elegant ballroom. There were uniformed federal officers wearing dress uniforms, polished scabbards at their sides. Their ladies were all attired elegantly in lavish ballgowns of every color. It was quite a spectacle.

There was a frivolity in the air, a brightness. Musicians were playing in the ballroom, the sweet tones of the violins floating out to greet the arrivals.

Her own gown drew attention, she knew, as she was the object of envious stares from the women and admiring looks from the men when she made her descent on Rance's arm.

"Mr. Taggart." An officer stepped forward, bowing with military snap in April's direction. His eyes took in her face, her silken hair, the marble smoothness of her white shoulders, glancing for just an instant to the swell of her breasts.

"Captain Devenaugh," Rance acknowledged coolly. "My pleasure. It's good to see you in more pleasant surroundings than a horse stable."

The officer laughed jovially, then glanced at April once more before saying, "I had heard what a gorgeous creature your wife was, but now I can testify to that fact, myself. She is magnificent."

April saw the proud look take hold of Rance's face, and she felt like screaming she was not a horse, not a "creature." But she merely smiled, as was expected, as had been instructed.

Other officers moved about, murmuring compliments, but Rance impatiently removed her from their flowery words and bold stares, leading her to the ballroom. He had gotten what he wanted from these important men—admiration for his lovely wife, and perhaps acceptance. But he did not want resentment from the officers' wives, so he had taken her away.

He pulled her gently into his arms. For so large a man, April had to admit that he danced quite well. As always, with a hoop, she had to pay close attention to her movements, lest the back of the hoop flip up, exposing her undergarments. She was glad for the preoccupation. It kept her from getting caught up in the sweet melody, or in the way Rance looked down at her. Warmth began to spread through her because of his touch.

"I always did think you were the prettier."

She raised an eyebrow. "I beg your pardon?"

He smiled. "When you were little. When I was no more in your life than the poor son of your father's groom. I thought you were much prettier than your twin. But that was when I believed you were sweet and innocent. I always knew she was cunning. Now I know you can be quite cunning, yourself, and vindictive."

She was aware that there were many eyes upon them, and she could only assume they made a striking couple. With a forced smile, she whispered, "If ever a woman had a reason to be vindictive, I do. You have humiliated me and interfered with my life. I have to dance with you. I have to pretend to be your wife. But damn you, Rance, don't push me too far. Everyone has a breaking point, and you are goading me toward mine."

His lips continued to smile, but his eyes betrayed the anger she had evoked. "Just keep on looking blissfully happy, my dear. That's all I'm asking—for now."

She allowed him to lead her into a delicate twirl, and when they passed close to each other, she hissed, "You need never ask for more. Remember that."

He raised their arms up high, fingers entwined as he twirled her in time to the waltz. "I won't ask, April . . . but you will."

The implication was maddening, carrying her to the point of explosion. The dance ended, and she was only dimly aware of the spattering of applause around the room, meant for them. She was grateful when Trella and Edward approached, greeting them like the close friends they pretended to be.

Edward and Rance steered them to a terrace overlooking the city, leaving them in the shadows while they went for glasses of champagne.

"My, but Rance is a handsome devil tonight," Trella gushed the moment they were alone. "I don't see how you can stay out of his bed, April. I should think—"

"I should think you could mind your own business," April said icily. "Really, Trella, do you ever think of anything except mating?"

Trella laughed, a high tinkling sound that grated. April had never known her to be truly angry. While she envied Trella her sunny nature, she also found her offensive.

"My heavens, I don't think of doing it with just any man, honey," she said. "Just those who appeal to me—like Edward and your Rance."

"He is not *my* Rance."

"Well, you could do it with him if you wanted to, and you know it. And don't tell me you haven't, because Edward says you have. I don't see why you don't want him again. A man has to have it, and if you don't give it to him, he's gonna go somewhere else. How can you even think of sending him to the arms of another woman? Edward says he thinks that's what he's doing, because there are plenty of nights when Rance doesn't come in till dawn, and he smells like perfume, and—"

"Trella, really!" April stared at her in wonder. "You and Edward seem to spend a great deal of time speculating about Rance's personal life. Why not use your energies to spice up your own activities?"

For the first time, Trella looked angry, but there was no time for a retort. Rance and Edward returned, carrying crystal glasses of sparkling champagne.

"Now tell Rance what you heard the women saying," Edward spoke to Trella urgently. With a smug look in April's direction, she made a smacking sound and began. "I overheard a woman saying that the White House seamstress, Lizzie Keckley, makes dresses for her once in a while when she has time. The Keckley woman told her about those say . . . say and sees. . . ."

"Seances," Rance corrected her, ebullient. "Go on."

"Well, this Lizzie, who's a nigra and used to be a slave, she even worked for Mrs. Jefferson Davis once, she said Mrs. Lincoln is having those things at the White House, and she's talking to that son of hers that died last February. And that's why the President won't be here tonight, because they're having another one tonight, and he went to it."

"You don't look surprised," Edward said to Rance.

"I'm not. I've heard the talk. There's been a lot of criticism, but Lincoln is said to be a very sympathetic husband who covers up his wife's erratic behavior."

"That's right," Trella rushed on breathlessly. "The woman was talking about that, too. She says she's heard that every time a new medium comes to Washington and Mrs. Lincoln hears about it, she has another one of those say . . . seances. Folks have tried to talk to President Lincoln about it, because they don't think it's right, having such goings-on at the White House like that."

Rance nodded. "He grieves over his son, too. The boy was only eleven. Evidently he's so concerned about his wife's grief that he's glad for her to receive comfort from any source."

"This nigra, Lizzie, is the one that got her started, according to the women I heard talking. She believes in all that stuff." She turned to Edward. "Do you believe they really talk to the dead?"

April had been silent as long as she could. "Will someone please tell me what's going on? You all act so excited. What's so important about seances at the White House?"

Rance narrowed his eyes, deep in thought, then said, "Edward, this is an opportunity we can't pass up. We're already here in the Union capital and we're accepted as businessmen, horse traders. All we have to do is arrange for a seance in the White House, and while all that table rapping and nonsense is going on, we can look around. We're bound to find some information of use to the Confederacy. It's worth the risk."

Edward started to speak in agreement, but April cut in quickly. "Aren't you going to tell me anything?" she asked, exasperated.

"We are going to have a seance at the White House," Rance said as though speaking to a child. "Have you heard of the Fox sisters? They started a national fad of communicating with the dead. People have begun to take it quite seriously, particularly since the war. There are plenty of widows and parents trying to communicate with men they've lost."

"I've heard about this," she muttered, "but I'm not interested."

"You will be, because you're going to learn all about spirit rappings and table tappings, eerie voices, flickering lights, mystical music, and speaking in trance." He gave her a lazy smile.

She shook her head. "Why should I learn? I don't believe in it—charlatans preying on the grief-stricken. It's disgusting."

"Well, it doesn't matter what you think, because you're going to be a medium and conduct a believable seance at the White House for Mrs. Mary Todd Lincoln, herself. With Trella's help, and, of course, the assistance of Edward and myself, you're going to give the most credible seance that has ever been held in the White House. Mrs. Lincoln will hold you in the highest esteem—and so will the Confederacy, *if* Edward and I can discover any valuable information."

"You're insane!" She stepped away from him, her back against the brick wall bordering the terrace. "I'll do no such thing."

Trella spoke up quickly. "Don't bother with her, Rance. I'll do it. I can do anything better than she can." She lifted her chin defiantly and gave April a brief look of disdain.

Rance rubbed at his mustache with his knuckles as his mind raced along. Trella was always eager to help, but the truth was that she lacked April's gentility. April would easily be accepted into the inner circle of Washington society. But Trella wouldn't. Too, April's ethereal beauty would make her seem spiritual, otherworldly.

"No," he said finally, firmly. "April will do it."

"I won't!" She looked at each of them in turn, eyes flashing rebelliously, defiantly. "I will not add to that poor woman's grief, and I think all of you are evil to even consider such a disgusting trick."

"But you'd be doing her a favor, really," Edward broke in. "It will make her feel good to think she's talking to her boy. We'll take care of all the details and make it believable. Just leave it to us."

"I will not be a part of this. It's absolutely out of the question."

Rance's fingers squeezed into her forearm as he jerked her away from the others. He pulled her into the shadows. Her lips parted in protest, but he spoke first.

"Before you give me a lecture on deception, April, let me remind you that you are a Southern woman in Union country, and that as long as you are here you are in danger of being accused of spying for the South."

She stared at him and he took a deep breath and went on.

"You need the rest of us, and we need you, for cover. We're all taking grave risks just being in Washington. And as for the seance, please remember that Mrs. Lincoln has held several before now and will doubtless continue to do so. You are not deceiving her any more than she has already deceived herself. And you may even ease her grief a little. What difference does it make to you whether she really talks to her son, or just thinks she does? If it makes the poor woman feel better, why should it matter to you?"

He had her on both points, and she hadn't the energy to

pretend otherwise, not to herself or to Rance. She sighed wearily. Would the nightmare ever be over? Or would things only get more and more complicated?

"All right, Rance," she sighed. There really was no choice. He led her back to the ballroom, explaining his plan as they moved.

"I'm going to get us introduced to one of the women Trella heard talking. You tell her you're interested in having some gowns made by this Lizzie Keckley. It may not be easy. I don't imagine a woman who works for the President's wife takes on new customers without a recommendation. So be charming, and maybe you'll be lucky. Understand?"

She gave him what she hoped was an arrogant grin. "I'm going to enjoy the day you get what's coming to you, Rance Taggart."

"That's the first hope you have given me, April," he said with a wink as he tucked her hand in the crook of his elbow. "Now I do have something to look forward to."

"That's not what I was talking about," she hissed. They entered the ballroom once more, and he whispered for her to smile. Play the game, she commanded herself. Play the game. For now, there is no other choice.

"That's one of them," Trella stepped close to Rance and whispered anxiously. "I think she's the one who has the same seamstress as Mrs. Lincoln." Rance nodded and told her to calm down, that he would handle things.

April watched as the woman approached. She was being led in their direction by a tall man wearing the uniform of an infantry colonel—a black coat with double rows of brass buttons, gold cord trimming the high collar and cuffs. Braided gold epaulets covered the shoulders. His trousers were light blue, with bright red stripes down the sides, and he also wore a bright red fringed sash at his waist.

He extended a white-gloved hand to Rance, the tips of his neatly curved mustache tipping upward as he smiled. "Mr. Taggart, I believe. We met yesterday at the cattle-yard."

"Ah, yes, of course, Colonel Truxmore," Rance countered, then began the introductions.

As the Colonel presented his wife, April saw instantly that they would not get along. She had seen the type before. She had married an officer, married "well," according to society, but what had she, as a person, ever done that was noteworthy? Had she married someone else, she might be out in the fields, tending a crop, or sitting at home with her children instead of attending a fancy ball, giving herself airs.

"April."

Rance's voice had an edge to it.

"This is Mrs. Truxmore," he said with meaning only she understood. "I was telling her that you have been admiring her exquisite gown."

"Oh . . . yes," April said quickly. Actually, she was not that enthused over the olive green velvet. The neck was too high, and the overall effect was austere.

"I was also telling her that you are in a quandary for a wardrobe, since we aren't that well established in Washington. Since we will be going to Europe next month, you would like her to recommend a seamstress."

Mrs. Truxmore did not look impressed. In fact, April thought impishly, she looked like she had just sucked a lemon. All sorts of wicked thoughts began to dance about in her head, like wondering what sort of expression she had on that prune face when the Colonel made love to her. Did she ever part her lips and sigh with ecstasy, or moan with delight? Or did she lie there, lips pursed in disapproval, with all the eagerness of a corpse in a coffin?

April had to stifle a giggle. Rance was glaring at her. "Yes, yes," she said in a rush. "I do so desperately need the services of a good seamstress here. I can get by with just a few things. Rance, darling that he is, has promised me a whole new wardrobe in Paris, but I don't want to arrive in the midst of the winter social season looking like a frump."

She decided to get to the point, wanting the scene to end. "Who is your seamstress?"

Mrs. Truxmore's neck stiffened even more, and her chin jutted higher until she was actually looking down her nose at April. "Well!" She was most offended. "*My* seamstress is Elizabeth Keckley, who also happens to be the White House seamstress. I hardly think she would take just anyone as a customer."

April bristled and clenched her gloved hands. Just anyone, indeed!

Rance felt her indignation and casually moved his hand to her back to give her a warning caress with his fingertips.

The Colonel coughed, embarrassed by his wife's effrontery. "My dear," his voice had an edge to it. "I think in this instance Elizabeth would consider taking Mrs. Taggart as a customer. After all, her husband has just delivered 50 artillery horses to three of my companies. Good artillery horses are hard to come by these days." He spoke with emphasis.

"How patriotic of Mr. Taggart," she said acidly. "But wasn't he paid for the horses? My goodness, if he's a businessman—"

"Yes, of course he was paid." The Colonel no longer tried to hide his annoyance. "But he did not have to sell the horses to *my* regiment. There are plenty of other regiments anxious for artillery horses. Now I want you to arrange for Mrs. Taggart to have an appointment with Elizabeth."

"But Elizabeth might not agree."

"She will agree. I've paid her enough money over the years that she better not *dis*agree." He looked at Rance and April in turn, smiled apologeticallly, and said, "My wife is so protective of Elizabeth. Doesn't want her overworked, you know."

"Of course," Rance nodded with understanding. April simply returned the woman's icy glare. "Tomorrow would be a good day for a fitting. My partner and I have some business appointments, so my wife won't have anything to occupy her."

Colonel Truxmore glanced at his wife, silently warning her not to object. With a little sniff and another lift of her chin, she murmured, "I will have a carriage sent for Mrs. Taggart at one o'clock."

"Wonderful!" The Colonel beamed. "Why don't you make it earlier so the two of you can have lunch? Are you staying here at the hotel, Mrs. Taggart?"

Rance spoke up quickly. "Yes, we are staying here. I'm sorry, but she won't be able to join your wife for lunch. She is entertaining the wife of another of my associates." He turned slightly and gestured toward Trella. "Mrs. Clark will be accompanying her to the fitting. The two are inseparable," he laughed softly.

"Tomorrow at one then," Mrs. Truxmore nodded stiffly, then turned to her husband. "I see some people we should speak to."

They said good night and walked away, and as soon as they were out of hearing range, April cried, "I have never met anyone so unpleasant in my entire life."

"Wonderful!" Rance beamed. "That means I no longer hold that position."

Edward and Trella laughed, and even April had a difficult time keeping a straight face.

"I think we should dance to celebrate our good fortune." He held out his arms to her as the orchestra began to play a lilting waltz. "We move together so well, my dear. It's as though we were made for each other."

He led her to the center of the floor, and April was aware of everyone watching in admiration as they began to glide in time to the music. Yes, she thought, a bit wistfully, it was a shame there had to be such animosity between them. They made a striking couple. They danced well together. And, she thought as shivers of warmth moved up and down her spine at his nearness, they did seem made for each other. She could remember the touch of his lips, the feel of his seeking hands, and a flush went through her as she remembered much more than that.

She was aware of the envious eyes of the women. Rance was quite handsome. He exuded strength, manliness, and charm. Why did there have to be such contention between them?

But, she reminded herself, it was not of her doing. He had interfered in her life, taken her by force that first time, made her beg. *He* had caused her resentment.

Their eyes met, held, and she looked away as he smiled knowingly. Damn him! He couldn't know what I'm thinking, she raged silently. He couldn't!

But, strangely, she knew that he did indeed know what she was thinking, and a good deal more besides.

🐚 Chapter Eighteen 🐚

RAIN slashed against the windows. Thunder rolled in the distance and lightning split the black heavens. An icy chill permeated the room, despite the roaring fire in the hearth.

"A perfect night for a seance," Trella offered as she stood before the mirror rubbing rouge into her cheeks.

April sat in a chair near the fire, staring down at the black bombazine dress she was wearing. A mourning dress, Rance had said it was befitting attire for a medium. "I don't think any of this is going to work," she murmured worriedly. "The whole idea is foolish."

Trella gave an unladylike snort. "You just don't have any faith in Rance, that's all. *I* happen to know what he's got planned. You just do your part, and everything will turn out just fine," she added accusingly.

April leaned back and closed her eyes. The only satisfaction she had derived thus far from the whole scheme was seeing the angry reaction on Mrs. Truxmore's face when she walked into her sewing room to hear Lizzie Keckley exulting over the fact that April was a medium.

"A . . . a *what?*" the arrogant woman had cried.

Lizzie had repeated her astonishing discovery while April remained silent. Mrs. Truxmore then opened and closed her mouth several times before exclaiming, "Well, I do not believe in such nonsense, and I will not have it discussed in this house."

"I believe in it," Lizzie said firmly. "A lot of people do. Including Mrs. Lincoln."

"Yes, I've heard of the weird goings-on at our White House," she said tartly, eyes narrowing in condemnation. "I happen to know that you take part in those affairs, Lizzie, but while you are in my house, you will honor my wishes. I do not wish to have such deviltry discussed here."

She turned to April. "Is it true? What she said? Do you profess to talk with the dead?"

"Of course," April regarded her coolly. "I have done so many times. I am pleased to hear that there are so many people in Washington who also believe."

The woman placed her hands on her hips as her face turned red. "I would never have allowed my husband to talk me into having you here, had I known this dreadful thing. Lizzie! How much longer will you be with the fitting? I prefer to have this over with as quickly as possible."

Lizzie had finished without delay, but not before she made April promise that she would conduct a seance for Mrs. Lincoln.

"It would be an honor," April had told her. "I have had strong vibrations within since arriving in Washington. The other day my husband and I passed the White House in our carriage, and I was overwhelmed by a feeling that told me someone was trying to communicate with me from beyond. Since I've heard of the death of Mrs. Lincoln's son, I know it was he who was trying to speak to his mother through me."

"Praise the Lord," Lizzie had cried, rolling her large eyes skywards and raising her arms. "It's a sign. I know it is. When I tell Mrs. Lincoln, she's going to have to see you. I just know it."

Mrs. Truxmore did not even bid her good-bye, and this caused April no distress. As soon as they were in the carriage, moving away from the house, Trella squealed with delight. "It's going to work out just like Rance said it would!" And April merely nodded, feeling dreadful. She still considered it a cruel scheme.

There was a soft knock on the door.

"April, we're ready," Edward called softly. She got to her feet, adjusting the black veil she wore over her face and she and Trella stepped into the hallway. Absently,

April realized how much she hated the wallpaper pattern—thousands and thousands of four-leaf clovers. She felt smothered in them, felt as though she were lying facedown in a never ending shamrock field. A nagging pain had begun in the base of her skull and was beginning to press against her temples.

"Drink this." She glanced up from her reverie to see that Rance stood in the open doorway of his room and held a snifter of brandy. "You look as though you need it," he said sympathetically.

Gratefully, she gulped it down. He went inside the room and returned with the bottle. He refilled her glass and she drank again. The pain lessened almost immediately, and a blessed relaxation began to course through her.

"April, this could be a very important evening to the Confederacy. Think of it in that light."

"I try to, but I still feel terrible, preying on that poor woman's grief."

"You aren't doing it for money," he pointed out. "Think of the people who do. You told me yourself that this Lizzie Keckley was astonished when you said you never charge for your seances."

April laughed shortly. "My seances, indeed. I'm sure everyone will see through me, despite all your coaching." She gave him a puzzled glance. "How did you come to know so much about seances, anyway? How do you know you've coached me properly?"

Trella and Edward had gone on ahead. Rance closed the door to his room, locked it, then took her arm. They began walking down the hall. "April, I'll be honest with you," he said quietly, thoughtfully. "I've had this planned for some time. It was no spur-of-the-moment thing. I did research. I asked questions. I listened. If you follow my instructions, your act will be quite believable."

"You aren't doing this just to 'prowl about' the White House," she said accusingly as they began to descend the stairs. "I think you have other motives."

"You're a smart girl, April," he beamed approvingly. "Actually, it's been my plan all along to be completely accepted in this city. What better way than making the President's wife happy? It could mean friendship for you with her, and the confidence of President Lincoln for me.

Then I'll be in a good position to trade with the Union army."

She bristled. "There's something else that doesn't make sense—your wanting to sell horses to the Yankees. I thought you wanted to supply the Confederacy. All of a sudden we move North and you become a traitor, and—"

He squeezed her arm so tightly that she winced with pain, and he ground out the warning: "Don't let me hear you say such a thing again, April. I'm no traitor to the South."

"Then why do you sell the Yankees horses?" she demanded. "Since we left Alabama, I haven't known you to deal with the Confederacy once."

"I told you I don't want to hear it."

"You're hurting my arm," she jerked against his grasp.

"Maybe I'm trying to squeeze some sense into you. I'll do more than that if you don't shut up and stop asking questions about things that don't concern you. I don't have to confide my every move to you."

"It does concern me if you're betraying the South and using me to help you do it."

They were halfway down the stairs. Edward and Trella were staring upward, eyes wide as they realized what April was saying so boldly. Rance turned to grip her shoulders, shaking her so roughly that her teeth clattered. "April, damn you, don't make me hurt you!" he whispered harshly, his lips so close she could feel his breath upon her face. "I don't want anyone overhearing you. Now if you don't shut up, we'll just go back upstairs, and I'll give you a sound lesson in obedience."

Tears of humiliation and fury sprang to her eyes. She lifted the veil to wipe them away with the back of her hands. He had reduced her to tears once again, and she hated him. "Dear God, why do you torture me by forcing me to stay with you?" Her voice cracked and shook with emotion. "Let me go, Rance, please. I can't tolerate this life. I've tried . . . I have. But I can't stand being around you any longer."

He was silent for several moments as she cried, shoulders heaving. Finally, he asked quietly, "Has it really been that terrible, April? Are you really so miserable? I haven't forced myself on you, and I've felt I was doing you a favor, looking after you. We both know what's waiting for you if you go back to Montgomery. Has it really been so bad, these last few months?"

She nodded, staring at him intently through the veil. "Yes. I'd rather go home and try to work things out there. Maybe the sheriff will help me, I don't know. If you won't take me there, then just let me go. Let me find my own way back, and I'll get help from someone, anyone. Oh, Rance," she gestured pleadingly as his hands fell away from her shoulders. "Can't you see what it's doing to me? Being so far from my home? Wondering how my father is? If he's even still alive?"

He glanced away, back up the stairway, gazing into space. Finally, with a deep sigh, he faced her once again. "All right, April. Cooperate with me tonight, and tomorrow I promise that you will be set free. I'll even give you the money to get you back to Alabama, and I'll make arrangements for you to get there."

For a moment, she could only stand there and stare at him, not believing her ears. Then she burst into tears once more. This time they were tears of joy. "Oh, Rance, thank you! Thank you! Dear God, you don't know what this means to me."

"We're going to be late," he said abruptly, taking her arm once more and moving on down the stairs.

April felt like singing. He would keep his word. Tomorrow . . . tomorrow . . . over and over again she sang the precious word silently, ebullient for the first time in longer than she could remember. She was going home!

The raw dark night was lit only by streetlights and an occasional zigzag of white lightning stabbing the black sky. The rain had turned to sleet, and the air seemed to become colder with each turn of the carriage wheels.

But April could not help being warmed by the sight of the White House, with all its impressive beauty. Even if it was the home of the Union President, there was still a stature about it, and she yielded up her respect with a silent apology to her homeland.

Rance descended from the carriage first, resplendent in a dark red waistcoat, the lapels heavily embroidered in gray satin. His trousers were black, matching his spit-polished boots. His dark hair curled slightly round his face, which had taken on a somber expression. Edward, too, was elegantly dressed. Trella faced the White House with sparkling eyes. She looked quite elegant in a dark gray dress, chosen by Rance for its conservative appearance. Still, it looked glamorous beside April's drab black bombazine.

A Negro in a red velvet coat and black satin knee-length trousers appeared from the gate to lead their horses and carriage away. They moved as quickly as possible through the sleet, hurrying up the stairs, where the door opened instantly.

A silver-haired Negro in austere black velvet bade them enter. He led them into a plush parlor, filled with heavy, ornate furniture of brocades, velvets, and leathers. April stared about, enthralled by the magnificent silver and crystal pieces on display, the oil paintings of past presidents which hung on the high-ceilinged walls. "Magnificent," she breathed. "Simply magnificent."

A young white woman appeared, wearing a long dress of pale blue cotton, a huge white apron, and a ruffled white cap perched on her dark auburn hair, which was pulled back in an austere bun. April noted that she, like all women, looked at Rance with admiration. She obviously found him attractive. Well, April reflected matter-of-factly, so do I. Another time . . . other circumstances . . . who knows what might have developed between us? But it was too late to contemplate that now. *Tomorrow—tomorrow— tomorrow,* her heart sang. *I will be free!*

"Mrs. Lincoln will be down shortly." The girl smiled pleasantly as she extended a tray filled with crystal glasses of liqueurs and wine. "There are appetizers on the sideboard. Please help yourselves."

Rance asked whether there would be other guests. When she said no, he asked if the President would be dining with them. She informed him that Mr. Lincoln was meeting with members of his cabinet at an undisclosed place and that Mrs. Lincoln would offer his regrets to them.

He exchanged looks with Edward, and as soon as the maid was out of the room, they stepped close together and spoke in hushed tones. "Wherever he is, that's where any important information will be," Edward said, disappointed.

Rance shook his head. "Not necessarily. There are

bound to be personal records here. A diary, perhaps. Could be to our advantage that he isn't around. With no other guests and only Mrs. Lincoln and the servants here, we should have more freedom to move around. I'm sure there are guards, but we'll watch our step."

April had a glass of wine, then a second, and a third, and just as Rance began to notice and frown, Mrs. Lincoln made her entrance.

She was small, fat to the point of dumpiness in a plain black dress. Her mouth was turned down at the corners, and her fleshy face wore a very unhappy expression. April thought her sweet and gentle, and her heart went out to her. The woman's grief was mirrored in her eyes.

When she introduced herself to April, she clasped her hands and gazed longingly up at her as though searching for something. The touch of a smile was on her lips, but it faded quickly and was replaced by the grimace of misery. "I am so happy you could come, my dear." Her voice was gentle, soft. "When Lizzie told me about your vibrations, a calling from the other side, I knew it meant Willie was trying to get through."

April swallowed hard, remembering everything Rance had told her. "Yes, I'm sure that's what it is, Mrs. Lincoln. I can feel an even stronger presence here, in this house. I am confident that Willie will reach through from the great beyond and speak to us tonight."

She squeezed April's hands. "Oh, I do hope so. It's been awhile now since any of the mediums I've had here could reach him. I think perhaps he did not feel comfortable with them. You're such a pretty young thing. I think Willie would have liked you, trusted you."

April bit her lip and turned away. She felt positively blasphemous to be talking this way. Why had she let Rance talk her into this? She was not even sure she could go through with it. Rance realized her state of mind and stepped forward before Mrs. Lincoln had time to notice her mood.

"We are sorry your husband can't be with us tonight," he said quickly. "I hold him in such high esteem. It would have been an honor to meet him personally."

That brief, fluttery smile touched her lips once again. "Thank you for saying so. Unfortunately, the war news is not good. It breaks my heart to see so much suffering on both sides, and it causes my husband even more distress. He has such a burden of responsibility on his shoulders." She glanced around anxiously. "Well, now. Shall we go into the dining room? I want us to enjoy good food and good fellowship, but I must admit to being in a hurry to get on with our seance. I imagine Willie is growing impatient, also." She looked at April, who nodded nervously.

The long mahogany table was covered with a delicate lace cloth. There were place settings for five. The china was fine bone, edged in gold. Ornate silver sparkled in the candlelight.

They took their seats, and a waiter helped the maid bring in huge platters of steak and onions, pheasant, and quail. There was also blancmange, pâte de foie gras, fruits, and a variety of rolls and crackers.

Only Trella appeared to have an appetite. She heaped her plate, while Edward glowered at her. Mrs. Lincoln was having only fruit. Rance and Edward had steaks.

"How long have you felt this calling?" Mrs. Lincoln inquired, eyes shining.

April repeated what Rance had instructed her to say. "Since I was a child. My grandfather had died, and he came to me one night in a dream. I felt such comfort that I began to call to him whenever I was lonely or had a problem. He always came and spoke to me. He still does."

"Oh, my, that must bring you such solace. I wish I had the gift! To think of calling Willie whenever I wanted to! It would be wonderful."

"The next best thing will be April reaching him." Rance reached to pat her chubby hand. "She has helped so many others."

April asked how many seances had been successful in calling Willie from the other side. "I can't be sure," Mrs. Lincoln replied quietly. "There have been charlatans, you know. That is to be expected, I suppose. But I like to think they only meant to help a grieving mother."

She shook her head sadly. "Much sadness comes from the criticism. My husband tries to shield me, but Lizzie tells me about it. My half-sister, Emilie Todd Helm, visits here often." She paused to take more fruit, then reached for a roll and slathered it with whipped butter before con-

tinuing. "I love her dearly, but it bothers me that she is so
harsh in her criticism. She complains to my husband, tries
to talk him into stopping the seances. If only she would
believe, then she would be comforted also. She lost her
husband not long ago. He fought for the Confederacy, a
brigadier general, Ben Helm. He was thirty-two years old
when he was killed in battle at a place called Chicka-
mauga."

She sipped from a crystal water glass, then said, "Emilie
is eighteen years younger than I. Perhaps she can bear up
better. I don't know. I do wish she would give Ben a
chance to speak to her. But she refuses to 'consort,' as she
calls it, with spiritualists."

She told them of her oldest son, Robert, and how he,
too, resisted any attempts to include him in seances. "He's
nineteen, a student at Harvard. He was so fond of Willie.
If only he would let Willie speak to him, they would both
feel better."

April saw Trella shudder. Smoothly, Rance got to his
feet and, with a polite nod to Mrs. Lincoln, told her how
much he had enjoyed the fine dinner. "Will you excuse Mr.
Clark and me while we have an after-dinner brandy and a
cigar in your lovely parlor? April always likes a few moments to relax after eating, in preparation for her seance."

"Yes, that would be nice." Edward stood also. "Rance,
did you see those lovely oils in the hallway? I want to see
them closer."

"Please feel free to look all you wish," Mrs. Lincoln
offered graciously. "I like to feel that the White House
belongs to all the people."

April held her wineglass out for a refill. There was a
warm buzzing coursing through her trembling body, and
she felt a bit light-headed. She could not remember ever
drinking so much wine at one time, but she liked the glow,
the feeling of confidence that seemed to be taking over.

She listened politely as Mrs. Lincoln told of other seances, other communications with her dead son, and all the
while, April wondered what Rance and Edward were
doing. Preparations would have to be made for the seance,
she worried, but they had disappeared.

"Do you feel ready now?" Mrs. Lincoln asked, touching
her arm.

April jumped, startled. She had not been listening at all. "No," she said quickly, hoping she had not spoken too sharply, for the woman was frowning. "You and Trella talk now, please. I want a moment to myself . . . to meditate, to prepare myself. There has to be the proper mood."

She got up and hurried from the dining room, not giving her hostess time to protest. The gas jets' soft, hissing sounds were the only sounds she could discern. Oh, dear, she thought, the house was so large, much larger than Pinehurst. Where had Rance and Edward gone? What would the servants think if they saw them prowling about where they had no business? Didn't they realize that they could all wind up in jail as spies?

She made her way down a narrow corridor and saw darkened stairs leading upward. She moved up them cautiously, hoping all the while that Trella would be able to keep Mrs. Lincoln occupied long enough for her to find them and tell them what a dangerous thing they were doing.

The second-floor was too dark to see where she was going. She had to grope her way along, resisting the overwhelming desire to call out to Rance. She dared not make a sound. Damn him, she thought furiously, where was he? Why was he taking such a chance?

Suddenly, she froze. Someone was coming down the hall, briskly. Pressing herself against the wall, she held her breath. Whoever it was was moving along as though he knew his way, even in the dark. A guard! It had to be a guard!

He was almost to where she waited, not daring to breathe. A few more steps, and he would pass. She would be safe. She willed him to move faster.

He was there, in front of her, had not broken his stride, had not seen her. She was safe.

And then it happened.

Something shot out of the blackness to squeeze her throat tightly, pressing her against the wall. She tried to scream, but the sounds were cut off by the ever-tightening force that held her. She could not breathe, could not move. The hold was paralyzing. She felt herself slipping away, knees buckling, losing consciousness. He was moving closer, pressing against her.

"Damn it, April!"

She felt herself being released. Strong arms held her up, pulling her body tight against his.

"I could have killed you," Rance hissed.

"You . . . you almost did," she whispered hoarsely, painfully, gasping for breath.

"I thought you were one of the servants, just waiting to sound the alarm. I couldn't take any chances. Not now. We're in too deep. What in the hell are you doing up here, anyway?"

"Looking for you. You were gone so long. I got worried. I told her I needed time to meditate." Her fingers touched her throat gingerly, and she winced.

He chuckled softly, suggestively. "Only you could feel so desirable in a bombazine mourning dress. Now get back downstairs and start setting things up the way I told you for the seance. Edward and I will be along in a few minutes."

She turned to leave, then saw the flicker of a light coming from a room nearby. "Who's that?" she asked, frightened once again.

"Edward. He's found the President's bedroom, and he's rummaging through his personal desk. Now go on, April. Get out of here. You almost ruined everything."

She hurried downstairs and entered the dining room just as Mrs. Lincoln and Trella were getting up. "Oh, there you are," Trella said nervously. "Mrs. Lincoln was just about to have the servants look for you."

"Yes, it's easy to get lost in this big house when you don't know your way around, my dear," Mrs. Lincoln said sweetly. "Especially when it's dark. Whenever we're having a seance, I keep down the light as much as possible throughout the evening. I want to set a welcome atmosphere for the spirits as early as I can."

"A . . . a very good idea," April stammered, frightened at having almost been discovered upstairs. "I think it's time to begin. I feel an urgency. It's this house, the vibrations—" She pretended to sway, which was not hard to do after all the wine she had drunk and the near-disaster of only moments ago.

"Yes, yes, of course." Mrs. Lincoln appeared flushed with excitement as she hurried to pull the bellcord. The same maid appeared and was instructed to make the parlor ready. "And get Lizzie. She was going to wait in the kitchen and pray for April."

April looked at Trella, saw the sick, unsure expression on her face. No time for that now, she felt like screaming. As Rance said, we're in too deep. There can be no slipups, no turning back.

Her head snapped up, new fingers of fear clutching her as Mrs. Lincoln asked, "Where is your husband, dear? And your friend, Mr. Clark? I do hope they haven't gotten lost. I'll have one of the servants go and look for them. I believe the guards are all outside, and—"

She reached for the bellcord once more, and April all but shouted, "No!" She took a breath, lowered her voice, and forced a smile. "There's no need. I saw them a moment ago. On the back terrace. Watching the storm. Please, let's move along. They will be here by the time we're ready to begin."

As they entered the parlor, Mrs. Lincoln moved ahead, and Trella stepped close to whisper in April's ear, "We hadn't planned on the nigra being here. Rance isn't going to like it."

The wine was subduing her own anxiety, and April murmured, "Rance will improvise. He has that way about him. Now stop looking so frightened. You're going to give us away."

She and Trella stood to the side as Lizzie entered and, with the help of the young maid, arranged chairs in a circle around a table in the middle of the room. Mrs. Lincoln pulled the thick velvet drapes across the windows.

"Darling."

April turned slightly and Rance rushed across the room to put his arms about her. "Darling, do you feel ready? Do you feel the calling?" he asked, a deeply concerned look on his face. Behind him, Edward appeared equally concerned.

"Yes," she lifted her chin confidently, wishing she had one more glass of wine. But it was now or never. "Let us begin."

With thudding heart, April directed everyone to a seat. Rance had also told her there would be no argument here, for it was always the medium's prerogative to designate seating. She placed him on her right, with Edward next to him, and then Trella, Lizzie, and, finally, Mrs. Lincoln on her left. They were in a tight circle.

"The lights," April whispered, closing her eyes and holding her head tilted backward. "We are ready."

The young maid extinguished the gas jets. They were suddenly consumed by total darkness. There was the sound of a door opening and closing as the maid left them.

Too late to back out now, April thought dizzily, fighting the nausea rising to her throat.

Taking a deep breath, April began the seance.

❧ Chapter Nineteen ❧

APRIL did not know what to expect. Rance had wanted it that way. He had instructed her in the basics of what she should say and do, but that was all. He wanted her just as awe-stricken as Mrs. Lincoln would be, as though she could not believe her own "powers." That way, the sitting would be quite believable.

Actually she felt rather foolish once the room was plunged into darkness. She held Rance's hand in her right, Mrs. Lincoln's in her left, wondering if they could feel the cold clamminess of her hands. They were all waiting for her to begin, and suddenly she realized that she could not utter a word.

It was too much. She could not go through with it. Dear God, she prayed frantically, what have I gotten myself into? She felt the firm squeeze of Rance's hand against her own, silently coaxing her. When still she did not speak, he nudged her with his elbow. Mrs. Lincoln and Lizzie were making small movements, their breathing harsh and raspy.

She urged the words upward through her ever-tightening throat, which was still sore from Rance's death-grip of only a short while ago. "We are here to speak to Willie. . . ." she whispered in the trembly, eerie voice that Rance had made her rehearse until it was believable. "We are gathered here, because Willie has sent signs that he is restless . . . he wants to speak to his mother."

She turned her head slightly to her left. "Speak to your son," she whispered sternly.

"Willie . . . darling . . ." The voice in the darkness cracked with emotion. "It's me, your mother. Speak to me, darling. Let me know that you are all right."

"Willie, that was your mother," April rushed on, making her tone excited now. "Did you hear your mother? Do you hear me? You have let me know you wanted to speak through me. We are here. We are waiting. If you are among us, then let your presence be known."

"Oh, my God!" Trella screamed to pierce the tense silence.

April had been sitting with her eyes closed, but at the sound, her lids flashed open, and a small cry escaped her as she saw the shining white object bobbing through the air above the table. What was it? She struggled to see. Mrs. Lincoln began to moan softly.

"That's his little bugle," Lizzie cried. "The li'l bugle his daddy had made out of silver, 'cause he wanted to be a bugle boy—"

"Do not break the chain!" April snapped tersely, feeling her grip on Mrs. Lincoln's hand slacken. The woman was pulling away, eyes riveted to the eerily glowing silver bugle that continued to dance above them. Then, just as quickly as it had appeared, it was gone. But the sound of its thinly pitched tone began to echo around them.

"He's playing. I hear him playing."

"Lizzie, please," Mrs. Lincoln whispered.

Suddenly the window clattered open, and a gust of icy wind and rain hit them full force at the same time the bugle sounded louder. The table began to rattle, and April realized it was rising.

"Oh, my God!" This time Trella's cry was more subdued.

Something whooshed by, brushed April's ear. It whooshed by again, and Lizzie screamed. "He touched me. I felt his touch. Praise the Lord, Miz Lincoln, he's here! Your boy is here in this room with us. I feel it stronger than ever before."

Softly, at first, the drumbeats began, rhythmically, over and over, filling the room with a sense of frenzy, wildness. Something bright and shiny flew across the room and hovered momentarily above the table before disappearing completely.

April did not know if the chill that was inching its way to her bones was from the open window or from fear. Rance was still holding her hand. How had he caused all this? It had to be a fake—had to be. Yet it seemed so real. It was becoming harder and harder to concentrate with the sounds of the bugle and the drum.

She began once more. "Willie is speaking to me." She strained to make her voice high-pitched. "Willie wants us to know he is happy. He describes his home as very beautiful, many stars, much gold. He says he is much happier than he ever was in this life."

"Oh, I want him to be happy," Mrs. Lincoln cried, then raised her voice. "Willie, darling, I want you to be happy. I do. I do."

"He says . . ." April paused for effect. "He says he is with Alex."

"Alex! My half-brother!" Mrs. Lincoln started to draw her hand away, but April held tightly. "Oh, praise the Lord. Alexander is my half-brother. He died fighting for the South . . . at Baton Rouge . . . not long ago. Oh, he always thought so much of Willie. They're together." She began to sob.

April squeezed her eyes shut, not wanting to see any more objects, hating herself for what she was doing. Charlatan! Liar! she accused herself. She was not charging a fee, and perhaps the seance would ease the poor woman's grief. But the guilt remained.

She saw a gray mist swimming before her. Strange, she thought vaguely, my eyes are closed, yet I see this mist. Slowly, ever so slowly, the mist became a cloud, and then the cloud was parting. She could see her father, so clearly, and, oh, dear God, no! She shook her head from side to side, moaning, felt Rance pressing harder on her hand, hurting her, but she could not open her eyes, could not speak. She saw him so clearly . . . lying in his coffin. The lid was being closed, and then he was being carried through those wrought iron gates with the scrolled "J." He was placed next to her mother. And it was so real she felt as though she could reach out and touch the rough wood of the casket, smell the musky odor of the mausoleum.

There were no flowers. No friends. No weeping relatives. Only Vanessa standing there, beside the casket, not even wearing a dress of mourning but a bright red ballgown. And there was Zeke, and he was smiling, showing the ugly yellow teeth she loathed.

It *was* real. She was there. She could see it. The steady beating of the drum began to match the beating of her heart. Real . . . real. Poppa in his coffin. "No!" She screamed suddenly. "No, Poppa, no!"

"April, stop it." She had dropped Rance's hand to cover her face and try to shut out the horrible scene, and he was reaching for her, shaking her.

"No—no—no," she moaned over and over, allowing him to press her face against his strong chest to muffle her cries of agony.

"Everyone sit right where you are. Don't move. I think she went too deeply into her trance. We're going to have to sit here until she returns to us. Don't anyone make a sound, please." He held her tighter, moving his lips to press against her ear and murmur, too softly for anyone else to hear, "It's all right. You can stop now. It's over."

But she could not stop, and after several moments, Rance said, "We can have light now. I think she needs some brandy."

Dimly, April was aware that the window was again closed. Cold air and sleet were no longer blowing across them. She continued to cling to Rance, even as the room was lit again. It was Lizzie who handed her a glass of brandy. April drank gratefully.

Mrs. Lincoln touched her shoulder gently and asked, "Are you all right now, dear? You gave us such a fright. I have never seen a medium travel so far from us."

April managed to nod, but her mind was on the vision. She closed her eyes, then opened them. It was gone. Perhaps, she told herself with relief, she had fallen asleep. She had dreamed of her father. Yes, that was it. She was sure of it. She had been thinking of morning, when she would be free to find her way back to him.

But why had she envisioned him in his coffin? Perhaps it was her instincts telling her to hurry home, there was no time to spare. He needed her.

"I would like to leave now," she looked at Rance, saw the concern in his eyes. "I don't feel well."

Lizzie, wide-eyed and quite shaken, backed toward the

door. "I'll get your wraps. I'll only be a moment. She does look like she could use some rest."

Mrs. Lincoln was saying something about hoping she could come back soon. She was so satisfied, she assured Rance, and happy to hear that Willie was with her half-brother. Perhaps next time, Rance responded politely, they might speak with Willie longer.

Just get me out of here, April implored him with her eyes. Take me out of here before I break down and let her know it was all a sham. I can't hurt her that way. Please, I don't want to hurt the woman.

Once they were in the carriage, Trella was unable to contain herself. "Rance, how did all those things happen? Oh, Lordy, don't tell me they were real. I was so scared, and I knew you and Edward never left the table."

"I'll explain, if you'll calm down," Rance laughed. "We had help. We do have some allies in Washington, you know. The window was forced open from outside. That's where the drumbeats and the bugle were being played. As for the bugle appearing to float from the air, Edward and I ran a string up near the ceiling when we first left the dining room, before we started prowling around."

"And the reason he insisted everyone remain calm at the end," Edward interjected, "was so I could grope about and remove all the strings that pulled all the objects."

She gasped. "Oh, my stars! It seemed so real. You sure had me fooled. I was so scared. But what about the table rising?"

Edward looked smug. "Rance and I dropped the hands that were holding you and April, and we lifted it from the floor. I think we did pretty good."

Trella clapped her hands together in childlike glee, then leaned across Edward to ask of Rance, "But did you find anything of importance?"

The carriage passed beneath a streetlight, the gas flame giving off an eerie glow that illuminated the grim expression on his face. In a dread tone, he murmured, "Yes, we did. I am afraid we are going to be too late to be of any help, though. Tomorrow, we leave Washington. I have to get beyond enemy lines so I can send a message."

"We need to leave, anyway," he continued, looking at

Edward as though conveying secrets. "There are other things to be done now."

Trella continued to bubble happily about the success of the seance, while everyone else fell silent, engrossed in private thoughts.

Arriving at the hotel, Edward and Trella went straight to Edward's room. April retired to her own without looking at Rance, but once inside, she was possessed by a strange feeling which she could not understand. She was free to go tomorrow morning, but nothing had been said tonight about any arrangements. Surely, he would not leave her destitute. They had a bargain, and she had kept her end.

Finally, she realized that she would have to talk to Rance. That, she told herself as she opened her door and left the room, was the only reason she wanted to see him.

She rapped softly on his door and did not have long to wait before he called, "Come in, April. It's not locked."

So, she thought, he had been expecting her. She turned the knob and stepped into faint darkness, the only light coming from the window and the gas lights beyond it. The storm had abated, and there was only silence to surround.

She took a deep breath and began, "I want to talk to you about how I am to leave tomorrow. I will need funds, but I will pay you back one day, I promise."

He was beside her so quickly that she did not see his movements. "That's not the reason you came to me tonight, and you know it!" His lips claimed hers, hard, smoldering. She stiffened in his embrace, pressed her hands against his chest and tried to pull away, but he held her tightly.

The desire she could not fight began to take hold. It began as a warm moisture in her loins, then spread upward to caress her insides. Her lips became soft, yielding, and she received his tongue.

In one easy movement, he lifted and carried her across the room, laying her on his bed. He removed her clothing quickly and then stripped off his own clothes.

His fingers danced upon her body, caressing, teasing, making her writhe and moan. "Take me," she whispered wantonly. "Oh, Rance, please, please take me."

"Show me!" he commanded gruffly. "Show me what you want me to do."

He rolled over on his back, grinning his smile. She shook her head in shy confusion.

He grasped her waist and pulled her over and up on top of him, spreading her thighs so that she was straddling him. He held her just above him and then, slowly, maneuvered her onto the probing shaft.

"Ride me," he commanded. "Ride me as you would your horse. I'll move with you. All the way."

At first, she moved slowly, still shy, but as the tingling sensations began to spread into spasms of delight, she undulated her hips to gyrate faster, harder. His fingers slid from her waist to her breasts, caressing, moving to pinch her nipples. She was free to set the pace, to move with him, against him, around him. And when she felt herself about to explode with the ultimate joy, he sensed it and quickly threw her over and onto her back. Then he took her wildly as though she were a mare daring to be tamed.

But tame her he did, until she was whimpering beneath him with inexpressible rapture. She clung to him tightly for a very long time, not wanting it to end.

Finally he rolled away but held her in his arms, her head tucked against his shoulder.

"Stay with me," he whispered, as the wind through the night. "Stay with me, April, and be my woman."

She blinked. "Are you," she began in wonder, "asking me—?"

"To be my woman," he interjected. "Nothing more, but nothing less. There's a war on, April. I've a job to do. I'll keep you safe, but I want you with me."

"But . . . but I have something to do, also, and we agreed. . . ." She felt her brain whirling wildly. It had all been settled! She would leave in the morning, return to Alabama, and try to help her father. Rance had promised to set her free. Yet now he was asking, *not telling her*, to stay with him. "I just don't understand."

He turned on his side, staring down at her face which was bathed in the pale light from the window. He brushed back golden tendrils of hair, kissed the tip of her nose. "I want you, April. I need you. That's all I can honestly tell you right now. When the war is over, we'll see what happens."

"But Vanessa—"

He sighed, exasperated. "April, you can't handle her by yourself, and with the war, nobody else is going to have time to help you. Wake up. If you go back there and get yourself in trouble, as much as I care for you, I won't be able to do anything about it. I've got a job to do for the South."

She nodded. As desperately as she wanted to go home, she could see the wisdom of his words. Hesitantly, she asked the question that was burning in her mind. "But will you help me when the war is over? Would you return with me then?"

He rolled once more to his back, staring upward into the darkness. "I don't like to make promises unless I know I can keep them. Like I said, April, I want you, and I need you, and if everything works out for us, then, yes, I probably will. More than that, I just can't promise."

"Then that has to be enough."

He was silent for a moment, then asked softly, "Are you sure?"

"I think so. I've hated you, Rance, you know that, but all the time I was hating you, a part of me was struggling against that, crying out that there was something between us . . . some kind of caring. I kept saying, 'another time, another place, and perhaps it would have been right for us,' but the part of me that hated overshadowed everything else."

"There were times that I didn't like you," he admitted, his voice softly amused. "You can be quite a handful, April, but I considered you a challenge, like a wild pony. Just when you think you've got him broke, he throws you. I wonder if I would ever feel in control of you."

She turned to trail her fingertips through the thick mat of hair on his chest. "You don't want to control me. Not really. If I were all sweetly obliging, then you wouldn't want me."

"Perhaps." He caught her hand, raised her fingertips to his lips, and kissed them. "One day, we'll find out."

Quickly, roughly, he gathered her in his arms and pressed his mouth upon hers. The kiss was long, stirring. He laughed softly as he pulled away. "We've got a hard day tomorrow. We're leaving, heading south. We need to get some sleep."

"You want me to sleep with you?" She pretended to be horrified. "What will Trella think?"

He muttered some obscenity as he reached to pull the folded blanket from the foot of the bed to spread over their naked bodies. She cuddled against him, a wave of peace settling over her. At last, she had given in to the secret cries of her heart.

The first waves of sleep were rocking her gently, and she had to struggle awake when the knocking began. Rance called out gruffly, "Yes? Who's there."

"Clark. I need to talk to you."

Rance uttered an oath, then called, "Can't it wait until tomorrow morning?"

"No," Edward replied firmly. "I need to talk to you now."

"Oh, damn!" Rance threw back the blanket and sighed, "Wrap yourself up in the blanket and go back to your room. Trella will be wondering where you are, and Edward obviously has some business to discuss. No telling when I'll get to bed now."

She nodded, disappointed. It had felt so wonderful to fall asleep in his strong arms. She pulled the blanket from the bed and wrapped it about her tightly, then opened the door, surprising Edward. Ducking her head with embarrassment, she whispered a good night and moved quickly down the hall. Behind her, she heard the door close, the lock snap.

She was almost to her room when she remembered the clothes she had left behind. They would have to be packed. She turned around and padded back to the door. She was just about to knock when her hand froze at the mention of her name.

"I thought she was leaving." That was Edward's voice. "All of a sudden, things look pretty cozy. What's going on?"

She leaned closer to hear Rance say in a flat tone, "Nothing to concern you. April wants to stay with me, that's all."

There was the sound of an exaggerated sigh, then, "What's the matter? Are you afraid if you let her go, you might find out later that you want her and then it'll be too late?"

"Something like that," came Rance's comment. "Look, Clark, it's not going to hurt anything having her along. You've got Trella. We look like two nice married couples. You and me alone look suspicious. Folks will start wondering why we aren't in uniform. With the women, we're more easily accepted as businessmen."

There was a long period of silence. April could not move. Rance made their union sound like a business arrangement.

She stood frozen, listening again. "There was a paper in the President's desk which gave the location of a nearby federal cavalry unit. We can round up our men and shouldn't have any trouble stealing them," Rance was saying. "Then we change the cavalry brand to artillery and sell the Yankees their own horses. They'll bring top price."

"Quite a nice profit," Edward agreed. "Then we take the money and go to Mexico and get prime stock for our Rebel cavalry. A nice deal all the way around."

April clamped her teeth together. So! Rance was stealing from the Yankees, then selling stolen horses right back to them, using the money to buy horses for the Confederacy and selling to them. He made it sound so noble, wanting to supply the South's cavalry with the best possible horses, when all the while he was making a tidy profit on stolen stock! Despicable! Oh, how she ached to scream it all out so that everyone in the hotel would know.

His words came flooding back and a new realization slapped her full in the face. "I want you. I need you. I want you to be my woman." He had not said "I love you. I want you to be my wife." Damn his charm! Damn his handsome face! Damn his wonderful body!

And damn me most of all, she thought, a smothering wave flowing over her. Damn me for being so weak as to even think about falling in love with a scheming bastard like Rance Taggart.

No more!

She whirled around and stalked down the hall.

No more! I'm going home. No matter what awaits me there, I'm going home.

And a little voice inside whispered that she was not running only from a man she considered a traitor—she

was running from the man who threatened to conquer her
heart, her soul, her whole being.

She could not let that happen.

Edward got up and went to pour them another glass of
whiskey, then returned to sit on the edge of the bed. Twirling his drink around in his hand, he watched the lantern's
glow catch the amber liquid and create dark, mysterious
dancing shadows. "Have you ever stopped to think how
much money you'd be making off this stinking war if you
charged the Confederacy for the cavalry horses?" he asked
thoughtfully, lifting his gaze to stare at Rance.

"Yeah," came his friend's quiet answer. "I have to admit
I have. It'd mount up to a tidy sum. A man could get rich
doing what I'm doing." He drew on his cheroot, watched
the smoke spiraling upwards.

"Others are becoming profiteers. Why not you?"

Rance gave him a sharp look. "I happen to believe in the
Confederacy. And the only reason I'm not in gray and
toting a gun and killing Yankees is because I feel I'm doing
the South a greater service by providing the Confederacy
with good horses."

He brought his feet down from where they had been
propped on the table, the heels hitting the wooden floor
loudly. "I'm also hurting the North by stealing from them
and then selling what I steal right back to them."

"Hell, don't get mad with me. I feel the same way. I just
wondered if you ever thought about the way you could be
making money."

Rance was quiet for a moment, then murmured, "I think
of a lot of things."

"Right now, I'll bet you're thinking about April and
wondering if you're doing the right thing in bringing her
along. I thought she was hell-bent to get back to Alabama.
How come she wants to stay?"

"I asked her to. She agreed. I guess she feels the same as
I do, which is *not* knowing what she feels. There's something between us that makes her want to find out which
way we're headed. If she goes home now, we'll never
know."

Edward gulped down his drink and stood. "I reckon I'd
better get to bed now. One more question?"

"You're pushing your luck, Clark. I don't like anybody nosing in my business."

"Sorry. But I have to ask this. Do you love April?"

Rance stared at him, eyes narrowing. Finally, he said flatly, "I can't say as I do. And I can't say as I don't. I guess we'll just have to wait and see."

"That doesn't make sense."

"Makes sense to me. That's the only person who's supposed to understand. Do you follow me?"

"Yeah," Edward laughed shortly and set his glass down before walking to the door. "It's your way of saying I've stuck my nose in your business enough for one night."

"Exactly."

"See you in the morning." He gave a snappy salute and walked out, grinning.

Rance poured himself another drink and went to stand at the window and stare out at the night. The storm had long ago abated, and a half moon had risen to cast a silvery sheen upon the sleeping city. A beautiful night. He wished April were still here. It had felt good to wrap his arms about her and feel her body snuggled next to him.

He thought about waking her and asking her to come back to his bed but decided against it. She needed to sleep. The White House activities had been exhausting for her. Let her rest. Tomorrow was only the beginning of many days together, with long nights of passion to follow.

With a confident smile on his lips, he went to his bed and lay down. One more night sleeping alone could be endured. All he had to do was think about what lay ahead with her in his arms.

It was good, he thought sleepily, that she had agreed to stay.

Because he had never intended to let her go, anyway.

❧ Chapter Twenty ❧

APRIL could make out Trella in the other bed. She stood inside, her back pressed against the closed door, until she could hear the even breathing that told her the girl was sleeping soundly. Then she walked over and sat on her own bed, commanding her screaming brain to calm down, to think, to plan.

There could be no mistake this time. When Rance discovered her missing, he would search for her. There was enough time between now and dawn that she should be able to put much distance between them. Washington was a busy place, with many roads out. He would not know which she had taken, and that was in her favor. He would surmise that she was heading for Alabama, but that was a long way off, and he was caught up in his traitorous war activities. He might not have time to go after her.

And, she thought with a triumphant smile, this time she would be smart. No barging in at Pinehurst. She would not even prowl about to see what was going on. No, this time she would go into Montgomery and seek help there. If the authorities did not care enough to give her aid, then she would try again to get in touch with Uncle James. And maybe a minister would help—surely there would be *some-one* to sympathize with her plight.

She would disguise herself. If Rance were angry enough to go after her, he would not have even the slightest chance of finding her, because she would be in disguise. The confidence surging through her made her smile. There was no need to stay a moment longer, no need to pack. She wanted nothing to remind her of this time with Rance.

She quickly donned a plain dress and then opened the door quietly and stepped into the hall. Glancing about, she moved quickly to the stairs and downward. To her left, in the main lobby, she could see a few people milling about. She would not take a chance on seeing anyone who might know her, remember her. It was far better to be unseen.

She turned to the right and made her way down the narrow, shadowy hallway past the kitchen, past the storage rooms, into the alley directly behind the hotel.

She stepped out into pitch darkness, bumped into a garbage barrel and sent an annoyed cat screaming to distant places.

She stiffened, commanded herself to calm down. A long night lay ahead, and excitement could cause mistakes. Perhaps the most formidable task would be just getting out of Yankee Washington. Women did not move about at night unescorted unless they were prostitutes. So, while she needed to cover as much distance as possible before morning, she knew she had to move carefully.

Pressing her back against the walls, she slowly ventured a few steps at a time, shuffling her feet along to feel her way and make sure no obstacle lay ahead. If she touched something, she was forced to move out a little and get around it, then press back into the shadows once again.

The silence was erupted by a woman's shrill, drunken laughter. Just ahead, she saw her—standing in the doorway of a dilapidated building and holding a lantern above her head as she bade her customer good night. "You're too good, soldier. I swear—I'll be sore for a week. I ought to be paying you instead o' the other way around."

"Well, that can be arranged," a man's voice slurred. "But I know you're only joshin' me, girl. You got others a'waitin'."

"Got to make a living. I'd rather lie with you all night. My, my, you are a lover. Now you come back and see me soon."

The door closed. April could not tell which way the soldier had gone. She held her breath and pressed herself as close against the building as possible. But where had he gone? She cursed him for the valuable time she was losing.

Then she heard the sound of a bottle smashing against the ground, followed by a loud oath. The door opened again, quickly, and the lantern the woman held illuminated the body of the soldier crumpled against the opposite wall in the alley.

"Well, you damn drunk, you can just spend the night there for all I care!" the woman snapped, annoyed. The door slammed, and darkness engulfed April's world once again.

She breathed a sigh of relief. She'd had just enough of a glimpse of the drunken soldier to tell that he was out for the night. He would pose no threat to her. She began to move along once more.

She was almost opposite the spot where he had crumpled when the idea came to her. He wore a Yankee uniform! She was stripping out of her dress almost before she realized it, then fumbling in the dark to find him and began stripping off his clothes.

Removing his pants and shirt, she struggled into them, nose wrinkling at the odor of cheap booze and the faint reminder of what had just taken place between him and the woman. She hated putting on the soiled garments, but they would get her safely out of Washington. There was no other way.

She tucked her long blond hair up inside the man's cap. Then she struggled into his boots, though they were much too large and would slip and slide uncomfortably. She would have to endure them, for she could not walk in bare feet, or wear her own slippers.

The drunken soldier snorted now and then but made no effort to resist. She left him lying in long-handled underwear, and stuffed her own clothes into a garbage barrel, making sure she went far enough down the alley that no one would suspect a woman had taken the soldier's garments.

Leaving the alley several minutes later, she stayed on side roads, refraining from moving onto main thoroughfares where there would be people. When she felt she was far enough away from the hotel that Rance, should he awaken and discover her gone, would not know which direction she had taken, April ducked into a doorway to catch her breath and assess her plight. It was with some irony that she admitted to herself that, in the process of making sure she would not be followed, she had lost her way! She now had no idea where she was.

The sound of footsteps caused her to glance up. Three soldiers passed beneath a streetlamp. They clung together, lurching and bumping, and she heard one say, ". . . hell to pay. Late . . . real late . . ."

They moved on, slowly, most likely heading for their camp. She decided to follow at a discreet distance. Perhaps she would be able to find out where she was, at which side of the city, so she would know which direction to take.

She had difficulty keeping up, even though the drunken soldiers moved slowly. Now and then they would stop for someone to be sick, and she would search quickly for a doorway in which to hide. But they had reached the outskirts of the city, and there were few doorways. Panic began to well in her as she thought of turning back. She surely did not want to talk to any Yankee soldiers, for her disguise would certainly be discovered.

A halo of light appeared as they topped a hill. Ducking behind a tree trunk, April peered out over a large campground. Tents dotted the landscape like sleeping birds, wings ready to fly should danger descend. Here and there campfires sent gray smoke twirling into the night. A sentry walked his post silently, crossing to and fro in front of the gate.

She watched as the three drunken men slowed their pace. One stumbled, fell, and the sentry was instantly alert, pointing his rifle in their direction and yelling, "Halt! Who's there?" The trio quickly sang out their names, which company they belonged to, and the sentry called to someone nearby, "We got three drunks here."

In a matter of seconds, other uniformed men were moving through the gates, taking the tardy, drunken soldiers in tow. April continued to watch, not knowing what to do next. Then she heard the rumble of a wagon passing through the gate, a soldier holding the reins. After being told what all the excitement was about, he snapped, "Well, let's get this road cleared. I've got to get these supplies all the way to Maryland. We got wounded men down there—"

Maryland! South! The right direction. The words danced feverishly in April's mind. She watched excitedly as the man got down off the wagon and moved to where one of the inebriated soldiers lay on the ground, heaving and gagging. No one was looking, and the wagon had stopped just beside a row of trees extending from the grove in which she was hiding. April did not really know how far Maryland was from Alabama. All that mattered was that the wagon was headed south.

She made her way along carefully, finally sprinting for the wagon. At last, she sprang quickly upward, clamped the back of the wagon with trembling hands, hoisted herself up, and dropped over among the cartons and boxes piled inside. Something jabbed her side painfully, and she ground her teeth together to keep from crying out. The commotion over the drunken soldiers had covered her drop into the wagon, but even so, the driver glanced back. Had she shaken the wagon? Would he come back to investigate? April held her breath, her heart pounding.

No, the driver was again berating the sentry for blocking the path. The two men argued while April got her breath back, and then the driver—Ryerson, the sentry had called him—shook the reins. The wagon lurched to a start.

April was extremely uncomfortable, but she dared not move about for fear of making the cartons fall. She forced herself to lie perfectly still, her body exhausted from her ordeal, lack of sleep, and anxiety.

After a while, it felt as though a part of her were sleeping, while the rest of her body were wide awake and would never sleep again. She stared upward into the darkness, and soon the images began—dancing, fluttering, vague, and vivid. She saw her father's face, and Vanessa's, and then, brighter and clearer than these, Rance appeared, desire shining in his eyes. He held out his arms, and everything within her cried out his name. She was moving toward him, her own desire melting through her body until she felt as though she no longer possessed a solid form, but rather a wild, weaving spirit seeking only the pleasure he alone could give.

But then, just as she reached his arms, felt herself being crushed against his chest, felt his eyes burning into hers, breath sweet and hot upon her face, his lips parted in that arrogant grin . . . his smile told her that he alone would possess her always . . . while she was nothing more to him than the satiation of his lust. That was all she would be, for as long as she pleased him.

He kissed her, long, hard, hungrily, and she whimpered with the passion he awakened. Then he was chuckling softly, thrusting her away, turning his back. He moved away, and she cried after him, but there was no sound except his laughter. He no longer wanted her.

She was left empty, alone, and anguished.

The sound of her own soft whimpering awakened her with a start. She lifted her head and glanced about, realizing sleep had come despite the overwhelming stress of the night. Had Ryerson heard any sounds? She was instantly alert. But the only sounds were the plodding hooves of the horses. The wagon had not slowed. He had not heard.

Suddenly, the sigh of relief that was about to escape her parted lips froze and terror made her cringe. Voices. Then she realized that she was hearing the sound of more horses than just the two pulling the wagon. Slowly, carefully, she raised up to peer over the pile of boxes. Up front, she could see nothing except the man holding the horses' reins. Looking to the rear, she saw them—framed in the soft moonlight which filtered down through gentle clouds. Six soldiers riding two abreast directly behind them.

She sank back out of sight. Of course, there would be a patrol traveling with a supply wagon. How could she have been so stupid as to not think of an escort? Now that was going to make her situation much more difficult. She had planned to leap from the wagon at the first opportunity toward dawn. Now it would be impossible without being seen by the escorting soldiers. There was no choice left but to remain hidden for as long as possible. And there was always the chance that she would be lucky and a chance to get away would come.

Now all weariness had left her as though washed away by cascades of rain. Alert. She had to be alert. If they found her, they would probably force her to leave, not caring that she would be stranded along the side of the road. Each turn of the wagon's wheels put her that much closer to the Southland, where, she felt confident, help could be found much more easily than here in the enemy's land.

". . . bad. Just terrible. Lord, there's no telling how many men we lost."

She stiffened as the sound of the voice from behind the wagon drifted in.

"Yeah," came another, sounding deeply concerned. "But think how bad it would've been if those two soldiers hadn't found the orders. I'd hate to be in the Reb officer's boots that lost them orders. And it was lucky for us there was an officer in General McClellan's headquarters who could identify Lee's assistant adjutant general's handwriting, so McClellan would know the thing was genuine."

Yet another voice chimed in. "It sure threw things into McClellan's hands, finding out that Lee's army was split into three separate fragments. Them orders told all about how the advance was at Hagerstown, Maryland . . . not too far from the Pennsylvania border, I'm told. Then there was another division sent back to a place called Turner's Gap, to make sure none of our men got through. And then the rest of 'em was split into three wings that was going to try to surround and capture Harpers Ferry."

The man who had spoken first cried, "Damnit, if McClellan coulda moved faster, we'd have won that damn battle. As it was, he broke through that gap and Lee was caught with his forces scattered. He still fought all day and didn't give much ground."

"Well, for all purposes, it was our victory," another interjected. "Thursday, the second day, Lee took his worn-out army back to Virginia. I hear we got plenty of recognition for how we come out in that battle."

"It was the bloodiest day of fightin' since the war started," a sad voice declared. "I hear that even though it's said we won it, we lost more men than the Rebs."

April bit her lip to keep from crying, pressed her fingertips against her throbbing temples. So! The information Rance had found in President Lincoln's desk had been valuable, but it was too late. Rance had not been sure just when the battle would take place and had wanted to get word to General Lee that his orders had been found by Yankees. Now it was all over, and thousands of good men were dead on both sides. Who could say how it would all have turned out if Rance had been able to get there in time?

Dawn came, the rising sun a sickly yellow hue encased by a gray mist. Crisp winds, heavy with the odor of sulphur, rustled the leaves of the trees alongside the road.

April felt stiff, but she dared not move. She tensed as the wagon stopped. Would they look beneath the arching canopy, she worried, find her hiding there? She waited, but no one came, and it was not long before she could smell coffee, hear the sound of bacon sizzling. She was dizzy with hunger. How long since she had eaten? She could not remember. Last night at the White House did not count. Nerves had kept her from doing more than picking at the food.

Glancing about, she wondered whether some of the cartons might contain food rations, then realized from reading the labels that she was surrounded by medical supplies.

Out the front of the wagon, she could see the men gathered at the edge of a creek bank. Four of them. All in blue uniforms. They were eating bacon and drinking coffee, but they constantly scanned the woods around them.

"We ain't really safe around here, you know," one of them said worriedly. "I wish those other wagons and men had kept up, but I reckon they've stopped somewhere. We'd lose too much time to wait for them."

"Right," Ryerson agreed gruffly. "We got to hurry up and be on our way. I got my orders, and I ain't lettin' no dawdlers get my butt in trouble. These supplies are needed by soldiers that might die if we don't hurry up and get there. Finish your coffee and let's move out."

"You always were a stickler for following orders," someone laughed.

"Yeah, go on and make fun," came Ryerson's defensive response. "But you better hope we do hurry up and get among our own. I 'magine it won't be long before we'll be close enough that some straggling Rebs could be in these woods. I'll feel a whole lot safer when we reach McClellan's army."

McClellan's army. April felt the dread chill move down her spine. They were headed straight into the battlefield! How was she going to explain being a woman in a Yankee uniform? She had to escape. But as her eyes darted about, she knew she could do nothing but remain right where she was. There was absolutely no way out.

She saw them kicking dirt over the flames of their campfire, gathering their things and preparing to move out. Her stomach gave a sickening lurch from sheer hunger, and she felt weak, dizzy.

"Hey, did you hear that noise?"

Now the lurch in her stomach came from fear. She had not made a sound. At least, she didn't think she had. Pressing her back against pointy edged boxes, she tried to sink even further down into the wagon.

"Yeah, I heard it. Over there. By them bushes. Move slow. I got my gun on it."

Slowly, cautiously, she raised her head to peer out once more. They had not heard her—but what then? She saw two of the men moving toward thick brush. She licked her dry, parched lips. A wounded Yankee? Rebel? Now she could hear the soft whimpering noise.

"Well, I'll be damned. Hey, Ryerson, look at this." The two men stepped back, allowing the wagonmaster to step forward.

"A damn mutt!" He leaned over, and she could see him dragging a scruffy, bony dog who had once been white. The pitiful creature offered no resistance. She could see the slight, hopeful wag of his tail, as though he were clutching one last hope that, through a show of friendship, he might be treated kindly.

"Well." Ryerson dumped him on the ground. "Don't waste no gunfire. Just kick him in the head—"

"No!"

The scream exploded before she was even aware of it. She scrambled over the back of the wagon and ran to where the four men stood staring, openmouthed and wide-eyed. One of them had his foot poised in midair, about to stomp the dog. She fell to her knees and scooped the pathetic animal into her arms and pressed him against her bosom. Only then did the impact of what she had done hit her full force. Lifting fearful eyes, she looked at them each in turn, then whispered, "I . . . I couldn't let you kill him. He's helpless."

"Well, I will be dipped in horse manure!" one of the soldiers cried. "A danged woman. Wearing a federal uniform."

Ryerson snarled, "And hidin' out in the back of *my* wagon, too." He reached down to fasten viselike fingers about her arm and jerk her to her feet. "What's your name, girl? And how long you been hidin' back there in my wagon?"

The dog raised his face to lick her chin gratefully with his pink tongue. She hugged him protectively and stared defiantly at Ryerson. "My name is April Jennings. I was being held against my will in Washington, and I escaped. I'm on my way home—to Montgomery, Alabama. I'd be pleased if you'd give me a ride as far south as you're going."

The men exchanged incredulous looks, then broke into rounds of convulsive laughter. April tried to pull away from Ryerson's grip, but he held her tightly, guffawing along with the others. Infuriated, she kicked his shin, and he stopped laughing and gave her a vicious shove that sent her sprawling to the ground.

"Just who do you think you are, you little spitfire?" He reached down to rub his aching ankle. "And you can let go that damn mutt, 'cause when we finish bustin' his head, we're gonna show you what happens to Reb spies, even if they are women."

"I'm no spy, you fool!" She got up on her knees, then managed to stand and face him defiantly. "I told you that I'm on my way home. I was taken to Washington against my will and kept against my will. You have no right to disbelieve me. And you aren't going to hurt the dog. He's one of God's creatures, and you can't."

Ryerson took a menacing step forward, and she instinctively moved back, only to find herself pressed against a smirking soldier who stood ready to move whenever he was given the word.

"You get out of that uniform," Ryerson ordered. "What'd you do to the brave soldier who was wearin' that blue? Stick a knife in his ribs after you robbed him? We're gonna teach you a few things."

"I want her after you, Ryerson."

She looked toward the man who had spoken, gasped when she saw him fumbling with his pants.

April screamed and tried to back away, but the four men were forming a circle about her, crowding closer, closer.

A shot rang out, and April blinked in stunned horror as Ryerson fell to the ground.

More gunfire. In a matter of seconds, all four Yankees lay dead on the ground in a spreading pool of blood. Then her vision cleared, the cloud of horror parting as the men in gray stepped out of the bushes, their guns still smoking.

"You all right, ma'am?" A tall, thin man with a scrubby beard spoke as he came closer. When she did not speak, he said gently, "We're not gonna hurt you now, so don't you be afraid. I'm Captain George Shoreham, and this here is Adam Pauley, Jarvis Ingram, and Dudley Harper. They're in my company, and we're about all that's left of it since the battle at Antietam. We've been wanderin' around, trying to find some more Confederates, and it's a good thing we happened along here when we did."

She stared at each of them in turn and was overwhelmed by their protection. She managed a nervous smile. "Thank you for . . . for saving me and my friend here." She gestured toward the dog.

"Well, now, looks like you've got quite a friend in that little fellow." Captain Shoreham grinned and reached down to pat the dog's head.

"He's lucky you came along, that's for sure."

April smiled down at the ragged dog. "He's filthy and he's missed many meals, but he's a lucky dog. I guess that's what his name should be—Lucky."

The captain said quietly, "Now, you better tell us just what's going on."

She told them all she knew, that the wagon in which she had been hiding carried supplies for wounded Yankees, and that other Yankees were probably not too far behind.

The men exchanged concerned glances and then the Captain said, "I reckon we'd best be gettin' along then, miss. We'll take their wagon, as we're bound to run into some of our own wounded. You want to come on along with us, or have you got a home to go to? You don't sound like a Yankee woman to me."

She explained briefly and he nodded with sympathy but said, "We can't help you none there, miss. Not now. Best we can do is take you along with us and keep you from harm as best we can. I got a spare shirt and a pair of trousers you can wear. You better get out of that uniform."

She went behind the wagon to change clothes, and then was helped up onto the wagon to sit beside Jarvis Ingram, who took the reins. Captain Shoreham and the others dragged the bodies of Ryerson and the Yankee soldiers into the bushes, then kicked dirt over the blood in the road.

They left the main road, moving into the wilderness. Jarvis told April they should not be lost much longer. "We figure we're close to Major General Hill's division, or some of 'em anyway. And we can't be too far from Richmond."

Jarvis gave her a sideways glance and asked, "Are you all right, ma'am? You look kind of funny—"

"I haven't eaten in quite a while," she told him feebly, her fingers absently running through the thin white fur of the dog as he lay curled beside her. "That awful smell in the air, it makes me feel sick. What is it?"

"Sulfur mostly," he said grimly. "With a little bit of death mixed in. A lot of men have died around here in the past few days, miss. I can't do nothin' about that smell, but maybe I can help your hunger a bit." He reached in the pocket of his shirt and brought out a stale biscuit and gave it to her.

After breaking off a bit for the dog, she ate the biscuit quickly, then thanked him, apologizing for being so gluttonous. "I can't ever remember being so hungry."

"A lot of folks are going to know the pain of an empty belly before this war is over," he said quietly. "And ever'-body thought it'd be over before it really even got started. We're all gonna suffer, one way or another."

They both fell silent, and it was not long before April felt her head nodding, her chin dropping as her eyes closed. She joined the dog in gentle slumber and was not even aware when Jarvis stopped the wagon long enough to lift her in his arms and place her in the back.

They continued to move steadily southward.

❧ Chapter Twenty-one ❧

A jubilant cry brought April to instant alertness. She sat up quickly and looked out to see the colorful stars and bars of the Confederate flag waving from the roof of a log cabin nestled in a grove of pines. Captain Shoreham and his men were cheering over the realization that they were now among their own kind. They were out of immediate danger from the Yankees.

"Godalmighty, I've always loved that flag, but never more than in this minute!" Captain Shoreham whooped with glee, following his proclamation with an ear-splitting Rebel yell.

A soldier in a dirty, tattered gray uniform approached and told them they were in Colonel Saul Whitfield's camp. "Don't look like much of a camp to me," the captain pointed out, seeing only a few other soldiers milling about.

"Most of our men are over that rise there," the soldier pointed to a hilly ridge. "Camp's really over there. The Colonel took over this cabin, 'cause his wife's bad sick. It's quieter here."

April had climbed down out of the wagon and walked around to stand before the soldier, the dog following her. Bewildered, she asked, "You say the Colonel's *wife* is sick? You mean she's here? Where you've been fighting?"

He gave her an insolent glare. "Lots of women follow their men into battle. The Colonel just happens to want his family with him. I might ask what you're doin' out here in the wilderness, wearin' men's breeches and traveling with a bunch of men," he added suggestively.

"Now wait a minute—" Captain Shoreham spoke up indignantly.

April interrupted quickly. "It's all right," she said to the captain, then turned back to the soldier. "It's really quite a long story, and we're all very tired. Do you suppose we could have something to eat? Then perhaps I could see the Colonel's wife. If she's ill, I might be of some comfort to her."

He frowned. "I'll have to check with the Colonel."

After all the months of running and sneaking and pretending, April basked in the friendly atmosphere of the camp. She was fed, and they even found a dress for her, a green muslin dress the Colonel's wife no longer used. She and Lucky thrived.

One afternoon, while she was trying to make arrangements to go to Alabama, she found herself talking with a garrulous older man who had been wounded at Harpers Ferry and was being left out of the fighting so that he could heal.

Glad to unburden herself, April told him about Pinehurst, and her father, and Vanessa, and he listened sympathetically, then began telling her about the fighting, what it was like to be right there inside it . . . and about the wounded and dead, the horrors he had seen.

"There was a boy from Alabama in my company. I knew lots of men from Alabama, but he sticks in my mind. I was talking to him one day about his home, and he got this funny look on his face. I asked him if he had a wife back there, or a sweetheart, and he just blowed up and said if I didn't mind my own damn business he was gonna bust me right in the mouth. I left him alone after that, but I couldn't get him outta my mind."

"Anyway." He paused for a breath and continued, "His name was Moseley, Alton Moseley. He got hit same time I did, but he got it pretty bad. They took him to that big hospital in Richmond, but I doubt they was able to save him. Some of the boys said he was blowed up pretty bad."

He stopped talking when he saw that she had gone white. She took a deep breath and said, "Alton . . . is—an old friend."

She turned beseeching blue eyes on him. "He's been taken to the big hospital in Richmond?"

"Chimborazo, yes," he replied.

"I must go there. At once."

Bidding him good-bye and mumbling good wishes for his health, she left him and sought out the Colonel. Luck was with her. There would be a wagon leaving for Richmond in a few days, and, yes, he promised, he would see that she was on it. It was unusual to provide transportation for a woman in an army wagon, but the Colonel liked her. He would help her out.

❧ Chapter Twenty-two ❧

"I am sorry, Miss Jennings. I do sympathize with you, but there is no way we can allow you to visit Lieutenant Moseley. His condition is extremely poor. He has been placed in our special unit for the critically wounded. It is absolutely impossible for you to visit him."

April sat on the edge of her chair, facing the woman who was in charge of visitors at the huge, sprawling Chimborazo Hospital.

Mrs. Palmer looked down at the papers on her desk, then lifted sympathetic eyes to meet April's searching gaze. "I hate to be so blunt with you, but he is not expected to live. I'm sorry."

"Not expected—?" April echoed, shaking her head from side to side wildly as she clutched the edge of the desk for support. "Oh, dear God. Then I must see him. I must! We were going to be married before he went off to war, and there was a terrible misunderstanding. I've got to see him and tell him what happened."

"It just isn't possible. I'm sorry."

April stared at her, foggily aware of her eyes, a warm brown. The laugh lines were evidence that she had probably smiled a lot once, before the war. Now she looked severe, bitter, almost merciless.

"Five minutes," she begged. "All I ask is five minutes with him."

"I'm sorry. He probably wouldn't know you. It's a miracle he's lived this long."

Mrs. Palmer stood, smoothing her long white skirt with an impatient flutter. "I do have work to do, Miss Jennings, and there is really no point in our discussing the situation any further. I wish there were some way I could help you, but there simply isn't. Come along, and I will show you out."

"I can find my own way out, thank you." She rose and walked from the room, head held high. Only when the door closed behind her did she slump against the wall and allow the dry sobs to rack her body.

How can I go home without seeing him, she cried silently. If he's going to die, then I must see him one last time and try to make him understand what happened.

She did not want him to think she had jilted him.

She glanced about furtively. No one was paying any attention to her. There seemed to be an air of greater urgency than when she had first arrived. Nurses scurried about, carrying trays of instruments, supplies, lint for bandages. Doctors looked weary, haggard, walking with their heads bent low, shoulders slumped.

Hurrying quickly down the hall, she slipped out a side entrance and onto the hospital grounds. Looking about, she saw the rest of the complex, sprawled out before her, a miniature city of hastily constructed plank and log buildings and an endless sea of tents. In the distance, she could hear the periodic screams now and then of the suffering and dying, and wondered if Alton were making any of those sounds. She prayed not.

Where would he be? There were so many buildings, and if she wandered around on her own, guards would become suspicious and escort her from the hospital grounds. Security all around Richmond was extremely tight. Word had it that General Lee's army was wheeling eastward, and there was speculation that he might be trying to invade Washington once again. When she arrived she had been questioned endlessly by the sentries at the front gate.

A sprawling oak stood nearby, and she moved beneath it. If anyone saw her, they would think she was on her way to or from somewhere, and merely catching her breath in the shade.

She thought about Lucky and just hoped she had him tied securely in the old deserted barn back in the field. It had not been easy to find food for herself, much less the large, shaggy white dog that she had come to love so deeply. In fact, it made her want to cry to think about the night he had run into the woods and stayed gone for hours, only to return and lay a dead rabbit proudly at her feet. She had managed to start a fire and roast him to a turn, and Lucky would not eat a bite until she had had her fill, even though she kept offering him a nibble every so often. It was as though he were silently trying to let her know that it was his intent to look after her, even if it meant his own starvation. The soldiers who had brought her along in their wagon had helped her search for a place. She'd been lucky to find the barn. And the men had left some food with her, enough for herself and Lucky, for a little while. How kind they had been!

Their little wagon had been caught in the woods while a battle went on nearby, only a few hundred yards from where they were hidden, behind a clump of trees. It was, she reflected, going through that battle together that had forged the friendship.

An explosion of artillery guns, belching furiously, had first signaled to them that a battle was going on. They hid their wagon and scrambled for cover, April holding on to Lucky. The smell of sulfur stung their nostrils, and through the veil of trees hiding them they could see smoke begin to cover the earth in a gray, darkening cloud. The roars and bellows of ten-pound Parrott guns and twelve-pound Napoleons swelled until there were no other sounds at all, and the little party hiding an impossibly short distance from annihilation felt it was being sucked into the very vortex of the sound, consumed, carried away to be evaporated, later, into thin air.

"Hey, miss! You all right?"

She jerked her head up and saw a soldier staring at her from the footpath.

"Yes, I'm fine," she forced a smile and called back to him. "I was on my way out and the heat became a bit too much. I couldn't resist this shade."

He did not return her smile. "Visiting hours are over for today. You move along now, you hear? I've got orders that nobody is to be wandering around."

"Of course. Of course." She hurried from beneath the tree, glancing over her shoulder until he disappeared inside a building.

Spotting a wooden building sitting off to itself, she turned in that direction. No one was about, and there were no windows. It had to be a supply shack of some sort, and she decided it would be a safe place to hide while planning her next move. If the soldier came back and saw that she had not obeyed his instructions to leave, he would, no doubt, escort her to the gate himself.

Just as she reached the door of the building, she heard voices from around the corner. Someone was approaching. She gave the door a hard yank, but it held tight. Frantically, she tugged. It jerked open just as their voices seemed to be upon her.

She slipped inside, desperation moving her with amazing speed. A putrid, rotting odor slapped her full in the face. Stuffing her fist into her mouth as bile rose from her stomach, she found herself shrouded in darkness. What was that horrible odor? Never had she smelled anything like it.

Behind her, the door began to creak open. She leaped to the side, felt something strike her leg. There was a stab of pain as a splinter tore through her dress. Something brushed her arm. Quickly she stooped down, out of sight as a shaft of light from the open door cut into the darkness. The two men entered, quickly closing the door behind them.

"This is a hell of a place to have to hide," a man complained. "As big as Chimborazo is, it looks like we could find a better spot to slip off to than this."

Another man's voice replied roughly, "Hell, Carter, don't gripe. I reckon we've tried just about ever' place there is, and they always find us. We've got to get a little rest. You know I ain't slept in almost thirty-six hours? Can't hold up much longer. Where'd you hide that bottle?"

"Same place. That little hole I dug in the floor about three steps to your left." His laughter was slightly strained. "We don't have to worry about nobody lookin' for us in here. Nobody wants to come in here lessen they have to, and I sure don't blame 'em."

"Who's idea was it to stack up bodies, anyhow?"

April's eyes widened in the dark. The hair on the back of her neck stood on edge.

"Dunno. I heard the government wants to give the families a chance to claim their dead kin before they're just dumped in the ground someplace. I hear only half is claimed, anyway. They keep 'em four or five days after they die. That's about as long as they can stand it before folks start complaining about the smell."

"Well, it's powerful rank in here now."

"You get used to it after a few minutes. I had the work detail in here a coupla weeks ago. You know, shifting bodies around, takin' out what ain't been claimed and buryin' 'em. Here. Take a drink. It'll make you feel easier."

April silently commanded her pounding heart to slow down, but it did not obey. It was foolish to be so frightened. These poor souls stacked all about her like sacks of flour could not harm her. She had to keep calm or be discovered. She squeezed her hands together tightly, clamped her teeth to keep them from clicking. Her body began to shake.

The man had been right. The smell could be gotten used to. It was not so noticeable any longer, for now the air was fetid with earth, mustiness, dust. The smell of decay merely blended in.

"How come everything has to happen around Richmond in this blamed war?" one of the men was saying. "We no sooner got the wounded in from that battle at Champion's Hill on the sixteenth of May when the cavalry skirmishes started. Every bit of the dadburn fighting seems to go on right around here, and we get all the results of it."

"Be glad you aren't out there in it," his companion pointed out. "We're lucky we got assigned to hospital duty. It ain't so bad. Sure, we dig ditches for all the arms and legs they cut off. And we haul bodies in here. It might not be the most pleasant job in the world, but if we weren't doin' it, we might be one of them poor fools stacked up over there waitin' to feed the worms."

April heard the sound of someone gulping liquid, then a worried voice say, "Grant got his butt beat twice tryin' to take Vicksburg, I hear. Then he got that long entrenchment line set up. I hear it's fifteen miles long, and he's plannin' on starvin' Joe Johnston and his men into surrenderin'.'"

"Yeah, but Lee's on the move, invadin' the North again."

"Yep. And you know what's gonna happen? I'll tell you, Carter. There's gonna be plenty more men brought in here. Ripped all to pieces. And that means more ditches for us to dig for arms and legs, and more bodies to come stack in here. I tell you, I'm sick of all of it. They brought in over two hundred wounded this mornin' in just one hour."

April then understood the reason for all the activity here. Everyone was too busy to pay her any mind.

Suddenly she snapped back to alertness as she heard Carter say, "The place where they put the ones they think is gonna die is full up. Usually they don't have but about a hundred in there, 'cause they mostly just go on and die when they're hurt that bad. Most don't take much time. They die or they don't. We're clearing out another building right next to it, 'cause forty-seven out of that bunch this mornin' is just waitin' to die. Can't do nothin' for 'em, 'cept make 'em as comfortable as possible. If it was up to me, I think I'd go ahead and put 'em out of their misery."

The other man gave a disgusted snort. "Naw, you wouldn't. You're just flappin' your jaws. And gimme that bottle. I'm the one what needs it. I got surgery detail this afternoon. I get to slosh a bucket of water over the operating table to wash the blood off every time they move somebody off it. Makes me sick."

April was no longer listening. The place for the dying was full. And one of these men was going to help prepare a building right next to it! He could be followed there . . . followed to the place next to where Alton was.

Oh, would they never leave? She winced with pain as she realized she was squeezing her hands so tightly together that her nails were digging into her own flesh. It had been half an hour, at least. The foul air was becoming overwhelming.

Finally, one of the men said, "Well, we best be gettin' back to work. I've stood it in here about as long as I can."

The other agreed. "It's the best hidin' place we've found yet."

She heard the sounds of them moving toward the door,

then a shaft of light plunged inside. She rose, fighting the horror of seeing, for the first time, all the shrouded bodies on either side of her.

"If you get sick of sloshin' blood, you can always come help me," the taller of the two called to his companion.

She hesitated just long enough that they would not notice the door opening. Slowly, she edged it open to step outside into the bright midday sun. Glancing to her right, she saw the man she wanted to follow walking slowly up a rutted, barren hill. Slowly, she started after him, keeping a leisurely pace so that anyone would think she was a hospital worker.

The soldier disappeared over a rise. She felt a wave of panic. If she lost sight of him, there was no way of finding Alton. She quickened her step, lifting her skirt above her ankles so she could run. Just then, a fat man in a checkered umber coat appeared and headed straight for her.

"Lady!" He waved. "I want to talk to you."

She froze. Ahead, up the rise, there was no sight of the soldier. With each passing second, he was getting farther and farther away. But she could not break into a run and follow. Not now. Not with this strange man striding toward her.

In what she hoped was a believable voice, she said, "I do not have time to tarry, sir. My brother has taken a turn for the worse, and I must get to him at once."

"You're heading for a restricted area." He spoke around a fat cigar. "What's your name, and who said you could come up here without an escort?"

He was a small, squat man, with narrow eyes hooded by thick folds of fat. He looked her up and down suspiciously as she frantically tried to think of a way out. Swallowing hard, pretending indignation and anger, she cried, "I just told you. My brother has taken a turn for the worse. My goodness, he could die."

She gave him a contemptuous look. "He did his part for the proud Southland, and why, might I ask, are you not in uniform doing your part?" She hoped the challenge would throw him.

The fat hoods above his eyes raised only slightly as a mocking expression took over his face. "I *am* in uniform, lady. Sort of. It's my job to see that people don't go where they aren't supposed to. It's not allowed for anyone to wander anywhere around here, no matter for what reason. Especially over that ridge there. See, we put wounded officers in a special section back there, and we want to make sure no Yankee spies slip in here to finish their job."

This time she did not have to pretend anger. "I will forgive your insinuations, sir, but surely it is not forbidden for a sister to visit her brother."

"No," he replied quietly, his gaze still inquiring and suspicious, "but you haven't told me just whose sister you are. What's your brother's name?"

"Lieutenant Alton Moseley," she snapped. Now it was going to be impossible to get away in time to find the soldier.

Suddenly, her furiously working mind conceived an alternate plan. She smiled faintly, speaking in a tremulous voice. "You could help me if you would, sir. I was being taken to my brother by a soldier who wasn't being very nice about it. He said it was time for him to go off duty. So I had an escort, don't you see?" She paused to give him a beseeching gaze, then continued. "Mrs. Palmer arranged everything. You know her, don't you? Well, she asked this soldier to take me, and he just kept walking faster and faster and wouldn't wait up for me." She was nearly sobbing by this time. "I was trying my best to keep up with him, but you called out to me, and now I've lost sight of him. Would you be so kind as to take me the rest of the way? I would be so grateful."

He rolled his cigar from one side of his mouth to the other and hooked his thumbs in his belt. "Well, I don't have any idea where your brother is, little lady. Let's go back to Mrs. Palmer's office, and I'll find out from her. Then I'll be glad to take you there."

"Oh, there's no time for all that. Don't you see? She would have taken me herself, but there are so many wounded coming in this morning that everyone is going in a hundred different directions. Don't *you* have more important things to do than delay me? If my brother dies before I reach him, I . . . I will never forgive you." She dabbed at her eyes with the back of her sleeves, and the tears she wiped away were genuine, for desperation was beginning to strangle her.

"I just don't have no idea where your brother is. In case you haven't noticed, this is a big hospital."

"I'm afraid," she began, letting the tears go on and stream down her cheeks, making no effort to brush them away, "that he's been taken someplace where they put people who . . . who might not live . . . Mrs. Palmer acted quite strange when I spoke with her. She was vague about his exact condition. Then the soldier who was supposed to escort me made some sort of remark about how I'd have to be taken to the most remote area of the hospital compound. Mrs. Palmer looked quite angry when he said that. I got the feeling they were hiding something from me. Why would my brother be taken to a remote area?" She blinked at him in feigned confusion.

For the first time, his expression softened. "You can believe I'll report that soldier for running off and leaving you. Now you come along with me, because . . ."—he paused to sigh and give her a look filled with pity—"I'm afraid I know now where he was taking you."

He held out his arm. She slipped her hand into the crook of his elbow, praying he would not think her trembling was strange.

They reached the top of the ridge. Below was sprawled a coarse, yellow, sandy soil, bearing scarcely anything but pine trees and broom sedge. In some places the pines were only about five feet high. This, then, was land that had been in cultivation before the war. There were patches of every age, also. Some of the trees were a hundred feet high. In the distance there were fields in which pines were just starting to spring up from the earth in beautiful green plumes. They were hardly noticeable among the sassafras bushes and blackberry vines. Yes, this had all been farmland not long ago.

Before them lay a clearing free of stumps, the ground covered with a deep mat of pine needles. Their footsteps could scarcely be heard. In the center there were two log cabins that looked as though they had been constructed hastily. At one end of each were chimneys made of split sticks. This was dangerous, April knew, for on cold nights when a large fire was built, chimneys made of wood often caught fire.

"I know it doesn't look like much," the man said as they walked toward the cabin on their right, "but I understand they wanted to put these men back here where they'd be comfortable, away from the others, and they made the arrangements in a hurry, thinking there would be time later to build nicer quarters. But there never was. Time has to be spent caring for the wounded, so nothing else ever gets done. I heard this morning that they're clearing out the storage cabin to move in more men."

April nodded, her excitement building as she realized she would soon see Alton.

A gentle breeze was blowing, a slight odor of balsam in the air. But above this, April could smell a strange scent, and she intuitively understood that this was the smell of impending death.

She stopped walking. Looking straight ahead at the cabin, she whispered, "I'll go the rest of the way myself."

She felt a pang of terror as he drawled, "No. Can't let you do that. They might not let you in. I'll have to let them know it's all right."

"No, really, I want to go in alone," she cried, too loudly, too nervously. His eyes turned to her curiously. She tried to make her voice calmer, silently commanded herself to get hold of herself. She gave him another tight smile and touched his arm gently. "Please. I have to do this alone. I don't want to be announced. If he's already dead, then let me be the one to find him. Don't make me have to hear it from someone else."

A loud scream pierced the air. She trembled. The man patted her shoulder. "That's another reason they put them back here, little lady, the screams. I heard a doctor say once it's like they feel the fingers of death reaching out to take them away. They're screaming in horror over dying. They're not in pain, 'cause they dose them up with opium and whiskey and anything else they can think of to give them peace. Come along now.

"By the way," he added suddenly. "My name is Clyde Thornsby. Like I said, we've got some important officers back here, and we just can't risk Yankee spies slipping in here."

"You told me that earlier. Now please. Let me go alone."

"They won't let you in unless they know you're approved." He was giving her that strange look again. "Come along."

April sucked in her breath, teeth biting into her lower lip as she fought for self-control. Oh, how she longed to just break away from him and run those last few yards to the cabin and rush inside to find Alton. But she was too close to risk exposure now. There was nothing to do but allow Clyde Thornsby to lead her.

They stepped inside, and a woman wearing a high-necked muslin dress and floor length apron, came rushing over. Her hair was pulled back from her face, and April could see that it was dirty, greasy, had not been washed in quite a while. She looked haggard, but beneath the deep lines of fatigue was a quality of kindness. She had seen far too much suffering, but she still struggled to meet the demands of her conscience.

"Yes, may I help you?"

April was straining to see in the dim light. Cots lined the walls, side by side, mere inches between. Some of the men were so horribly deformed that nausea bubbled in her throat. One of these, she thought in terror, was Alton.

Behind her, Clyde Thornsby was reaching into his pocket to display a badge and explain the circumstances of finding April.

"Well, who is she here to see?" the woman asked in a tired voice. "We had no notice anyone was coming."

Her words were drowned out by an agonizing moan that echoed through the cabin, awaking men who had managed to fall asleep. Soon screams and moans rang out and the woman was raising her voice above the din, explaining that this was why visitors were discouraged. It would take her quite a while to calm the men down again.

April moved away, ignoring Clyde and the nurse. She took slow, faltering steps, pausing at the foot of each cot to stare at the man lying on it. Behind her, she heard Clyde say, "Leave her be. She's all right. It's her brother. She may not have much time."

"She may not have any," the nurse responded crisply. "I've had three die this morning. They're back there covered up with sheets waiting to be moved to the Dead House. He could be one of them. What's his name?"

"Let me see. Now what did she say it was—"

April froze. Her fist flew to her mouth to attempt to stifle the rising shriek. Before her lay Alton, staring upward. His face was intact. He was not moving. Beneath the sheet, she could see lumps of what? Bandages? The stumps of limbs? Dear God, just how badly had he been torn apart?

She forced her trembling legs to move, taking shuffling steps to the edge of the cot. "Alton . . ." she whispered in a voice too low even for her own ears. "Alton. Alton, please hear me."

"Alton Moseley?" the nurse cried sharply from behind her. "She's here to see Lieutenant Moseley? That must be the Jennings woman. I was told to be on the lookout for her. She's not his sister!"

Clyde Thornsby moved quickly. He ran toward April, calling for her to stop. But she ignored him as she knelt beside Alton's cot and cried, "Please, please hear me, Alton. It's me, April."

He turned his head ever so slightly, trying to focus his eyes. His breathing was shallow, labored, and grating sounds came from his chest. His eyes were dull and unseeing.

"It's April. I've come to see you, to tell you—"

He opened his mouth, mustering every ounce of strength left in his ravaged body. The searing scream that came from his lips seemed torn from his very soul.

"Get thee behind me, Satan! Get thee behind me! Thou shalt not have my soul!"

"Alton." She reached to touch him, but he shrank away, sobbing wildly, and she gasped in horror as he used the stumps of what had once been his arms to shove the sheet away from his emaciated body, struggling desperately to retreat from her.

"Satan! Satan! Satan!" he screamed over and over, tears flowing from his wildly rolling eyes. "Help me, God. Help me, Jesus. Satan's here in the form of an angel!"

April bowed her head and sobbed, just as the hand of Clyde Thornsby clamped down painfully on her shoulder.

And she prayed as she had never prayed before.

❧ Chapter Twenty-three ❧

APRIL's arms were being twisted painfully behind her back as she struggled against the strength of Clyde Thornsby. She watched in horror as Alton writhed in terror on his cot, moving only stubs where arms and legs had once been. Saliva oozed from the corners of his mouth as a nurse attempted to hold his heaving torso. "God! God! Take this she-devil away," he screamed in agony. "Please, please, don't do this to me."

"You little Yankee bitch!" Clyde yelled, giving her a vicious shake. He yanked her around from the cot so that she was no longer facing Alton. "Is this what you came here to do? Do Yankees stoop so low as to torture a man who's lost his arms and legs?"

She whipped her head from side to side, her long hair streaming across her face, covering her eyes. "No, no, no! We were going to be married. You must let me talk to him."

"You've done all you're gonna do to that poor boy. Now you're coming with me, and we're going to find out just who put you up to this."

She brought her foot up high, then slammed it crashing backward into his shin. With a scream of pain, he loosened just enough so that she could wrest quickly away. Running back to Alton's cot, she gripped the edge and leaned forward, her body convulsing in sobs as she pleaded,

"You have to know me, Alton! April! It's April! Remember? You loved me once. We were going to be married, but it was Vanessa who stopped us, Alton."

Clyde grabbed her once again, just as a guard, alerted by all the screams, came charging into the cabin. "Help me," Clyde yelled. "Grab her feet. Get her out of here. She's trying to kill this boy."

"I'm not! I'm not. Oh, please God," she screamed. "Make them listen to me, please."

The guard lifted her feet from the floor while Clyde gripped her beneath her shoulders. They carried her to the door, while Alton sobbed, "The Devil! Torturing me by pretending to be April. Oh, God, let me die. Don't make me suffer this way. Not fair . . . not fair . . . not after all I've been through. Oh, God, hear me, kill me. . . ."

His wails echoed through the building, shutting out the moans from the other patients.

Once outside, the soldier dropped April's feet, but Clyde held onto her. "Get me some rope," he said hoarsely. "A gag. We're taking her to headquarters. She's a spy."

"I'm not a spy or a Yankee!" she shrieked, trying to kick him once again.

He released her and spun her around, his hand cracking across her face once, twice, three times. She felt a ringing in her ears and swayed dizzily, spots dancing before her eyes as the pain settled into every bone in her face.

"Now I'm not listenin' to your lies. I don't want to hurt you, but by damn, I will. Now you just calm down. You've done your dirty work."

"I'm not a Yankee!"

He hit her again, this time sending her sprawling on the ground. The soldier came running with a scarf and a piece of rope. "Hey," he protested. "She's a woman—"

"Stay out of this." Clyde yanked the rope away from him and bent down to jerk April's wrists behind her back. He looped the twine tightly, then stuffed the scarf in her mouth roughly before straightening up. April's head was bobbing about limply as she struggled for consciousness over the stunning pain exploding inside her head.

"Now let's get her to headquarters. You got a horse nearby? I want to get there in a hurry."

The soldier nodded and disappeared around the building, at the same moment one of the nurses came outside to see what was going on.

"Is he all right?" Clyde asked quickly. "Is he still havin' them fits?"

She gave April a hating glare as she answered, "No, thank God. He fainted." To April, she said coldly, "You should be ashamed. What kind of witch are you that you could torture the poor man that way? How could you?"

April struggled to speak against the gag. Her head slumped. What did it matter? They would not believe her. The memory of Alton lying there, all his limbs gone, screaming that she was a she-devil—that picture would haunt her for as long as she lived.

The soldier returned with a small wagon pulled by one horse. Clyde dumped April unceremoniously down in the rough wood bed, then climbed up on the bench beside the soldier, who popped the reins and started moving them toward the ridge.

April's lips were burning. She had tasted blood after the second blow, knew that her mouth was cut.

Soon they arrived at the headquarters, a large two-story white frame building with a proud red and white Confederate flag flapping in the breeze atop a pole just outside the porch. Clyde got down out of the wagon and then reached inside and scooped April up.

Two gray-clad guards were standing at attention just outside the double-front doors. When they saw a woman being dragged from the wagon tied and gagged, their muskets snapped to point directly forward, and one of them cried, "Hey, what's going on here? What're you doin' to that woman?"

"Yankee spy!" Clyde hoisted her over his shoulder. "Tell your commanding officer that Clyde Thornsby wants to see him."

The second guard spoke up. "He's okay," he said to the soldier beside him. "He's security, all right. You go tell General Hepple."

"Where can I put her till the General decides what to do with her?" Clyde inquired, glancing about. "We don't have a jail here, and she's liable to run off if she isn't put somewhere. You should've seen what she just did." He

proceeded to give them his version of the horrors she had
inflicted.

The guard frowned down at her. "We got an ice house
around back," he said. "It's about twelve foot deep. Put her
in there and pull up the ladder, and she won't go nowhere.
We've put a few men down there till we could get 'em to
Libby prison in Richmond."

April attempted to scream her protests against the gag in
her mouth, but made only a muffled sound. She kicked her
legs wildly as Clyde dragged her around the headquarters
to a wooded area beyond.

The structure around the ice house was made of split
logs and was about eight feet square. She watched in horror as the guard pulled a peg from the drop door, opening
it to display the damp, dark pit beyond. He descended the
ladder and held his arms up. "You can stop that kicking,"
he yelled. "Or I'll just let you fall all the way to the bottom
and break your neck. It sure as hell don't matter to me."

Frozen with terror, April ceased struggling as Clyde
passed her to the guard. She felt the sawdust scraping at
her bare arms as she was dumped roughly the last remaining few feet to the pit floor. The air was close, damp, the
odor a mixture of rotting wood and earth. She could feel
the chill of the nearby ice, packed down in the sawdust to
delay its melting in the summer heat.

Clyde jerked the gag from her mouth, warning her that
if she started screaming, he would replace it and leave her
tied. She made no sound, and he untied her hands, then
scurried up the ladder. She was helpless to do anything but
watch as he stepped through the doorway and pulled the
ladder up behind him. He leaned back in to stare down at
her and call, "When I find out what's to be done with you,
I'll be back. Till then, you're just wasting your breath if
you start yelling, because no one will hear you down
there."

He swung the hatched door shut, and she was plunged
into darkness.

God alone knew what her fate was to be.

The light filtering through the slatted roof of her prison
grew dimmer as the day wore on. Then there was no light
at all, and she shivered as the dampness worked its way
into her bones. Hunger had become a great, gnawing pain,

and the trembling from being cold made her stomach ache even more.

She tensed as the sound of footfalls reached her ears. Someone was coming. Scrambling to her feet, she stumbled. Her legs were numb from crouching for hours.

A ball of light hovered over the slatted covering. As it was swung open, she saw a lantern, held high. There was a man's outline, but his face was not visible. An unfamiliar voice called down. "You all right, woman?"

"Yes, yes, but I'm cold and hungry," her voice quavered as she fought to keep from breaking into sobs. "Please let me out of here. I haven't done anything. I swear I haven't. Please believe me, and in God's name, have mercy—"

"Stop your whining, Yankee bitch!" he yelled. "They ain't gonna get you out of there till tomorrow morning, so you might as well settle down for the night. Here. I brought you something to eat."

Something hit the ground nearby.

"If it was up to me, you'd starve, but I was ordered to feed you."

The hatch door fell shut with a loud bang, and she stared at the disappearing ball of light, her body shaking with dry sobs, anguish choking her.

For a long while, she stood staring upward. Then she lowered herself to the ground once more and groveled for the bundle. It was a burlap bag. She reached inside and found the food—a sweet potato, some cold, greasy concoction made of swine's flesh, and a hunk of cornbread. She forced herself to eat slowly, afraid of nausea after going so long without eating. The food was barely palatable, but that did not matter.

As she ate, crouched there in the damp sawdust, she thought of Lucky, and tears stung her eyes. The poor dog. Surely he would find a way to take care of himself. But what if he could not get loose from where she had tied him, inside the old barn? If she had left him running free, he would have followed her. Now, she wished she had. Perhaps he would have caused her to be discovered before finding Alton. Then she wouldn't be here in this pit.

When the food was gone, she lay down and tried to think of other things. Poppa. Was he still alive? If so, how was he faring? Was Vanessa still at Pinehurst, or had she given up?

Rance. Where was he? Did he think of her, or was he too angry to care any longer? She felt a stab of pain. The only time she had meant anything at all to him was when they became one entity in lovemaking. And when an entity is divided, is there any real feeling between the two divisions until the entity is created once more? In their case, she had doubted it.

But why was she wishing she had never left him? Desperation? Yes, that was all it was. She cursed herself for thinking about Rance. What good would it do? Then, suddenly, the answer was clear. Thinking about Rance was helping her keep her sanity. Dreaming about Rance would keep her from becoming a babbling madwoman by morning.

Sleep would not come. Even when the roll of thunder began to disrupt the quiet of the night, and the slash of white lightning gave momentary illumination within the pit, she did not close her eyes.

Then the rain came. Slowly at first. Tiny drops, just a few of which made their way through the cracks above to fall on her shivering skin. Then came the downpour, cascading through in a torrent to soak her. Her teeth chattered and her hair hung wet and dripping on her shoulders, but there was nothing she could do for herself.

They shot spies, didn't they? Would they come in the morning and take her out and line up the soldiers to shoot her? And if so, she pondered recklessly, what difference would it make now? The sawdust was becoming saturated. She could feel the water beginning to creep up about her. Perhaps she would drown, and then they would be disappointed because, when they came, they would find her already dead.

Just as a faint gray light began to work its way downward, the rains slackened, then ceased. She was sitting in mired sawdust then, half covered in water. How much longer, she wondered miserably, how much longer must I endure this hell?

The light grew brighter. She struggled to stand but fell backward. It was impossible to stand in the slush beneath.

Perhaps, she began to think, they were not coming at all. This was to be her fate—to die here in this pit. They would not come until they were sure she was dead. They had wounded Confederates to care for. They would spend their time caring for their own before worrying about a Yankee spy.

Panic took hold. The trembling was beginning again, this time causing her body to jerk uncontrollably. Although sunlight streamed down now, she began to feel darkness descend about her. She knew it was hysteria but was unable to stop it.

"Maybe she drowned last night. Save us a lot of trouble if she did."

At the sound of voices, her head jerked upward, eyes growing wide.

"Aw, don't talk like that. You're letting the war make an animal out of you. Damn. You want to see a woman drown like a rat?"

"Don't matter to me. Not after what I hear she did. Wonder why? I mean, Moseley wasn't no important officer or nothin'. He was just a lieutenant. Why bother with him?"

The hatch was opened. She squinted at the great blast of sunlight and covered her face with her hands.

"Good Lord! She's about drowned in that damn sawdust. Look at her. That ain't no way to treat a dog!"

Dog. April was fighting to clear her mind. Hysteria was threatening to jumble her brain.

"Dog," she whispered as the man reached her after climbing down the ladder. "Save my dog, please," she gasped.

"Lady, you don't have no dog here." His hands on her shoulders were as gentle as his voice. "Now I'm going to get you out of here, so just put your arms around my neck and hang on. Lord, what a mess. I can't hardly stand in this muck."

She clutched him as tightly as her dwindling strength would allow, and as he climbed the ladder slowly, holding her with one hand, clutching at the rungs with the other, she whispered, "Please. Save my dog . . . I left him tied . . . in a barn. . . . He might die there . . . please. . . ."

"What's she mumbling about, Blackmon?" a soldier leaning over the opening asked as they neared the top. "She whining about going to Tarboro? Well, that's too bad. That's the place for a hussy like her. She—"

"Shut up, or I'm going to throw you in that goddamn pit." He reached the top, stepped through the opening, and set April on her feet. She swayed, and he quickly slipped a strong arm about her to hold up her upright. Facing the other soldier, who was watching with a crooked, smug grin, Blackmon yelled angrily, "Just what kind of an animal are you, Hester? Putting a woman in a hellhole like that all night long, and it poured down rain last night, too."

Saul Hester snickered. "You trying to tell me your place is any better? I hear Tarboro ain't fit for hogs, Blackmon."

"My prisoners can keep dry," he lashed out in retort. "We don't stick 'em in goddamn holes in the ground. She could've drowned down there."

Hester stiffened, frowning. "Look, I was only doing what Thornsby told me to do. He was the one what stuck her in there and said to keep her there till the officers decided what to do with her. I wasn't gonna get in trouble by letting her outta there."

"Shit, you didn't care."

April looked up with weary eyes as the tall, heavyset man began brushing her matted hair back from her face. He had black eyes beneath bushy brows. The heavy beard which covered the lower part of his huge, round face concealed the bottom line of a jagged scar running from the corner of his nose downward. His hair was shoulder length, as dirty and tangled as her own. His gray uniform was soiled and worn. He towered over her.

He was ugly. There was simply no getting around the fact that this man was the ugliest she had ever seen. Had she come upon him unawares, the sight of him would have provoked a scream of terror. He was huge. The hand he touched her with was almost as big as her head. His shoulders were twice the width of her own. And body hair. Dear Lord, he reminded her of a giant, hairy spider! With his sleeves rolled up, she could hardly see his skin for the thick down that grew all the way to the base of his fingernails.

She tried not to show her revulsion. Despite his raw, coarse appearance, she knew that he felt some pity for her plight.

He was obviously used to reactions like hers, for he laughed and murmured, "Yeah, I know I'm ugly, but you ain't. I think you're just about the prettiest woman I ever laid eyes on. If you were cleaned up, I bet you'd really be something to look at."

She could not help but tremble at that. He was not only ugly, he could also frighten a person quite easily.

"You ain't got to be scared of me, darlin'. I can think of other things to do with you besides hurt you. That's why I'm so mad at these squareheads for treating you like they did." He smiled, displaying teeth so decayed they were almost completely blackened. "Say, are you all right? Did they give you anything to eat?"

"Hell, yeah, we fed her!" the other soldier cried indignantly before April had a chance to reply. "Fed her good, too. Same as what we ate."

Blackmon ignored him. "Now you ain't got no reason to be scared, darlin'. I can feel you shaking. My name's Blackmon, by the way. Sergeant Kaid Blackmon. And from now on, you got to do everything I tell you. Then there won't be no trouble. You just remember I'm the boss. You mind me, and we'll get along fine. You get sassy, and I got ways of making you wish you hadn't. You understand?"

She could not speak but hoped the cold resentment she felt for this creature was mirrored in the hating glare she gave him. Evidently it was, for he gave her a hard smack across her shoulders with his beefy hand that almost sent her sprawling. "I asked you a question, darlin'. I expect an answer. You understand me?"

"Yes, damn you!" she hissed between clenched teeth. "I understand you just fine. Now where are you taking me?"

"See that wagon over there?"

She looked to where he pointed and gasped. It was a cage. That's all she could call it. There were bars on all four sides of the wooden structure, which was drawn by two horses so wasted their ribs were sticking out pitifully.

"A cage!" she whispered in horror. "You're taking me to that cage?"

He dropped a muscular arm across her shoulders and she had no choice but to allow herself to be steered along. With a lopsided grin, he told her, "Now you ain't got nothing to be scared of, like I told you. Just follow orders, and me and you will get along real fine. I know I'm ugly, but I can be real nice to you, if you'll let me."

He punctuated his statement with a secretive chuckle, and she fought a wave of revulsion.

"Now what was it you was saying to me back there about a dog?"

She whipped her head around to stare up at him, feeling a sudden flash of hope. "I left my dog tied in a barn in the woods. Where are you taking me? Please . . . I can't leave him tied up to just starve to death."

"Well, no siree," he chuckled again. "We sure can't do that, 'cause I'm afraid you're going to be gone for a mighty long spell. Those officers didn't take too kindly when they heard what you done, and they're sending you to Tarboro Prison for a long, long time. I'm not even going to tell you just how long, 'cause it'll make it a whole lot easier if you just don't think about it. Just take one day at a time. You know what I mean?"

He displayed the rotting teeth again, and she looked away in disgust.

Once more he slapped her shoulder, hard, and this time her knees buckled, but he reached down and grabbed her just before she fell to the ground. "Now you just quit acting like you're gonna puke every time you look at me, darlin'. I can't help being ugly, and you can't help having to look at me. We're gonna be together for a long, long time, just like I said, and you'll make it a lot easier on yourself if you'll just calm down."

She took a deep breath and prayed that he would listen to her side of the story. "It isn't like they say it is. I'm not a spy. I came here to see my fiancé, and—"

He covered her face with his hand, gently, but it was enough to cease her words. "Now I'm not going to listen to you going on and on about how you really ain't guilty, Miss Jennings. I can't help you, anyway, even if I believed you. I'm in charge of this special prison set up for women, and I was told to come get you and take you there. So you just get on up in that wagon, and we'll have you tucked in your cell by noontime. I'll see to it you get some extra rations for your lunch. Got a nice prison dress for you to put on, too. You like brown? I hope so. All your clothes from now on is gonna be brown. Just like all my women wear."

Suddenly, she could stand no more. Maybe there was no chance of escape. Maybe she was no match for this gorilla-like man. But she could try. By God, she could try.

Suddenly she snaked her head downward to clamp her teeth in his arm at the same time she brought her knee up to his crotch. Then, expecting him to release her, she jerked around to be ready to run—where, she did not know—just run as long and as fast as possible and pray she could get away.

Sergeant Kaid Blackmon did not move.

She stared up at him in stunned disbelief. He was smiling as though she had done something really quite humorous.

"Now did you think a puny little thing like you was gonna hurt a big, ugly bastard like me? Darlin', you got a lot to learn." And he swung her up in his arms and started toward the wagon.

"If that's all it took to catch me off guard," he said matter-of-factly, "I couldn't handle . . . let's see now . . . I got twenty-two of you lovelies in my little home away from home now. Naw, I couldn't handle all of you practically single-handed. The other girls know that, just like you will. But if you keep on trying, then I'll get pissed off, and I'll have to get a little mean. I don't like to do that. I get carried away, and I don't know when to stop, and I guess I don't know my own strength."

Effortlessly, he rolled her over and under to hold her with one arm while he opened the back of the jail wagon. Then he shoved her inside, closed the door and bolted it. "It's not a far piece. Maybe a three-hour ride. Like I said, we'll be there by lunchtime, and we'll get you bathed and cleaned up and fed. I just know you're going to be a pretty thing when you're all cleaned up." He winked and walked around to climb up on the seat.

She stumbled forward to clutch the bars immediately behind where he sat. "You bastard!" she screamed, squeez-

ing the steel bars and attempting to shake them in her
grasp. "You dirty, common bastard. You're like all the
rest. You won't believe me. All I wanted to do was see
Alton . . . tell him . . . oh, damn you, what's the use?"

She slumped to the wagon floor and began to sob, hating
herself for her weakness . . . hating him and everyone
connected with her misery.

He popped the reins, started the horses lumbering forward slowly. Turning his head around to stare down at her,
he casually asked, "Now where did you say your little dog
was tied, darlin'?"

She lifted her face to stare at him incredulously. "What
. . . what did you say?" she whispered, not sure she had
heard right, or, if she had, wondering how he could play
such a cruel trick as to make her think he would actually
go after poor Lucky.

He laughed, enjoying her surprise. "I asked where it was
you left your little dog tied. You said you didn't want to go
off and leave him to starve, didn't you? Well, if you don't
tell me where you left him, then I can't go get him to take
him with us, now can I?"

"Oh, dear Jesus, if you mean that—"

"Of course, I mean it. Now where is he?"

She gave him the directions, her heart pounding. Was it
a trick? Lucky was just a mutt, a mongrel, but he was all
she had, and he loved her and trusted her, and it was
horrible enough that she was being taken to prison for a
crime she did not commit, without having to bear the
tragic knowledge that he would be left behind for God
only knew what fate.

"Well, we'll just go get him," he drawled, winking at her
once more. "I may be ugly, darlin', but I ain't altogether a
sonofabitch."

He turned the wagon, following her directions to Lucky.

❧ Chapter Twenty-four ❧

APRIL sat in the rusting tub of cold water, hating the feel of the harsh lye soap against her skin but knowing Kaid Blackmon would make good his threat to scrub her personally if she did not bathe herself. One of the first rules of "his" camp, he had said, was that each of the women prisoners would bathe daily.

"I may be ugly," he had said sardonically, "but I ain't going to put up with them damn nits. Not on me, and not on my prisoners. So you can get used to scrubbing every day, like it or not."

She had dared to complain about the lack of hot water, and he had laughed at her, saying she should be grateful that a tub was provided. "Otherwise you'd be washing in that creek back yonder."

"Back yonder." As she splashed the water over her body she could see out one of the two windows of the rotting log cabin. "Out yonder" was a wilderness. Trees in every direction, the trunks hidden by thick weeds and undergrowth taller than she. The clearing where the prison was located was hardly a clearing at all. There was a stump every few feet.

Tarboro Prison was appallingly isolated and small, even for a prison. The prisoners had just one cabin, the one in which she was bathing. Twenty dilapidated cots lined the walls with scarce inches between them. There were no sheets, blankets, or pillows. Only rotting canvas to lie on.

A long, crudely constructed wood table sat at one end of the narrow room. The rusting tub and several chamber pots occupied the other end. There was one window on each side, and only a single door.

"Used to be a church," Kaid had told her. "There weren't many folks around to start with, and when the war came, these people moved closer to Fredericksburg, not wanting to be out here in the wilderness if the Yankees came."

She had looked about her in horror and murmured, "This place isn't fit for pigs."

He snorted contemptuously. "That's just about how the government feels about the prisoners we get here. Pigs. Animals. Lowlife. Scum. In most cases, they're right. We got a rough, mean bunch of women here." His voice softened as he suddenly trailed his stubby fingers down her arm in a gentle gesture. "I think you're different, April. A cut above them others. I sure hope so—"

She had jerked away from him, rubbing the flesh he had touched as though to wipe away filth. "Just don't touch me," she bit out the words. "For now, I'm a prisoner, I know, but that doesn't mean I have to put up with your abuse—"

He grabbed her so quickly she did not even see him move. "You listen to me, and you listen good, 'cause I'm getting tired of telling you. I'm boss here. Lord. Master. What I say goes. I touch you and anybody else, any time I feel like it. Now, I can be good to you, or I can be a real sonofabitch. It don't matter to me."

He gave her a sharp whack across the shoulders with the palm of his hand, propelling her forward. "Now you get inside and get that bath, and I'll get your clothes for you. You can rest today, 'cause I know that was quite an ordeal last night in that pit, but tomorrow you'll be out in the fields with the rest of the women—growing the food you're gonna have to eat."

Lucky had growled ominously at the roughness with which his mistress was being handled. Kaid paused to pat the dog on the head and say, "Now you just calm down, boy. Me and you are gonna get along just fine. I've been wanting me a dog. I think you'll just stay with me in my cabin."

April looked toward the edge of the clearing, and saw a fairly new cabin. Though small, it was, by far, much nicer than the prisoners' cabin. On the other side, there was another structure, also made of split logs and just a bit larger.

"That's my place." Kaid had pointed to the smaller cabin. "My men stay in the other one. Don't be so curious now, 'cause you're gonna have plenty of time to get used to things around here."

He had surprised her by leaving her alone to take her bath, taking Lucky with him.

She was grateful for the brief respite. The man puzzled her. He was ugly and ominous, true, but there was something slightly gentle about him as well.

She was drying herself on a scratchy burlap bag, the only thing available for a towel, when the door opened without warning. Gasping, she jerked the bag about her to cover her nakedness, thinking it was the sergeant returning. Instead, she saw a tall, skinny woman, her hair hanging limply about her pale, sallow face. There were deep circles beneath green eyes that once might have sparkled. Now they were dull, as lifeless and miserable-looking as her entire appearance.

"I heard Blackmouth was going after a new prisoner," she said tonelessly as she walked slowly to a cot and lay down across it on her stomach, facing April. "My name's Selma. What's yours?"

April replied thinly, warily, "April Jennings. And who is 'Blackmouth'?"

"That's what we call Blackmon, because of his nasty rotting teeth. He opens that big mouth of his, and all you see is black teeth." She propped her chin in her hands. "How come you're here? What'd you do?"

"I didn't do anything," April replied bitterly. "They said I was a spy, but that's not true."

"Ahh, they think everybody's a spy. That's what happened to me. I was doing just fine till a pipsqueak captain screamed to high heaven that I'd given him the clap. So he had me sent off here. That was almost a year ago."

April blinked in confusion. "The clap? I don't know what you're talking about."

"Oh, honey, you are green, aren't you?" Selma threw back her long brown hair and laughed. "You never heard of the clap? It's the pox or whatever you want to call it. They got all kinds of names for it. Anyway, it wasn't me that gave it to the little bastard. But he was yelling that I was a Yankee spy, sent south to give the clap to every Rebel officer I could get in my bed. Like I said, I didn't give it to him. He was such a horny little creep that he'd lay with any woman who'd spread her legs for him. He had it in for me, 'cause I don't come cheap. I charge plenty, but I do plenty, but then he really got mad when I wouldn't do some of the weird stuff he wanted me to.

"So . . ." She spread her hands in a helpless gesture as a sad little smile twisted her lips. "Here I am for God only knows how long. The only good thing about it is that the guards believe I've got the clap, and they don't mess with me."

April clutched the burlap bag tighter around her nakedness as fright shot through her body. "You mean the guards—"

Selma interrupted with a high-pitched giggle. "Fuck you? Sure, they do. Anytime they want, which is all the time. There's six guards besides Blackmouth. There's twenty-two of us. Twenty-three now. So that means that sixteen of us get lucky every night and don't have to roll with them sons-of-bitches till daylight. That's all they got to do, anyway. They stand over us while we sweat in the fields all day, getting blisters on our hands. They just stand around, making sure we don't try to escape, and when night comes, they flip a coin to see who gets who."

"Oh, my God!" April swayed and sat down quickly on the nearest cot, the water from her body trickling down about her. "Oh, my dear, dear God."

"Yeah, I know what you mean." Selma looked at her with genuine pity. "It's gonna be rough on you. You're younger than the rest of us, and you're pretty. I can't see much with that bag over you, but I'll just bet you got a damn nice body, too. Those bastards are really gonna go crazy over you. But you'll have a while before they pass you around. Blackmouth always gets the new prisoners first, and they don't get passed around till he gets tired of them. I don't imagine he'll tire of you anytime soon."

Tears of rage and desperation flooded April's eyes as she stared at the woman in horror. "Just what kind of place is this? How can the Confederate government allow this kind of savagery to go on?"

Selma shrugged. "I don't think anybody knows what goes on outside of our little 'home' here. You see, Tarboro is for women only—women considered spies and traitors by the South. They consider us outcasts of the worst kind, and they just want to get us out of the way. They don't want to execute us, or do anything that would get them criticized. After all, we are women. So they just shuffle us off and forget about us. Blackmouth and his little army are perfectly happy with the setup. They not only don't have to take a chance on getting their guts blown out in the war, they've got their own harem."

"Actually," she went on matter-of-factly, "it's really not that bad. If it weren't for having to work in them damn fields and thinking about all that money I could be making in the brothels back in Richmond, I wouldn't mind the life. I hear some of the guards are pretty good, too. Some of the girls fight over them."

April looked away, repulsed. "It's horrible. I didn't know such a thing could exist. . . ."

"Oh, it can, and it does. Just make the best of it. If you're smart, you'll make Blackmouth as happy as you can, for as long as you can, 'cause, honey, once you start getting passed around, you're gonna lose that innocent honeydew look of yours mighty fast."

Neither of them had heard the door open. They did not know Kaid Blackmon had returned until his booming voice echoed from the rotting walls about them. "Selma, what're you doing here? You're supposed to be out in them damned fields. You want me to beat your worthless hide?"

Selma withered before his anger-glazed eyes, shrinking backward on the cot as he approached menacingly. "Casper told me I could come here and lay down. I fainted out there in that hot sun. And I got a splinter as big as a fence post in my foot, and—"

"Just shut up!" he snarled, lunging forward to strike her across her face with his huge hand. "I'm getting sick of your whining. There ain't nothing wrong with you. Now

get out of here and back in them fields or I'll take skin off
your ass, you understand me?"

"Yes, Sergeant, yes. I'm sorry—"

She scrambled from the cot, hurrying toward the door,
and April was horrified to see that she was limping on her
right foot, leaving a trace of blood from the splinter she
had tried to tell Blackmon about.

When the door had closed behind her, Kaid tossed the
garments he was carrying into April's lap. "Put these on.
Everybody has a special dress here. Like I told you—"

Suddenly everything within erupted as April screamed
out at him. "She was sick, you bastard! You could look at
her and see she was sick! And she did have a splinter in her
foot. There's the blood right there on the floor!" She
pointed an accusing finger downward. "Tell me, Sergeant,
does President Davis know about Tarboro prison? Does he
know what goes on here? Selma told me about how the
guards rape the women, and—"

"Now you wait a damn minute, you little wildcat!" He
jerked her roughly to her feet and the burlap cover fell
away. "It ain't your place to say nothing about what goes
on around here. And as for President Davis, a traitorous
spy like you ain't got the right to mention the name of a
fine man like that."

His eyes dropped to her breasts, then lower, scanning
her naked body as she cringed in his grasping hands. "Lord
. . ." he whispered hoarsely, as though suddenly struck by a
deep, inner pain. "Lord, Lord, I've never seen a woman put
together like you before."

"You get your damn, dirty hands off of me, you filthy
bastard!" She began to kick at him and struggle as he held
her. "Don't you touch me, damn you—"

A strange, dazed look had taken over his face. He
scooped her naked body into his arms, oblivious to the
blows she flailed at him, her nails raking down his cheeks,
as he strode to the door.

"Please, no!" she begged, anger fading to desperate pleas
as she realized once again how futile it was to attempt to
fight this hulking brute.

He gazed down at her hungrily. "Got to have you, darlin'. I've never seen a woman as pretty as you."

They reached his cabin, and he kicked the door open, then shut, behind him. He removed his clothing and guided her to the bed. "It's gonna be good, darlin'. I promise you it's gonna be good. I'll be gentle."

His pulsating manhood unleashed, he grasped it in his hand, shaking it roughly as he crawled on top of her. "You were made for a man like me."

April felt as though she were suffocating as he lowered his heavy body to hers. She tried to scream for mercy once more but could not breathe.

He grunted and shifted his body. Then suddenly, he gave a little cry of anguish and tore himself away from the bed. She watched, stunned, as he staggered across the room. He threw his bulk into a wooden chair, his weight causing a threatening creak. Burrowing his face in his hands, he lowered his head to the table and became very still.

For a long time Kaid Blackmon sat without moving. Damn it to hell, he thought, miserable, confused. Why hadn't he been able to take her? Never in all his years pleasuring himself with women had his body failed him. Why had he suddenly been unable to take the most beautiful and desirable woman he had ever seen?

He shook his head and stared at the floor, ashamed. He gave her a sullen glance, then lowered his eyes once more. Maybe he loved her. Maybe, damn it, he cared. He only knew that he could not take anyone that pretty and use her like a common trollop.

He stared at her with red-rimmed eyes as she clutched her blanket tightly under her chin, trembling. With a tight, sad smile, he whispered raggedly, "You ain't got to be scared of me, April. Not now."

He struggled to his feet, turning his back as he adjusted his clothing. Then he shuffled from the cabin, shoulders slumped.

Dear God, April thought wildly. He had been about to take her but then he had run from her suddenly. Something must have happened to him. But what?

There was no time to wonder about it. Now was the time to run.

Cursing herself for not acting sooner, she leaped to her feet. In that instant the door opened and Kaid stepped inside and tossed a bundle of prison garb on the table. "Put these on, April. Can't have you running around without clothes. I'm going to fix you something to eat, then take you out to the field. You might as well get used to the way things are around here."

She watched him as he went to a cabinet and took out hardtack and a cold potato, then poured her a cup of water from a large jug. "This ain't much, but you'll get more for supper." He glanced at her sharply. "I told you to put them clothes on," he snarled.

She turned her back, let the blanket drop away and struggled to pull the baggy dress over her head. It hung loose all the way from the shoulders with no fit at all. It did not go all the way to her ankles. "This . . . this is indecent," she said, eyes misting with humiliation. "It's too short. I have no undergarments, no pantalettes or chemise."

"Just shut up!" He pounded the table with his fist. "We don't have fancy balls and teas around here, and as close as we live, the guards will see you bathing anyway. Just be thankful I'm going to put the word out that they ain't gonna have you. Now get over here and eat this cold tater and hardtack so I can get you out to the field."

She obeyed, partly because of the stabbing hunger pains churning within and also because she did not want to rile the man further. He was glaring at her. Moments before, he had been filled with desire. When he had taken her to get Lucky, he had shown tenderness. He was a man of many faces, and because she did not know what triggered each emotion, she found him deeply frightening. He could change moods without notice or any apparent provocation.

"You work from sunup to sundown," he said as she ate. "You work the fields to grow the food you eat. Keeps you out of trouble, too. Everybody takes turns with the cooking. On Saturdays you get to go to the creek and wash your clothes, but you still take a bath every single night. Always make sure that whore, Selma, gets in the water last. She's eat up with the clap."

"Sundays you can rest," he went on, "if you've done your share all week. If you ain't, then you'll be put to work doing something, believe me."

He paused to give her a long, searching look. Then he took a deep breath and said, "Now I let my boys do just about what they want around here. We got a good thing going being assigned to run this prison, and we know it. So we all get along real good, and nobody gives anybody any trouble. The boys can have any woman they want, any time, but when we get a new one, like you, I get firsts for as long as I want it. So they won't be bothering you. And don't you tell me one of 'em is if he ain't, 'cause if I find out you lie about something that could make me kill one of my own men, I'm liable to just go crazy and break that pretty neck of yours. You understand me?"

She turned blazing blue eyes upon him as she slowly rose from the table. She had had enough of his intimidation. She had had enough of the mess her life had become. "No, damn you to hell, Kaid Blackmon, I don't understand you!" She spat out the words, unwavering before the flush of anger that crept into his face as he towered above her. "One minute you're kind to me, and the next you're screaming and threatening to beat me or kill me. One minute you're tender, and the next you're a brutal bastard. I'm sick of every damn bit of this. I'm not guilty of what they say I did. I never did anything against the Confederacy, and I hope every damn one of you who think I did will rot in hell!"

She paused for a quick breath then rushed on. "I will play your filthy little games here, but heed me well, you big, ugly bastard! I'll stick a knife in your back the first chance I get—and any other man who touches me. And I swear on my mother's grave that I will find a way out of this hellhole—"

She stopped her tirade as he threw back his head and laughed uproariously. And he kept on laughing, his huge body convulsing as he bent forward from his waist, then backward, in delighted guffaws. "Oh, April, April," he cried finally, tears of amusement streaming down his cheeks. "I've never met a woman like you. I swear! Beautiful, and a spirit to boot. You are a delight!"

He reached out and pulled her into the circle of his arms and gave her a squeeze that made her gasp. "I'm gonna like having you around, darlin'. I really am.

"Now then." He gave her a pat and released her. "Put your shoes on, and let's get on out to the field. You and I both know you're my favorite, but if I keep you out of the fields, it's going to make the other prisoners hate you right from the start, and that'd be real bad. You got to try to get along with them, you know. Come along now."

She put on the wooden shoes that pinched her feet, and when she gave a cry of pain, Kaid apologized. "That's the best we can do. The government more or less forgets us out here, and we have to make do. I took them off a scrawny little Yankee boy I found in the woods and shot awhile back. I just saved 'em figuring sooner or later we'd get a woman with feet small enough to wear 'em. You're such a tiny thing, I'm surprised you can't."

"And just how 'scrawny' was the little Yankee boy?" she asked scornfully.

He frowned. "No matter. He was a Yankee. Don't matter to me if they're ten years old or a hundred. If he's a bluebelly, I'll kill him."

He clamped his hand around her wrist and all but dragged her from the cabin. The rough wooden shoes pinched painfully as she struggled to keep up with his fast pace. They moved through the stump-littered clearing toward the forest, then down a path leading around a swamp. Fallen trees and thick underwood bordered on both sides, and April thought she had never seen a more dismal place. She cast wary eyes upward to low-hanging tree limbs, sure that a slant-eyed snake lay in wait on every branch.

"When you start planning your escape," Kaid taunted, "remember there are swamps all around us. Lots of poisonous snakes, quicksand, and wild razorback hogs that'll cut you to pieces before they start eating you. And you'd never make it down the road we come in on. Somebody's always watching it. You may not see 'em, but they're there. So if you want to try to get away, you're going to have to go through the swamps."

"Maybe the snakes and the quicksand and the wild hogs would be better than what I have to endure with you, Kaid Blackmon."

"Now, April," he chuckled and turned his head to give her an amused look. "I'm not all that bad. You be nice to me, and I'll be nice to you. That's the way it works. And don't you be mad at me about what happened a little while ago. I was just tired, that's all. I'm going to make it all up to you tonight."

Too furious to speak, she could only hope that whatever had stopped him from ravishing her would happen again.

They stepped out of the forest, and she saw that they were in another clearing. This one was devoid of stumps. There were, she guessed, at least two or three acres here, lined with neat rows of green plants of all descriptions. The women, dressed in humiliating garb identical to hers, were scattered about the field. Some were using implements like hoes and shovels, while others were on their knees working the soil with their hands. They all stopped what they were doing to stare at her.

A soldier in gray was sitting nearby beneath the cooling shade of an elm tree, and he got lazily to his feet and walked to where they were standing. "This here is Private Ellison," Kaid told her. "You do what he tells you to do. He's in charge of the fields."

April looked at him, saw glazed desire in his eyes as he looked boldly over her body. The dress was thin. She knew her nipples protruded, and she moved quickly to cover her bosom as best she could with her free arm.

The soldier laughed. "Well, we got us a real lady here, ain't we? Don't want nobody seeing her bosoms." He made a smacking sound with his lips. "How's about a li'l kiss to say hello, sweet lady? And there ain't no need in you being shy, 'cause in a little while, when it gets real hot, you'll peel down and work in the raw like the rest of them hussies—"

With a movement so fast April never saw till he struck, Kaid sent Ellison backward with a vicious blow to the chest. Towering over him as he lay sprawled in the dirt, Kaid cried, "You keep your filthy mouth shut to this one, you hear me? She's a cut above the rest. She'll be doing her share in the field, but only in the field. She won't be doing it in your bed or out in the bushes. Now do you understand me, or do I need to rattle that so-called brain of yours a little?"

Ellison's eyes narrowed to angry slits. "Yeah," he drawled as he slowly got to his feet. "No need to get all riled up."

Kaid did not smile, but there was a gentle note in his

voice as he said, "Get to work now. I'm gonna go back and let your dog out. I put him in the barn so he wouldn't wander off. Don't worry. I'll keep an eye on him till he gets used to his surroundings."

April shook her head, bewildered. He cares about my dog, she thought as she stumbled along behind Private Ellison, and Lucky seems to like him. But why did he lock him in the barn? So he wouldn't come to my rescue when he heard me screaming? And why is he being nice to him? None of it makes any sense. A man like that, so brutal and callous, caring about a mongrel dog. . . .

"Here. Jewel will show you what to do."

April turned to look down at a woman kneeling in the dirt. Her face was streaked with grime, as were her hands and arms. Once, April thought, she might have been pretty. Now her skin was baked by the sun, dried and leathery. Her dark hair was dull, lifeless, and pulled haphazardly into a bun on top of her head, damp strands clinging to her perspiration-slicked neck.

She looked up at them with flashing eyes and gave April a look of hate. "What's the matter? Don't Miss Hoity-Toity know how to pull weeds? It don't take no fancy education for this, you know."

Ellison raised his hand as though to strike her. "Don't you get sassy, Jewel. I ain't listening to that smart mouth of yours."

Jewel did not shrink away but continued to stare at April defiantly, furiously. She smirked. "What's the matter? Can't she tell the difference between a weed and a bean plant?" She looked at April. "Are you a Yankee?"

"No, I'm from the South," she replied quickly, wanting to make friends, for she did not understand the hating way the woman was looking at her. "I'm from Montgomery, Alabama, actually, and it's a long story how I got here. But I'm not a spy, and—"

"I didn't ask for the story of your life, bitch. Just get your ass down here and start jerking plants. I'll bet you lived on a fancy plantation, and your daddy whipped his slaves to work in the fields, and you never had to get those dainty hands of yours dirty."

"Jewel, I'm warning you!" Ellison took a menacing step forward.

She stared up at him, undaunted. "You don't scare me, you sonofabitch. And the only reason you brought her over here to work with me is to rub in the fact that Kaid's got a new sweetie to keep his bed warm for a while. Well, it don't make any damn difference to me, understand? And if you think I'm going to warm yours for you—"

He swooped down to slap her, but she had seen the blow coming and was ready for it. April gasped and jumped back, but Jewel held herself steady and kept the taunting smirk on her face.

"You'll do anything I tell you to, you bitch." Ellison's face was red with ire. "Now if you want me to strip that worthless hide of yours and tie you up and beat you till you bleed, then you keep running that smart mouth.

"And I'll tell you something else," he went on, pointing his finger in her face. "Tonight I'm taking you out to the barn where nobody can hear you scream, and I'm going to fix you good."

"Oh, shit, Ellison, you ain't got what it takes to fix no woman good," she laughed. "Now get out of here, or I'll go screaming after Kaid and tell him how you're acting. I might even tell him you're trying to feel up his new sweetie. You know what would happen then," she added with a wink.

He sucked in his breath, straightened. It was obvious her threats had registered. He gave April a rough shove and sent her sprawling down beside Jewel. "Just get to work," he said between gritted teeth. "I'll take care of you later. You can believe that, bitch."

Jewel threw back her head and laughed, long and loud and shrill, but April could tell that it was only an act. She could see the glimmer of unshed tears in the woman's eyes.

When he was out of hearing range, she told her, "I'm sorry, Jewel. He shouldn't have hit you like that—"

"Don't worry about it," she snapped. Pointing to a yellowish green plant nearby, she said, "That's a weed. We have to crawl all over this damn field and pull them up. They've got stickers on them, and they'll really prick your fingers. So try to be careful."

"My name is April Jennings." She held out her hand and

smiled wanly. "I hope we can be friends. It can't be very pleasant here, and if we get along—"

She gasped as Jewel slapped her hand away, then pointed an accusing finger. "Let's get something straight. You and me ain't never gonna be friends, 'cause I ain't got no friends here, see? I do my job, and I keep my mouth shut, and I leave everybody alone. The only reason that bastard brought you over here to work with me was to goad me, to let me know Kaid's got somebody else to lay with and won't be calling me to his bed.

"But that won't last long," she rushed on. "It never does, 'cause there ain't nobody else can satisfy him like I can, 'cause I understand him. He's a good man. But you and the prissy little sluts like you think he's just an ugly old creep without a heart. I know different. And if I ever catch you flirting with him or leading him on, I'll kill you with my bare hands. You understand me?"

April could not believe what she was hearing. She fell back on her knees staring, openmouthed, as the woman's tirade continued.

"I got sent here because I was a spy for the Union. I'd do it again. But as long as I'm in this hellhole, I'm going to make the best of things, and that includes claiming Kaid Blackmon for my man. Sure, he may fool around with the rest of you once in a while, but ask any of them, and they'll tell you it's *me* he really likes to do it with.

"I get the best of the food, and I get just about the best of anything that's to be had around here, because it's *me* he cares about. You're pretty. No doubt about that. But just don't think you're going to move in and take over, 'cause you ain't."

Ellison quickly walked back down the row. "You just won't learn to shut up when I tell you to, will you, Jewel?" he cried, reaching to scoop her up roughly by her elbow and slap her once again. She tried to fight back, but he quickly twisted her arms behind her back with one hand, fastening his other hand in her hair. "I'm gonna teach you a lesson. In front of everybody. Now let's just go over to that tree yonder and tie you up good, and then I'm gonna take off my belt and beat your worthless hide."

"No!" April clambered to her feet and began tugging at

his arms. "Don't do it! She wasn't doing anything. You can't!"

He turned on her viciously. "You better stay out of this, woman, or you'll get a beatin', too. Now you get back to work."

"No, I won't. She wasn't doing anything." She reached to grab a handful of his hair and jerk as hard as she could. With a cry of pain, he released Jewel and struck out to knock April away from him.

"You're gonna get it now, you slut—" He stepped toward her as she and Jewel backed away together.

"No, she isn't, Ellison."

April recognized Selma. She still looked pale and wan, but she was approaching, a shovel in her hand. "You aren't going to do a thing to April, because if you do, Sergeant Blackmon will have *your* hide trussed up and beaten, and you know it. So why don't you forget the whole thing and everybody get back to work?"

He looked at them, red-faced, chest heaving. At last he took a deep breath and said hoarsely, "All right. Just get back to work. All of you." He pointed a finger at Jewel. "I know you're just upset about having a new girl around, so I'll let you go this time. But you sass me again, bitch, and I'll beat you so bad Blackmon won't want to touch you for a month."

"Oh, go to hell!" Jewel dropped to her knees and began plucking at the weeds. This time she was unable to hold back the tears, and they began to stream down her face, mingling with the grime to make crooked muddy paths along her cheeks.

Selma patted April on the back and murmured, "Come on over here and work with me. Jewel likes to keep to herself."

Jewel's head whipped up, eyes flashing once more. "You're damn right I do, and you just remember what I told you, woman. I catch you trying to play Kaid for a fool, and I'll claw your goddamned eyes out."

"I . . . I wouldn't. . . ." April stammered helplessly.

"Oh, come on. No point in arguing with her." Selma led April away. When they had reached the far side of the field, she bent down and started jerking at the weeds, showing April how to do it.

They heard a long, low whistle from a guard and looked up to see one of the women taking off her dress. Naked, she continued with her work, oblivious to the taunting remarks.

April was aghast. "How can she?"

Selma laughed softly, bitterly. "You got a lot to learn, honey. When the sun beats down and your skin sticks to your dress, you're glad to come out of it. Besides, these guards have seen everything we got, anyway. It don't matter."

"It . . . it does to me," April cried, frightened.

"It won't after you've been here awhile. You get to the point where nothing matters and you don't even give a damn if you wake up in the morning. Welcome to Hell, honey, 'cause if this ain't it, then there ain't one."

Incredulously, April glanced around and saw several other women prisoners giving in to the torturous rays of the sun. They, too, stepped out of their clothing.

"How can the Confederate government allow this?" she whispered in anguish.

"The government don't know the conditions here," Selma answered. "They think Tarboro prison is a nice little agricultural farm for women prisoners. They'd have Blackmouth's head on a platter if they knew the shit that goes on here. Why do you think he keeps a guard posted on that road out of here? It sure ain't 'cause he worries that one of us is going to escape. He wants to make sure he gets warned if a surprise visitor shows up.

Things are different when there's a visitor, you can bet on that. All of a sudden we get our undies back, and suddenly everything becomes pleasant. The visitors see a happy bunch of women doing easy little chores and living good. And we know better than to let them know otherwise, because the sergeant would see anybody dead that squealed on him.

"You see," she went on, yanking at the weeds as she talked, seemingly oblivious to the blood oozing from her hands as the thorns pricked her flesh, "Blackmouth has it made, and he knows it. He lives pretty easy, and he's got a woman any time he wants one. As ugly as he is, you know he has a hard time finding one on the outside. He's also out of the fighting, and he don't have to worry about getting his guts blown to hell on a battlefield. The soldiers under him know they've got a nice setup, too."

"But the . . . the women," April stuttered, still astonished. "What about when their time is up? Don't they report him then?"

Selma laughed harshly. "Now who do you think they'd believe? A respected Confederate officer or an ex-prisoner? Besides, not too many ever get out of here. If Blackmouth figures he can't trust somebody, they just disappear."

"Oh, God." April fell forward on her hands, shaking her head from side to side. "You . . . you're talking about murder."

"That's strong language, honey. I'm talking about 'accidents,' you know? Like falling in quicksand or getting bit by a moccasin. Those things *do* happen."

"But what if a woman . . . you know . . . gets in the *family way*? Wouldn't the government wonder how she got that way here?"

Selma shrugged. "It happens. They just keep her tucked away till she has the baby. Then they take the baby away someplace. There are lots of women who've never been able to have their own, and they're glad to get one."

She jerked her head toward a soldier who was approaching them, a scowl on his face. "Look, we're doing too much talking. They *do* beat your hide around here for not working, so let's get busy. We'll have all the time in the world for talking later, honey, 'cause believe me, you ain't going nowhere."

April forced her trembling hands to reach out and grab at the weeds, pausing now and then to swat at the gnats that swarmed her face, or to brush at the sweat that dripped from her forehead to sting her eyes.

Welcome to Hell, she thought in anguish, for surely she had died and been sucked into the very pits of Hades.

Chapter Twenty-five

APRIL lay on the rough canvas cot, tossing and turning now and then as the relentless humidity of the night caused her to itch and prickle. Now and then a mosquito's incessant whine would cause her to slap out wildly in the darkness.

No breeze stirred through either of the two windows, and they were not allowed to have the door open at night. Snakes, Sergeant Blackmon had said. In the daytime, they could be on alert for the silent black snakes that roamed out of the swamps every now and then.

Her hands stung from the thorns and blisters suffered working in the fields. Her muscles ached painfully. Selma had told her that she would get used to it, but almost a month had passed since arriving at Tarboro, and she still suffered the miseries of the damned.

In the distance, she could hear the sounds of shrill laughter caught on the wind. Each night, it was the same. After they had eaten supper and taken their baths, the guards would come in, one by one, and select the woman of their choice for the night. Some of them actually seemed pleased at being chosen, but, for the most part, they resisted.

She thought of little Redora Grimsley, hardly more than a child. Fourteen, she said she was, as best as she could remember. She had come to Tarboro only a week after

April's arrival, having been caught slipping through the enemy lines at night to forage for the Yankees. Though not exceptionally pretty, she had such wide brown innocent eyes that she seemed adorable. A sprinkling of freckles across her upturned nose accentuated her youthful look.

She was from a small town in Pennsylvania. Her father had been killed in one of the first battles of the war, and her mother had died that winter of the fever, though Redora suspected her heart was broken and she gave up the will to live. Having no family, Redora was befriended by a Union soldier, who promised to take care of her. He had, she told them firmly, promised to marry her when the war was over. In this time of turmoil, with the cloud of death always looming over everyone, she saw nothing wrong in giving herself to him wholly, to prove the love that quickly grew in her.

When Jasper Wiley was killed in a battle, Redora told April and Selma, sobbing brokenly, the rest of his regiment kept her with them. They were her friends and Jasper's, and they wanted to look after her. Besides, she said, there were things she could do, like cooking and cleaning utensils, doing laundry for the soldiers. She even learned to clean their guns. They never touched her "that way," she swore, out of respect for Jasper.

Then the soldiers found themselves cut off from the rest of their company. It was Redora's idea to sneak through the woods and steal food for them from the Rebels until they could find their way back to their own lines. If captured, she was sure she could convince the enemy that she was merely lost and trying to find her way home. Unfortunately for everyone, she was discovered. The Rebels suspected the truth, so they followed her, capturing her friends and charging her with spying. She was quickly shipped off to Tarboro prison.

She was left alone the first two nights, but then Private Ellison came for her. She had screamed and fought, and even though they were slapped and shoved aside, Selma and April tried to save her. He had called other guards to hold them back while he took the shrieking girl away. During the seemingly endless night that followed, they heard Redora scream . . . and they knew what torment she was enduring.

The next morning, the fresh, innocent look was gone from Redora's eyes. She looked older, wiser, bitter. And after that night, Redora never smiled anymore. It grieved April to watch the girl wither, like a flower plucked and tossed aside.

She still struggled when they came for her, just as she had tonight, but not fiercely, for she was no match for them.

April heard another shrill laugh. On the next cot, Selma muttered, "That's not Redora. We'll never hear her enjoying it. That's probably that whore, Jewel. She always makes a lot of noise, hoping Blackmon will hear and get jealous."

April folded her arms behind her head and stared into the darkness thoughtfully. "Why does she care about him, Selma?" she asked. "Do you think she loves him?"

"I don't know," came the sighing reply. "He's chosen her more than any of the others. Once or twice he's even taken her for a wagon ride on Sunday afternoon. I've seen them laughing some together. You know, he's really not so bad when you catch him in the right mood. Unfortunately, that isn't very often."

"Mmmm," April considered. "He's taken my dog away from me. Lucky would rather be with him than me. I always heard to be leery of a man a dog *doesn't* like."

"Blackmouth's got a mean streak to be sure, but maybe he's always kind to Lucky. Who knows? But one thing I do know—he's sweet on you. What I can't figure out, though, is how come he never sends for you to go to his cabin. Hasn't he ever tried anything?"

April had never confided to Selma about that first day, when Kaid had been about to rape her, then stopped abruptly with no explanation. It had been so strange, and somehow she could not bring herself to talk about it. He had acted oddly since. He spoke gruffly to her, ordering her about like the other prisoners, but when he thought she was not looking, she would catch him staring at her with a tender look on his face.

"No," she lied, finally answering Selma's question. "He hasn't."

She heard her sigh, then, "Well, he will sooner or later. He's been acting downright weird lately. He's always taken the new ones for himself for a few weeks. First it was you he left alone, then Redora. Something funny is going on, and Jewel's noticing, too. That's why she's out there screeching like a cat, hoping he'll hear and get jealous, like I said."

"It could be Redora."

"No, whoever's making that noise is enjoying it. Redora would be crying."

They fell silent. April closed her eyes and tried to sleep but, as always, miserable worries prevented slumber from coming easily. And, as happened so often, Rance Taggart invaded her thoughts. Memories of kisses like warm sweet wine caused her to lick her lips in ecstatic remembrance.

"April?"

Her eyes flashed open, blinded momentarily by the sudden illumination. Terror prickled through her body.

"Come with me, darlin'."

"No!" she cried out, involuntarily.

From the next cot, Selma spoke nervously. "Go with him, honey. Don't make a fuss."

April knew she had no choice. She stumbled along, and when they reached his cabin, Kaid Blackmon set the lantern down on a table just inside the door, then told her to go and lie down on the bed.

She did as she was told, pulling up a blanket to cover herself. She could hear the sounds of his boots hitting the floor and movements as he undressed.

"Look at me!"

She cringed.

"I told you to look at me!" With his lips mere inches from her own, he spoke in a strained, ragged voice. "Tell me I'm not ugly. Tell me you like me, April. Tell me you want me to make love to you."

"I can't" she screamed. "Damn you, I won't say those things to you! I won't!"

"I'll make you want me! I'll make you want to love me."

Then, suddenly, just like the other time, he moved abruptly away from her.

He stumbled across the cabin, this time throwing himself on the floor and beating on it, sobbing, his huge body heaving.

April huddled under the blanket and continued to stare. What could have happened to this man?

Finally, he sat up and sighed. "It's you doing it to me, darlin'."

"Me?" April blinked.

"You're different from any woman I ever wanted before."

His voice broke, and he jerked his head to one side so she could not see the tears. "Damnit, girl, I must be in love with you. I can't stand the thought of . . . doing anything that might hurt you . . . anything you don't want me to do."

He forced himself to look at her once again. "I don't even want another woman. I could have Jewel or any of them whores, but I don't want 'em. I want you, because I love you. But when it comes right down to couplin' with you, something inside just won't let me. I've never had this happen to me before, never, and I've been bustin' women since I was twelve years old and found out what this thing was good for."

April winced, embarrassed.

"You've gotta understand me," he went on miserably, searching her face for some sign of understanding. "You think I like being ugly? You think I like being so big? I can't help the way I am. I'm not ugly inside. Leastways, I don't try to be."

He took a long swallow from his jug of popskull. "If I was good-lookin', you wouldn't want to throw up every time I touch you, would you? You'd want me to sling you down on that bed and really put it to you."

Suddenly, April had had enough. She quickly got to her feet, anger giving her the courage to face him. "It wouldn't make any damn difference to me if you were the handsomest man on earth, Kaid Blackmon! Did you ever stop to think that maybe I'm not a whore? That maybe I don't want you to 'put it to me,' as you so crudely call it? That I just don't want you or any other man raping me? If I loved you, then your looks wouldn't matter. Do you understand me? Can you stop feeling sorry for yourself long enough to understand?"

He blinked in surprise.

"You mean you could care about me if I treated you like a lady? It wouldn't matter to you if I was ugly?"

She shook her head frantically, wanting to tell him that was not exactly what she had meant, but not wanting to hurt his feelings.

"I won't try to do it to you again, April." He reached for her hand, but she snatched it away. He went on quickly, "I can make you want me. I know I can. I'll be good to you. I won't make you work in the fields no more. We'll spend some time together, me and you, and it won't make no difference what the others think. You're the woman I've always wanted all my life . . . a real lady. And I'm gonna make you love me, like I love you. I swear I am."

He reached out and pulled her down to sit beside him once more, stroking her long golden hair back from her face lovingly as she sat rigidly still. "Before the war," he said quietly, "I was a blacksmith. You know what that is? It's a person that makes horseshoes. I was good at it, too, because I've got big arms, and I can stand the heat of the fire. Then when the war broke out, I wanted to do my part. Didn't have no family. Ma died when I was little, and I can't remember having no pa."

He sighed, reaching for her hand once more, and this time she allowed him to take it. "I was powerful lonesome, April, and now I know why. All those women I tussled with, night after night, them actin' like they loved it, squealin' and clawin' and kickin' their legs in the air and diggin' their heels in my back—it was all an act. I know that now. With you, it'd be different. I know it would. You'd never put on an act. You're a lady."

He put his arms around her and pulled her close. "I think I loved you from the minute I laid eyes on you, huddlin' down there in that goddamn ice pit. It made me so damned mad to see what they was doin' to a beauty like you. And I wanted you then, and I want you now."

Suddenly the cabin door banged open, and Kaid jerked away from her to reach for his gun propped against the wall. Ellison yelled from the doorway, "Hold it, Blackmon. It's me. Didn't you hear me yelling?"

Kaid snarled, "Hell, no, I didn't hear you yelling, you sonofabitch, and you better have a damned good reason for bargin' in here."

"It's that damned dog of hers!" Ellison yelled. "I think he's run up on some wild hogs. Come out here and listen. Sounds like the damnedest fight you ever heard."

"Lucky!" April screamed, struggling to get off the bed as Kaid reached to hold her back. "They'll kill him!"

"You just stay put." Kaid jumped up and reached for his pants. Grabbing the lantern and his gun, he hurried to follow Ellison, who was already on his way.

April looked around quickly and spotted an old shirt of Kaid's. It barely reached her knees, but it was better than running naked.

Stepping outside the cabin, she heard the grunts and snorts of the wild hogs and Lucky's growls and cries of pain, and her blood ran cold. Ahead, she could see the two men running through the darkness, and she moved to follow, ignoring the rocks that cut into her bare feet as she hurried behind them. Tears streaked her cheeks and her heart pounded wildly. He was just a mutt, she knew, but they had been through a lot together, and dear God, she did not want him to die.

"It ain't far. Down in that ravine there," she heard Ellison yell. "It ain't been going on long. I was just gettin' Redora back to the cabin, when I heard all hell bustin' loose."

They fought their way through the thick brambles and thorns, and April struggled to keep up. The shirt caught and tore, and as she twisted away, she felt her own flesh being ripped painfully, but still she fought to keep up with them.

"There!" Ellison yelled. "There they are! Damn, there's only one, but he's a big one. How you gonna get a shot in? He's ripping that dog all to pieces."

April pushed forward, bumping into Kaid's back and almost falling. He gripped her elbow, holding her upright and cursing her for following. She looked down into the ravine, saw the two thrashing animals, and screamed at the sight of the snake-headed, hairy, wild hog. His sharp, up-turned tusks kept jabbing at Lucky.

Lucky, covered in blood, his own and the hog's, was flung to one side suddenly but quickly got to his feet and took up a stance, teeth bared, a low, guttural snarl coming from deep within him.

Kaid shoved her into Ellison's arms and cried, "Hold her, damnit, I'm gonna try to shoot that bastard—"

"You'll hit Lucky," April screamed in panic, for just at that moment the dog sprang for the hog once more, aiming his sharp teeth for the beast's throat. The hog ducked, dipped, slung him to the side and then made another charge, penetrating once again with his tusks.

"Damnit, he's gonna kill him!" Kaid slung his gun aside and charged down the ravine, drawing a knife from his belt as he went.

"Don't wade into that, Sergeant," Ellison cried, still holding April. "Goddamn, he ain't nothing but a dog!"

April screamed as she saw the hog backing up for one final charge toward Lucky, who was lying in the blood and the mud whimpering helplessly. This time, the grunting wild beast would finish him.

But then the hog saw the man running toward him, and he split the air with an angry shrieking grunt and charged toward him, head down, bloodied tusks pointed for the kill. Kaid sprang to the side, rolling over on his back and slashing the knife's blade upward just as the hog charged over him.

Blood spattered as the brute's stomach was laid open, but he had enough life left in him to turn sharply and make one final, desperate lunge. April watched in horror as a tusk gouged into Kaid's thigh just as he brought the knife slashing across the hog's throat with every ounce of strength he had in him, twisting, gouging, thrusting again and again.

The beast lay on the ground, blood pouring from the fatal wound.

"I will be damned!" Ellison cried, releasing April, who tumbled down the side of the ravine in her haste to get to Lucky and the man who had saved his life.

"He charged right in there to save a damned dog," Ellison said in wonder.

"Get help!" April screamed up to him as she saw the bloodied wound on Kaid's thigh. "And hurry!"

"I'm going to be all right," Kaid told her, grimacing with pain as he mashed down on the wound to attempt to stop the flow of blood. "We got to see about Lucky. He's hurt bad. We got to get him back to the cabin."

He yelled up to Ellison to carry the dog, adding quickly, "We don't need to get the others stirred up. Some of the prisoners might use this as a chance to try to escape, and I don't want to haul a bunch of snake-bit bodies out of them swamps tomorrow. Let's just move quietly."

April attempted to help Kaid from the ravine, but he brushed aside her efforts, saying, "You know a little thing like you can't help a big bastard like me, darlin'. Now I'm gonna be fine. I been hurt lots worse than this and lived to tell about it. This fellow's the one I'm worried about. That hog ripped him all to pieces, looks like."

He struggled to hold his wounded thigh with one hand while using the other to grab at rocks, exposed roots, any thing to aid him in his climb up out of the ravine. Once out, he called softly, "Follow me and watch out for snakes."

There was no sound in the night except for their gasping breath and the thudding of their feet upon the ground as they ran. Just as they reached the cabin, April trailing by perhaps twenty yards, Ellison appeared, holding a lantern. He had brought an anxious-faced guard, wearing only pants. She recognized Delmer Compton, a private.

"Man, you're soaked in blood," Delmer cried as Kaid pushed by him and through the cabin door. "You better sit down and let me tend to that leg. Lord, look at the blood!"

"Get me something to bandage it," Kaid snapped as he brushed everything from the wooden table in the center of the room to the floor with a loud clatter. Ellison had laid the dog down by the table. Now the animal stared up at Kaid with pain-clouded eyes and gave a feeble whimper. Kaid patted his head and said, "I'm gonna fix you, boy. Don't you worry none."

Ellison frowned. "Sergeant, let that dog go till we can bandage your leg. You're losin' an awful lot of blood."

"It ain't deep," Kaid snapped, shoving him aside as he came forward to bend down and inspect the wound. "It just looks bad, because of the blood. Lucky's the one who needs tending to, or he's gonna die. Now get the hell out of my way. Somebody hand me that jug over there," he ordered.

April watched from the doorway, chest heaving at the sight of the bloodied man and dog before her. Kaid whipped his head around and yelled, "April, you got any thread? A needle?"

She shook her head, feeling completely helpless.

"Compton," he barked, "Go over and ask the women if anybody's got a needle. Don't let on anything's wrong. Then go to the barn and get me some horse hair, from the mane or tail, and get back here as quick as you can."

Ellison handed him the jug, and he took a quick swig before holding Lucky's muzzle up and parting his mouth to pour in a good-sized dose.

"You givin' that popskull to the dog?" Ellison asked in wonder, eyes bulging.

"Hell, yeah. If it makes it easier on a man when he's hurtin', it's bound to make a dog feel better, too. Hold that lantern. April, get me some rags—shirts—a sheet—anything. I got to mop up this blood so I can see what I'm doing."

She moved around the cabin, gathering cloth, and when he yelled for a basin of water, she got that for him, also. Ellison just stood nearby with his hands on his hips, watching in amazement as Kaid worked feverishly.

Compton returned with a needle and a handful of horse hair. By then, Lucky's wounds were cleansed, revealing four long slashes, one of them quite deep. Blood continued to flow. Kaid packed rags into the opening to stifle the oozing as he began to work with the other cuts. Threading the needle in the light of the lantern, using a long strand of horse hair, he quickly and deftly pulled the split skin together and began stitching it closed.

"Sewing up a danged dog." Ellison shook his head back and forth. "I just can't believe it. And you risked your life to charge down there in the middle of all that fightin', too. And you're still bleedin'."

Kaid paused, needle in hand, long enough to cast a menacing look in the soldier's direction. He snarled, "I can take care of me, but this dog can't take care of himself. Now just shut up, Ellison, 'cause you're botherin' me."

Ellison snickered as April caught his eye suddenly. She still wore Kaid's shirt, and perspiring from running caused the garment to stick to her skin. Her large breasts heaved, nipples moving provocatively up and down as she breathed.

"Lord . . ." he whispered under his breath, "I'd strangle that dog if he'd stopped me from gettin' some of that."

Kaid did not hear him, and April ignored him. She folded her arms across her chest and stepped closer to the table. "Is there anything I can do?" she asked anxiously.

Turning his head only slightly from his intent stitching, he gave her a lopsided grin. "Just stay close to me, darlin'. Right now, I can't ask for anything more than that." Then the smile faded as he noticed what she was wearing. He yelled to Ellison to get her clothes from the cabin.

Long, tense moments passed as Kaid worked over the dog. It was perhaps a half hour later that he finally stood back and motioned to Compton to bandage the dog. "He's stopped bleeding. I think he's gonna be all right—"

And then he toppled forward, Compton leaping forward to catch him just before he hit the floor. Dragging him to the bed, a trail of blood behind him, he lifted him up and snapped at April to get the jug, the needle, and more horse hair. "Now we gotta try to save him," he said, giving her a condemning look.

She did as she was told while Compton ripped open his sergeant's trouser leg, exposing the gaping wound. "You know anything about sewing a man up?" he asked her. She shook her head wildly from side to side, and he snapped, "Well, you better learn fast. Thread that needle. I'm going to hold the skin together, and you start stitching. Then we're going to get some whiskey in him, and I'm going to burn it shut."

When he had the ragged edges of skin together, April took a deep breath and poked the needle through, joining the edges. After that first stitch, she knew she could do it . . . would do it. He had saved Lucky. He deserved saving, in turn. April breathed deep, even breaths while she worked. Compton's eyes never left Kaid's face.

When it was done, she stepped back, swaying dizzily. Ellison had returned, and he caught her elbows and helped her to a chair.

"Good job," Compton said, surveying her work. "The bleeding has stopped, and I don't think we'll have to burn it. Now all we got to do is sit and wait and see what happens."

"Ahhh, he'll make it," Ellison said breezily, settling down with the remainder of the jug. "The Sarge is tough. I'll wager they both make it. Let's take a drink."

April picked up the prison dress he had brought to her and slipped outside the cabin to put it on quickly in the darkness. Then she returned, ignoring the two drinking soldiers as she walked over to kneel beside Kaid. He was breathing heavily, but evenly. There was no more blood oozing from the bandage wrapped around his leg. He would, she reflected gratefully, survive. And so would Lucky, thanks to a man who cared about one of God's own creatures more than himself.

"A giant," she whispered so low that Ellison and Compton could not hear. "A *gentle* giant."

She touched her fingertips to his forehead. His eyelids fluttered, then opened. Smiling wanly, he reached to caress her hand. "How's the mutt?"

"He's going to be fine. So will you, if you'll lie there and get some rest. You lost an awful lot of blood."

He nodded, then emitted a feeble snicker. "Maybe it was ugly blood. Maybe all the ugly blood drained out, and now I won't be ugly no more."

"Anyone who did what you did can't be ugly, Kaid."

He closed his eyes, head dropping wearily to the side. "Stay with me," he whispered, still holding her hand. "Don't leave me tonight—"

"I'll be here," she assured him. "Just sleep. I'm going to look after you and Lucky."

Just when she was sure he was finally asleep, he opened his eyes and turned to stare at her once more. "When I'm back on my feet, I'm going to get you out of this, April . . . get you out and make you love me."

Soon, he slept.

🜲 Chapter Twenty-six 🜲

RANCE crawled slowly along the ground on his belly, pausing every few yards to listen for some sign that they might have been detected by Yankee sentries. Behind him, Edward Clark followed, moving equally as cautiously.

The only sounds were the occasional mournful hooting of an owl, and the night wind dancing through the forest. Ahead, they could hear the restless pawing of horses' hooves in the Pennsylvania dirt.

They were getting close.

Edward scrambled forward to plop down next to Rance, their arms touching. "How much farther?" He whispered so low Rance had to strain to hear him.

"Maybe fifty yards. There's only one sentry posted at the corral. You know the plan."

Edward whispered that he was ready, and Rance hoped he was telling the truth. There could be no slipup now, for they were right in the middle of a hotbed of Yankees, and if spotted, would be killed on the spot. Everything had to go exactly the way he had planned.

Ahead, in a hastily constructed corral of split rails, a hundred Union artillery horses were waiting, horses that would bring a small fortune when rebranded and resold to the Union army. There was no time for the ploys he had used in the past—steal the cavalry's horses, rebrand them as artillery, resell their own horses to the Yankees; then use the money to buy prime stock for the Confederacy. Hell, no, the war had busted wide open, this summer of '63, and Rance knew he had to move fast. The object was to get the best possible horses for the Rebel cavalry. There was no time to waste on playing fancy tricks—or for making money for his own pocket, he reflected with a touch of chagrin. He would not come out of this war broke by any means, but he'd had to forego much of a profit as he became caught up in the war itself.

Beside him, Edward waited quietly. It was part of the plan that they would crawl this far in the dark and then wait at least a half hour to make sure all was calm before making the final move.

He slapped at a pesky mosquito and wished for a jug of popskull. Licking his upper lip, he tried not to realize that death could come at any moment. The march was on. There was no time to think about anything except getting these fine horses for Jeb Stuart. After Stuart's current mission, his whole cavalry unit was going to need horses badly.

Besides, Rance thought with a wry grin, he was in uniform now. Confederate gray. President Davis, himself, had bestowed the commission, saying he wanted to make sure he was duly made a part of the Confederate army. He could have been an officer of just about any rank, he knew, but he would accept nothing higher than Captain. Being an officer, he had been allowed to sit in on conferences with General Robert E. Lee, himself, as Lee planned the next move for his Army of Northern Virginia.

Lee had begun his move in early June, by shifting his troops northwest from Fredericksburg behind the line of the Rappahannock River. His aim was to reach the Shenandoah Valley and then cross the Potomac River west of the Blue Ridge mountains. He had divided his army into three corps. One was led by James Longstreet, and the others were being commanded by two new Lieutenant generals, Richard S. Ewell and A. P. Hill.

Rance knew that Longstreet's corps had led off, pausing at a place called Culpepper Court House in Virginia, while Ewell's corps leapfrogged it and moved on to drive a few scattered Union detachments out of the lower valley. Meanwhile, Hill had stayed in Fredericksburg to keep an eye on the enemy there.

The Union Army of the Potomac, under General Joe Hooker, was taken by surprise when Lee split up his army. The first thing Hooker had wanted to do was march on Richmond, since Lee's army was divided. Washington had said no. They were still sore over the way Hooker had been beaten all to hell at Chancellorsville in May. Rance had heard that the Union was not about to let Hooker try a new offense. The Confederacy had managed to learn that he was to act strictly on the defensive and follow Lee wherever he went. Defend, but not attack.

Rance was worried. It had been ten days since Lee had heard from Stuart. Which meant ten days had passed with no word of Hooker's movements. By invading enemy territory Lee was, in effect, moving blind. He had gotten into Pennsylvania, but his three corps were widely separated. The advance was near a town called York, and the rear was at Chambersburg.

Beside him, Clark hissed, "Is it time yet? I want to get this over with, Taggart."

Taking a deep breath and straining to hear around them one last time, Rance said, "Yeah. We'll move out. I'll take care of the sentry on the north gate. You hit the south. When I whistle, leap on one of those horses and start shooting, and let's move them out."

Clark started forward, and Rance shot out a hand to hold him back. "Remember," he warned. "Once those horses start stampeding, you ride like the devil is on your heels, because once those Yankees hear the commotion and wake up and realize what's going on, you're going to think the devil *is* on your heels."

Rance listened until Clark had crawled out of hearing range. Then he moved forward. Crouching in a thicket, he could see the Union sentry slouched against the corral gate in the faint moonlight. His chin rested on his chest, and Rance watched for several moments to make sure he was sleeping. Good. He had expected to find him asleep at his post. It was late, and the Yankee didn't have to worry about being discovered lax on his duty.

Well, Rance thought as he sucked in his breath and pulled his knife from his boot, the man would never wake up again.

He slithered along the ground until he was only a few feet from the guard, then rolled beneath the bottom railing of the corral. A few of the horses standing nearby pawed nervously and sounded nervous whinnies, but the guard never moved.

Rance crawled until he was directly behind the soldier, then sprang up to hold him steady against the post with one arm, while he moved with his other to bring the knife slashing across his throat in a single swift movement.

The soldier struggled only briefly, then slumped lifelessly to the ground.

This is the crucial moment, Rance thought as his heart pounded wildly. If Clark hasn't done his job, then we've blown the whole mission, and we're dead. He gave a long, low whistle, then quickly unfastened the corral gate and swung it open. Instantly, he leaped onto the nearest horse, wrapping his legs under the belly and digging his fingers into the mane, holding his knife in his teeth.

Edward's shots exploded the silent night. Rance grinned and kicked the horse's flanks with his heels. Behind him, he could hear Edward screaming the Rebel yell as he continued to fire. The great thunder of horses' stampeding hooves was like a million drums beating at once. And Rance was leading them, heading down the ravine to where his men waited. They were going to have to ride hard and fast, driving the herd across the Rebel lines, where the Yankees would dare not follow.

He could hear the angry shouts as the sleeping Yankees awoke and realized what was going on. There was no time to look back and see if Edward was following. He had to hang on, to get as far away as possible.

They charged through the night. A low-hanging branch slapped Rance painfully across the face. He struggled to dig his fingers tighter into the horse's mane, stunned. Blood trickled into his eyes.

On and on he rode, and just as panic began to spark— had they taken the wrong trail? had he missed his men altogether?—he heard triumphant shouts and gratefully jerked his mount to the side, then slid down to run for Virtus, who was waiting nearby.

Once in his familiar saddle, Rance began to relax. The

run was over. His men would now take the horses to a prearranged hideout in the mountains. His job was done.

Rance reached into his saddlebag and brought out the small bottle of whiskey, treating himself to a long, satisfying swallow. He mopped the cut on his forehead with his sleeve. The run had been successful. Stuart would have good, fresh horses waiting for him when he finished his present mission. But how damn long was this blasted war going to go on? How many more lives were going to be lost before they could all get down to the business of living in peace? Rance was thoroughly aware that each morning he awoke could be his last.

He waited for Edward to join him for the return to camp, and his mind began to wander, as usual, to thoughts of home—and April. Where was his golden-haired, blue-eyed beauty?

He took another swig of liquor. Damnit, why had she run away? What had he done? He had asked her to stay and she had agreed. And then she had simply disappeared.

He knew she had not made it back to Alabama. He had paid a man a thousand dollars just to ride down there and find out. There was only one woman living at Pinehurst, Vanessa. There were some surly fellows hanging around her. No one named Carter Jennings was about, but Rance's informant had heard that the plantation owner was dead.

So where the hell was April? What if she had made it back there and Vanessa had killed her? And how the hell was he supposed to find out when he was stuck in the middle of a goddamned war?

He shook his head and ground his teeth together. Blast her, anyway. Why couldn't she have stayed with him? Eventually, he would have taken her home, done what he could to help her reclaim her home. Well, there was little he could do now.

He had passed the word that he would pay five thousand to any man bringing news of her. It was a long shot—but it was his only shot.

"Well, we made it." Edward's face was beaming in the faint moonlight. As he approached, his mount slowed to a walk. "Now all we got to do is get back to camp and, if we're lucky, we'll get a few hours sleep."

Rance tugged at his mustache thoughtfully. Suddenly, he asked, "What do you hear from Trella?"

"Huh?" Edward blinked, surprised at the question at this, of all times. "What brought that on?"

"Is she still in Richmond?"

"Of course, she is." Edward cocked his head to one side and strained to see Rance's face. "What's this all about? You know damn well I took her to Richmond and left her there, because she got mad when we went in the army active, and I wouldn't marry her. She's working in some bawdy house trying to make me jealous. I won't fall for that. No woman is going to rope me in, not for a while, anyway. And it damn sure ain't going to be a whore like Trella."

"Is that a big house she's working in?"

"Yeah. About the biggest in Richmond. Damnit, Taggart, you getting a yen for a woman? Hell, you can screw her for all I care."

"No, it's not that. Don't get your dander up. You pretend you don't care, but you do. It's April. You know I put the word out I'd pay five thousand for anyone that could tell me where she is."

"Yeah," his companion drawled slowly. "So that's it. I figured you were being eat up inside more than you let on. You think maybe Trella could help you find her?"

"That's about it." He kneed Virtus to begin lumbering forward, and Edward followed. "Maybe we can get a few days' leave and go see if she's learned anything. She knows about the money, doesn't she?"

He laughed. "Hell, yes. I imagine she's keeping her ears open. That woman loves money almost as much as she loves men."

"We'll pay her a visit."

They rode in silence until they reached a gurgling stream. Rance got down from his horse and began to splash water over his face and arms.

Dawn was beginning. A pale gray light covered the earth, heralding a new day. Soon, the sky would turn pink, then bloodred, and the sun would erupt from the horizon.

"You love her, don't you?" Edward asked quietly, watching Rance carefully as he bathed.

Without looking up, Rance muttered, "I don't think I've ever loved any woman, Clark. You know that. But April belongs to me. Fair and square. Maybe you think that's stupid, but it's my way. I want her back. I want her with me until I get tired of her, for however short or long a time that might be."

He glanced up sharply. "I don't want to talk about it any more, all right?"

Clark nodded silently, feeling no resentment. They had been together for a long time . . . long enough for each to respect the other man's privacy.

When they got to camp they unsaddled their horses and immediately fell on their blankets to try and catch as much sleep as possible.

Rance had just dozed off when the bellow came, "Fall out! Fall out, everyone! We're under attack!"

Rance leaped up, instantly alert, to see one of their soldiers charging through the camp on a large black horse. Troopers were jumping up from around campfires and beneath trees. Somewhere a bugle began to play the first blaring notes of "To Arms."

The sound ended abruptly as the bugler fell forward, a bullet in his neck.

"It's an all-out attack!" someone screamed just as an exploding volley of fire erupted from the woods, only a few hundred yards behind them.

A major came riding up as Rance and Edward scrambled for cover. He yelled hoarsely, "Damnit, we didn't get the word! Lee's army has collided head-on with Meade's."

"Meade?" Rance cried. "What happened to Hooker?"

"Lincoln replaced him with George Meade. What damn difference does it make now? We're under attack." He galloped away to attempt to gather his men for the counterfire. Rance watched helplessly as a bullet caught him squarely in the back and he toppled headfirst from his horse dead.

"No time to saddle," Rance yelled to the men within shouting distance. "Fall into battle line on foot." They rushed to the edge of the field and fell forward, prone, to begin firing at the charging Yankees.

A screaming Union soldier leaped over a blackberry

bush, and Rance raised his revolver and fired, kicking away his tumbling corpse as the man fell on them. Beside him, a Rebel soldier shrieked as he was caught from behind by the swing of a Yankee saber. Rance jerked his own knife from his boot and drove it into the attacker's throat.

He emptied his gun at Union soldiers around them, clicking on the empty cylinders before throwing it aside and grabbing the dead Yankee's saber. Charging forward, he felled four of the enemy soldiers and was about to dart for cover when a movement caught his eye to the left. Edward Clark was running right behind him, but he did not see a Yankee approaching from behind, wielding a bloodied sword.

"Clark, hit the ground!" Rance screamed, lunging for the attacking soldier just as Clark swung out of his path. With one fierce chop, Rance severed the Yankee's arm, his hand still clutching his sword.

He tore his gaze away from the sickening sight as Edward cried, "I'm hit!"

He saw the blood streaming down his friend's arm and moved swiftly to support him as they ran for cover. Clark's legs buckled twice, and Rance had to drag him along. They reached a grove of trees and were out of danger, but only for a short time. The battle was erupting on all sides.

They watched as four Rebel soldiers, their guns emptied, did battle on foot with charging Yankees on horseback. The Yankees wielded swords. Each of the Rebels was hacked down and killed.

"We've got to get out of here," Rance said harshly, anxiously. "You're hit, and all I've got is a sword. We're outnumbered. We've got to make it back to the main company. We've got a chance there. Here, we're going to be cut down. How bad are you hit?"

Edward clutched his wounded right arm, blood oozing through his fingers as he shuddered with pain. "I'm pretty sure the ball went all the way through. I'm bleeding on both sides. Got to stop the bleeding—"

"We can't worry about that now. Lay down on your belly. All we can do is play dead and hope some gun-happy Yankee won't ride by and decide to make sure we really are. Here, let me smear some of your blood on my back so I'll look wounded."

They lay down, a few feet apart, and Rance positioned his body in a grotesque arch. Clark followed suit. "If you hear someone coming, stop breathing," he ordered. "Lay real still. It's our only chance."

"Oh, God, somebody is coming," Clark said, gasping one last breath and holding it.

The Yankee soldiers slowed their horses as they maneuvered through the thick grove of trees. Seeing two lifeless bodies in their path, they rode right over them. Rance gritted his teeth and struggled to keep from crying out in agony as a hoof crunched down squarely in the middle of his back. He prayed they wouldn't ride over Clark. Since he was already suffering, he would never be able to hold back a cry of pain.

The Yankees rode on. Soon Rance was dizzy from holding his breath. When they were out of sight, he gulped in the sweet, precious air and rolled toward Clark. He was not moving. "Are you okay?" He gave his friend a gentle shake. "Let's go."

Then he saw the mangled arm, crushed into the mud by a horse's hoof. Cursing, he squeezed Clark's throat slightly, to feel the pulse. He was still alive, but unconscious. He had probably held his breath, fought to keep from screaming, and had passed out. It had saved his life, but only for the moment. If Rance did not get help for them quickly, Clark was going to die.

He raised up on his knees and stuck two fingers in his mouth to give an ear-splitting whistle. In seconds, Virtus came crashing across the clearing, heading straight for them. "Good boy," he whispered, patting him absently as he held him steady, checking to make sure the great horse was not wounded. Then he reached down and lifted Clark to place him belly-down across the animal's back. When he was in position, he swung himself up, clutching the long mane of hair on Virtus's back as he jerked him around.

Beneath him, Clark moaned. "We're going to make it, my friend. Hold on," Rance said tensely. "Just hang on for a little while longer."

The smell of sulfur and smoke stung his eyes as he guided the horse over the corpses of Yankees and Rebels. The smell of blood was an overpowering stench, battling with sulfur to make a nauseating wave.

Ahead, behind, all around him echoed gunfire and the screams of the wounded. Rance moved the horse as fast as he dared while alert for the enemy.

"Here!"

He jerked his head up, tears of relief sparking his eyes as he saw the men in gray waving to him from where they had taken refuge behind a picket line.

He gripped Clark's body with one hand, Virtus's mane with the other, and kneed the horse forward, leaping the last remaining yards to safety. Landing solidly, he lurched to a halt, hanging on to Clark.

"It's bad," one of the soldiers told him as they pulled Clark from the horse. "It's a head-on attack, but we've got 'em outnumbered. Lee got just outside Gettysburg, and Meade hit him there this morning."

Rance slid down and directed that someone see to help for Clark. "The ball passed through his arm. But we were playing dead, and a goddamn Yankee rode his horse over both of us. I feel like my back is broken, but it's just bruised. He's the one I'm worried about. The damned horse mangled the arm that was already wounded."

He turned to the soldier who had been telling him of the attack and asked, "What happened to Stuart? Why weren't we warned that Meade was moving to meet Lee head-on?"

The soldier, hardly more than a boy, shrugged. "All anybody can figure is that Hooker's army was bigger than we thought, and it's taking Stuart longer to get around him. It don't matter now, does it? The battle is on."

A terrible wave of foreboding moving through him, Rance nodded in solemn agreement.

On the first day of the Battle of Gettysburg, July 1, 1863, the Federals were greatly outnumbered and the Confederates were victorious. General Lee was attacking at both flanks and in the center of the federal lines, using everything he had in an attempt to crush the Army of the Potomac once and for all.

It was not until late that night that Rance was able to get to the hospital tent to ask about Edward. He had gone out to join in the fighting and lost count of the number of Yankees who died by his hand. Exhausted, he walked toward the medical area. He tensed at the anguished

shrieks of the wounded and dying. He had to pick his way
through the men lying side by side on the ground. Some
were on stretchers, some lay on blankets. Others, waiting
for treatment, were lying on the bare ground.

Some were already dead and lay with unseeing eyes. It
would be a while, he knew, before the dead were discovered and carried away.

A fire flickered to his left, and he grimaced at the sight
of corpses stacked like cordwood, nearly eight feet high.
Barebacked soldiers worked wearily nearby with shovels,
digging a large pit for a common grave.

The sight to his right sickened him even more. Here
was the disposal area from the surgical tents. Arms and
legs . . . hands and feet . . . when there was time, they
would be buried. For now, they were food for flies in the
hot July evening.

The scene inside the tents was grisly. Surgeons in bloodied aprons worked frantically over wounded men placed on
wooden operating tables. Some held their big knives between their teeth as they used their hands to feel wounds.
If a bone were smashed, if the wound was gouged and
arteries ripped open, then there would be a quick swipe of
the knife, the chilling grind of saw against bone, and another human limb was tossed outside.

They had run out of anesthetic. Now there was nothing
left but whiskey. It was not enough to deaden the excruci-
ating pain of surgery. Soldiers stood around the tables
holding down the screaming, frantically fighting men who
swore they would rather die than be dismembered. Some
were restrained with ropes.

Rance paused to watch, and respect grew in him at the
sight of the surgeons, their pain over the task mingling
with determination. Now and then one of the assistants
would turn away, retching. Twice Rance saw strong men
pass out at the gory sight.

The yellowish glow from lanterns hanging overhead cast
an eerie halo over the scene. Rance moved on to where
patients already treated lay on the ground. The smell of hot
tar and seared flesh touched his nostrils. He had seen the
black substance slapped on freshly cut stumps to stop the
bleeding.

Some of the men lay moaning softly in anguish. Others

had passed out from their ordeal on the table. And, as always, the sightless eyes of the dead stared past him.

"What are you doing here, soldier?"

Rance jerked around at the sound of the belligerent voice. A man much larger than he, heavy, with square-set hulking shoulders, glared at him. The pressures of the day and his present surroundings had taken their toil.

"I'm looking for a friend of mine who was hit this morning. Lieutenant Edward Clark," Rance explained.

The soldier sneered. "Well, it ain't visitin' hours, soldier, and it ain't tea time, neither. So why in the fuck don't you get outta here? I got enough to do without—"

Rance's hand shot out to wrap around the big man's throat and slam him backward, pinning him against a tree trunk.

"It's 'Captain' to you, Private," he said between clenched teeth, "and I'm in no mood to take your guff. This goddamn war wasn't my idea. So back off."

The man's eyes bulged as Rance exerted pressure on his throat.

"Do you understand me?" Rance leaned forward and stared straight into his eyes. "Or do you want the two of us to fight our own battle?"

The private tried to nod but could not. Rance released him, and he clutched his throat with both hands and coughed several times before whispering hoarsely, "Hell, I didn't mean nothin', sir. It's been a hard day, and—"

"And you aren't taking it out on me. Now who around here can tell me where to find my friend?"

The soldier took a few steps in retreat before saying, "I'm sorry. I wish I could help you. But there's maybe a thousand men lying around here, and I don't know how you're going to find him."

"*We're* going to find him," Rance said quietly. "Just walk around and call his name—Edward Clark. It'll give you something to do, besides get yourself into trouble. Now move."

The private moved quickly away, calling out Edward Clark's name as he went. Rance went in the opposite direction. He had gone only a few paces when a wounded soldier lying nearby called out, "Hey. You sure got guts."

"How's that?" Rance paused to look down at the man.

"That's Hugo Pauley you just slammed. He's a bad one. You coulda got killed."

Rance smiled. "I didn't though, did I?" He started to move on, then turned to say, "And he's not bad, soldier. Just big."

"An hour later, Hugo Pauley came rushing up to Rance to tell him he had found Clark. He led Rance to where Clark lay, on a blanket near the edge of the field.

"I'm lucky," Edward told him with a crooked smile. "At first, this dumb-ass surgeon wanted to take my arm off, because it would've been the easy thing for him to do. But I raised hell and said it was my arm and if I got gangrene, it was my business. So they bandaged me up, and here I am."

Rance knelt beside him. "You could die from gangrene, you know," he said anxiously. "I know you don't want to lose your arm, old buddy, but you don't want to lose your life either."

Edward grinned wryly, a little drunk, Rance knew, from whiskey. "Hurry up and whip those Yankee asses out there, and then get me to Richmond. Between Chimborazo hospital and Trella's tender, loving care, I'll be just fine."

"I'll do my best, buddy. Just hang on."

Rance told him about the day's battle, wanting to get his mind off his injury, but he had not been there long when a soldier rushed over and said, "Are you Captain Taggart? Private Pauley told me I'd find you over here. There's some men looking for you, wanting to know about those horses you all stole from the Yankees this morning. They want to know what to do with them."

"They're for Jeb Stuart," Rance told him.

The soldier looked puzzled. "But nobody's seen Stuart. Everybody's pissed because he ain't showed up. So they want to know what they're supposed to do with the horses."

Rance was becoming angry. "Keep them for Stuart. He'll be here. Believe it."

Edward touched his arm. "Go along and do what you've got to do. I'm not going anywhere."

Rance got to his feet reluctantly. "Maybe I'd better. Things are in a pretty bad state of confusion around here."

Edward managed another wan smile. "I'm gonna make it. Just don't leave me behind. I want to be there when it happens."

Rance raised an eyebrow and looked down at him, puzzled.

"You're going to have to explain that."

"I want to be there when you find her. You won't admit it, you stubborn bastard, but you're in love with her."

"Me?" Rance laughed. "No way, my friend. I want her because she's my property . . . just like my horse. As for loving her—or any woman—I think you know me better than that. I'm not going to settle down."

"I didn't say anything about settling down. I just said you're in love. That's why you want to find her. All this talk about her being your property is bullshit and you know it. You just won't admit it."

Rance shook his head. "I think you've had enough whiskey for one night, Lieutenant. Why don't you just go to sleep? You'll be thinking more clearly in the morning."

He turned on his heel and walked away, not looking back even when Edward chuckled.

In love, indeed, he scoffed silently. She was property. Like his horse. His gun. His saber. He had a claim on her. She had an obligation to him. They had made promises— her loyalty to him for the remainder of the war in exchange for his help with Pinehurst afterward.

But there was no denying that he yearned for the feel of her firm body . . . the touch of her lips upon his.

Despite the horrors about him . . . the screams . . . the stench of the wounded and dying . . . he felt desire welling.

But that had nothing to do with love.

He laughed, walking through the night. Clark was crazy. Love had nothing to do with it. Nothing at all.

✂ Chapter Twenty-seven ✂

RANCE maneuvered the wagon carefully over the rutted road, trying to avoid the deep holes, as the jolt would cause the wounded men in the back to cry out in agony. It was rough going. This was a section that had not been corduroyed—lined with logs—and while corduroy strips were bumpier, wagons moved faster on them, and there were no great, dropping jolts.

He turned in his seat to look back at the six men lying in the wagon bed. He had been given special permission to take them into Richmond, to the big hospital there. These were but a few of those wounded in Gettysburg who had refused amputation. Their wounds were not healing. Green pus oozed from their bandages, which had to be changed constantly. Still, they refused amputation. As a last resort, the doctors agreed to send them to Chimborazo. Rance figured the field doctors were just glad to get them off their hands.

One of the soldiers Rance carried was Edward Clark, and he frowned to see how pale and gaunt he looked in the midday sun. His arm was in bad shape. Rance had changed his bandage the last time they had stopped, roughly an hour before, and already the yellowish green discharge was oozing through.

There were closer hospitals, but he had especially asked to take the men to Chimborazo, and not strictly for personal reasons. He had heard that the best facilities were there, and that's what he wanted for his companions. But he could not deny that he wanted to see Trella.

Edward moaned. Rance called to him and asked if he wanted water. "Just keep moving," came the feeble reply. "Get me out of Pennsylvania and further south—"

"We'll be there by sundown," Rance reassured him. "Just hold on."

He popped the reins and picked up the horses' gait as they came upon a smoother stretch of road. Virtus, in harness on the left, flipped his tail insolently, angry, Rance thought with a smile, over being relegated to the indignity of wagon pulling.

Rance reflected painfully on the terrible three-day battle of Gettysburg. It had been hell. There was no way of knowing exactly how many had been killed, but everyone acknowledged that losses were enormous. Some said that there might be as many as twenty thousand on both sides. If that were true, then Lee had lost nearly a third of the whole Confederate Army.

Jeb Stuart's absence had proved costly. He had finally reached Lee on the evening of that second day of battle, but Lee had been forced to fight before he was ready. And he had not been free to maneuver because, due to Stuart's absence, he had no way of knowing the Yankees' exact position.

Rance rubbed at his left arm and winced. It was a slight wound, but still sore. He had caught the slash of a saber wielded by a man whom he was killing.

Rance had not had to go with Major General George Pickett on that last afternoon of the three-day siege. He had killed his share of Yankees. But he had wanted to go. It was to be an assault on the central federal position on Cemetery Ridge. It might have won the battle. And it nearly succeeded.

But, Rance lamented ruefully, "almost" was not good enough. There had been fifteen thousand Rebels in that assault, but they suffered terrible losses and the troops were separated, their column finally falling back to Confederate lines existing before the battle.

The battle of Gettysburg was over, and there was nothing left for General Lee to do but retreat, which he did. Meade followed, but his own army was mangled, and he was too cautious an officer to force another battle with Lee north of the Potomac. Rance was relieved. Like all the other battle-weary Rebels, he knew that Lee's army could not have withstood another head-on clash.

One of the wounded called for water, and Rance brought the wagon to a stop beneath a shaded grove. He got down off the seat and took a canteen. Clark opened dazed eyes and lifted his head.

"Are we out of Pennsylvania?" he demanded, a surprising strength in his voice. "Damnit, Taggart, get me out of this goddamned Yankee territory."

Lifting the canteen to Clark's lips, Rance said, "General Lee made it back into Virginia. The campaign is over for now, Clark. You just rest. I told you, we're almost into Richmond. I'll have you tucked safely into bed at Chimborazo Hospital by sundown."

Clark's eyes focused sharply upon him, and Rance was relieved to see a bit of his old spirit return. "Yeah, and then you'll head for Trella, you dog. You been so long without a woman, you'll steal mine."

"You don't worry about her working in a bawdy house, you son of a gun," he laughed, gently tousling his hair, "but you worry about *me* having a tussle with her. Now that's a friend for you."

"Hell, yes." Clark nodded. "The women you take to bed have a way of falling in love with you. I don't have to worry about her falling for one of those other rowdies."

Rance shook his head and returned to start the wagon. They lumbered forward again.

He snorted and thought, fall in love, indeed! Maybe there had been a few who had run after him. And most wanted a repeat performance. But there was one, he reminded himself, who had not fallen under any charms he might possess. April. *She* hadn't minded leaving his bed.

Maybe that was why he found her so enchanting, he suddenly realized. She was actually the only woman he had never been able to possess totally.

He shook his head. They had enjoyed each other. She was one hell of a woman. But she had left him. Why? Damn it, he was going to find out why. There weren't too many things he set his mind to that he didn't wind up doing, and by God, this was going to be one of them.

Soon they came upon what Rance knew was called "old fields," a coarse, yellow, sandy soil that bore scarcely anything but pine trees and broom sedge. There were some places where, for acres, the pines would be only about five feet high, so he knew this was land that had been in cultivation probably no more than six or eight years before. He could also see patches where the trees were perhaps a hundred feet high. Then, for long intervals, there were fields in which the pines were just beginning to spring from the ground into beautiful green plumes, growing among the grass and sassafras bushes and blackberry vines.

He found Virginia a beautiful state, but not nearly as appealing as Alabama. He felt a twinge of homesickness. One day, by God, he would return to the peace of Cheaha mountain and raise his beloved horses. And he would raise them, not for war or strictly for profit, but for the sheer love of the animals.

It was almost sundown when the wagon rolled through the gates of Chimborazo Hospital. Rance had been stopped several times as they approached the outskirts of the Confederate capitol, as sentries made sure that he was, in fact, a Rebel and carrying true Rebel soldiers. He hated the delay and the answering of questions but understood the need for security.

When he arrived, the gate soldiers immediately sent for someone to escort him inside. He moved on past rows of identical white buildings until he was signaled to stop. Then, while his men were unloaded by soldiers who seemed to appear out of nowhere, he unhitched Virtus from the wagon and led him to a water trough. He found a place to secure him, then went back to inquire about Clark.

He saw a harried doctor walking away from the cot where Clark had been placed, and he touched the doctor's shoulder. "I'm Captain Taggart. I brought these men here. I want to know about Clark." Rance pointed.

"He's in bad shape, just like all of them," the doctor snapped. "Damnit, who do they think they are, refusing amputation? And what kind of stupid doctors did you have out there on the battlefield that they let patients tell *them* what to do? When the bone is split and shattered, there's nothing to do but cut off the limb."

"There were plenty of others who didn't argue," Rance

told him quietly. "I think the doctors were glad enough not to worry about those who did. Now just tell me how my friend is."

The doctor frowned. "All right, Captain, I'll tell you straight. Your friend's arm is mangled—"

Rance interrupted, "He got a minie ball straight through the muscle. It was an ugly, jagged wound, but a clean one. I was there when it happened. Then we had to lie down and play dead when some Yankees rode through. They rode right over us. One of their horses stomped on Clark. That's what mangled it, not the minie ball."

"It doesn't matter now. It's mangled. Gangrene has set in."

"He won't let you amputate. He'd rather die."

The doctor raised an eyebrow. "Well, he may just get his druthers, Captain."

The nerve in Rance's jaw tightened, and he fought down the impulse to smash his fist into the cocky-talking doctor's mouth. "Spare me your sarcasm and tell me what you can do for him," he snapped.

The doctor shrugged, glanced at Clark, then said, "I'm going to give him a cathartic to keep his bowels open, first of all. He's complaining about stomach pain. Then I will give him some opiates for the pain in his wound. As soon as I can get to him, I'll make an incision to drain the pus and wash it out with chlorinated water. About all I can do then is apply tincture of iodine or a tannic acid solution and camphorated oil."

"I saw some maggots in his wound the last time I changed the bandage."

"Yes, I saw them, too. We'll get them out."

"Leave them."

The doctor's eyes widened. "Maggots are an infection of the worst kind. I'll get them out with injections of chloroform."

"No, you won't," Rance said quietly. "They may be his only chance."

The doctor started to brush by him, but Rance spun him around. Speaking low enough that no one else around them could hear, he said, "Now you listen to me, doc, and you listen good. You leave those maggots in there. You think he's going to die, so what's it going to hurt to try something? I heard about a group of surgeons tending gangrene cases in a prison stockade in Chattanooga. The Yankee surgeons wouldn't give them bandages and supplies, so there was nothing the Rebs could do but leave their patients' wounds unbandaged for the flies to blow. As it turned out, the maggots ate the infection, cleaned the wound out, and the men were cured."

The doctor sputtered, "That . . . that is the most insane thing I have ever heard of! And you unhand me at once before I have you thrown into jail. I'm a Colonel, and—"

"I don't give a damn if you're General Robert E. Lee." Rance's upper lip quivered. "That man over there is a friend of mine. I don't want him to die, and he doesn't want his arm cut off. So you just leave the damn maggots in his wound. Now, I'm going into town. But I'm coming back first thing in the morning, and if either his arm or those little white maggots are gone, I'm going to come looking for you, and you just better hope I don't find you. Do we understand each other?"

"All right," the doctor sighed, taking a few steps to the side. "Just don't blame me if he's dead when you get back. It's your responsibility, not mine."

Rance nodded. "Good."

He walked over to Edward and touched his shoulder. "I'm going into Richmond to find Trella. You rest, and I'll see you in the morning."

Edward managed a weak smile. "Thanks for getting me here. I don't . . ." He paused to take a gasping breath. ". . . even care if you make love to my woman. Just don't make her fall in love with you."

"It's information about April that I want from your woman. Nothing more." He gave his shoulder a gentle squeeze and turned to leave.

"Captain. May I have a word with you?"

He walked over to where the doctor was standing.

"We were never formally introduced. My name is Dr. Gilstrap."

"Captain Taggart."

The doctor nodded curtly, eyes stormy. "I want you to know that I plan to report you for threatening me. I don't appreciate anyone telling me how to practice medicine."

Rance sighed impatiently. "Do whatever you like, doctor, I don't have time to discuss it."

He started to walk on by, but the doctor placed his hand against Rance's stomach, hard. Rance saw that two guards stood nearby and quickly figured that the doctor had asked them to be close by for this confrontation.

He slowly dropped his eyes to look at the doctor's hand, then raised them. "I don't like anybody touching me except women."

Dr. Gilstrap jerked his hand back quickly and said, "Look here, I want you to know that I am going to treat that man as I see fit. I don't intend to be intimidated by you. The very idea! Leave the maggots in the wound! Why, if that were reasonable treatment, I would have heard about it, and—"

"Then you're saying you know everything."

"Why, no . . ." he sputtered. "Not at all, I'm saying—"

Rance cocked his head to one side and grinned. "Did it ever occur to you that there just might be a few medical advances being made out there on the battlefield that you don't know about, doctor? Haven't you got enough wounded soldiers to tend to without worrying about a few maggots crawling around in Clark's arm? Are you so goddamn stubborn you aren't willing to try something new?"

"I . . . I . . ." Dr. Gilstrap swallowed hard, glanced around to make sure the soldiers were still nearby, then cleared his throat. "I'm saying that I will treat that man and any man in this ward the way I see fit, and I will not be intimidated by you, Captain. That is my privilege, and I intend to exercise it."

"And my privilege, doctor," Rance smiled, "will be to make good my threat. I'll see you tomorrow."

He tipped his hat to the soldiers, then walked away.

When he arrived in Richmond, he found the city teeming with boisterous soldiers. Respectable townspeople had long since retired to their homes as darkness fell. The night belonged to the men of war, who were attempting to drink away their sorrows.

After checking into a hotel and taking a hot bath, Rance changed into the fresh uniform he had carried in his saddlebag—a gray tunic with black facings and stand-up collar with tiny gold stars adorning. The trousers were dark blue, a black velvet stripe bordered in gold cording running down the outside of each leg. He pulled on scuffed ankle boots, yearning all the while for the casual dress he had always worn around the ranch. Officer's dress, he had decided long ago, was not to his liking. He had to wear the uniform, for he did not want to be thought a nonsoldier. That would be dangerous in a town full of drunk, battle-weary men.

The streets were crowded with drunken, jostling soldiers as Rance made his way to The Bed of Roses. He looked neither right nor left as he walked briskly along. Soon he found himself in front of a two-story house set back from the street and painted fiery red. He shook his head in disbelief. The front porch and the columns supporting it were covered with climbing roses. The yard was filled with thick, flowering rose bushes. The aroma was overwhelming.

He took the steps two at a time and rapped on the front door. A moment later a woman with a heavily made-up face and wearing a bright red satin wrapper appeared. Her eyes sparkled as she gazed up at him. "Well, hello, big boy. Welcome to The Bed of Roses," she cooed, taking a deep breath so that her fleshy breasts would rise above the low-cut gown. "Ain't seen you around here before. My, my, you are a handsome devil. Big, too."

She waved him inside. "You come on in here, big boy. My name's Paulette, and I just happen to be available for the evening. We're going to have us a fine time."

Rance glanced around at the entrance foyer, saw that the wallpaper was of red and pink roses. Pots of red roses were everywhere. Beyond, he could see a parlor decorated in pink and white and yellow; candlelight cast a mellow glow around everything. Despite the apparent effort at sophisticated decor, it was obviously a cheap house. Paulette, who was tugging at his sleeve, was an example of the low-quality woman employed here. He had been to some houses where the girls were actually pretty, but there was no way that he could ever make love to the fleshy blob beside him.

He took a deep breath and said, "I'm looking for Trella Haynes. I was told she works here."

The woman's eyebrows raised in surprise. "Well, she don't," she responded quickly, red-tinted lips turning downward. "She's here, but she don't *work* here, if you know what I mean." She yanked the front of her wrapper together in a haughty gesture as though announcing that, if he did not intend to buy, then he would get no free looks.

"I don't know what you mean." He stood with legs spread wide apart, arms folded across his massive chest, eyes stormy. "Maybe you'd better explain."

"She's a maid." Paulette walked over and picked up a glass of amber liquid and took a long swallow. "Helps in the kitchen, cleans the rooms, does the wash. Stuff like that. I get so damn tired of men coming here and wanting *her* when she thinks she's too goddamned good for selling. I keep telling Annie she ought to get her out of here. She gets in my way."

"Would you call her for me, please? Tell her Captain Taggart is here."

The front door opened and a soldier lurched in, drunk. He saw Paulette and grinned broadly, opening his arms. She hurried across the rose-scrolled rug to greet him. "Paulette, baby, I was hopin' you'd be free. I need me some of that hot lovin'—" Oblivious to Rance, the soldier jerked Paulette's wrapper open to fill his hands with her fleshy breasts, kneading them roughly as his lips came down to devour hers.

They clung together for a moment. Then Paulette stepped back to pat his crotch with a grin and declared proudly, "I can get it up quick, can't I, Lonnie Earl? Come on. I'll take care of this one fast, and then we'll have all night for more fun."

Laughing together, they ran up the stairs and disappeared. Rance walked over to where Paulette had left her glass, lifted it, and took a sniff. Brandy. He downed the rest of it. Glancing about for a bottle, he found one, halfful, on the chipped mahogany sideboard. He lifted it to his lips and finished it all in one long swallow.

Rance smiled. So, this was Trella's ploy. And a very dangerous one. But then, Trella was not very smart. She could not bring herself to actually become a prostitute, but by working as a servant in a whorehouse, she figured that Edward would think the obvious. He was, of course, supposed to become so enraged at the thought of other men having her that he would demand she leave and marry him. But she was the one becoming angry, as Edward made no show of jealousy, allowing her to do as she pleased.

Rance walked through the entrance foyer, listening to the giggles and the moans of ecstasy audible from upstairs. He moved around the stairs to a door at the end of the narrow hallway. He did not knock. Twisting the glass knob, he swung the door open into darkness. Feeling his way along, he found a single lantern burning in a large room off to the right which served as a kitchen. In a corner of that room was another door.

He stood outside and called softly, "Trella? It's me, Rance Taggart."

"Oh, God!" came the pleased cry from inside. In an instant she was throwing open the door to fling herself into his arms. Whimpering with joy, she cried, "It *is* you. Oh, God, it is you, Rance! It's been so long. So damned long—" She squeezed him hard, then stood back to look up at him. Her tearstained face was framed by long silky black hair.

He led her back into the tiny room, his arm about her shoulders. The furnishings were drab—a cot, a chair, a small crate serving as a table. There was a lantern on the crate, illuminating the dreary scene. She pulled him down beside her on the unmade cot and cried, "Oh, Rance, I just can't believe it's really you!" and threw herself into his arms once more.

He hugged her again, then pushed her gently away and stared down into her anxious eyes. "Why did you tell Edward you were working as a whore, Trella?" he demanded quietly.

She shrugged, sniffed, dabbed at her eyes with the sleeve of her plain muslin nightgown. Then she gave her long raven hair a toss and said, "I want Edward to marry me. I thought he would come after me and demand that I leave this place. But he didn't. And I found out I couldn't . . . you know . . . do it. . . ." Her voice trailed off, embarrassed, and she shuddered.

"Edward isn't ready to marry you or anybody else. Besides, he's hurt. He may lose his arm."

She broke into fresh sobs, and he held her against him

and patted her back. She cried against his chest. When she had calmed down enough to listen, he told her of Edward's injury. "The maggots are a chance we have to take," he explained. "He won't let them take his arm off. But I won't let him die. If he isn't better soon, I'll just tell the surgeons to knock him out and amputate."

She pulled away from him and dabbed at her eyes once more. "Damn the war! It's messing up everybody's lives."

How childlike she sounded! He cared nothing for her romantically, but he felt drawn to her in her helplessness. He asked for a drink of whiskey. She said she knew where the madam of the house kept her stock, and went to get a bottle. When she returned, he took several long, deep swallows before speaking again. "Have you any news of April? I passed the word around that there's a reward if anyone can tell me where to find her."

She made a face. "Are you still looking for her, Rance? Why don't you just give up? She doesn't love you, or she never would've left. A man like you, you could have your pick of women. Like me, for instance," she added with an impish grin, but the look in her eye told of her seriousness.

He took another swallow, and knew the whiskey was hitting him fast and hard, for he hadn't eaten all day. No matter. He liked the feeling, liked the way he was beginning to drift away from the stench of war and the cloying smell of roses. "Yes, I'm still looking for her, and it hasn't got anything to do with love. Now that woman out there, Paulette, she said men had come here asking for you. Has anyone come with word of April? I let a few people know that they could find you in a whorehouse in Richmond."

She leaned back, resting against the wall behind the cot, entwining tiny fingers around his large hand. With lowered lashes, she gave him an inviting look. "You never made love to me, Rance. I let you know lots of times that you could, any time you wanted. The only reason I hung around with Edward so long was to be close to you. I'll bet you knew that, didn't you?"

"I didn't think about it." He took another drink. Damn it to hell, he didn't need this. "Just tell me if you've heard about April."

"Maybe I have, and maybe I haven't," she whispered huskily, then demanded, "Look at me, Rance Taggart!"

He turned his head, gasping as he realized she had pulled up her gown to reveal long, bare legs, exposing a triangle of soft, dark hair at her crotch. She took his hand and placed it there, pressing hard.

"Do what I know you want to do." She thrust herself against him, pushing his hand downward. "Take me, any way you want me. Then I'll tell you what I've heard about your precious April."

He jerked his hand back as though it were burned and got to his feet. "Stop playing games, Trella. I came here to ask about April, not to make love to my best friend's woman."

She stuck out her tongue petulantly and stretched her arm to place an accusing finger against the telltale bulge in his crotch. "You want me. You can't lie about *that*." She pressed against him.

"That's a normal response. It doesn't mean I'm going to take you up on your offer. Just tell me what you know, Trella, and I'll be on my way."

"Do you really want to be on your way?" She stood on tiptoe to brush her lips against his. Her arms wound about his neck, pulling him close. "I haven't had a man since I left Edward, and I'd be lying if I said I didn't want one. I enjoy it as much as a man, but I ain't no whore, Rance. And God, how I've dreamed of doing it with you. I know you'd be good—"

He unwrapped her arms and thrust her away from him, pushing her into a sitting position on the cot. God, but it was taking every ounce of self-control to keep from taking what she was so all-fired determined to give. It had been a long time since that last night in Washington, with April.

"If you want to know what I heard about April, then you're going to have to be nice to me. You're going to have to be real nice, Rance Taggart. And nobody is ever going to know. Especially Edward, 'cause he's the man I want to marry. He'll be good to me. You're in love with April. I know that. But that don't mean you and me can't have a hell of a good time together."

He knew he should turn and get out of there—fast. But he could not be certain that she was only teasing about April. Maybe she did know something. He kept his eyes on her, trying to see inside that scheming little head, as he tipped the bottle up once more. He was feeling hazy, thick-tongued. Soon, he would be dog-assed drunk, he knew, and when he passed out, he damn sure didn't want to be here.

But it was *she* who saw inside *him*, and she taunted, "You're standing there wondering if I'm lying . . . wondering if I've really heard anything. And you want me. Oh, Lordy, how you want me. And there's a battle going right inside you, 'cause you're trying to keep from taking me, and it's getting harder and harder."

"Look at these!" She yanked her gown over her head and displayed her naked breasts. Cupping them in her hands, she gave them a shake. "They ain't as big as April's, but they're nice, aren't they? Don't you want to try one? Just fasten your mouth around this—" She flicked her left nipple and giggled softly.

Rance could not tear his eyes away from the rosy red tip hardening before his eyes. Roses. Damn the roses. He could smell them everywhere. Even here in this tiny dungeon of a room. And that girl was lying there naked, playing with her breasts, opening and closing her legs to display that downy venus of joy.

"I'm going to make you feel so good," she cried suddenly, falling forward on her knees and working deft fingers on his trousers. He stood hypnotized, unable to move, gazing down to watch her release his swollen manhood.

"Oh, my heavens, just look at that!" she cried, wrapping her hands around it to stroke eagerly, squeezing ever so gently. "Why, a woman would be a fool to leave a man like you, Rance. I'm going to make you so happy."

He closed his eyes as he felt her lips close about him. He knew it was wrong . . . knew he should run like hell . . . for a she-devil was casting a spell on him.

His knees felt weak. He lowered himself to the cot. She continued to caress him hungrily with her mouth.

Soon he could only sigh deliciously, thrusting his hips to match the movements of her lips. Later, there would be time to feel guilty. For the moment, he could apologize only for being a man.

❧ Chapter Twenty-eight ❧

APRIL felt the first hint of autumn in the air as she stepped from the cabin into the crisp morning. Gathering a woolen shawl around her, she began walking toward the chicken pen at the edge of the dense woods. Soon, she thought, looking up longingly at the swinging leaves, fall would arrive. She had always loved fall back home in Alabama.

She went into the leaning shed, picked up an empty wooden bucket, and began filling it with corn from a burlap sack. Kaid had given her the chore of tending the chickens, and while she enjoyed it, she realized that the other women resented it. At first, they had openly criticized her, assuming she was sleeping with Kaid in order to get an easier life than theirs. But they were wrong.

Since the night when Lucky and Kaid had nearly died, Kaid had not approached her except to tell her what work to do around the prison. But the others couldn't, of course, know that. Even Selma had turned against her. "A smart one you are," she had sneered. "Making like you're too fine to bed down with one of the guards. Said it was sickening, you did. Then you let that ugly Blackmouth have your sweets, so's you could stay out of the fields and keep them lily white hands nice and soft."

April had not complained to Kaid . . . not when they stole food from her plate and dared her to object . . . not when they forced her to be the last in the bath water, after

Selma. She only prayed that God would get her out of this misery soon, or let her die.

One night Kaid had called her to his cabin. The others exchanged knowing looks when Private Ellison came for her. But Kaid only wanted to show her that Lucky was completely healed, proudly displaying the skin he had sewn together, now merely a crooked scar that the dog's fur would eventually cover.

They talked awhile. He told her about the terrible battle of Gettysburg. He offered her a cup of hot tea, which she accepted gratefully, for it had been one of those nights when someone snatched her supper.

He watched her curiously as she gulped down the tea, then offered a bit of fried corn pone, staring at her while she ate, a strange expression on his face. Then he sent her back to her bed.

When she opened the door to the cabin, Jewel confronted her, nails arched, lips turned back in a menacing snarl. "You're using him, you bitch!" she screamed. "You damn hussy! He's too good for the likes of you!"

Jewel pounced on her, raking her long, chipped nails down her cheeks, wrapping them in her hair to yank and pull as April shrieked in pain and terror and tried as best she could to get away. The others gathered around, gleefully clapping their hands and cheering for Jewel.

Even now April shuddered to think what might have happened had Private Ellison not been nearby and heard the commotion. He waded right into the fight and jerked Jewel away, tearing at her hair. When she did not obey his command to stop struggling, he hit her with his fist, knocking her to the floor, unconscious.

He took April, bleeding and bruised, to Kaid's cabin.

"From now on you stay here," he said angrily as he bathed her wounds and rubbed on camphor. "I'll move in with the other men. I can't let you be around them damned witches. They might kill you. Some of 'em are real hellions."

Kaid explained their accusations. "They're jealous of you, darlin', because you're a lady, something they never will be. And you're also beautiful. As for you sleeping with me, we both know that just can't happen as long as I know you feel like you do about me."

She had protested moving into his cabin, but he reminded her firmly that she would do as he said. Since then, she saw the other women only from a distance. Kaid made sure of that. She even ate her meals in the cabin. But whenever they were within shouting distance, the other women would yell threats and obscenities until one of the guards forced them to stop.

April pushed the gate open, and the hens began to flutter and cackle around her feet. Scattering the corn upon the ground, she looked about for the rooster and smiled when she saw him. So regal and proud, he strutted among his harem, knowing they were his for the taking any time he chose. And they adored him, seemed not to mind sharing such a marvelous male.

It made her think of Rance. Yes, she thought with a deep sigh, Rance could keep many women happy, and they would be grateful for the opportunity to share his favors. Rance was cocky and proud, too, like the bright red rooster.

Where was he, she wondered sadly, as she had wondered so many times. And how was he? Did he hate her terribly for leaving? He was arrogant, yes, but he could also be so loving, so kind and tender. Wrapped in his arms, her head upon his chest . . . had she ever known anything more glorious? Damn, why had she been so proud? She shook her head in silent bewilderment.

She watched as the rooster selected one of the plump white hens for his morning's delight. But, instead of allowing him to have his way, the hen shook her tail feathers and ran. The rooster followed, ignoring all the dozens of other willing mates.

Maybe, she thought with a wry smile, that kind of behavior would have taken Rance by surprise. Perhaps that was the only way a woman would ever be able to capture his heart—by refusing to be conquered.

On the other side of the fence, Lucky whined and pawed at the ground. "You're just going to have to wait, boy," she called to him as she scattered the last remains of the bright yellow corn kernels. "I can't have you chasing my chickens. You might catch one, and then there'd be the devil to pay—" Her voice trailed off as thundering hooves broke the silence of the morning. She soon recognized the rider as Corporal Forbes, the night sentry. He was in a terrible hurry. As he got closer, she could see panic on his face. He galloped by her without a glance, charging to an abrupt stop in front of the soldiers' quarters and leaping from the horse. He shoved the door open with outstretched hands.

Bewildered, she stepped out of the pen and latched the gate. No sooner had she turned around than the men came running out of the cabin.

Kaid was coming straight toward her, as fast as his legs would carry him. He had a slight limp from his battle with the wild hog and, as he moved, he skipped along on one foot. "Get in that shed!" he yelled to her, his face red, arms waving. "Get in there and don't you dare come out. Take Lucky with you. I don't want him sniffing around the door and trying to get to you."

"What is going on?" She froze where she stood, apprehension making her hands tremble.

"That damn sonofabitch fell asleep on his post, and he didn't wake up till the patrol was right on him. He told them the road was out due to the hard rains last week, so they're taking the long way around. But they'll be here any minute. Now you get in that cabin and stay hid."

"But why?" she cried as he shoved her along roughly. The feed bucket went clattering to the ground. "What difference does it make if they see me?" Around her, Kaid's men were routing the other women.

"We ain't ready for no inspection, and anything could happen. I've been afraid of this. Just do as I say, April. I want to make sure you aren't seen."

He jerked open the door to the shed and pushed her inside, then motioned for Lucky to follow. She heard the bolt slide into place and cried out when she realized he was locking her in.

"Don't you worry. I'll come back for you. Just be quiet."

She heard him running away and leaned forward to peek through a crack between the door slats. The men were passing out fresh clothes to the women, yelling at them to change and make themselves look okay, warning them they would be punished severely if they did not move quickly. Beside her, Lucky whined in confusion, and she reached to give him a comforting pat. "I don't know what's going on, either, boy. We can't do anything but wait and see."

She did not have long to wait. Within moments she counted twelve horses and riders coming into the camp. The men all had a grim, set look. An officer rode in front. She could not tell his rank. Kaid ran forward to snap to attention and salute, and the officer dismounted and returned the salute.

"We're here to inspect, Sergeant," he said, motioning to his men to dismount. "Where are the prisoners?"

Kaid smiled too broadly and sounded too jubilant as he answered, "Just getting up, Major. By the way, sir, we're real proud to have you out here. We've never had such a high rank inspect us before."

The Major withered him with a look. "You may not be so proud when I'm finished, Sergeant. We've had reports comparing this camp to Sodom and Gomorrah. The women are treated worse than animals. Your men take their pleasure with them whenever they feel like it. The food rations are no better than garbage. And you make them work the fields till they're exhausted and bleeding."

"Sir!" Kaid stiffened, aghast. "Wherever did you hear a bucket o' lies like that? True, it ain't no social gathering out here. I don't think I have to remind you that this is a prison. These women have been found guilty of treason and spying and God knows what else. They were sent out here to be punished, not coddled."

"I believe *detainment* is more what the Confederacy had in mind. Farming their own food is one thing, but making them produce enough for you to sell for your personal profit is *not* what the government had in mind."

Kaid's face turned a fiery red, and he sputtered, "I . . . I ain't got no idea what you're talkin' about, sir. We barely grow enough to get by out here. I know food's scarce now, and I haven't wanted to ask the army for any more."

The Major turned to sweep his men with a knowing smile, then faced Kaid once more. "You sold some potatoes to an old man. One of your soldiers was drunk. He offered to sell him something else. One of your prisoners. The old man was appalled. He told his son, who also happens to be a soldier, and he, in turn, reported this to the proper authorities. His father was asked to see just how much he could learn of the goings-on here. He learned a great deal. That is why we are here today. To see for ourselves."

"Well, now, I reckon I remember that old man. Caught him trying to steal some of my chickens." Kaid appeared to calm down. "Made my boys mad, and they roughed him up a bit to teach him a lesson, so's he wouldn't come back. He wanted revenge, so he made up some lies. You just come along with me and see for yourself how nice everything is here."

April watched Kaid lead the Major and his men through the camp. She knew the women would not dare answer any questions truthfully. But would the Major realize that or not?

"Things aren't too clean right now," she heard Kaid say as they moved away, his voice growing fainter. "We got crops comin' in, and the rains last week helped things along, so we've all had to pitch in and do our share to get 'em in so's we'll have plenty to eat this winter."

She could hear no more, but she continued to stare through the crack, watching as they moved in and around the other buildings. A half hour or more passed, and finally Kaid and the Major came close enough that she could again make out what they were saying.

"I still don't like what I see here, Sergeant," said the Major. He was an older, distinguished-looking man, with a quiet authority about him. "It's not a good environment for ladies."

"Ladies?" Kaid chuckled. "There ain't a lady in the bunch. You know that."

The Major regarded him coolly. "They are women, and Southern gentlemen regard their women with a protective attitude. It would be a disgrace to the South for it to be known that women are being kept in a place like this. I may as well tell you that it has already been decided that Tarboro prison will be turned into a compound for Yankee prisoners. These women will be moved within the week to a new unit set up near Richmond. It's larger, and you will probably have three times as many women there, as we are combining several smaller compounds."

Kaid's voice was worried. "Am I going to be in charge of the new one?"

"If not in command," he was told, "you may still have a responsible position. That will all be decided later. In the meantime, I want you to get these women ready to move. A special company of men will be sent here to harvest your crops. We can't let them go to waste."

The Major's men were mounting their horses. "We'll be leaving now," their commanding officer announced. "I have a report to file, and there are arrangements to be made."

"It wasn't like you thought, was it?" Kaid asked, smiling. "It ain't like that . . . Sodom and something?"

The Major returned his smile easily. "It probably is, Sergeant. I imagine your prisoners have been informed of the consequences they could expect for answering my questions honestly. Do you take me for a fool?" His voice rose. "I could tell they were scared to death, and I saw the way you and your men hovered around them."

Kaid quickly shook his head. "I don't understand, sir. We're strict, of course, but—"

"Do you honestly think I believe these women haven't been forced to submit? Raped at will? Give me credit for having some intelligence, you idiot!"

"But, sir—"

The Major had allowed full vent to his fury and would not listen. "That won't happen at the new prison. There will be women matrons to serve as chaperones to make sure the prisoners are not abused by the guards. I don't like what I've seen here, Sergeant."

He mounted his horse, reined him around in a complete circle, then snapped, "Just be glad you have properly intimidated your women, or the Confederacy would have your head."

He signaled and his men followed in a swinging column. The Major called back with a sardonic grin. "We will go out through the main road, Sergeant. I've a feeling all that water has miraculously dried up by now."

As soon as the soldiers were out of sight, Kaid hurried to the shed and unlocked the door. April rushed out, crying, "Why did you lock me in there? I wouldn't have told them anything."

He fastened possessive fingers about her arm and led her toward his cabin, motioning the anxious guards away as they started toward him, boiling over, he knew, with questions.

"I've been expecting a surprise inspection," he told her as soon as they were inside. "It was just a feeling I'd get when I'd go in for supplies. The top dogs were startin' to ask a lot of questions. I think what happened was that somebody got jealous of my setup out here."

"All right, so you were expecting it," she said, exasperated, "but that doesn't tell me why you locked me in that shed."

"They did a head count of the prisoners. I figured they'd do that, too."

"Well, why didn't you want them to count me, for heaven's sake? They know I'm here. There are records—"

"Hell, yes, I know that!" He spoke so sharply that she stepped away from him, watching as he began to pace furiously up and down before the fireplace. "I want 'em to come up one short. Then, when they come to take the others to the new prison camp, they'll find the same number they found today. You won't be counted."

"Then what do you plan to do with me? I can't believe you're going to set me free."

He stopped pacing and stared at her as though she had lost her mind. "Let you go? You know better than that, April. I don't never intend to let you go." He walked over to pull her into his arms, and she did not resist. She was too frightened. His eyes searched hers adoringly, and the little smile on his lips was sad. "I know you don't love me. You don't even like me touchin' you. But you're the prettiest thing I've ever seen, darlin', and I can't let you go."

He brushed her golden hair back from her face as she watched him fearfully. "Don't worry," he laughed. "I'm not going to hurt you. I'd never hurt you. I'd kill anybody else that tried. I want to take care of you, April, and make you happy. I'd do anything in the world for you . . . except let you leave me."

Dear God, she had known that he was in love with her, but this was worse than she had ever imagined. He would never let her leave now, even when the war was over, or she had served her time. He intended to keep her with him forever!

Deciding to attempt reasoning with him, she reminded

him of the long talks they'd had in the evenings while he and Lucky were mending. "I told you that, someday, somehow, I'm going home, Kaid. I'm going back to Pinehurst. If Poppa is alive, then I want to get help for him."

He nodded, running his hands up and down her bare arms, knocking away her shawl. "You told me. And I understand. I think what your sister did was rotten. I ain't scared of her or those scalawags you told me she hired. I'll take you back there myself, and I'll get your home back . . . straighten things out for you."

Her heart suddenly leaped with joy. "You would? Kaid, you would do that for me? Oh, I'd see that you were well paid, believe me. I mean, I know there's probably no money at all now. Things were going down so quickly once Poppa got sick, but if you could see Pinehurst, you'd know that it can be a rich plantation again someday and—"

She fell silent, realizing how deeply she was involved in her dream. She hadn't been paying attention to him.

Kaid was standing very still, his hands on her tiny waist, just staring down into her eyes as though trying to read her mind.

"You don't have to pay me. I don't want money from you. I want you to be my wife."

She cocked her head to one side. "You . . . you want me to *marry* you, Kaid?"

"I sure do, April. You and I both know the problem I have when : . ." He paused, swallowed hard, then continued, ". . . when I try to make love to you. It's because I love you so much. I can't just jump on top of you. It's got to be because you *want* me. If you were my wife, everything'd be all right."

He picked her up and swirled her around, then set her on her feet, a wide smile on his face displaying the chipped, blackened teeth. "You might even stop thinkin' about what an ugly bastard I am, darlin', when I show you how good I can be to you." He winked. "You'll never be sorry, I promise. Oh, it's going to be the happiest day of my life when I stroll down the street with you on my arm, telling the whole world you're my wife."

"I can't marry you, Kaid."

"Why, sure you can." He walked over to glance out the window, and a frown creased his forehead. "Those fools.

I'm going to have to get out there and get them into the fields. If we don't get them crops in, the army will take 'em, and I still stand to make some money sellin' 'em myself."

He glanced back at her. "It's going to be wonderful, April. You'll see. And I promise to take you back to Alabama, back to your home. I'll get things straightened out with that sister of yours."

He sat down and pulled her into his lap, squeezing her gently as she fought to hide her revulsion. "I've got it all figured out," he said, "and I've had plenty of time to think about it, 'cause, like I said, I had an idea something like this was gonna happen. What I'll do is, I'll fix your prison records to say you died. I'll say you tried to escape and got killed by a snake in the swamp. We'll even fix you a grave, with your name on a headstone and everything. Meanwhile, you'll be living in Richmond, as my wife, and nobody will know nothing.

"I'm not asking you to love me," he went on in a rush. "I'm asking you to give me a chance, April. Maybe in time, you can love me, once you find out I'm not really so ugly."

She took a deep breath and prayed for the right words. Looking away from him, she said, "I don't find you ugly, Kaid. You showed me what a gentle person you can be when you risked yourself to save my dog. You've been good to me when we both know you could have had me any time you wanted. I would be most obliged if you would take me back to Alabama and help me reclaim my home. But I can't marry you."

"You can't?" he roared. "Then, damn it, you don't want to go home very bad. You'd rather rot in prison than marry me? Hell, I don't need you then!"

He stood so quickly that she fell to the floor. He made no move to help her up but strode to the window and stared out in angry silence.

April doubled up her knees and propped her head against them, clenching her fists. Finally, she could control herself no longer and screamed, "Damn it, Kaid, you just can't see it, can you?"

He whipped his head around, stunned by the outburst.

"I could promise to marry you, get you to take me

home, then change my mind, you fool! But even if I don't love you, I'm your friend. I don't want to use you, or hurt you. Can't you see that? You say you don't want to hurt me, but what do you think you're doing when you blackmail me into marrying you, for God's sake? How can you be so blind?"

He scratched at his beard. "I never thought of it like that. You could trick me, couldn't you?"

"Yes," she pleaded, "but you've been kind to me, and I don't want to hurt you. Can't you just help me, anyway, even though all I can promise is that I will try to desire you? I'll try to give you what you want."

They stood staring at each other, Kaid wearing a look of veiled hope.

Suddenly a fist began hammering against the door and a man's voice called out frantically, "Sergeant, get out here, will you? We want to know what's going on. The men are threatening to just get on their horses and run away. They're afraid they're gonna get in trouble for fuckin' the prisoners."

Kaid screamed so loud the walls quaked. "Get the hell out of here, boy. Don't bother me right now!"

They heard the murmur of the soldier's curses as he moved away from the door.

Kaid walked over to grip April's shoulders. "You're saying that you'll try to desire me, but you won't marry me?"

"If you agree to take me to Alabama."

"But there's a war."

"As soon as you can. That's all I ask." She turned away, then glanced back at him sharply. "Oh, Kaid, it would be so easy to deceive you. Then, once I was free, I could refuse to keep my part of the bargain. But you've been too good to me. I can't betray you. I know that, in your way, you do care for me."

"Oh, hell, yes, I care," he responded quickly, his tongue flicking over his lips once more. "You just don't know how much. Maybe I'm a goddamn fool to even think a woman as pretty as you could ever want me to touch her, much less be my wife, but a man's got to dream, darlin'. When he stops dreamin', he might as well die."

Swallowing hard, she slipped her arms about his neck.

"Oh, darlin', darlin', it's gonna be so good. I just know it is. I may be ugly, but I know what a woman likes."

She could contain herself no longer. "Will you just stop talking about how ugly you are, Kaid?" she cried, staring up at him. His hold loosened in surprise. "Will you stop telling me how ugly you are? I don't see you that way—not till you remind me. Can't you just for God's sake stop talking?"

"Blackmon! Open up!"

April recognized Private Ellison's voice, urgent and demanding.

"Open up or I'm gonna bust this door down."

"You're fixing for me to bust your head!" Kaid's huge body was shaking with fury. "I said I'd be out there in a minute. Leave me alone."

"You better get out here now if you want any men left by dark. They're plenty upset. And the prisoners are givin' us sass, too. They think we're gonna get in a heap of trouble, so they're actin' real cocky. They say they ain't goin' in the fields and we don't dare make 'em."

Kaid muttered a vile obscenity, and moved away from her. "I'm gonna go straighten everybody out, darlin'. But I'll be back later, I promise." He grinned, and left her.

❧ Chapter Twenty-nine ❧

IT was a grim time for the South, that spring of 1864. After the battle of Gettysburg, during the previous July, forty-three thousand men on both sides had been listed as killed, wounded, or missing. Too, this was the first clear-cut victory for the Union. With the fall of Vicksburg on the fourth of July, Southern morale sank to a new low.

In addition, the Confederacy was suffering from low supplies of everything from food to drugs to men. Hospitals were so desperate for chloroform, morphine, quinine, paregoric, and laudanum, that profiteers were smuggling drugs through enemy lines in empty coffins. Women were also able to smuggle drugs by carrying them within the confines of their hoop skirts. For men were reluctant to search women.

Field medics learned to improvise. A concoction of dogwood, poplar, and willow bark was used as a quinine substitute. Opium was extracted from the red poppy flower, when the flower could be found at all.

Starved, often without shoes, many of the troops were covered with lice, filth, and dirt. The men did not want to bathe in the freezing air, even before a fire. As a result, they developed "camp itch" and were treated with a strong concoction of poke root and an ointment made from elder and sweet gum, lard, olive oil, and sulfur flour.

Some of the women imprisoned at the new Dobbsville Stockade had been assigned to make these ointments, as well as the concoction believed helpful in the treatment of venereal disease. They mixed poke roots, elderberries, wild sarsaparilla, sassafras, jessamine, and prickly ash to form a potion. Then there was silk weed root to put in whiskey, and rosin pills from pine trees.

If lack of drugs was a problem, lack of food was a desperation. Horse meat was being issued to some companies. The soldiers sometimes went for months without receiving any rations besides salty bacon, rice, flour, and tough horse beef. As a result, they were driven to slaughter mules and horses and eat them. Some men even ate large wharf rats. It was a last resort before starvation.

One company said they had cooked a cat for two days, but it was still too tough to eat. The only thing that kept them alive till rations finally arrived were the two wild dogs they found roaming in the woods, and they were skin and bones.

The meal they were given was sour, dirty, weevil-eaten and filled with ants and worms.

Many soldiers were turning to whiskey when they could get it, to dull their senses so they would not think about food so much. Whether they called it "busthead," "popskull," "red eye," or "spill skull" it all meant the same thing—a little respite from the misery that seemed to have no end.

When whiskey also became scarce, they doctored it, concocting the brew from apple brandy, made up of a third of genuine alcohol, while the rest came from water, vitriol, and coloring matter. The old and mellow taste was developed by the addition of the raw flesh of wild game.

Desertion had become a serious problem. Many Rebel soldiers felt that their commitment to the Confederacy did not include the invasion of Northern soil. And after the twin disasters of Gettysburg and Vicksburg, the number of unauthorized absentees was estimated at between fifty and a hundred thousand, from both sides.

The women at Dobbsville Stockade had better conditions than they'd known at Tarboro. They still mourned their lives, but at least they were not subjected to the lust of the guards.

The women were housed in small log huts, chinked and daubed after the fashion of pioneer cabins. There were no floors, just the bare earth. They slept in triple deck bunks. There was one door to each cabin, but no windows. A large fireplace was added for heat. All cooking was done in one large building where men and women prisoners ate together. Meals were the only time the men and women were together, and they were not allowed to converse.

On a sunny day in early March, a cold wind blew across the work-bent bodies of the women prisoners as they prodded the ground with their hoes. They would have preferred winter tasks—assigned to making lint and bandages —but with a hint of spring in the air, it was time to begin planting. They, like everyone else, desperately needed whatever food they could sprout from the earth.

They paused in their digging to stare at the man on horseback who approached along the outside of the fence. He was well-built, muscular but lean. Long dark sideburns were neatly trimmed to accentuate the firm, angular jaw. His nose was slightly aquiline, well formed, and beneath it were tightly set lips framed by the mustache and closely cropped beard. Brown eyes, as mellow and rich as Louisiana coffee, were fringed by lashes seemingly too thick and long to belong to a man. The face was golden-bronzed by the sun.

He wore a dress gray uniform with shiny brass buttons and gold epaulettes bearing the rank of captain. A red sash was bound about his waist, and he wore both a black gun belt and a scabbard. White-gloved hands held the reins of the great black stallion clipping his hooves at a determined gait.

"Now that's a fine figure of a man," Jewel murmured to Selma, who was working the row next to her. "A woman would never forget what it was like to have him inside her."

"Is that all you think about?" Selma snapped. "I honestly think you miss all the mating you got to do at Tarboro."

Jewel shot her a look of scorn. "And I think you miss mating at all since you got marked for having the clap." She stepped over the lumps of upturned soil and moved closer to the fence as the man approached. "Hey, Captain. You're a good-looking rogue, you know that? It's not often we scum get to see a handsome gentleman like you," she called out in challenge, hoping he would stop to talk.

Captain Rance Taggart reined Virtus to a stop beside the woman. He stared down at the ragged, torn nails, the long, bony fingers clutching the fence. Long, grimy hair clung to her lined face. What, he wondered, had been her crime? What had brought her to this end? Most of these women, he knew, were guilty of treachery to the Confederacy, and, since there was no cure for those who carried the clap, many of those afflicted were confined in stockades to keep them from the soldiers.

"Thank you for your kind greeting." Rance tipped his hat politely and gave her a slight smile. "Perhaps you could be so kind as to help me. Where would I find the officer in charge of this stockade?"

Jewel looked him up and down, liking what she saw. Striking what she hoped was a seductive pose, her fleshy breasts thrust forward, she replied, "Well, now, Captain, you'd be looking for Major Whitley, and he ain't never around much. Stays in Richmond, where it's more comfy-cozy, he does. Look around and you can see we ain't got much here in the way of comfort. No saloons. No place to gamble. No women except the likes of us, and we ain't supposed to be messed with. Not that way." She cocked her head to one side and gave him a leer. " 'Course, if a real smart officer knew what strings to pull, he could make arrangements to have the lady of his choice. There are ways. . . ." She let her voice trail off in a husky drawl.

"I imagine that would be possible, madam." He gave her a wink, which made her giggle. "And if I had the time for such a pleasure, rest assured you would be the lady of my choice. Unfortunately, I've business to tend to and no time for luxuries. Could you tell me who would be in charge in the Major's absence?"

"Blackmouth." She spat the hated name.

"I beg your pardon?"

Jewel laughed raucously. "That's what we call the no-good sonofabitch because, when he opens his mouth, all you see is a big, black hole. He's got rotten teeth. His name's Blackmon, Sergeant Kaid Blackmon. I reckon that's what you better call him."

He was amused by her candor. "I *reckon* I had. Now where would I find him?"

She pointed down the road. "If you keep ridin', you'll come to a nicer building than the rest. On the left. He'll be in there, probably takin' a drink, if he thinks nobody's lookin'."

"Tell me," Rance pushed for information. "Weren't some of you women in Tarboro Prison before being moved here last fall?"

"Sure were. A hellhole it was, too. 'Blackmouth' was top dog there, for sure, and he ran things the way he wanted. Then the real top dogs got wind of things and closed it down. Moved us here. We still got it rough, but it's better'n it was back there, believe me."

"Were *you* one of the prisoners there?"

Her eyes narrowed suspiciously, and she stepped back from the fence and placed her hands on her hips. "Yeah, I was. But don't go askin' me no questions about what went on. It was a hellhole. That's all I'm going to say."

Rance thought a moment, then decided that he might get more information from one of April's fellow prisoners than he would from the officer in charge. "I'm not trying to make any trouble, madam. I'm looking for someone. A young woman by the name of April Jennings. The last information about her was—" He stopped talking and stared down at the woman. Her face had suddenly twisted in a grimace of rage. Her hands were opening and closing at her side, fingers arching as though clawing. Her eyes flashed wide then narrowed to angry slits.

"The only thing I know about that bitch is that she was a snake in the grass. Used people. You ain't gonna find her around here. I can tell you that."

"Well, where can I find her then?" Rance was puzzled. April was not the sort to make enemies. Whatever had she done to make this woman hate her so?

Jewel turned and started walking back toward the others.

"Hey," he called. "Can't you at least tell me where she is?"

"If I knew, I wouldn't tell you," she yelled over her shoulder. "You ain't got no business gettin' mixed up with a bitch like that. Just turn around and go back where you come from, Captain, 'cause 'Blackmouth' ain't gonna tell you nothin' neither."

He gave Virtus a gentle nudge, urging him forward. The woman's response was yet another upset in an already mysterious situation. April's being in prison seemed beyond understanding.

April, a Union spy? Ridiculous! Rance had learned the whole story of Alton Moseley, had been told that she caused him untold agony while he was dying. She had been sent to Tarboro.

The next morning, after Rance learned the story from some soldiers, he had gone to check on Edward and found Trella standing beside his bed. She had looked away from Rance, cheeks coloring slightly. She needn't have worried, he thought. She was just another woman, and as long as his best friend never found out, then no one would be hurt. He had simply lost his control and his good intentions.

"They aren't gonna take my arm off," Edward had mustered strength enough to say, determination in his voice. "They're gonna leave them things in and see what happens."

Rance explained briefly about April, saying that he was going to get her released from prison. He warned Edward that, if leaving the maggots in the wound did not take care of the infection, then he would have to agree to amputation. "And don't tell me you'd rather die, you bastard," he snapped. "That's the coward's way out."

"Why, you're man enough for me with one arm, anyway," Trella cooed, avoiding Rance's gaze. "My goodness, you just wear me out sometimes."

Rance left shortly after that, unable to stomach the two-timing wench any longer.

Immediately he went to the hospital military post to get help with his quest, but as soon as he introduced himself, the soldier behind the desk cried, "Captain Taggart, you're to report to Major General Jeb Stuart in Richmond at once. He sent word that you could be found somewhere around here, something about your bringing in wounded soldiers. The orders were marked urgent, and they came in yesterday morning. You'd best get moving."

Rance silently cursed the news. The thought of April suffering in prison made his guts burn, but Stuart would not have sent for him unless it was extremely important. He could only hope that whatever Stuart wanted would not take long, so he could return to Chimborazo quickly and start fighting to free her.

Rance sat in a tent on an outpost of Richmond and listened to the great cavalry general explain that his men were in immediate need of horses. Good horses. "We've quite a winter before us, Taggart. I plan to busy my men giving the Yankees hell. They won't hole in like sleeping bears. Not with us around to ride rampant."

Rance knew he meant it. He had a lot of respect for Stuart. He had fought hard in just about every major battle so far.

Though not six feet tall, Stuart was built heavily and wore a massive flowing beard that people said was meant to cover a receding chin and to camouflage his youth as well, for he was only thirty years old. But his personal bravery, endurance, and high good humor had made him a magnificent cavalry leader. He surrounded himself with an excellent staff and trained his subordinates with a sober professionalism. He had a reputation for being deeply religious.

"One of my scouts tells me the Yankees have a good supply of horses just across the Rapidan River, Taggart," he said, tugging at his bushy brown beard as his eyes bored into Rance's. "I could send some of my men. They're damned good, and you know it. But nobody's got an eye for horse flesh like you have. I don't want to send a patrol behind enemy lines, risking their lives, only to have them come back with a bunch of worthless nags. You go pick out the best. That's all I'll have for my men. The best.

"You served me well once before," Stuart reminded him. "You got me damn good horses. I'm counting on you, Taggart."

Rance could not refuse. It was his duty to the Confederacy, and he wanted to help this man.

So, through the winter months, he rode with Stuart's cavalry. He was proud to be a part of that gallant band. If he had not been haunted by thoughts of April, he would have been content with his life.

It was mid-February before Stuart allowed his men a respite from fighting. All indications pointed to fierce fighting with the spring thaw. He wanted his cavalrymen rested for it. So, while the others recuperated, Rance rode at full speed to Richmond.

He found Trella, who told him that Edward had recuperated fully and been reassigned to duty. He was fighting somewhere, though she did not know where . . . did not seem to care. They'd had a fight of their own, she said, before he left. She doubted that he would return to her. This time, she was really working as a prostitute.

He had left her, heading for Chimborazo. There, thanks to intervention by General Stuart, he was able to secure the pardon for April.

He had the pardon when he knocked on Kaid Blackmon's door.

Rance approached the headquarters and dismounted. A guard snapped to attention and saluted. Rance returned the gesture and asked to see Sergeant Blackmon.

"Inside, sir. Go right in," he was told, a bit reluctantly.

He pushed open the door and saw the swarthy, heavyset man leaning back against the wall in a precariously balanced chair. The front chair legs hit the floor at the same time the big man did. Saluting smartly, he said, "Sergeant Blackmon, sir."

Rance removed his gloves, reached inside his coat, and withdrew the official pardon. Handing it to Blackmon, he felt an immediate dislike for the man.

"A pardon for Miss April Jennings," Rance told him as the sergeant scanned the papers. "She was unjustly imprisoned some time ago. That's a full pardon. She is to be released to me. Send for her at once, please."

He was glancing about the room, noticing the sparse furnishings, the empty whiskey bottles lying in dust-cluttered corners, when he became aware that the sergeant had made no move. Turning, he saw Blackmon looking at him with a strange expression on his face, a mixture of anger and . . . what? Sadness? *His wrath.*

"Well, sergeant?" Rance asked impatiently. "Have Miss Jennings brought to me at once."

"Can't." Blackmon spit a wad of tobacco into a dark corner and wiped his mouth with the back of his hand. He glared openly at the intruder.

Rance was about to ask why in the hell he could not send for her, but the man spoke up first.

"She's dead."

A full moment passed before Rance could find his voice. Dear God, he thought wildly, it was like that other time . . . that other time when he returned for a woman he dared believe he was capable of loving, only to find her dead. It was happening all over again.

"What . . . what happened to her?" he managed to choke, reaching for the bottle on the desk without asking. He tipped it quickly to his lips and took a long swallow of whiskey, listening as Blackmon told him how April tried to escape before they moved out of Tarboro, ran into the swamps and was lost. A few days later, an old farmer told them of finding her body, snake-bitten and alligator-chewed. Blackmon had buried her.

"I made out the report. It's all here if you want to see it, Captain," Blackmon offered, reaching toward a drawer.

Rance shook his head. He was feeling sick, fighting the bile rising in his throat.

"I didn't go mark the grave or nothing. I mean, she was just a prisoner, and I'm real sorry that it's come out now that she shouldn't have been in prison, but you gotta understand that *we* didn't know none of that. We were just doin' what we was told to do, and that was to keep her in the stockade. Her dyin' was her own doin'."

Rance never spoke. He continued to down the contents of the bottle as quickly as possible, racing to blot out the horror.

"Here. You can read the report."

He thrust some papers forward, but Rance pushed them away. "No," he whispered hoarsely. "I don't want to see them. I've got to be going." He forced himself to walk rigidly from the cabin. Later, there would be time for a big drunk, to souse himself with as much liquor as his body would hold. It was going to take a hell of a drunk to ever get over this, he thought dazedly. God, not April. Not April.

Virtus seemed to sense his master's grief, and he moved along slowly without being prodded. Rance stared straight ahead, seeing only a vision of laughing blue eyes and golden blond hair, and a smile like an angel's.

He had not heard the woman calling his name. Only when he felt a small stone strike his arm did he glance around sharply, drawing his saber, ready for a fight. Then he saw her standing at the fence, far away from the others, glancing back over her shoulder nervously as she called to him once again. "It's Taggart, ain't it? Ain't your name Taggart? You look just like she said Taggart would look. Nobody could be as handsome as she said you was. I had a feeling you'd come for her one day."

He started to dismount, heart pounding wildly as he realized this woman knew something of April. Perhaps she could tell him of her life during those last weeks. . . .

"No, don't get off your horse," she said sharply, glancing around wildly. "I can't let nobody see me talking to you. I'd be killed for sure . . . or worse."

He started to speak, but she waved him to silence. "Don't ask me nothing, 'cause there's no time. Just listen. My name's Selma. I was a friend of April's . . . for a while. Then, like all the others, I turned against her, 'cause I really didn't understand how it was. But that's not important. I can make it all up to her now."

She took a deep breath and went on so rapidly that he had to strain to grasp each harshly whispered word. "April ain't dead."

His eyes widened. His heart began to pound even faster, this time with hope. "How do you know this?"

"No time to explain!" she snapped harshly. "When you find her, you'll understand. Just follow Blackmon. No matter how long it takes. Follow him. He'll take you straight to her. I gotta go now. He might see me. He'd figure what I was telling you, 'cause we all know the truth about Blackmon. I only told you 'cause of what she said about you . . . how she missed you and all. That's all I got to say."

She turned and ran back to where the others were working under the hot sun, bent over with their hoes, chopping at the hard-packed soil.

Dazed, Rance moved Virtus forward. Why not believe the woman? Kaid Blackmon had acted strangely. And this might explain why that first woman had reacted so violently when he asked about April. Selma said they had all turned against April. But why? And what happened to make Selma change her mind?

None of it made any sense, but he was certain of one thing—he was going to take Selma's advice and follow Kaid Blackmon when he left Dobbsville stockade.

Riding with Stuart's cavalry had given him valuable experience in undercover maneuvering. He rode perhaps five miles down the road before turning back, wanting to make sure that if Blackmon had had him followed, he would be satisfied that Rance was on his way.

He moved through the woods, dismounting only far enough away from the headquarters building that he would be able to keep a watch on foot, yet not have to run too far for his horse when the time came to follow Blackmon.

The day wore on. He climbed a tree, hiding among the leaves for cover. Though it was only early March, it was damn hot.

Finally, the sun sank, leaving a murky sea of yellow pink waves in the horizon. Rance was tired and hungry, but he was not about to leave his perch in the tree. He had watched the women being led back to their quarters and tried to single out the one called Selma, but could not. They all looked the same in their drab, shapeless, toe-length garments.

Suddenly a movement caught his eye and he strained to see in the gathering darkness. Yes, it was Blackmon, all right. No mistaking the bulk of the man. Fury surged through Rance's body as he scrambled down from the tree. If he were hiding April, then there was little doubt as to why. And by God, he would have his revenge.

He watched just long enough to see the sergeant mount a horse and head toward a mountain to the northwest of the stockade, and then Rance was running for Virtus.

He rode along at a safe distance behind, skirting through the woods in the shadows to make sure he was not observed. He rode for nearly an hour. Damn, but it was a long way, he swore impatiently. If Selma had led him on a wild-goose chase, he was going to go back and tell her a thing or two. But somehow, he sensed that she wasn't lying. She had no reason to. And there was no denying the wild, frantic look in her eyes as she darted furtive glances around to make sure no one saw her talking to him.

Finally, Blackmon wound his way through a thick grove

of trees toward a small cabin nestled deep within. Rance left Virtus behind and went the rest of the way on foot, careful not to make a sound. As he got near the cabin, Rance crawled on his belly to just beneath a small, narrow window. He crouched there and waited.

His heart soared when he heard her voice. She was alive!

"I fixed a stew," he heard her say in a thin, defeated voice.

"Ahh, it's not a stew I'm after, darlin'," came the sergeant's lusty reply. Damn his soul to hell, thought Rance.

"One of these days you'll want me as much as I do you and then you'll thank me for keeping you here."

"I'll thank you when you take me home," came her emotionless voice. She sounded exhausted, as though she had lost all will to live. "Kaid, you promised—"

"Damn it, don't start in on me again, woman. I told you—when the time is right, I'll take you. Not before. I can't risk nobody finding out you ain't dead, or it'll be my head for sure. There was a man at the stockade asking about you just today."

"There was?" she echoed, her voice much stronger. "What was his name? Why was he looking for me? Tell me everything, Kaid, please."

"Forget about him. It ain't important."

"But it is!" she cried.

Rance could hear signs of a struggle, then silence. He raised slowly up on tiptoe to peer inside. He could just barely make them out as they tussled on the floor on a pine straw mattress. He could see April struggling against the man, hear her moans of protest.

Rance drew his sidearm and made his way around toward the door. He heard Kaid's cajoling voice going on and on. "Now come on, darlin'. We made a bargain, and I'm going to keep my end of it, but you gotta give me time. Now come on and let me love you, please. Tell me you want me to love you."

At the sound of the cabin door crashing against the wall, Kaid sprang backward with a guttural cry of surprise. Rance stood pointing his pistol straight at him. "We meet again, Blackmon," he said with deadly quiet.

"You! How did you—"

April interrupted with her own cry of surprise. Scrambling to her feet, she ran straight for Rance, arms open wide, tears of joy streaming down her cheeks. "It's you! Oh, praise God for answering my prayers, Rance! It's you."

He held out one arm to wrap her protectively against his chest as he held his weapon unwaveringly on Kaid. Kaid looked from the gun to April, his mouth opening and closing in silent rage.

"You falsified records because you wanted her for yourself. Once Tarboro closed and things tightened down, you kept her your own personal prisoner." His voice raised to a cry. "I ought to kill you, you bastard . . . cut your balls off and leave you to die."

Kaid did not wince. He just continued to glare. Nodding to April, he asked quietly, "Do I deserve that, darlin'? Have I been mean to you? Do I deserve to die? Have I ever forced you to love me?"

Rance felt her shudder, heard her quick intake of breath. Just then a movement at the door caught his eye and he glanced quickly to see the big white dog standing there, teeth bared, hair standing up on his back.

"Don't shoot him, please," April cried. "He's my dog. We . . . we've been through a lot together."

"So have we," Kaid said quietly. "You gonna let him kill me, April?"

Rance removed his arm from about her and pushed her away so his eyes could rake over her. She realized that she was still naked, and she tried to cover herself with her hands. "Do you want me to kill him, April? Maybe you better explain."

"I don't want him to die," she said quickly. "He saved my dog's life at the risk of his own. He kept my life from being completely miserable. He never let the other guards have their way with me, and I never suffered the way the others did. Oh, Rance, let him live. Just get me out of here. Take me home, please." She was sobbing with exhaustion and near hysterics.

"I can't take you home, April, but I can take you with me." He motioned for her to get her clothes on. "Take your dog and wait outside. I'll be right out."

Darting anxious glances at the two men who stood eyeing each other warily, April dressed quickly, then hurried out into the darkness with Lucky.

When they were alone, Kaid said, "Look, Taggart, no matter what you think, I never harmed that girl. I tried to make things easy for her. Maybe I did lie and say she was dead so I could keep her for my own, but it was doing her a favor. Anything could've happened if she'd been left in the stockade. I swear I ain't never hurt her."

"All right. I won't kill you. We'll just go peacefully."

"No, you won't. I'll track you down. I won't let her go. Maybe you better go on and kill me right here and now."

Rance saw that the man had guts to be talking so boldly with a gun pointed right at him. But he also knew that he was challenging him to ruthlessly shoot him down in cold blood after April had made a plea for him to be spared. But the decision did not require much thought. He had never feared any man, and the thoughts of this one, big and ugly though he was, coming after him, would not cause him to lose any sleep.

He replaced the gun in his holster. With narrow, slitted eyes, he asked, "You want to settle this now?"

A slow smile spread across Blackmon's face. "Naw. You just keep lookin' over your shoulder, Taggart. One of these nights, I'll be slippin' up on you."

Rance shrugged. "Have it your way. Now or later, it doesn't matter to me."

Rance simply turned and walked away, and Blackmon could not help but marvel at the gut courage of the man. He might have just shot him, got rid of him easily.

Rance took April's hand and silently led her through the woods to Virtus. He could feel her trembling once more as he lifted her, seating her behind the saddle.

"Will the dog follow?" He looked down at Lucky, who seemed quite at ease now. April nodded. "His name is Lucky. And he'll follow."

They had not gone far through the night when he felt her place her hands about his waist and lean her cheek against his back. "I still can't believe it," she murmured dreamily . . . happily.

He said nothing.

"You do love me, don't you, Rance?"

He stiffened.

She lifted her head from his back, removed her hands from his waist. "That is why you came after me, isn't it?"

she asked in a strange voice, "Because you realized you do love me . . . after all?"

He turned in the saddle to look at her beautiful face in the moonlight, ire in her bright blue eyes. "Love you?" he echoed arrogantly, his mocking smile flashing in the night. "Love doesn't have a thing to do with it, April."

"Then why . . . ?" she gasped. "Why did you go to so much trouble to find me?"

He gave her a maddening smile and turned back around to face the road ahead.

"Answer me, Rance Taggart, damn you!" she exploded, beating on his back with her fists. "If you don't love me, then why didn't you just leave me where I was? Why can't you admit you care about me?"

He reined Virtus to an abrupt stop and whirled around to pull her in front of him. Cradling her tightly in his arms, he stared down at her moon-bathed face and whispered huskily, "What's it going to take, blue eyes, for you to realize that you belong to me? You are my property. I always claim my property."

His lips came down upon hers, in a bruising kiss. At first she squirmed and struggled against him but soon she surrendered to his strength and her own desire. She began to return his kiss, to part her lips and receive his hot, probing tongue.

"Don't get excited, little one," he laughed, abruptly releasing her. "We don't have time for that right now, but later, we'll make up for all the nights we were apart."

"You . . . you pompous, arrogant ass!" she hissed, twisting and almost falling from the horse.

"Damnit, April, get still," he snapped, jerking her against him tightly with one arm, using the other to snap the reins. Virtus began to move along.

Despite the rebellion smoldering within, April felt a wave of desire for him. Damn him, she thought, damn him all the way to hell.

Because, though fury boiled within her, April had to admit—if only to herself—that for whatever time she spent with Rance Taggart, she would glory in it, glory in each hour spent in his arms.

Later there would be time for hating the man.

🐚 Chapter Thirty 🐚

APRIL heard a key fumbling in the door, but she continued to lie on her side in the bed, staring at the wall. It was midafternoon, but what difference did it make what time it was? She had not been out of this blasted hotel room in the four weeks since Rance had brought her here. Nothing ever changed. He came three times a day to bring her meals, and each morning a young Negro girl brought in a tub of hot water and fresh clothes.

She heard him enter the room but she did not turn. She hated him, the war, and Richmond, Virginia, in that order. She wished everyone would just go away and leave her to wither and die.

"Still in bed, I see," he commented, amused.

It was the amusement in his voice that caused her to roll over and glare at him. "And what else am I supposed to be doing? Pacing up and down the floor? Staring out the window at the guard you keep posted below to keep me from running away? Just what would you have me do, Rance?"

He was wearing a casual gray uniform but still displayed the captain's stars. He was carrying a large package which he tossed unceremoniously on the bed. He walked over, sat down, and crossed his legs lazily as he watched her. She glanced down at the package but made no move to touch it. "Go ahead," he urged. "See what I bought for you this morning. I had to guess at your size. Waist like this . . ."

331

He cupped his hands together in a small circle. "Breasts like this . . ." He grinned and spread his hands wider.

"You think you're so damn smart!" She reached out and shoved the box to the floor. "I don't want anything from you—except to be rid of you."

He frowned. "April, how long are you going to keep this up? You were plenty glad to see me when I came to get you away from Blackmon, but as soon as you found out I didn't plan to take you straight to a parson and marry you, you started acting like a spoiled brat."

"I wouldn't marry you if you were the last man on earth, Rance Taggart. I just can't understand why you insist on keeping me around. Why don't you go ahead and rape me and be done with it?"

He raised an eyebrow, dark eyes flashing with annoyance. "How many times did I ever rape you? And is that all you've got on your mind, woman? You think that's all any man wants from you, isn't it? Maybe deep down it's what *you* want, and it's just sticking in your craw that I haven't leaped into bed with you."

"Damn you!" She chopped the words out between tightly clenched teeth. "Damn you, Rance Taggart, you are a sorry excuse for a gentleman."

He threw back his head and laughed. "I never claimed to be a gentleman. At least I make no pretenses, lovely lady." He stopped his laughter and looked at her grimly. "Now get out of that bed and open the box. Your bath will be brought to you shortly, and I've someone coming to do your hair. We're going to a ball tonight, and I want you to look your best."

"I'm not going anywhere with you!" she sputtered, turning her face to the wall once more after pulling the spread up to her chin.

Without another word, he crossed the floor, jerked down the covers, and yanked her roughly to her feet. He ripped off the flimsy nightgown, shoved her back down on the bed, and tore open the package. The gown he laid out on the bed was beautiful, made of powder blue silk, with a daring décolletage. The wide skirt was edged in a band of delicate lace, and scallops were caught up in tiny white velvet bows.

Forgetting her anger entirely, she fingered the gown lovingly, whispering, "It . . . it's the most beautiful dress I've ever seen. Why ever would you buy it for me?"

"There's a lavish ball being held tonight," he said casually, taking a long, thin cheroot from his pocket and lighting while she continued to admire the gown. "Everyone of rank and importance will be there. I want a beautiful woman by my side. It looks good for an officer to be seen with beautiful women."

"Since when did you care about rank, anyway? You're nothing but a damn privateer."

He looked at her for a long time, quietly, thoughtfully, and then decided to explain. "April, it doesn't make any goddamn difference whether you believe me or not, but I never pocketed any money I got from selling Yankee horses. I used whatever I got to buy better stock to *give* to the Confederate cavalry." He paused a moment, then continued, "Now just get dressed, and I'll come for you later."

He started for the door, but she called out, "You're right. I don't believe you. The only thing I want to hear from you is when you plan to set me free."

"When I'm good and damn ready." Without turning to look at her, he walked out and locked the door behind him.

The Negro maid brought her bath and helped her dress, and all the while April was thinking that maybe, just maybe, there would be someone at the ball who would listen to her story and help her.

Suddenly she was aware that the young girl was speaking to her. "I'm sorry, what did you say?"

"The war." The girl said as she stood behind her, brushing April's long yellow gold hair. "It's bad for the South. That's how come they're havin' this heah party tonight. I hear tell it might be the last party evah. The war is fixin' to bust wide open. The Yankees might just march right into Richmond."

"Would you like that?" April asked suddenly, curiously.

"No'm. Not really. I mean, I got a job heah at the hotel. If'n the Yankees come, they gonna burn evahthing. What me gonna do then? Starve or get kilt, I reckon."

April pointed out that it might not be that bad. "And you would be free. Don't you want to be free?"

The dark eyes rolled upward as she shook her kinky head back and forth. "Not if'n it means I gots to look after myself. Somebody's lookin' aftah me now, and I ain't goin' hungry. I'd just as soon evahthing stayed like it is."

"But nothing ever stays the same," April said quietly, more to herself than to the girl. She was thinking of the days at Pinehurst before Vanessa became so discontent . . . before Poppa became ill. "No," she repeated, "no matter how happy you think you are, nothing stays the same. It gets worse or it gets better, but everything always changes."

The girl said nothing more, eyeing her strangely as she continued to work on her hair. When she had finished, golden ringlets hung in a cascade from the top of her head, held in place by fragrant gardenia blossoms tied with blue silk ribbons and bows. "Cap'n Taggart gonna like that," she said proudly, standing back to admire her work. "He one handsome man, and he gonna have one pretty lady with him tonight."

April stood before the gilt-edged oval mirror and stared at her reflection. In the weeks since coming to Richmond, her coloring had improved. She looked rested. The gaunt, frightened look was gone from her eyes. For this much, she was grateful. Of course, she could stand to gain a bit of weight, but judging by the neckline, she had not lost anything *there*.

Rance knocked on the door, and the servant girl let him in. He was splendidly attired in dress grays and white gloves, a shining saber held by an ornate scabbard at his side. Three bars on his collar and four rows of gold braid on the sleeve of his coat denoted his captain's rank. He was, April was forced to admit, quite a splendid man.

His eyes swept over her, mirroring his pleasure. He held out his arm and murmured, "Never have I been graced by so beautiful a companion, Miss Jennings. I think it's time the Captain and his lady joined the others."

She did not return his smile but allowed him to lead her from the room and out to the sweeping, curving stairway. They paused, staring down the stairway as light from hundreds of candles in crystal chandeliers and lanterns filled with whale oil and set along the walls cast a mellow glow over the colorful array of dancers. Fragrant bouquets of gardenias, roses, and magnolia blossoms were tied to the stair railings with garlands of greenery and ribbons. The scent of flowers mingled with expensive French perfumes floating through the air.

The men were resplendent in their dress uniforms. Some, like Rance, wore their sabers. But it was the ladies who adorned the scene the most brilliantly. Their rainbow-hued ballgowns and hooped skirts swirled gaily to the sweeping music of a military band.

They laughed, chatting with the officers who held them as closely as propriety allowed. Some, April supposed, were visiting sweethearts. But most were probably wives, come to see their husbands before they marched off to yet another battle. It was obvious that all were making a determined effort at a happy time, an effort not to think of war. Some of these men would die before the war ended, if it ever did.

Rance led her down the stairs. Revelers nearby turned to stare. April nodded politely, eyes scanning the crowd for someone, anyone, who might lend a sympathetic ear.

"Don't try it, April," Rance growled close to her ear.

"I don't know what you're talking about," she snapped.

"Yes, you do. You think you might find someone who will believe you're being held against your will. If you dare try, I'll let everyone here know that you've been in prison, sentenced as a Union spy."

"You wouldn't!"

He smiled confidently. "Oh, yes, love, I would. And I would leave out the part about your having been pardoned. I would merely say you were released to my custody for the duration of the war."

He moved to stand before her and bowed slightly. "May I have this dance, lovely lady?" His crooked smile made her want to slap his face. She suppressed her ire and moved into his arms.

He held her closely, too closely, and she cursed herself for the warmth spreading through her body. Once, he danced her behind a huge potted plant and kissed her. She complied, thinking dizzily how his kisses always tasted of warm, sweet wine. He left her shaken, and the twinkle in his eye announced that he was aware of her reaction.

In the weeks since taking her from Blackmon, he had never tried to seduce her. What did he have in mind? It was maddening.

And once more, as though reading her mind, he whispered, "I'm waiting for you to ask me, love."

"Ask you what?" She bit out the words, trying to move away. But he continued to hold her tightly.

"I'm waiting for you to invite me to your bed. I won't give you the pleasure of claiming that I forced you." He cocked his head to one side and stared down at her. "It's going to be good. We both know it. How much longer do you intend to hold out? Your stubbornness is causing both of us misery."

Suddenly she jerked out of his arms, not caring who saw or heard, but there was no one within earshot. "You let me tell you something, you pompous, arrogant privateer! I'll rot in hell before I invite you to my bed."

She whirled and walked away. Strangely, he did not follow. Glancing over her shoulder, she saw that he was talking to an officer of higher rank. He cast a worried glance in her direction but continued to talk with the other man.

Now is the time to escape, she thought frantically, almost falling in her haste to get to the front door of the hotel. A soldier stepped forward to block her path. "You must be Miss Jennings," he said politely, without smiling. "Captain Taggart said you might be wanting to leave, and he left orders that you were to remain here. He doesn't want you roaming the streets alone at night. It isn't safe, nor proper for a lady."

Exasperated, she tried to push by him, but he clamped a firm hand on her shoulder. "I am sorry, Miss Jennings." He sounded impatient. "If you persist, I've orders to return you to your quarters upstairs."

She turned away, thinking to try the rear of the hotel, but he called out softly. "There are guards back there, too, ma'am. Why don't you join the other ladies and help yourself to some champagne? The meeting the officers are having now was unexpected. But, I can assure you, it is important."

"Well, maybe I'll just return to my room," she said haughtily, starting for the stairs.

"Wouldn't advise that, either." He sounded amused now, rather than annoyed. "The Captain will probably prefer you to wait with the ladies. The ball will continue when the meeting is over."

"Well, I don't prefer to wait with the ladies," she snapped, stomping in unladylike fashion through the ballroom and to the open doors of the veranda. Of course, there was a guard there also, but she assured him that she wanted only a breath of fresh air. "I am not going to leap over the balcony, if that's what you're worried about."

He nodded and leaned back against the wall, watching her suspiciously.

The gentle night breeze kissed her burning cheeks as she moved to grip the balcony railing with angrily shaking hands. Beyond, just down a few bricked steps, lay the courtyard. Bathed in moonlight, the air was sweet with the floral gardens. It would be nice, she told the guard, if she could just go for a little walk, alone.

"Fine with me," he drawled. "There's guards all around those walls out there, and they've got orders to watch you, Miss Jennings. And, believe me, they know who you are."

With a defiant set to her face, she whipped around to face him and ask, "Just how would they know who I am?"

His grin was slow, lazy, and annoying. "Captain Taggart spread the word that the most beautiful woman at the ball might want to leave, and we were to stop her. You're easy to spot, ma'am, 'cause you're easily the loveliest flower around."

With a flip of her hooped skirt, she moved quickly down the steps, almost stumbling in her haste to rid herself of his vexing company. In the courtyard, she inhaled deeply of the sweet night air, enjoying, for a moment, a sense of peace. Continuing to move, she walked toward the shadows where excited voices issued from an open window. She paused just far enough away to overhear, without appearing to eavesdrop.

". . . sorry to take you men away from the party," an apologetic, yet gruffly authoritative voice was saying. "We were afraid this would happen. We've been waiting for word from General Lee's staff."

April pretended to examine an ivory magnolia blossom

while she listened. Inside, against the glow of the oil lanterns, she could see them—officers in dress uniform, brows knit in consternation. Rance was among them, a thin cheroot dangling from his tightly set lips. The man speaking, a ponderous figure with bushy gray sideburns matching his wiry beard, wore the three stars of a Colonel.

"We have known all along, of course," he was saying, "that the Army of the Potomac has been encamped on the northern side of the upper Rapidan, near Culpepper Court House."

"I reckon we do," one of the officers interjected to a round of laughter. "They've been there for three damn years, and they're only a few miles farther south than they were when the war started."

The Colonel's glowering eyes quelled the robust reaction, and everyone fell silent once again. "As I was saying, the Army of the Potomac is camped there, and we have reason to believe its mission now will be to head south and attack. Since Lincoln named Grant commander of all the Union armies, we have felt that his strategy will be one of extreme aggression.

"His objective will be our armies, not our cities and strategic points. He will try to put our armies out of action as quickly as possible. His theory is what our strategists are basing their defensive tactics on. There are, we feel, two armies that will concern Grant the most—the Army of Northern Virginia, under Lee, and the Army of Tennessee, under Joe Johnston."

April glanced through the window quickly as another man spoke. She could not denote his rank. "Has President Davis finally realized that Braxton Bragg just can't win a battle? He made a big mess of that Kentucky invasion back in the summer of '62, and good Lord, he let victory slip right through his fingers at Murfreesboro."

"As you are aware," the Colonel answered in a condescending tone, "the President removed him after Chattanooga, and he now serves as his chief military adviser." He paused to take a deep breath and sweep the men circling him with a fierce gaze. "Let me remind you, gentlemen, that we accomplish nothing by criticizing our fellow officers. Our purpose right now is to attempt to thwart Grant's inevitable advance."

He continued, "Johnston is now entrenched on the low mountain ridges northwest of Dalton, Georgia. Lee's army is just below the Rapidan River in the central part of Virginia. These two armies are the only ones that matter. We have sizable forces west of the Mississippi, under Edmund Smith, but that region is cut off now that the Yankees control the river. Gentlemen . . ."—he paused for effect—"the fate of the Confederacy depends on the fate of Johnston's and Lee's armies. We have every reason to believe that Grant knows this, and that he is going to try to destroy them."

April saw him reach for a bottle of brandy and pour himself a drink, as though needing it. He took a long swallow. All eyes were upon him as, with a grim expression, he announced, "Gentlemen, I regret to have to inform you tonight that the Army of the Potomac has begun its move. With over a hundred thousand men, Grant is moving now toward the Army of Northern Virginia and the city of Richmond."

Gasps went up, but before the excitement could drown him out, the officer cried loudly, "Listen to me. There's more. Sherman is reported to be moving toward Georgia, after Johnston. Our scouts have told us that Grant is crossing the Rapidan and is on the move. We have just received this word, and each of you is to return to your companies for further orders now."

The men began leaving the room. A few stayed behind to confer with the officer who had been speaking. April saw that Rance was one of these and knew she had a few moments respite before he would look for her.

She felt a chill beginning deep within, a chill of terror. The Yankees were heading for Richmond! Would the Rebels be able to stop them? And Sherman. What was it that officer had said about Sherman? He was marching for Georgia. Did that mean he would eventually attack Alabama . . . and Montgomery . . . and possibly destroy Pinehurst? Now she felt the need to return home more strongly than ever. There was nothing she could do in the way of defense, but at least she could *be there*. It was better than doing nothing. It was certainly better than sitting and waiting for Grant to attack Richmond.

She turned and hurried through the courtyard, heading

back toward the ballroom. Rance would have to see the wisdom in letting her go. He would be going to battle. What was to become of her? He could not leave her locked in the hotel room.

Word had spread quickly. Even the guard at the door looked alarmed. She pushed by him, eyes scanning the room for Rance. Everywhere the officers were taking their ladies in tow, preparing to leave. An air of suspense and, yes, stark terror was bearing down on them with an invisible but smothering force.

Then she saw him, striding purposefully toward her. She caught his arms, stared up into his stormy brown eyes and cried, "I heard, Rance. I know what's happening. You must let me leave. You can't expect me to just sit here and wait for Grant to attack the city. And with Sherman marching toward Georgia . . . my God, he could attack in Alabama, too."

His face contorted angrily as he demanded, "Just how the hell do you know all this, April?"

"I was outside the window, in the courtyard. I heard it all. Oh, does it matter?" She implored, "Rance, please. Let me go. There's nothing for me here."

He stared at her for a long time before speaking, then murmured, "No, I guess there's not. I guess I've been wrong about a lot of things. But you're crazy to want to go running back to Alabama and that devil sister of yours. You'll be safer here. I have to ride with Stuart. I want to ride with him. All hell is about to break loose in this infernal war, and every man will be needed. I'll see that you're taken care of here. Richmond will be well defended, rest assured."

"No!" She gripped his arms. "I'll find a way, somehow, to leave. Damn you, why do you insist on keeping me? I don't love you. You don't love me. It's madness, it's—"

He grabbed her arm, squeezing painfully as he steered her toward the stairs. "I've listened to all of this I'm going to, April. I'm a fool. I dared to think—"

He stopped short. They had reached the second floor. April looked up at his face, saw the tight set, the quickly narrowing eyes, felt his tension. Slowly she followed his gaze.

Kaid Blackmon was standing before them, towering ominously, legs spread wide apart in a challenging stance. His right hand was poised only inches from the gun in his holster. "I come to talk to you, Taggart," he said quietly. "No trouble. Just talk. Had a time trackin' you here, but I did. And now we're goin' to talk."

Rance showed no fear of the man. "Do you want to talk here or in my room?"

"Wherever. Might be best in private."

A few people were hurrying by, officers with anxious faces, women crying.

Rance led the way to his room, keeping April close to him. Inside, Rance pointed toward a chair and she took it gratefully, sitting down to grip the arms and watch the two men as they faced each other.

Rance removed his spotless white gloves. "All right, Blackmon. What's on your mind?"

"I just heard the word from a lieutenant headin' out. Grant's crossing the river. I'll get to the point." Tobacco dripped from the corner of his mouth. He looked around for a spitoon and, not finding one, crossed to the window and spat. Wiping his mouth with the back of his hand, he faced Rance again. "April wants to go to Alabama. I'll take her."

Rance sneered. "Even if she wanted to go with you, how do you figure you can take her? We've got a huge battle coming up. Every man is needed."

"I'm desertin', Captain. It's that simple. I've done my share for the Confederacy. And I'm sick of this damn war. I'll kill any man that tries to stop me."

Rance laughed. "I doubt you'll even be missed, Blackmon. From what I hear, you were never good for anything anyway, except raping helpless women prisoners."

Blackmon took a menacing step forward. "That's a goddamned lie." Rance did not retreat. He did not move a muscle. Blackmon sized him up, then snapped, "I didn't come here to jaw with you. April wants to go with me, and I'm takin' her back to Alabama, just like I promised her I would."

April was a storm of emotions. She desperately wanted to leave Richmond. But go with Kaid? The thought sick-

ened her. Still, Rance did not love her, and whatever feelings she had for him were, she knew, probably never to be
returned.

"You won her in a horse race, and that's how come you
figure she belongs to you, right?" Blackmon asked.

She closed her eyes and took a deep breath. Damn! She
was getting tired of being nothing more to any man except
a possession. Was she simply going to sit here and let them
talk about her? Decide her fate as though she were a mule
to be traded from one to the other? Before she would allow
any further indignities, she would make up her mind.
Quickly, she said hoarsely, avoiding Rance's eyes, "I will
go with him. I choose to. Let's not talk about it anymore."

Rance was silent, and she began to feel panic well up in
her. Well, why didn't he *say* something? Would he try to
stop her, tell her he *did* love her? Was he finally going to
admit his feelings for her?

A second passed and then another, and when she could
not stand the silence any longer, she rose from her chair—
still avoiding Rance's gaze—and moved a step toward
Blackmon.

"There is nothing for me here. Yes, I'll go with you,
Kaid," she said, her voice quavering. She hoped to God
that she could trust him not to touch her. But there was no
way she could stay here now, knowing how little Rance
cared for her. "I'll meet you in the morning, at the stables.
Good night."

She still had not looked at Rance. Now she walked to
the door and through it without a single glance backward,
keeping her back straight and her face set. She went into
her own room, closed the door behind her, and leaned
against it, staring ahead without seeing.

A few hours later, when the hotel was quiet for the
night, April lay in bed, wide awake, studying the ceiling.
When she heard her door open softly, she knew who it was
without turning to look, and joy began gathering in her.

He stopped at the foot of her bed and gazed down at
her. She returned his gaze. Neither spoke for several moments.

"I won't see you again after tomorrow," Rance said
finally. "I came to say good-bye . . . and to wish you luck

with your protector." He did not try to keep the sarcasm from his voice, and she bristled instantly.

"Will I be worse off with Kaid than I have been with you? He'll keep his hands off me."

"Aren't you tired of pretending you don't want me, April?" he asked quietly. Without waiting for her answer, he sat down beside her and drew back the covers. Looking deeply into her eyes, he reached over and touched her thigh, feeling the warmth of her through the thin cotton nightgown.

April shuddered. She wanted to return his touch. But if she did, would he taunt her, make her admit that she wanted him? His hand moved upward and he leaned over to kiss her, a burning kiss that went on and on. She responded, returning his passion with hers, and her arms twined around his neck, pulling him closer. In that one endless kiss, the world receded and there was only their desire.

Rance moved back slowly, briefly touching her face with his fingers, letting them trail down over the smooth cheek to her stubborn little chin.

Suddenly he chuckled softly and began dancing his fingers slowly over her thighs and belly.

"Years ago," he murmured huskily, "I used to have fantasies about taming your wild spirit. Whenever I saw you at Pinehurst, I wondered about you. I think I desired you even then."

A puzzled frown furrowed her brow and he said, "No, I never cared for Vanessa. It was always you who intrigued me."

April relaxed again, and his stroking became hotter, more insistent. She writhed beneath his hands, and he bent for another kiss.

She felt his fingers parting the soft flesh between her thighs and could not suppress the moan of pleasure which escaped her trembling lips as he began to caress her. Sweet hot flames of ecstasy shot into her innermost recesses.

He continued to stroke rhythmically while they kissed. Then, raising his head, he whispered harshly, "Say you want me, April. Say you want me."

She could no longer resist him. "Yes, damn you," she whispered hoarsely. "I want you."

No man, she thought, *has ever made me feel this way
. . . like living and dying all rolled into one.*

He wanted her as desperately as she did him. Quickly
shedding his clothes, he mounted her, plunging himself all
the way in, thrusting his hips to and fro, forcing himself to
hold back . . . hold back until he felt her heels digging
into his back, her nails clawing at the flesh of his shoulders. Only then did he allow himself the ultimate glory.

Afterward, he held her against him. She cradled her
head against his shoulder, her fingertips entwining the
damp curling hairs of his chest. She could not fight him,
not ever again. She was happy here, happier lying in his
arms than she had ever been in her life, and she would not
let pride keep her from admitting that. She would tell
Rance she loved him, and pray that he would not taunt her
any more.

"Rance," she began.

Rance held her lovingly, gazing down into her face. "I
love you, April," he told her, letting go to touch her face
lovingly with one hand. "I think I always have, but I
thought that damned plantation meant more to you than
me or any man ever could."

"I guess I was foolish enough to think that, too," she
admitted, her heart pounding tremulously at his nearness,
at the realization that he did, truly, love her. "And I
thought I was just a possession to you . . . something to
own."

He laughed softly, smiling down at her in adoration.
"Oh, yes, you are a possession, my beauty, and you always
will be. I intend to own you, in bed and out, for the rest of
my life. But I was ready to give you up, because I figured
that's what you wanted. I needed to know that you really
loved me, April. And that's all I was waiting for."

They kissed again for long, precious moments. Then he
said, "Let's declare a truce, my love. There never was any
question of my letting you go—not with Blackmon or anyone else. You're mine, and I'll never let you go."

A splintering crash drove them apart, Rance leaping to
his feet. Framed in the doorway stood Kaid, his face black
with rage.

"So, *Darlin'*," he sneered, his voice shaking with fury,

"you enjoy doing it with this one! You never cared for me, not at all, no matter how much I loved you."

As Rance turned away, reaching for his gun, Kaid shrieked at April, "You never cared for me! You just used me, damn you! Used me!"

She was never sure, later, exactly how it happened. Kaid was screaming at her, his face contorted with the most awful fury she had ever seen. The next instant, a shot rang out and she was covered with blood. As she heard her own terrified screams, she realized it was not her own blood but Rance's blood that splashed onto her face, her neck, her bosom. And then she knew no more.

❧ Chapter Thirty-one ❧

NUMBED by sorrow, April had lost track of the time they had been traveling. Each time she closed her eyes the image of Rance lying in a spreading pool of his own blood returned with stark horror. *Dead.* The word ripped its way through her mind, stunning her with grief. Dead, and only moments after they had both realized how deeply they really loved one another. It was unspeakably cruel. She silently cursed the God who had let this happen.

She no longer cared whether they ever reached Alabama. She did not care if Kaid made good his frequent threats to kill her. She numbly did as she was told, riding the train, being tossed up onto a stolen horse once they reached Wilmington, riding through swamps and woodlands with the sun beating down fiercely.

At night, Kaid would camp far away from the main roads, forcing her to eat whatever he could kill in the woods. A rabbit. A squirrel. Once, there was only a rattlesnake, cooked over a fire after it was skinned.

He would laugh evilly. "Me and you are gonna be together for a long, long time. We made a deal. I take you back to that fancy plantation of yours, and then me and you just might even get married."

Strangely, he never tried to touch her, not ever. His love for her had turned wholly to hate, but he didn't molest her or even suggest it. It was the single mercy in April's life, and she was grateful.

It took them almost a month to reach Montgomery, traveling slowly so as to avoid anyone who might ask why Kaid wasn't fighting. Letting him lead her, pretending to be subservient, April gave Kaid the directions to Pinehurst.

They had made their way through the woods, staying off the main road, as always. As they sat atop the fresh horses Kaid had stolen just outside Columbus, Georgia, April drank in the sight of her once-palatial home.

The grounds were overgrown with weeds. The mansion, itself, was but a shell of what was once a splendid structure. Gone were the roses that had entwined the proud columns of the wide front porch. All of Pinehurst cried out in pain over having been neglected and allowed to die.

"It looks deserted," Kaid said, more to himself than to April. He tugged at his beard thoughtfully. She started to nudge her horse forward, but he reached out to block her way and snapped, "Don't you go no further. I said it *looks* deserted. I can't be sure it is. We ain't gonna just go ridin' up there. Not after what you told me once about your sister and the men she had working for her."

"I doubt they're still here," she said quietly, almost sadly. "I doubt that anyone is here anymore."

"Well, I'm gonna nose around a bit and be sure. These woods circle them grounds all the way around?"

She nodded.

"Then we hang back in the woods and poke about till it gets dark. We can tell if somebody is inside when it gets dark, 'cause they'll be lightin' up."

For the next several hours, they moved about the woods. April's heart constricted as the utter decay of her home became more and more apparent. The servants' quarters were entirely empty. The cattle pens were deserted and knee-high in weeds. The stables held no horses, either. The high-bred stock her father had taken such pride in were simply gone.

"There ain't nothing here, it don't look like to me," Kaid said finally, as they returned to their best vantage point. The blue sky began to pale to a darker shade, heralding the night. He looked at her for a long time, as though deep in thought, then said, "I think there's some riches here to be had, darlin'. The slaves might've run off, and your sister may not have hung around when things got poor, but we

can make something of this place, you and me. I'm gonna
like livin' here. I know how to rebuild this place into what
it looks like it once was, a real palace. I'll live like a
goddamn king."

Suddenly, he jerked around straining to see through the
thick foliage. April followed his gaze, a tremor darting
through her as she saw a light in the window.

"What room is that?" he demanded.

She could not speak. She was overcome with the realization that someone was still living in the house! But who?
Poppa? Vanessa?

He hissed, "I asked you a question, damnit."

"The parlor," she replied, not turning away from the
house. "It's the parlor."

"We're gonna sneak up there, real quiet, and I'm gonna
get the drop on whoever's in there. We're gonna go by *my*
rules, darlin', not theirs. The first thing I'm gonna do is kill
whatever stud she's got living in there. There won't be
nobody left 'cept me and you and your sister.

"And you know something else?" He peered intently at
her upturned face. "If your sister is nicer to me than you
are, then she's gonna be the one to share my kingdom, and
you'll be feedin' the buzzards. Understand me?"

Without waiting for a reply, he fastened his burly hand
about her wrists and jerked her along. When they reached
the weed-covered grounds, he forced her to crawl along
with him on hands and knees.

There was no sound save for the crickets chirping their
early summer song, and even this ceased as the insects
became aware of intruders in their realm. Above, the sky
was blue black, and there was no moon to cast shadows. It
was a night of total darkness. A night, April thought fearfully, created for murder.

Kaid pulled her through the blackness to the rear of the
house, groping his way, pausing now and then to ask her
where they were in relationship to the parlor. They were
heading for the back door of the house.

She shivered in the night breeze. Somewhere along the
way, she had lost her shawl, and her thin muslin dress was
frayed.

They reached the back porch steps. She felt the cold
steel of a blade against her throat and held her breath in

terror as Kaid whispered, "Now you're gonna lead me
inside. You're gonna take me straight to that room where
somebody is sitting. And you ain't gonna bump into nothin'
on purpose just to make noise and let 'em know we're
here. I've got a knife in one hand and a gun in the other,
and even though you're still the prettiest woman I ever laid
eyes on, I'll kill you so quick you won't have time to
scream. You understand me?"

She could only nod slightly, feeling the sharp blade nick
her flesh. But the terror was gone. She was no longer afraid
of dying. Rance was gone, and she saw no future for
herself. He had killed the only man she had ever loved.
Never before had she felt capable of taking a life, but, God
forgive her, she knew she could snuff out Kaid's without a
second of remorse. The time, she vowed fiercely, would
come.

She led him up the stairs and opened the back door. The
hinges squeaked loudly, and Kaid jerked her back, hissing,
"Slowly, damn you, bitch. I told you not to make no
noise!"

This time, she pulled the door gently, and the squeak
was faint. They stepped into the kitchen. He wrapped his
fingers around the knife, making a fist which he held
tightly against her throat. She could only take tiny, halting
steps, as he kept holding her back, waiting long moments
for any sound, any sign that their presence had been detected.

It seemed to take forever to cross the kitchen and enter
the hallway. April had to grope for the doorway. Then,
toward the middle of the long corridor that ran the length
of the house, she could see a pale golden light. The doors
to the parlor—which stood between the main hallway and
the front foyer—were open. Kaid could see the rest of the
way himself and no longer depended on her to lead him.
He continued to move cautiously, slowly, hesitating every
few steps.

Suddenly they could hear voices. April recognized
Vanessa's and, despite all that had happened, felt a warmth
stir in her.

She realized at once that Vanessa was drunk.

". . . don't care what you hear in town," Vanessa was
saying. "The Yankees aren't heading this way. Why do

you have to look for trouble, Zeke?" She paused to hiccup. There was the sound of glass hitting glass as she poured herself another drink.

"You haven't had to fight in the damned war. You've lived here damn good, you bastard."

"You call this good? You even call this living?" He sounded angry. "The slaves run off. You've about sold all the silver. I'd like to know what the hell else is left besides the goddamn land. And when the Yankees come, they're gonna take that."

"No, they won't. I'll give them shelter. Tell them I'm a Union sympathizer. They won't take my land. Besides . . ." She hiccuped once more. "They aren't coming."

"Damn you, Vanessa. Listen to me!"

They heard the sound of glass shattering. April envisioned Zeke knocking Vanessa's drink from her hand, sending it smashing into the fireplace.

"I told you the war news isn't good for the South. That crazy Yankee General Sherman is heading south. Some say he's heading straight for Atlanta. And Grant is moving on Richmond. Damn it, let's sell off the rest of the silver and get the hell out of here. We'll go to Mexico."

"You're crazy," came her blistering retort. "Pinehurst is the biggest, richest plantation in all of Alabama, and I'm not leaving it. Not ever. Do you hear me? You get the hell out if you want to, but I'm staying! I've fought too hard to gain control here, and when the war is over, I'll build this place back to what it once was. If you don't want to be a part of all that, then to hell with you."

"You aren't having another drink—"

"You don't tell me what to do, you bastard!"

There was the sound of scuffling, and Kaid took advantage of the moment. Shoving April to one side, he rushed the rest of the distance into the arched doorway of the parlor, a weapon in each hand, and stood there, legs spread, face alight with triumph.

April hurried after him, standing just behind him and a few feet to his left.

Vanessa's eyes widened in shock, then narrowed to stark, freezing hatred as she saw April. Zeke demanded, "Just who the hell are you?" Nodding to April, he said, "You oughta know better than to come back here."

Vanessa quickly regained her composure. "I'll handle this," she snapped, eyes flicking over Kaid. "How dare you come storming into my home this way? I'll have you arrested. And get that girl out of here. She was disowned by my father and has no right to be in this house!"

"I'll do the talking!" Kaid waved his gun ominously, and Vanessa fell silent. She was not, he decided at once, as beautiful as April. She was elegantly dressed in a rose satin gown, the bodice cut low, exposing a generous, appealing bosom. Her hair hung about her face in golden ringlets, a lovely sight. But there was just something, he thought, something ugly about her . . . ugly and undesirable. He made his decision easily. She would die. He would keep April.

"April, here, can prove she was meant to have this place," Kaid told them brusquely. "She told me about the ring her daddy give her. Whoever's got that ring is the rightful owner here."

April cursed herself silently for that long ago day when she had so foolishly confided the story to him. Vanessa and Zeke exchanged anxious, alarmed looks. At least, April thought with some satisfaction, she had not told Kaid where the ring was hidden. That was *her* secret.

"Now, the way I see it," Kaid continued, enjoying his power, "you two ain't nothin' but poachers, and I figure the best thing to do is just go on and get rid of you so you won't be around to make no trouble. I've come a long way and been through hell and back to get here. I've deserted the army, and I aim to sit out the rest of the war right here in this house. I sure don't need nobody making trouble—"

April saw him raise his hand slightly, knew instinctively that he was about to fire the gun. There was no time to think—only to act and act quickly—and she hurled herself against his side. He fell against the door opening. The gun exploded, the bullet shattering into the chandelier above them, sending down a shower of glass.

Zeke leaped forward, hands outstretched, and April jumped backward into the foyer, out of the way. The two men thrashed wildly on the floor. Zeke had seen the knife in Kaid's left hand, and it was this he was after, using every ounce of strength he could muster to fasten his hand around Kaid's and twist downward, plunging the blade into the big man's throat.

April could not scream. She stood there in silent, frozen horror, hands clutching her own throat in revulsion as she watched the blood gurgling rapidly from Kaid's. She closed her eyes and envisioned her beloved's blood, blood let by the hand of the man who was now dying.

"Get him out of here!"

Her eyes blinked at the sound of Vanessa's hysterical voice.

"Get that son-of-a-bitch out of here. Dig a hole. Bury him. Do something with him. Just get him out of the house."

Zeke got to his feet and stood glaring menacingly at April. "What about her? You gotta do something about her."

Vanessa regarded her coldly. "The first thing we're going to do is have her hand over that ring."

April shook her head from side to side. Finally able to find her voice, she said, "The ring isn't important, Vanessa. You and I are going to share Pinehurst. Poppa will approve. I'll talk to him, beg him to understand—"

"You little fool!" Vanessa laughed harshly. "Poppa died in '62."

"No . . ." April moaned, refusing to accept what she had really known since the White House seance.

"Yes, he's dead, and Pinehurst is mine, and there will be no sharing. I told you that a long time ago. Hand over that ring."

Suddenly, a spirit she had thought long dead arose in her fiercely and April faced her sister defiantly. "No! No one knows where that ring is hidden except me, and I won't tell you. Go ahead and kill me, but relatives will come one day to claim this estate, and they will want to see the ring as proof of your ownership. The whole family knew you were disowned, Vanessa. As long as you don't have that ring, you'll never own Pinehurst!

"I've tried to love you. . . ." she rushed on, tears stinging her eyes. "I've begged you to forgive the way Poppa treated you. But you won't *let* me love you. You choose to hate me. I honestly believe you would kill me and never know a moment's remorse."

She turned to Zeke and lashed out, "Did you know he held me prisoner the last time you sent me away? Held me prisoner in that shack down by the creek. If it hadn't been for someone rescuing me . . . someone I loved more than my life . . . someone who is dead now . . . I would still be there. . . ." She covered her face with her hands, sobbing uncontrollably, her whole body trembling.

"You no-good bastard!" Vanessa screamed, reaching out for a tall vase and throwing it at Zeke. He ducked, the vase shattering against the wall behind him. "I'll deal with you later," she shrieked, then turned to April once more. "Damn you, April, tell me where you hid that ring!"

April raised her tear-streaked face and screamed, "I'd rather go to my grave than give it to you."

A slow, evil smile spread across Vanessa's face. "Then go to your grave you shall, dear sister—but alive, not dead. We'll just see how you like living in the family mausoleum. You can be with dear Poppa, be close to him. You will stay there until you tell me where you hid that ring!"

April shook her head wildly from side to side in horror and fear. "No, you wouldn't put me there . . . you wouldn't."

"Oh, yes, I would. We'll let you stay there with the rats and the spiders, and we'll feed you just enough to keep you alive so you can enjoy your surroundings."

She smiled at April with glittering eyes. "After a few days with the dead, dear sister," she murmured, "you'll wish you were one of them."

I already do, April thought. *Dear Lord, I already do.*

⚜️ Chapter Thirty-two ⚜️

APRIL began to fear that she was losing her sanity. She had wept until there were no more tears, only an utter hopelessness that pervaded everything. Her only respite from the living nightmare of the mausoleum was the blessed sleep that became almost constant. It was, she reasoned feebly, her mind's way of taking her away from her torturous plight.

Twice a day they came, always together. The first visit would be at midmorning, when the sun was high. Vanessa would beat upon the iron mausoleum doors with a large rock, sending metallic reverberations through April's prison. She would laugh as April struggled to awaken, clamping her hands over her ears.

Then Vanessa would ask if she were ready to tell where the ring was hidden. The answer was always the same. No. She would rather die.

Then Zeke would step forward to taunt her with descriptions of what he was going to do to her if she did not cooperate. But April knew that Vanessa would not allow him to ravish her. She was jealous of Zeke, for reasons April couldn't begin to understand.

Their second visit always came in midafternoon. Each time, they slipped just enough food through the wrought iron gates to keep her from starving to death. A crust of molded bread, or a half-rotten potato. Sometimes a bit of soured meat or a piece of rotting fruit. There would also be just one swallow of water. No more.

354

"We can keep this up forever, you know," Vanessa would tell her over and over. "This can go on for years. If you don't die, you will eventually go insane, just like Poppa. Then I can bring you back to the house and invite all the neighbors in to see that you lost your mind, just like Poppa. There will be no question about my being the rightful heiress. I can say you stole the ring and hid it, and you will be such a babbling lunatic by then that no one will doubt me."

She would stand outside the gates sometimes for an hour, taunting her. "Why don't you make things easier for yourself, April? You tell me where the ring is, and then I'll set you free. I will give you clothes and money. Yes, there will be money. I promise to send you away with a nice share."

Without much hope, April would reply, "Let me go, and I promise you I will share everything with you. I will forgive everything you ever did to hurt me."

"Well, I haven't forgiven *you* and I never will," Vanessa snarled through the iron bars. "I will have what is rightfully mine."

When she was not asleep, April would sit close to the gates, wanting the warm sunshine to touch her body, wanting to smell the sweet outer air, for the moldy odor within was overwhelming. What month was it? Too hot for May. The days were getting longer. Was it June? How many days had she been here? How many weeks?

Sometimes she would catch herself talking out loud to herself, or to her dead parents who lay inside those stone-covered caskets, and she would become frightened. Maybe she was going insane. But never, she vowed, hands squeezing the iron bars as she stared toward the hazy green forest with yearning, never, *ever*, would she give the ring to Vanessa. Poppa had given it to her. Vanessa had tormented Poppa, probably even hastened his death. This much, she could do for him, and she vowed she would, even if it meant her life.

One morning they did not come at the usual hour, and April felt a deep panic. Perhaps they had decided to leave her there to starve to death. She knelt beside the gate all day long, thin, bony fingers curved tightly about the bars, her eyes burning from straining toward the footpath for the sight of them, ears tuned to the sound of their approach.

Sleep had finally taken her when the sound of Zeke's derisive voice woke her. "Well, now, I'll bet you're good and hungry, ain't you, precious?"

He knelt before her, grinning down into her face with shining eyes, enjoying her misery. "No, Vanessa ain't with me. She sent me down here with your food. I got you a nice rotten peach. See?" He held up the yellowed fruit, mottled black, and squeezed it. The juice dribbled down his fingers. "We've decided you're gettin' too much to eat, so we won't be coming around but once a day. Maybe before long you'll feel like talking."

"Never," she whispered, as he continued to squeeze the peach in his filthy hands.

Dropping the peach to the ground, he mashed it into the red clay with his foot. "You know," he said matter-of-factly, drawing a cheroot from his pocket and lighting it, "it's a real shame to see a beauty like you turn into such a hag. I guess that's why that jealous sister of yours don't care if I come down here alone. She knows no man in his right mind would want somethin' that looks like you. Look at you! Skin and bones. Eyes sunk into your head. Hair matted and full of them crawly white things. And you stink, too. Stink just like them rotten corpses in there."

He laughed tauntingly, rocking back and forth on his heels. "I can't believe I ever did want somethin' like you. But then, you was a real beauty once. I don't figure you can last more'n a few more days. Then we can take you back up to the house and call in folks and say, 'Hey, look at the crazy! Just like her pappy!' Then everybody will say, 'Sure, so now there's nobody to claim Pinehurst except Vanessa, and it don't matter none what her daddy told ever'body about disinheriting her, 'cause he was as crazy as his other daughter is now."

April did not know why she wanted to know, but something made her ask suddenly, "What month is this?"

"Oh, I don't know if I should tell you that. Vanessa told me not to talk to you none. Just give you that peach and get the hell back to the house. But I don't reckon it'd do no harm to let you know it's almost July. Hot, ain't it? But I reckon it's plenty cool in there."

He handed her a cup of water through the bars, waited for her to drink it down quickly and then return it to him. Then he got to his feet and stretched his arms high above his head. "Well, I'm goin' back up to the house and have me a nice glass of whiskey and a plate of that chicken stew Vanessa cooked for dinner. Then I'm gonna crawl in that big old bed of hers and get me some. You settle down with the spiders and rats and have yourself a nice night now, you hear?"

He winked, laughing long and loud, before turning to walk back up the path, whistling as he went.

April did not move. She was staring at what was left of the peach. Green flies began to buzz noisily about it, settling down to scurry over the remnants. She watched as one ant, then two, found the treat and began to sample the juicy puddle. Her stomach rumbled with hunger, and she licked her lips. How sweet the peach would have tasted, even if it was rotten! Then she saw that there were two small pieces that had not quite been pulverized. It would be better than nothing, for she would have to endure the rest of the day, the entire night, and most of the next day before Zeke would return. Even then, he might destroy her food again.

She stretched her thin arm through the bars of the gate, stretching until her torso pressed painfully and she could reach no farther. Trembling now in ravenous eagerness, she saw that her fingertips were but an inch away from the tiny lumps. A little farther . . . just a bit farther . . . and she would have them. No matter about the flies or the ants or the dirt. Just one bite was better than nothing. Dizzily, she realized that she could soon become desperate enough to eat the flies and ants.

She closed her eyes, took a deep breath, and tried with all her might to stretch one more time. She felt something wet. She had touched them! She wriggled her fingers. No. It was not the peach bits. The wetness was higher up than her fingers . . . higher than her wrist. Something was licking her forearm! She tried to open her eyes but did not want to see the wild animal that was about to bite down into her flesh. A great, choking scream caught in her throat and her whole body froze.

Then she heard it. The whimper, a mixture of sadness

and joy. Her eyes flashed open and she screamed, not in terror, but in delight. It was not a wild animal licking her arm—it was Lucky!

"Oh, God, oh God, oh God!" She cried over and over, reaching to stroke his thick fur, laughing and sobbing all at once. "Lucky! How? How did you find me? Where did you come from?"

She scrambled up on her knees, her joyful heart overcoming the weakness of her body as the dog pushed his muzzle through the bars to lick her face happily. "Lucky, bless you," she whispered, "Bless you, boy, you found me. But how did you?"

"He loves you," the husky voice spoke quietly. "And so do I."

Time stood still. April looked up to see the dear, handsome face . . . the coal black hair and warm brown eyes . . . the strong, powerful body she knew so well. . . .

She felt herself slipping away, but he bent down quickly to reach through the bars and cup her face in his hands and command, "April, stay with me, sweetheart! Don't go out on me now. I've got to get you out of here. Goddamn, what have they done to you? You look like a corpse."

He slapped her cheeks gently. Her eyes flashed open, her gaze on his dear face mirroring all the overwhelming love that was in her heart. "Rance, I thought you were dead," she choked out the words, barely audible.

His laugh was short and brittle. "So did I. I lost a hell of a lot of blood, and it was quite a while before the doctors thought I'd make it. I tried to catch up with you sooner, but—oh, hell, sweetheart." He shook his head in dismay. "So much has happened. Right now, I just want to get you out of here. I just turned Lucky loose and bless him, he found you. Now, how—"

He froze at the sound of Lucky's sudden snarl. The dog's hair was standing straight up as he prepared to lunge forward. April looked up just in time to see the gun butt come whipping down across Rance's head. It happened in a flash and, just as quickly, she saw Zeke turning the gun around, about to point at Lucky, and she screamed, "Run, Lucky, run!"

The dog obeyed. The gun fired just as he leaped into the thick brush, running into the woods.

Zeke turned the gun on Rance.

"No!" April shrieked, struggling up on her weak legs to clutch the bars and plead. "No, please don't kill him. Dear God in heaven, Zeke, don't kill him."

Zeke was about to pull the trigger, but suddenly his eyes narrowed. Very quietly, he asked, "Who is he, April? And you better give me some answers."

The words rushed from her trembling lips. "Rance Taggart."

"He's the same bastard that came and took you before, ain't he?"

She nodded fearfully.

"Thought I recognized him." A slow smile was spreading across his face. "He must have it bad, traveling this far twice to try to find you. And from the way you're acting, I'd say this guy means a lot to you."

"Please, Zeke," she begged. "Have mercy. He's hurt—"

"Oh, I'm gonna help him all right. I'm gonna lock him up with you and then I'm gonna go get Vanessa. I've got an idea this is just what we've been hoping for—something to make you tell us where that blasted ring is hid."

He fumbled in his pocket and brought forth a key which he inserted in the lock. The gates swung open with a loud, grating sound. April tried to push through to get to Rance, but Zeke roughly shoved her back inside and she fell to her knees. Afraid to rile him, she crouched and watched anxiously as he picked up Rance's feet and dragged him inside. Then he walked out, slammed the gates, and locked them again.

She cradled Rance's head in her arms, carefully parting his thick dark hair, matted with blood, to see how seriously he was hurt. She heard Zeke say he was going for Vanessa. "And when we get back, honey, you're either going to tell us where that damn ring is, or you're going to watch your lover die. I'll take great pleasure in blowing his head off."

April knelt and pressed her lips to Rance's forehead. it was hopeless. One moment he was there to rescue her and now he was a part of the nightmare.

She cried his name over and over between great, gulping sobs praying to God to help them.

Joy washed through her as she saw his thick lashes fluttering. Then his eyes opened, slowly focusing on her face. He lifted his fingertips to touch her tears and whispered, "I hope I never have to see you cry again, April."

"He's gone to get Vanessa," she told him quickly. "And then they're coming back." She explained about the ring, why she was being kept prisoner, finishing in desperation, "They'll kill us, anyway, when I tell them."

She was stunned to see that familiar, lazy smile touch his lips. It faded as he pursed his mouth in pain and touched the back of his head.

"They won't be coming back, honey," he said, pulling himself up to a sitting position and glancing around. "What a grim place! Your parents are buried here?" He looked at the stone-covered biers.

"What makes you think they aren't coming back?"

He told her then, that he and Edward Clark and three other men had ridden in together. He had taken Lucky to go and search for her. But Clark and the others stayed by the house. "They'll take care of those two. Your nightmare is over."

He pulled her into his arms and kissed her gently. "Hang on, sweetheart," he murmured huskily, holding her against him as he glanced around. "I wish Clark would hurry up."

Anxious to keep her from passing out, he began to tell her about the war and all that had happened since Kaid had shot him. It was best to keep her from worrying, for he did not like the look on her face. She was ill, physically and mentally, and he was anxious to get her out of there.

He told her how General Grant and the Army of the Potomac had crossed the Rapidan river in early May, marching down through a stretch of junglelike terrain and isolated farms known as "The Wilderness." Grant had hoped to bring Lee's army to battle out in open country, farther south, but it had always been one of Lee's philosophies not to fight where his enemy wanted to fight. So Lee had marched his army straight into the "Wilderness" and attacked the federal columns before they could get across the junglelike lands.

"It was a bad place for a fight," Rance told her, his eyes grim. "There weren't many roads. There weren't many farm clearings, either. Mostly, it was nothing but dense

woods, with underbrush so thick it was impossible to see
fifty yards in any direction. There were ravines and water-
courses and brambles and creepers, and you could hardly
move. The Yankees had more men, but that didn't mean
anything, not when they couldn't move, either. And they
had no advantage in artillery, either, because the big guns
were useless in that place."

He paused to take a breath and look at April closely.
She was listening. Good. That meant she was not slipping
away. If he could just hold onto her for a little while
longer!

"It was blind and vicious," he went on. "Then the woods
caught on fire. Some of the wounded on both sides just
burned to death. The smoke from the battle and the fire
was so bad it choked us, and it made a fog so bad it was
impossible to see anything. That lasted two days, and we
all thought Grant would retreat. Go north of the Rapidan
and reorganize. But he moved south, toward a crossroads
at Spotsylvania Court House. It was about eleven miles
southwest of Fredericksburg and on Lee's road to Richmond. Grant moved all night, to get there first, so Lee
would have to do all the attacking.

"Damn Grant," Rance swore loudly, wanting to keep
April's attention. He swung his head from side to side.
"When his soldiers, exhausted though they were, realized
they weren't retreating but advancing, they really got excited. Grant turned the Battle of the Wilderness almost
into a victory. He wasn't even pausing to lick his wounds.
He was going to force the fighting, knowing he had Lee's
army outnumbered.

"Next thing that happened," he went on, "was a rolling
battle at that crossroads that went on for twelve days.
There was one day of nothing but hand-to-hand combat.
There was no letup."

His voice dropped, as though he could not bear to go on,
but knew he must . . . must keep April alert. Her eyes were
growing hazy. Damn, he swore silently, where was Clark?

"Stuart heard about Phil Sheridan, an infantry officer in
charge of Grant's cavalry corps," he went on. "Sheridan
took his cavalry off on a driving raid toward Richmond,
and Jeb Stuart took us and we galloped off to meet Sheri-

dan. We met him head on at a place called Yellow Tavern, but . . ." He paused, fighting for composure, but he couldn't hide his grief. "Stuart got killed."

"No!" April spoke for the first time. She reached to touch his dear cheek. "How you must ache, Rance! I know how you admired and respected Jeb Stuart."

He nodded. "Yeah. It hurt. It hurt the South, too. Jeb Stuart was one hell of a man."

April felt herself slipping away again—from starvation, from all that had happened. Rance gave her a gentle shake, then bent and kissed her. "Hang on," he whispered.

"Hey, there's no time for that!"

The jovial voice jolted them. Edward Clark was peering at them through the mausoleum gates, grinning. Beside him, Lucky panted happily, his tail swishing jauntily.

"Let's get you out of here."

He told them to stand back, then aimed his gun at the lock and fired. It burst open and he wrenched apart the gates.

As Rance and April stumbled out, clinging together in the twilight, he told them of the scene at the house. Zeke had been shot and killed, and Vanessa had run away. "We couldn't just shoot her in the back," he explained, looking at them beseechingly. "I mean, she *is* a woman."

"No, I don't want her killed," April said quickly, and then her legs began to give way. She felt herself falling, the black shroud engulfing once again.

Rance lifted her in his arms and Edward on one side, Lucky trotting along on the other, they made their way up the path to where their friends were waiting at the house.

"We'll spend the night here," Rance decided after he had placed April on a bed. "I'm going to rummage around and find some food. She's wasted away."

Edward frowned, then murmured hesitantly, "I hate to say it, Taggart, but she don't look good. No telling how long she's been locked in that place. She just might not make it."

"She's going to make it," Rance said fiercely, reaching to brush her hair back from her face. "I'm going to see that she makes it. We've been through too much to lose now."

"Yeah. I reckon the South feels the same way, even though Sherman's moving full steam on Atlanta."

Rance took a deep breath and stared down at April's pale, thin body, so skeletal that she looked dead. Quietly, he said, "I know there's a war going on, Clark. And I'm getting back into it just as soon as I take care of April, I swear it. We'll leave for Cheaha as soon as she's able. Meanwhile, I just hope that she-devil sister of hers comes back. I want to deal with her myself."

"If she does make it, maybe April won't want to go live on your mountain. I mean, all she ever talked about was coming back here and claiming what was rightfully hers."

"That was when she hoped her father was alive."

"She might not like you dragging her off again."

Rance smiled to himself.

"She'll want to come with me," he said with finality, pressing his lips against her sunken cheek. "For her, the war is over."

Outside, in the night, hidden in the thick underbrush around the slaves' quarters, Vanessa crouched, staring toward the great house. The hatred flowing through her was as poisonous as snake venom.

She could see the lighted window of April's bedroom, knew that he had taken her there to nurse her back to health. Zeke was dead. And she still did not know where the Pinehurst ring was hidden.

How long would they remain in her house? There were too many of them for her to fight now, especially without Zeke.

There, crouched in the shadows, Vanessa was sure of only one thing. For her, the war was just beginning.

❧ Chapter Thirty-three ☙

WHILE Sherman wrought hell throughout Georgia, Alabama was suffering its own hell at the hands of plundering Yankees who were waging smaller raids.

Even as Rance settled April in at the ranch on Cheaha, a raid led by the federal officer was striking deep into the heart of Alabama, destroying important iron furnaces, cotton mills, and the railroad running from Montgomery to West Point.

As word spread that Rance intended to "run his guts" out to get horses and supplies through to the Rebels, his band of followers grew. Most brought their families, for there were stories of women being attacked in their homes.

It was a time of terror for Southern women. As April healed and grew stronger, she urged Rance to move them to a higher spot on the mountain. There would be weeks, perhaps even months, when he and his men would be away. The women were far too vulnerable living at the base of the mountain. He agreed, and his band, now grown to fifty-seven men, moved up the mountain and began chopping down trees and building cabins. Fall was in the air and winter would soon be upon them.

He found a place for them on a high peak, confident that Yankee foragers would not take the trouble to climb so high.

Just as the little mountain village was being completed, word came from one of Rance's scouts that Atlanta had fallen to Sherman. The city was in flames.

April was sure that Montgomery would be next. "They will burn Pinehurst. I know they will," she cried. "Rance, what can we do? I want so desperately for us to go back there one day. I want us to live there . . . see our children grow up there."

He held her against him, his bearded chin resting on her head. "I feel the same way, sweetheart," he told her gently. "If they burn it down, then we'll rebuild it. We just can't worry about that now. We have to think about our own survival. I have to leave you and find a way to help the Confederacy in any way I can. You must be strong and help the other women be strong."

Now that there was shelter for the women and children, he and the men would soon leave. "First, I'm going down into Talladega and find food and supplies for all of you, even if I have to steal it. Then we'll go, and I don't know when we'll be back."

"Or even whether you ever will come back." She fought her tears. Then, breaking the promise she had made to herself, she cried, "Rance, sign a pledge of loyalty to the Union. Let's leave here and go home."

He gripped her shoulders and held her away from him so that he could stare down into her face. "April, you don't mean that. I know your home means a lot to you, but to ask me to turn my back on the Confederacy, now, in its most desperate hour? Turn away from what Stuart and all the others fought for?"

She asked evenly, "Would you do it for our child?"

He blinked, not understanding.

"Rance," she sighed, "I'm trying to tell you that I am going to have a baby. In the spring. I want the baby to be born at Pinehurst. And I want the baby's father to be alive when he's born! Haven't you given enough to the Confederacy? Haven't I?"

He ran his fingers through his long, thick hair, then through his beard, a slow smile touching his lips. "Well, I'll be damned! I'm going to be a father!"

April stamped her foot in exasperation. "Will you listen to me? I don't want to be left here on this mountain to give birth alone. I don't want my baby's father dying. Damn you, Rance." She threw herself against his chest, sobbing.

Feeling him stiffen, she pulled back to stare up into his face and see anger there.

"I don't want my baby's mother to be a coward, either, April," he said stonily. "Now grow up. Look around you. There are plenty of other women around you in the family way, and they aren't whining to go back to some fancy mansion to have their babies. They aren't asking their men to turn yellow, denounce everything they believe in to get out of fighting."

He cupped her chin in his hand, forcing her to meet his fiery gaze. "What has happened to your spirit, April? I know you've been through all kinds of hell, but your spirit's still there, I'm sure of that. I love you, April, but I swear I'll die before I ever sign an oath of loyalty to the Union. You do whatever you want. I've got a war to fight."

He stalked away, leaving her there alone. She had never felt such shame. If he were not the man he was, proud, brave, believing in a cause and willing to die for it, then she could never have given him her heart. And she had never been a coward before. She wouldn't be one now!

"Rance, I didn't mean it!"

He turned, holding his arms open to catch her as she threw herself against him.

"I'm just frightened. To have a baby. To see you leave me. But I love you, and I'll stay, and—"

He silenced her with a kiss, then, not caring that others were watching, he lifted her in his arms and carried her toward the cool, green forest, disappearing into the thick foliage and underbrush. Neither spoke. It was not a time for words. Everything had been said.

When they were deep enough in the woods, far away from the others, Rance laid her gently on a bed of fragrant pine needles. Slowly, he undressed her, his eyes gazing adoringly upon her face. She trembled beneath his touch, her body already beginning to shiver with anticipation of the ecstasy to come.

They lay side by side, naked, the sun beaming golden light through the foliage above. A bird sang his song of joy, sharing in their glory.

His lips touched her forehead, her cheeks, finally pressing down upon her mouth. She received his tongue, arching her back to move even closer as his warm, possessive hands closed about her breasts. She sighed as he squeezed her nipples, feeling them quickly move to hard, taut, eagerness.

He lowered his seeking tongue, trailing downward to flick teasingly about the succulent tips, then sucking each hungrily into his mouth.

She wanted him. Heaven above knew how much she wanted him. Her hands began to explore, and she found what she was seeking, that proud flesh of manhood, erect and taut, quivering in eagerness to claim her with force and tender fury. And it was this, she thought in wonder, drawing the swollen organ toward her, thighs spreading to receive it, that had planted the seed of love within her. And it was from here, she thought, touching her own self as she guided him into her, that the product of that love would be born.

He rocked himself in and out of her, lifting himself up on his hands, his arms straight and rigid. He wanted to see her face, delighting in the waves of joy that she did not try to hide. "Mine . . ." he whispered triumphantly, thrusting himself harder, faster, causing her body to move roughly against the ground. "Mine . . . forever . . ."

They came together, and only then did he lie against her breasts, the love sweat of both their bodies mingling as they reveled in the wonder of their union.

That afternoon, Rance left with half his men, leaving the other half to finish the cabins. It was his intent to go for supplies, for he had no way of knowing how long they would be away.

He returned two days later, bringing a stranger, a tall thin man with kind eyes.

"This is the Reverend Mister Fowler. He was good enough to ride up here with me. He's going to marry us, April." His voice was deep with emotion as he smiled at her and whispered huskily, "If I must leave you now, I want to leave you as my wife."

April clung to him, smiling through tears of joy, as the others gathered around to cheer their approval.

They were married at sunrise the next morning, the sky turning from pale gray to watermelon red as dawn erupted on the mountaintop. The birds sang, the winds danced through the treetops, and it was as though God, Himself, blessed the scene.

There was no time for lovemaking . . . no time to re-affirm that which had already been vowed long ago. The men hastily prepared to leave, and Rance explained, "The South is being choked to death." His misery and worry were obvious. "Sherman is proving what he was trying to prove all along, that if the war is carried to the Southern people themselves, then the Confederacy stands a good chance of collapsing. He's slashing through the very heart of us, April."

"And what do you plan to do?" she asked. "What *can* you do?"

"I'm going to run horses, and I'm going to get supplies to the Confederate troops. I may not be able to do much, but I can do something.

"I'm depending on you to keep things going here. We've brought hogs and chickens and flour and salt and a few other things to see you through the winter. I'll come back when I can. I'll send messages to you when I can. I'm leaving a dozen men here to guard you and the other women."

He pulled her into his arms, almost roughly. "And I make this one vow to you, blue eyes." He sounded almost angry. "If there's any way possible, our baby will be born at Pinehurst. I can't promise you it will happen. I can only promise you I'll try to make it happen."

The proud Stars and Bars of the Confederate flag were soon held aloft, snapping in the cool fall winds, as the men marched away down the mountain. And she was left with the memory of his kiss, tasting, as always, of warm, sweet wine.

Fall quickly became winter. There were weeks without any news at all, and then one of the men guarding the women would sneak down the mountain and bring back whatever information he could.

Sherman, they were told, had left Atlanta in flames in mid-November and marched for the Georgia coast. For Christmas, it was said that he had telegraphed President Lincoln,

I beg to present you, as a Christmas gift, the city of Savannah, with 150 heavy guns and plenty of ammunition, and also about 25,000 bales of cotton.

April had never met the man but wished him dead . . . wished all Yankees dead.

And she prayed each night and each morning, and sometimes several times each day, that Rance was alive and would return soon. She felt their baby move beneath her heart and wondered if it would be born at home. Then she chided herself for worrying about that. There were much more important things to be considered.

April wept when they were told about Sherman's march to the sea. Nowhere in Georgia was there any force to give Sherman serious opposition. He and his men had laid the land to waste as they moved, making good Sherman's prediction that a crow would starve in the path behind him.

It was even worse to hear about the lawless stragglers, some of whom were deserters. They were on the fringe of the army, and among them were soldiers temporarily absent without leave who returned to duty later. These were marauding just for the fun of it. These hoodlums, called "bummers," were far more dangerous than Sherman. They robbed, burned, and pillaged from Atlanta to the sea, not because they particularly hated the South, but because they had no morals.

Anything that lay in Sherman's path was destroyed either by him or by looters—bridges, railroads, warehouses. Barns were burned. Animals and food were taken.

Lee's army was starving, eating dead, rotten horses, rats, roaches, anything to battle the starvation that was taking more lives than the war itself.

Despite the constant fears over the war, April found peace on the mountain. She walked alone in the woods, reveling in the fragrant, colorful wild flowers, the sweet song of the birds. She would stand for hours gazing at the magnificent view from the mountain peaks, her eyes scanning the sprawling Alabama countryside. Was Rance down there somewhere? Or was he in Georgia, or Virginia? Or was he even alive?

She could not believe that he would not return. And it

was this belief and the beautiful world about her, that gave her more peace than she had known in years. She began to regain her strength after the several ordeals of the last few years.

The older women in their little hideaway camp calculated that her baby would be born sometime in late May. A beautiful time for birth, April thought happily, placing her hand often upon her swelling abdomen. A new season, a new life.

In February, they heard that General Sherman was moving northward to strike through the Carolinas. There was no word from Rance. Was he alive? Then, on a Sunday morning in early April, the lookout below gave his special whippoorwill call to signal that someone was coming. April ran with the others, as fast as her heavy body would carry her. Peering down the scrub-lined narrow path, she could see them—men in tattered gray uniforms, some of them being supported, half-carried, half-dragged, by their comrades. And above them, hanging in shreds but still there, was the remnant of the Confederate flag.

Wives and sweethearts screamed with hysterical joy as they recognized the anguished, war-weary faces of their loved ones. April's hope dimmed. She did not see Rance. Finally, unable to see through her tears, and too frightened to ask any of the men about him, she crept away from the others, toward the woods. She sat down in the field, drinking in the sweet fragrance of the earth. The air smelled so sweet, and she drank of it, then hung her head and wept.

"No one cries among flowers, blue eyes."

She could not move. This was a dream. It was not happening.

She felt a hand on her shoulder. And just then, a dirty, shaggy dog bounded forward to cover her face with eager licks.

"No," he murmured, kneeling beside her, staring down at her with warm eyes. "No one cries among the flowers."

They clung together, laughing and clutching each other as though to reassure themselves that this was real. They were together at long last.

"For me, the war is over," he told her, gesturing to his heavily bandaged leg. She gasped in fear, but he said, "It will heal in time. I caught a Yankee ball, and the doctors were afraid to remove it. Said it was too deep, and they might wind up having to take the leg off. I'm as stubborn as Clark was.

"It's going to be over in just a few days, honey," he said tightly, stroking her long golden hair, pausing now and then to brush his lips against hers. Then he moved his hand to her swollen belly, eyebrows raising in wonder. "He's going to be here soon, isn't he?"

She nodded, smiling. "A month, maybe. According to the other women."

"Then we're going home." He got to his feet and pulled her up and into his arms. Together, they walked to the edge of the mountain and stared down. "It may be a while in coming, but this land will know peace one day. We'll be a part of it. So will our child.

"Are you ready?" he asked her then, gazing down at her with so much love that she trembled, feeling it penetrate to her soul. "Are you ready to go home and have our baby?"

"Anywhere," she murmured tremulously, as his lips came closer. "Anywhere, my darling, with you."

They stood there, among the flowers, smiling at one another. And the white shaggy dog chased a butterfly through the forest, sensing his master and mistress needed time alone.

No one, the wind seemed to whisper, cries among the flowers.

❦ Chapter Thirty-four ❧

RANCE would not urge the horses pulling the buck-board to move any faster, despite April's anxious prodding.

"It will take days to get home moving this slowly," she complained, wriggling impatiently on the splintered wooden plank seat.

He glanced at her in amusement. "You want the baby born at Pinehurst, don't you? If I bounce you around any more I'll be delivering the baby myself. And I don't think I'd be any good at *that*."

His bandaged leg was propped up, and now and then pain crossed his face. "It's bad, isn't it?" she asked quietly. "Your leg. It hurts, doesn't it?"

"I told you it will heal in time. There's no gangrene. I'm thankful for that. Someday maybe a surgeon will come along who's smart enough to dig the bullet out without shattering the bone. Till then, I guess you're just going to have to put up with a husband who walks a bit stiff-legged."

She leaned over to kiss his cheek, laughing as her bonnet slipped and she quickly reached for it. The sun was scorching and she was tired, but she would not complain. They were going home! After the hell they had both endured in the past four years, nothing would mar this journey.

Familiar fields and forests were green and still, and an unearthly quiet hung over the land. Death was in the air—

the death of the Confederacy—death of the South as they had known it. "Is there no hope?"

He shook his head grimly. "We will hear one day soon that Lee has surrendered. It's over, April."

"We aren't surrendering," she said with a stubborn tilt to her head, folding her hands across her swollen abdomen. "I will never admit defeat. I will never let my children or my grandchildren say that the South was defeated by the damn Yankees."

Chuckling, he turned to look at her. He loved the expression on her face when her mind was set and nothing could change it. "And what, my darling, will you tell them?"

"That we just got tired of killing Yankees and quit fighting."

He roared with laughter, but she glared at him so angrily that he forced himself to stop. She meant it, by God, he realized in wonder. Like thousands of other Southerners, she would never be able to accept the fact that the Confederacy had been soundly whipped.

And he wondered about that, himself. Had there been enough food, enough ammunition, then the story would have been quite different. What would future generations have to say about the war? A hundred years from now, what would be the impact of the North's victory upon America? He would long be in his grave, but perhaps, there might be a way of knowing. Who could say what happened after death? Was there awareness? Whenever such thoughts found their way into his mind, he pushed them aside, for the attempt to comprehend was overwhelming.

They occasionally passed a house still standing, then passed a smoke-blackened ruin. No cattle lowed, and no birds sang here.

"I liked it better on the mountain," she said, whispering, for the grim scene seemed to demand silence.

"We're going to see evidence of plundering Yankees, April. Let's just hope they didn't reach Pinehurst."

"And what of Vanessa?"

"When we reach Montgomery, I'm going to go to whatever government is there and ask what's the proper thing to do. You will have the family ring to prove your ownership. I have money buried back on the mountain to pay any taxes due. I hear that's how the Yankees will take our land, if we can't pay the taxes. And you can bet there will be plenty of Southerners who won't be able to come up with anything. The Yankees will be swarming down here like vultures after bodies on the battlefields."

"I wish you had brought the money with you. I know I won't feel like riding back, and I don't want to be alone."

"You won't be. I'm going to find a midwife to stay with you. And I couldn't bring the money. It's pure gold, and I am not riding into Montgomery with pure gold. Right now I just want to get you home. Then I'll worry about other things."

He was silent for a moment, tugging at his beard. Finally, he looked at her somberly and said, "If Vanessa is there, I'll deal with her. She's insane, and I don't trust her around you."

"You mean if she's still living at Pinehurst, you'll ask her to leave?" She shook her head. "Oh, Rance, I can't do that to my sister. Where would she go?"

"Damnit, woman, why do you care?" he yelled, unable to control his temper. "What has that bitch got to do to you for you to realize just how goddamn mean she is? She'd kill you and never bat an eye. I don't want to hear one word out of you about how I handle her if she's there. Do you understand me?"

She nodded, aware that no amount of pleading could sway him when he was riled. His strength of character was admirable, but she often found it annoying to have it directed at her so forcibly.

In midafternoon, Rance turned from the main road onto a deeply corrugated clay road. The horses were barely moving, for the way was rough. In the distance was an old cabin of rotten logs, several having fallen out, giving the structure a precarious lurch to one side.

"We're going to have to ask for shelter," he explained to her. "You need the rest. Let's pray there's food to be shared."

A woman, old beyond her years, appeared in the doorway. Her faded dress hung shapelessly on her thin body. Behind her, five small children peered out curiously.

Rance introduced April and himself, then said, "My wife, as you can see, is in the family way, and we need a night's sleep before continuing on our way. If you could oblige us, I'll go into the woods and hunt for our supper."

The woman's deeply shadowed eyes stared at them without interest. She shrugged, then said tonelessly, "Lost my man at Gettysburg. Lost one son up in Tennessee. Another in The Wilderness, two more in Atlanta. Ain't got much. You're welcome to what I do have."

Rance and April exchanged looks of shared sorrow for the pitiful woman. Then he helped her from the wagon, took his musket, and headed for the woods.

They ate the four rabbits he killed for supper, and the woman, Mrs. Mattie Kirkwood, offered them corn cakes and fried dove eggs.

There was little conversation. The children were quiet, subdued, retiring to their worn pallets on the floor as soon as supper was finished. Mrs. Kirkwood could offer not even a blanket, but Rance had a worn one in the back of the wagon. April slept in the curve of his arm, uncomfortable on the hard clay floor, her back aching from the weight of the child.

They were on their way at sunrise, having eaten more dove eggs and fried salt pork.

They reached Montgomery at noon. Rance immediately went to the office of the provost marshal and returned with the grim, final news that on April 9, General Lee had surrendered to General Grant near Appomattox Court House in Virginia.

The bloody war was over. The Army of Northern Virginia had stacked their muskets before silent lines of federal soldiers. Lee's surrender left Johnston and his Army of Tennessee with no place to go. On April 26, near Durham, North Carolina, General Johnston surrendered to General Sherman.

April could not cry. In the four years of hell, there had been too many tears. And tears would not change any of the anguish. She carried a new life within her, soon to be born, and it was a new life that she and Rance were seeking. No, she would not cry.

"We'd best be getting to Pinehurst," she said softly, reaching to touch his arm as though to reassure herself that he was still beside her . . . would always be. "We've much to do, and I must know whether it still stands."

"I found out that the Yankees didn't do too much plundering around here. Right now, I'm going to use what money I did bring to try and buy food and supplies. Then I've got to find a midwife to stay with you so I can return to the mountain for the gold. Edward was staying to help the others get their things together and make plans to return home. Some of them may be wanting to come here, to live at Pinehurst, if their own homes have been destroyed, or if they're afraid to return."

"I've told them they will be welcome," she assured him. "There's much work to be done, and we'll need all the help we can get. If we hurry and plant now, and get some cows and hogs, we can have food for all."

It did not take long for Rance to find an old Negro woman who was delighted to stay with April in exchange for food and shelter.

Jessie was a freed slave. She had stayed on at the Atlanta plantation where she was born until Sherman burned it. Her husband was dead and her children were grown and scattered. She remembered having cousins in Montgomery. Rance and April were amazed that she had found her way to Alabama, for she could neither read nor write and had been eating out of trash barrels and sleeping in barns.

"You'll be just fine with Jessie lookin' after you," she said with a grateful grin as she heaved her body up into the back of the wagon. "And if'n a doctor ain't around when yo' time comes, Jessie can birth that baby. I birthed maybe hunnerds o' babies in my lifetime."

April glanced nervously at Rance, and he gave her a reassuring smile as he whispered, "I won't be gone over a few days, sweetheart. Then I'll be back with the others. Don't worry. You said the other women figure you have another month to go."

"The way I feel now," she responded wearily, "I can't make it another day."

He patted her knee and gave the reins a snap to start the horses. "You'll feel better when we get you home."

Soon they rounded the last curve before the mansion would come into view, and April squeezed her eyes shut and held her breath.

"We're here!" Rance cried triumphantly.

Only then did she look, shrieking with joy at the sight of the stately columnar house still standing regally upon the hill, still a sentinel of awesome beauty overseeing everything within its realm.

The grounds were still unkempt, but that was of no consequence. All that mattered was that the Yankees had not destroyed her home.

"Will you go faster?" she cried excitedly. "Oh, Rance, I can't believe it—"

From the rear, Jessie saw the awesome house and exclaimed, "Lawdy, what a big place. Why that's bigger'n what my mastah had over in Atlanta. I sho' hope you gonna get some mo' help, 'cause I'll never be able to take care of that big place by myself."

Rance laughed and told her not to worry. "We'll clean up living quarters on the first floor and worry about the rest after the baby comes."

The moment the wagon stopped in front of the wide marble steps, April tried to stand up, but he held her back, snapping, "Will you wait till I get down first and help you, April? Try to remember you're in a delicate condition."

"How can I forget?" She grinned, trembling with joy. She was home at last! Home! How wonderful the moment.

He lifted her to the ground, then kept a protective arm about her as they walked slowly up the steps. Jessie hung back, staring about in awe.

They found the front doors locked, but April remembered that a key was always hidden in a large stone urn at the end of a porch. The rose bush once held by the urn was now blackened.

Unlocking the door, April hurried inside, glancing about excitedly in the semidarkness. There was an overwhelming musty smell, but she cried, "The furniture is still here. The Yankees didn't come at all! I'll have to check on the silver, and—" Her voice trailed off as her gaze dropped to the dark stain on the oak floor in the parlor. The memory of Kaid Blackmon's body lying there, blood oozing from the wound in his throat, made her shudder. Sensing her thoughts, Rance placed his arm about her shoulders in a protective, comforting gesture.

April turned toward the stairs, struggling to dismiss the awful past. "It . . . it looks lived in," she said.

"Of course, it's lived in, you fool. *I* live here. It's my home!"

They stared upward to see Vanessa on the landing, blue eyes luminous with rage. Her knuckles showed white as she gripped the dusty mahogany railing. Long golden hair was tousled about her flushed face.

April could not speak. Rance's arm tightened about her.

Vanessa was wearing a green satin dressing gown, which she boldly allowed to fall open, exposing her naked breasts. He pretended not to notice as he spoke quietly, ominously. "This is not your home, Vanessa. It's April's. Mine and April's. Get your things and get out. You have brought enough misery to this place."

Vanessa laughed shrilly, tossing her head, her hair flying about wildly. "So you want me to get out, do you? We shall see about that, you arrogant cripple." She gestured towards his bandaged leg. "This house is mine. Everyone knows that. It is you and that snit who shall leave. At once."

"I understand there is a family heirloom to prove the claim. Do you have that ring, Vanessa?" he challenged.

She answered coolly. "Why don't you leave before you force me to have you arrested?"

"Vanessa, don't make me drag you out of here bodily." He took a step forward. "I'm not going to argue with you. The war is over and—"

"Yes, it is, isn't it?" she cried gleefully. "The Union won, and you're nothing but a dirty Rebel. A traitor to the noble Union. I think there is someone you should meet, before you continue threatening me in my own home."

She turned slightly, her eyes still fastened upon him, glittering. "Ernest," she called. "Would you come here, please? There's a dirty Rebel down here making threats. I think he needs to be reminded just who won the war, and then be properly chastized."

Rance motioned for April to step into the parlor, and she complied, frightened to see him draw his sword. Soon a tall, thin man appeared and stood beside Vanessa, bare-chested, wearing only the blue trousers of his federal uniform. Rance was standing at the foot of the stairs, legs wide apart, sword held tightly, ready for confrontation.

Vanessa pointed. "See? He draws his weapon against a Union man. Take him to prison or whatever it is you do with die-hard Rebels who refuse to admit the war is over and make threats against private citizens."

Rance sized the man up immediately. His Adam's apple was bobbing up and down nervously. It was obvious that he wanted no fight. Had he been backed up by other soldiers, it might have been different.

"I'm Lieutenant Gant." The stranger spoke in a thin voice, eyes fearful as he sized up Rance. "What seems to be the trouble here?"

Before Vanessa could repeat her complaint, he spotted April peering out the parlor door. "Who's she?" he demanded, eyebrows raising. "Why, she looks just like you—"

"She's my twin sister," responded Vanessa with venom in her tone. "My father disowned her years ago. Now she's come back with this Rebel trash to make trouble. Get rid of them both."

Rance moved to end the situation. He advanced slowly toward the stairway and said, "I've no quarrel with you, Lieutenant, and this has nothing to do with you being a Yankee and me being a Rebel. I don't know who you are or why you're here, but this woman is my wife, and she is the legal heir to this property and can prove it. Your friend here has no proof of ownership, I assure you. If you want trouble, it's trouble you'll get. And unless you have a real interest in that slut you're standing with, I'd suggest you get your blue belly out of here about as fast as those skinny legs of yours will carry you."

Lieutenant Gant whirled and disappeared from sight, and Vanessa screamed after him, "You come back here, you gutless coward. Don't you run out on me after all I've done for you."

Gant was back in seconds, yanking on his shirt, fastening the buttons with nervous fingers. Without looking at Rance, he told Vanessa, "Look, we're getting out of here. You told me you had claim to this property, and that man down there seems to think he can prove you don't. I can get in a hell of a mess with the Union brass if I hang around here and get mixed up in a family brawl. We're supposed to occupy this territory peacefully. So I'm leaving, and you can go with me or stay and fight your own battle."

They locked eyes, each blistering with anger. Then Vanessa threw hating glares at Rance and April in turn and cried, "I'll go, damn you, but I'll be back. I'll be back to stay."

The Lieutenant slung her roughly down the hall, and she reached out to steady herself lest she lose her balance and fall. "You get your stuff together and do it fast," he snapped. "I told you, I'm not getting mixed up in all this. I thought something funny was going on all along."

Boots in hand, he hurried down the stairs to Rance. "Look, whatever your name is—"

"Taggart. Captain Taggart. Confederate States Army . . . or was," he said unwaveringly.

"Captain Taggart." Gant ran his fingers through his hair, nodding apologetically toward April. "Look, I am sorry about all this. Vanessa . . . Miss Jennings . . . opened this place to the Union army. She allowed soldiers to stay here, cooked for them. She said she was a sympathizer. All the servants had left, she said, and she was alone. She and I . . . well, we sort of got together, understand?"

Rance nodded, expressionless, his hand still fastened on his sword.

"I just don't want any trouble. The General would have my head, and—"

"That's fine," Rance cut him off crisply. "Just take Vanessa and go. I can assure you that I will be in the provost marshal's office tomorrow morning with the necessary proof that my wife is, indeed, the legal heiress to this property."

"Fine, that's fine." Gant kept bobbing his head up and down as he backed toward the door. "Just remember, when you talk to him, that I don't care. It doesn't matter to me one way or the other."

Vanessa flounced angrily down the stairs carrying a small bag which the Lieutenant quickly took from her. He opened the front doors. With one final, hating glare, she turned to April and snapped, "The place is in ruins, anyway. And you needn't bother looking for the silver. I sold every piece. Sold all Mother's jewelry, too. You won't be able to pay the taxes, and the Yankees will take the rest of Pinehurst."

April started forward, but Rance held her back. "Vanessa, please . . . can't we stop all this? I never hated you. We're sisters. We can forget the past and start over if you will only stop this insane—"

"Never!" Vanessa screamed so loudly that Jessie, still standing in the driveway by the wagon, jumped at the sound. "I will hate you till I die," she raged.

Lieutenant Gant grabbed her arm and jerked her roughly out the door, casting one final apologetic glance toward Rance and April. "I won't let her come back and bother you, I promise," he said quickly. "I'm beginning to think she's a bit daft. I suspected as much all along."

Rance walked over to slam the door. He did not want to hear any more. Turning to face April, he quietly said, "It's over. She won't be back. The Lieutenant will see to that because he knows he can't afford any trouble here. Tomorrow morning, I will take that ring into the provost marshal and settle this once and for all. I just hope the ring is considered valid proof. It's a bit unusual."

"It's a part of legal records," she explained, lowering her heavy body into a nearby chair. "And the records are probably still at the courthouse. And Poppa left a will, I'm sure. He wanted to make certain that Vanessa would never have a claim."

"Then there's nothing to worry about."

"I'm worried about my sister and what will become of her," she whispered, blinking back tears.

"She'll get by. Don't worry about her. Now then, I'd like for you to get that ring right now. I'll feel a lot better once I have it in my hand."

"Then follow me," she told him, taking the hand he extended to help her to her feet. "We need to go before it gets dark."

They walked out the front door, and Rance paused to instruct Jessie about unloading the supplies. She nodded eagerly, knowing that she would soon have her first decent meal in months.

The sky had turned to a purple haze, and silver clouds skipped across the sky. The smell of rain was in the air, and the wind was picking up. They would have to hurry, she knew, to be back in the house by dark.

She saw the wistful expression on Rance's face as she led him around to the path. He was thinking, she knew, of the wonderful, purebred horses he had once cared for there. She prayed that he would someday know once again pleasure in the animals he loved.

They moved down the sloping hill. The dogwoods had long since bloomed but were still lush and green. The azaleas had also put forth their glory for the season.

"April, you're going to the cemetery," Rance exclaimed. "What on earth for?"

She did not answer but kept on walking. The graves at the front of the burial grounds were now overgrown with weeds, and some of the stone monuments had cracked and fallen. That, she decided at once, was something they would take care of as soon as possible—the restoring of her ancestors' graves.

She walked to the red brick building with its double iron gates across the doorway, staring up at the scrawled "J" in the ironwork. Anguished memories came flooding back, and she stopped and trembled, not wanting to go on.

"It's in there, isn't it?" Rance squeezed her hand. "The ring."

She nodded mutely, then forced herself to move to the little niches built into the brick that still held tiny marble statues. Pointing, she whispered, "There. The statue of the kneeling angel. There is a chipped brick there that will slide out. There's a key hidden there."

Rance moved swiftly to follow her directions, then, without hesitation, inserted the key in the lock and swung the gates open, a loud, grating sound filling the air. "Now where?" he asked brusquely.

"You aren't afraid, are you?" She stared at him in wonder. "I was always afraid to come here, but you don't seem to mind. In fact, I don't think I've ever seen you show fear in all the time I've known you."

"When a man has to live in fear, April, then it's time for him to die," he sighed. "Now where is the ring hidden? I want to get you back to the house, fed, and in bed. It's been a hard trip, and a nasty homecoming, thanks to your sister."

She took a deep breath, closed her eyes, then opened them. "There. That bier on the end."

"You hid it in a coffin?" he asked incredulously. "I thought you were scared of this place. Who's buried in there?"

"No one. It is where I am to be buried one day. I didn't think the Yankees would like it here any better than I do. And if they came, they wouldn't desecrate a coffin. All you have to do is slide that marble slab to the side and reach inside. It's at this end, wrapped in a piece of cloth."

Effortlessly, he moved the slab, reached in, and brought out the ring, sparkling in the twilight. He gave her a crooked smile as he tossed it up in the air and caught it. "You were lucky, April. The Yankees have been desecrating graves, just like the Rebels, when they realized that people thought they were safe hiding places.

"This mausoleum would have been the first place they'd have looked if they had come plundering through here. You have something to be thankful to your sister for, after all, because she welcomed them with open arms. They didn't do any damage because she welcomed them."

He tucked the ring in his pocket. "Let's go home, blue eyes," he whispered. "It's all over now."

Arms about each other, they walked through the purple night to the house.

Lieutenant Gant leaned forward in the buggy, one hand holding the horse's reins, the other popping the whip across the animal's rump. It was getting darker, and rain drops were starting to fall. He was anxious to get back to Montgomery, eager to forget he had ever been fool enough to become involved with that strange woman.

She had been good in bed. There was no denying that. She was also quite beautiful. But he had always sensed something peculiar about her, and the scene a short while ago had borne out his suspicions.

He was well rid of her. And damn it, he thought, popping the whip harder, if she wanted to jump out of the buggy and go running off into the woods just as darkness fell, then let her.

He was glad to wash his hands of the whole mess.

🐚 Chapter Thirty-five 🐚

APRIL awoke and stared about, blinking rapidly, bewildered. Then, slowly, happily, it came to her. Home. She was home in her own bed. It was too good to be true.

She turned, smiling, arms outstretched to reach for Rance. That side of the bed was empty.

She heaved her swollen body up, crying out for him. Where was he? What time was it? Padding quickly to the windows, she jerked open the heavy drapes to see that the sun was already high in the sky. Why, it was probably almost noon, she realized with a start. Why had Rance let her sleep so long? They were supposed to be going into Montgomery first thing.

She reached the stair railing, clutching it as she leaned over to call. "Rance, where are you?" Desperation made her voice tremble.

Jessie appeared in the foyer, a dust cloth in her hands. "Well, good mornin', Miz April," she called up pleasantly. "I thought you was gonna sleep the day clean away."

"Jessie, where is Mr. Taggart?" she asked, making her way carefully down the stairs.

"Well, he left early this mornin'. Said you was sleepin' so good, he was just gonna let you alone. Said he was goin' into town on some business, and he'd be back later on. He told me to just let you rest, 'cause he knowed you was tired, and he told me to start cleanin' things up."

"Damn," she swore under her breath, reaching the landing and looking about. Jessie had been busy. The parlor was spotless. Vanessa, she and Rance had realized the night before, had not attempted to keep the house clean once the servants ran away.

"I got some eatin' waitin' for you in the kitchen," Jessie smiled. "Fried some of that fatback Mr. Taggart bought in town, and I boiled some beans. You need to eat and keep up your strength. Ain't gonna be long 'fore you birth that baby."

"I've several weeks," April said absently, but then her stomach rumbled slightly and she admitted, "I'll have a small portion, Jessie. Bring it to my room, please. I'm going to lie back down."

"Yes'm," she nodded, hurrying away. "You just get all the rest you want. Mr. Taggart, he told me it was my job to look after you, and that's sho' what I'm gonna do."

She stopped, a sudden strained look appearing on her plump face. April prodded, "Yes, Jessie, what is it?"

Jessie looked down at the floor, sucked in her lips, then said, "Well, it ain't none of my business, I know, but that woman what ran outta hear screamin' yesterday . . ."

April felt a stab of alarm. "Have you seen her? Has she been back?"

Jessie shook her head quickly. "No'm. Mr. Taggart said if I saw her not to let her in. I was just wonderin', is she as mean as she sounded? I mean, I need this job, and Lord knows I need a roof over my head, but that woman scared me, and—"

"Jessie, I think we have seen the last of Vanessa," April told her, hoping it was true. "There have been family problems, but the business Mr. Taggart is taking care of today will eliminate them. Someday, quite honestly, I hope my sister and I can make peace between us, but that will be up to her."

"Yes'm. I just don't want no trouble. Like I said, she scared me somethin' fierce, and I seen enough trouble for my lifetime."

"So have I, Jessie." April forced a smile. "Don't worry."

She made her way slowly back up the stairs. God, she hoped Vanessa did stay away until she was ready to make peace. Rance had said the night before that he doubted she

would ever change. He had asked what it would take for
April to realize just what an evil person her twin really
was.

There were no words to make him understand. Despite
everything, Vanessa was still her sister, her twin sister,
and if there were any way at all they could get along, then
she wanted to find that way.

She lay down across the bed. How many weeks till the
baby would be born? She placed her hand lovingly on the
swollen mound of her stomach as the baby gave a kick.
She smiled. God, she loved the child already, almost as
much as she loved Rance. And despite the South losing the
war . . . despite the hard times that were sure to lie ahead,
life was good, and she was grateful to be alive.

"My, don't you look like the regal queen."

April sat bolt upright in terror, a silent scream gushing
from her trembling lips. Vanessa stood in the doorway, her
dress tattered, her hair matted with leaves. There were
bruises on her face.

But it was her eyes that stunned April the most. Never
had she seen such hatred. They seemed to bulge from their
sockets, a brilliant blue sparkling with red and gold fires.

"Did you really think I would give up so easily?"

April was too terrified to speak.

Vanessa gave her long hair a toss, lips curling back in a
snarling grimace. "So he married you, did he? I suppose
you're real proud of that. And you're going to have a baby.
Isn't that sweet?"

She took a step forward. "I suppose you're lying there
thinking what a grand life you're going to have here after
you rebuild Pinehurst into the finest plantation in Alabama. You're thinking how wonderful everything is going
to be.

"But you forgot one thing," she cackled, the sound chilling. "You forgot about *me*!

"I jumped off that wagon last night," she whispered, eyes
still glittering, "and fought my way through the woods all
night long to get back here. Did you think you could get
rid of me so easily? Did you think all you had to do was
have that sonofabitch order me off *my* land? Oh, no. I've
been through too much to give up."

April choked as she struggled to speak, "Please . . . please, Vanessa . . . hear me out. . . ."

"Hear you out!" she mimicked, sneering. "You cunning little harlot! I don't want to listen to your lies. You can't wheedle around me the way you do men. I know you for what you are!

"And I know something else—" She took another step forward. "I know Rance took that goddamned ring into town. I was hiding outside the kitchen window this morning when he told that nigra where he was going. He's going to file a claim to this place. I tried to change them, but it's in the records that the rightful heir must have possession of that goddamned ring. I couldn't change those records."

"We can share—" April was slowly forcing her terrified body to move from the bed.

Vanessa laughed shrilly. "Share? Oh, no, dear sister. You and I aren't going to share anything. If I can't have this place, then neither shall you."

That was when April saw the gun she had been hiding in the folds of her skirt. "No . . ." she whispered, shaking her head from side to side in horror. "No . . . you wouldn't . . . you couldn't. Please, God, no—"

In that instant, Jessie appeared in the doorway and screamed. Vanessa whirled around.

"Lawdy, Lawdy!" The Negro covered her face with her apron and began to back out of the room. "Don't kill me. Please don't kill me. I ain't got nothin' to do with none of this."

"Get out of here," Vanessa hissed. "I've no quarrel with you."

Slowly, she turned back to face April, lowering the gun and pointing it straight at her. "Now, damn you, I'll be rid of you once and for all."

April used every ounce of strength within her to leap to one side, trying to move quickly enough to dodge the bullet.

The gun exploded in a blinding flash.

She felt a hot, searing pain . . . but that was nothing compared to what she saw on her sister's face. The last vision she had before oblivion swept her away was of her sister's twisted, insane face. *God forgive her,* April thought as she gasped for air. *God forgive my sister. She has lost her mind.*

From far, far away, someone was calling. April whirled around and around in a spinning pool of light . . . grays, blues, reds, yellows. It was pretty here. She did not want to leave. Couldn't they leave her alone? Why did they want to bring her back? She wanted to stay. Peace was here, not there.

"April, can you hear me?"

Her eyes opened, closed. Was that Rance? So handsome. So dear. God, how she loved him. But couldn't he allow her to remain here, where it was so nice and calm? No one hated her here. No one wanted to hurt her. And there was music. She could hear singing. Such a pretty sound.

"April, honey, wake up, please—"

He sounded hurt. She did not want him hurt. She forced her eyes open, wanting to beg him not to be hurt . . . not to care . . . to let her remain here. Didn't he know how wonderful it was not to be afraid anymore? And Vanessa was not here to torment her.

"Vanessa," she whispered suddenly. The peace was gone. There was no longer any music. No pretty colors. The whirling had stopped. She tried to raise up, but strong hands held her down. She felt a sharp pain in her chest and cried out.

"Don't move around, sweetheart," Rance was commanding. "You've been hurt. You'll only harm yourself if you don't lie still."

"Vanessa," she repeated, looking about wildly, realizing she was in a strange place. And there were other people there, too. People she did not know.

"Vanessa won't hurt you again, April."

Her frantic gaze settled upon his face. "Tell me . . ." she whispered.

"Vanessa is dead."

"Dead? Oh, God," she moaned, moving her head from side to side.

"Listen to me." He caught her face, held her. Then he told her. Vanessa had tried to kill her and believed she had. Jessie had run from the room and was halfway down the stairs when she heard Vanessa screaming over and over, asking God what she had done. Jessie heard another shot, then silence.

"She went back upstairs and found Vanessa on the floor," he said quietly. "She was dead. She killed herself. She thought she had killed you, April. And in the end, she just realized she couldn't live with her torment and the final act of killing her own sister. She was insane. That's the only way to explain her."

He leaned over to kiss her. "Too late, April, your sister found regret in all she had done. I suppose it's best this way. She's at peace now."

The tears began to trickle downward, and Rance murmured, "Go ahead and cry, sweetheart. Cry one last time, and then let go of the past."

Silently, she gave thanks for having been spared, spared to live, to love Rance, to give birth. . . .

She touched her stomach. It was flat. "My baby!" she screamed, struggling to rise once more. "My baby! My God, no, not my baby!"

He forced her to lie back once more and he cried, "The baby is fine. A little boy. We have a son, April. Do you understand? A baby boy! He's small, but the doctors say he's going to live."

She stared at him in wonder. "A boy," she whispered, dry, parched lips moving to smile up at him. "We have a baby boy."

Rance nodded, his tears glistening. "Jessie brought you into town herself. You were wounded in the chest, but the bullet went clean through . . . missed your heart. But by then you went into labor, and there was nothing they could do but deliver the baby and hope for the best. Well, honey, we got the best. He's a beauty."

He nodded with pride to a woman who had been standing back in the shadows. Stepping forth, she laid a blanketed bundle in April's trembling arms.

April raised her head in wonder to stare down at the tiny scrap. His head was covered with thick, black hair. She laughed through her tears and cried, "He looks like you!"

"Well, that's the first of many problems he's going to have," Rance laughed with her.

The others moved out of the hospital room, leaving them alone. April held her son close to her bosom and looked up in wonder and love to meet Rance's adoring gaze.

Their nightmare was over. Their dream had become a living reality.

And he leaned down to press his lips to hers in a kiss that tasted of warm, sweet wine.